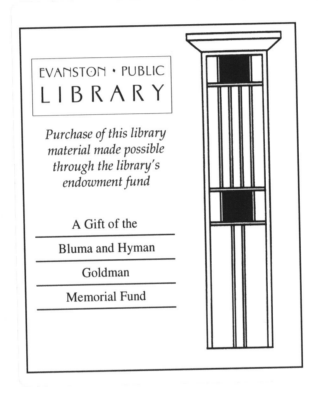

The Last
Werewolf

The Last Werewolf

Glen Duncan

ALFRED A. KNOPF

New York

2011

THIS IS A BORZOI BOOK
Published by Alfred A. Knopf

www.aaknopf.com

Knopf, Borzoi Books, and the colophon are registered trademarks
of Random House, Inc.

Originally published in Great Britain by Canongate Books, Ltd., Edinburgh.

Grateful acknowledgment is made to Farrar, Straus and Giroux, LLC, for
permission to reprint an excerpt from "The Discovery of the Pacific" from
Selected Poems by Thom Gunn, copyright © 2007 by The Estate of Thom Gunn.

Library of Congress Cataloging-in-Publication Data
Duncan, Glen, [date]
The last werewolf / by Glen Duncan.—1st American ed.
p. cm.
ISBN 978-0-307-59508-9
1. Werewolves—Fiction. I. Title.
PR6104.U535L37 2011
823'.92—dc22   2011011667

Jacket design by Peter Mendelsund

Manufactured in the United States of America

First American Edition

For Pete and Eva

First Moon

Let It Come Down

2

"It's official," Harley said. "They killed the Berliner two nights ago. You're the last." Then after a pause: "I'm sorry."

Yesterday evening this was. We were in the upstairs library of his Earl's Court house, him standing at a tense tilt between stone hearth and oxblood couch, me in the window seat with a tumbler of forty-five-year-old Macallan and a Camel Filter, staring out at dark London's fast-falling snow. The room smelled of tangerines and leather and the fire's pine logs. Forty-eight hours on I was still sluggish from the Curse. Wolf drains from the wrists and shoulders last. In spite of what I'd just heard I thought: Madeline can give me a massage later, warm jasmine oil and the long-nailed magnolia hands I don't love and never will.

"What are you going to do?" Harley said.

I sipped, swallowed, glimpsed the peat bog plashing white legs of the kilted clan Macallan as the whisky kindled in my chest. *It's official. You're the last. I'm sorry.* I'd known what he was going to tell me. Now that he had, what? Vague ontological vertigo. Kubrik's astronaut with the severed umbilicus spinning away all alone into infinity . . . At a certain point one's imagination refused. The phrase was: *It doesn't bear thinking about.* Manifestly it didn't.

"Marlowe?"

"This room's dead to you," I said. "But there are bibliophiles the world over it would reduce to tears of joy." No exaggeration. Harley's collection's worth a million-six, books he doesn't go to anymore because he's entered the phase of having given up reading. If he lives another ten years he'll enter the next phase—of having gone back to it. Giving up reading seems the height of maturity at first. Like all such heights a false summit. It's a human thing. I've seen it countless times. Two hundred years, you see everything countless times.

"I can't imagine what this is like for you," he said.

"Neither can I."

"We need to plan."

I didn't reply. Instead let the silence fill with the alternative to planning. Harley lit a Gauloise and topped us up with an unsteady hand, lilac-veined and liver-spotted these days. At seventy he maintains longish thinning grey hair and a plump nicotined moustache that looks waxed but isn't. There was a time when his young men called him Buffalo Bill. Now his young men know Buffalo Bill only as the serial killer from *The Silence of the Lambs*. During periods of psychic weakness he leans on a bone-handled cane, though he's been told by his doctor it's ruining his spine.

"The Berliner," I said. "Grainer killed him?"

"Not Grainer. His Californian protégé, Ellis."

"Grainer's saving himself for the main event. He'll come after me alone."

Harley sat down on the couch and stared at the floor. I know what scares him: If I die first there'll be no salving surreality between him and his conscience. Jake Marlowe is a monster, fact. Kills and devours people, fact. Which makes him, Harley, an accessory after the fact, fact. With me alive, walking and talking and doing the lunar shuffle once a month he can live in it as in a decadent dream. *Did I mention my best friend's a werewolf, by the way?* Dead, I'll force a brutal awakening. *I helped Marlowe get away with murder.* He'll probably kill himself or go once and for all mad. One of his upper left incisors is full gold, a dental anachronism that suggests semicraziness anyway.

"Next full moon," he said. "The rest of the Hunt's been ordered to stand down. It's Grainer's party. You know what he's like."

Indeed. Eric Grainer is the Hunt's Big Dick. All upper-echelon members of WOCOP (World Organisation for the Control of Occult Phenomena) are loaded or bankrolled by the loaded for their expertise. Grainer's expertise is tracking and killing my kind. *My kind.* Of which, thanks to WOCOP's assassins and a century of no new howling kids on the block, it turns out I'm the last. I thought of the Berliner, whose name (God being dead, irony still rollickingly alive) was Wolfgang, pictured his last moments: the frost reeling under him, his moonlit muzzle and sweating pelt, the split-second in which his eyes merged disbelief and fear and horror and sadness and relief—then the white and final light of silver.

"What are you going to do?" Harley repeated.

All wolf and no gang. Humour darkens. I looked out of the window. The snow was coming down with the implacability of an Old Testament plague. In Earl's Court Road pedestrians tottered and slid and in the cold swirling angelic freshness felt their childhoods still there and the shock like a snapped stem of not being children anymore. Two nights ago I'd eaten a forty-three-year-old hedge fund specialist. I've been in a phase of taking the ones no one wants. My last phase, apparently.

"Nothing," I said.

"You'll have to get out of London."

"What for?"

"We're not going to have this conversation."

"It's time."

"It's not time."

"Harley—"

"You've got a duty to live, same as the rest of us."

"Hardly the same as the rest of you."

"Nevertheless. You go on living. And don't give me any poetic bollocks about being tired. It's bogus. It's bad script."

"It's not bad script," I said. "I am tired."

"Been around too long, worn out by history, too full of content, emptily replete—you've told me. I don't believe you. And in any case you don't give up. You love life because life's all there is. There's no God and that's His only Commandment. Give me your word."

I was thinking, as the honest part of me had been from the moment Harley had given me the news, *You'll have to tell it now. The untellable tale. You wondered how long a postponement you'd get. Turns out you got a hundred and sixty-seven years. Quite a while to keep a girl waiting.*

"Give me your word, Jake."

"Give you my word what?"

"Give me your word you're not going to sit there like a cabbage till Grainer tracks you down and kills you."

When I'd imagined this moment I'd imagined clean relief. Now the moment had arrived there was relief, but it wasn't clean. The sordid little flame of selfhood shimmied in protest. Not that my self's what it used to be. These days it deserves a sad smile, as might a twinge of vestigial lust in an old man's balls. "Shot him, did they?" I asked. "Herr Wolfgang?"

Harley took a fretful drag, then while exhaling through his nostrils mashed the Gauloise in a standing obsidian ashtray. "They didn't shoot him," he said. "Ellis cut his head off."

2

ALL PARADIGM SHIFTS ANSWER the amoral craving for novelty. Obama's election victory did it. So did the Auschwitz footage in its day. Good and evil are irrelevant. Show us the world's not the way we thought it was and a part of us rejoices. Nothing's exempt. One's own death-sentence elicits a mad little hallelujah, and mine's egregiously overdue. For ten, twenty, thirty years now I've been dragging myself through the motions. How long do werewolves live? Madeline asked recently. According to WOCOP around four hundred years. I don't know *how*. Naturally one sets oneself challenges—Sanskrit, Kant, advanced calculus, t'ai chi—but that only addresses the problem of Time. The bigger problem, of Being, just keeps getting bigger. (Vampires, not surprisingly, have an on-off love affair with catatonia.) One by one I've exhausted the modes: hedonism, asceticism, spontaneity, reflection, everything from miserable Socrates to the happy pig. My mechanism's worn out. I don't have what it takes. I still have feelings but I'm sick of having them. Which is another feeling I'm sick of having. I just . . . I just don't want any more *life*.

Harley crashed from anxiety to morbidity to melancholy but I remained dreamy and light, part voluntary obtuseness, part Zenlike acceptance, part simply an inability to concentrate. You can't just ignore this, he kept saying. You can't just fucking *roll over*. For a while I responded mildly with things like Why not? and Of course I can, but he got so worked up— the bone-handled cane came back into play—I feared for his heart and changed tack. Just let me digest, I told him. Just let me think. Just let me, in fact, get laid, as I've arranged to do, as I'm paying for even as we speak. This was true (Madeline waited at a £360-a-night boutique hotel across town) but it wasn't a happy shift of topic for Harley: prostate surgery three months ago left his libido in a sulk and London's rent boys bereft of munificent patronage. However, it got me out of there. Tearily drunk, he embraced me and insisted I borrow a woollen hat and made me promise to call him in twenty-four hours, whereafter, he kept repeating, all this pathetic sissying cod Hamlet bollocks would have to stop.

It was still snowing when I stepped out into the street. Vehicular traffic was poignantly stupefied and Earl's Court Underground was closed. For a moment I stood adjusting to the air's fierce innocence. I hadn't known the Berliner, but what was he if not kin? He'd had a near miss in the Black Forest two years ago, fled to the States and gone off-radar in Alaska. If he'd stayed in the wilderness he might still be alive. (The thought, "wilderness," stirred the ghost animal, ran cold fingers through the pelt that wasn't there; mountains like black glass and slivers of snow and the blood-hot howl on ice-flavoured air . . .) But home pulls. It draws you back to tell you you don't belong. They got Wolfgang twenty miles from Berlin. *Ellis cut his head off.* The death of a loved one brutally vivifies everything: clouds, street corners, faces, TV ads. You bear it because others share the grief. Species death leaves no others. You're alone among all the eerily renewed particulars.

Tongue out to taste the cold falling flakes I got the first inklings of the weight the world might put on me for the time I had left, the mass of its detail, its relentless plotless insistence. Again, it didn't bear thinking about. This would be my torture: All that didn't bear thinking about would devote itself to forcing me to bear thinking about it.

I lit a Camel and hauled myself into focus. Practicalities: Get to Gloucester Road on foot. Circle Line to Farringdon. Ten minutes flailing trek to the Zetter, where Madeline, God bless her mercenary charms, would be waiting. I pulled the woollen cap down snug over my ears and began walking.

Harley had said: Grainer wants the monster not the man. You've got time. I didn't doubt he was right. There were twenty-seven days to the next full moon and thanks to the interference Harley had been running WOCOP still had me in Paris. Which knowledge sustained me for a few minutes despite the growing conviction—*this is paranoia, you're doing this to yourself*—that I was being followed.

Then, turning into Cromwell Road, the denial allowance was spent and there was nothing between me and the livid fact: I *was* being followed.

This is paranoia, I began again, but the mantra had lost its magic. Pressing on me from behind was warm insinuation where should have been uninterrupted cold: surveillance. Snow and buildings molecularly swelled in urgent confirmation: *They've found you. It's already begun.*

Adrenaline isn't interested in ennui. Adrenaline floods, regardless, in my state not just the human fibres but lupine leftovers too, those creature dregs that hadn't fully conceded transformation. Phantom wolf energies and their *Homo sapiens* correlates wriggled and belched in my scalp, shoulders, wrists, knees. My bladder tingled as in the too fast pitch down from a Ferris wheel's summit. The absurdity was being unable, shin-deep in snow, to quicken my pace. Harley had tried to press a Smith & Wesson automatic on me before I'd left but I'd laughed it away. Stop being a granny. I imagined him watching now on CCTV saying, Yes, Harley the granny. I hope you're happy, Marlowe, you fucking idiot.

I tossed the cigarette and shoved my hands into my overcoat pockets. Harley had to be warned. If the Hunt was tailing me then they knew where I'd just been. The Earl's Court house wasn't in his name (masqueraded instead as what it was perfectly equipped to be, an elite rare book dealership) and had hitherto been safe. But if WOCOP had uncovered it then Harley—for nearly fifty years my double agent, my fix-it, my familiar, my friend—might already be dead.

If, then . . . If, then . . . This, aside from the business of monthly transformation, the inestimable drag of Being a Werewolf, is what I'm sick of, the endless logistics. There's a reason humans peg-out around eighty: prose fatigue. It looks like organ failure or cancer or stroke but it's really just the inability to carry on clambering through the assault course of mundane cause and effect. If we ask Sheila then we can't ask Ron. If I have the kippers now then it's quiche for tea. Four score years is about all the ifs and thens you can take. Dementia's the sane realisation you just can't be *doing* with all that anymore.

My face was hot and tender. The snow's recording studio hush made small sounds distinct: someone opening a can of beer; a burp; a purse snapping shut. Across the road three drunk young men hysterically scuffled with one another. A cabbie wrapped in a tartan blanket stood by his vehicle's open door complaining into a mobile. Outside Flamingo two hotdog-eating bouncers in Cossack hats presided over a line of shivering clubbers. *Nothing like the blood and meat of the young. You can taste the audacity of hope.* Post-Curse these thoughts still shoot up like the inappropriate erections of adolescence. I crossed over, joined the end of the queue, with Buddhist detachment registered the thudding succulence of the three underdressed girls in front of me, and dialled Harley on the secure mobile. He answered after three rings.

"Someone's following me," I said. "You need to get out of there. It's compromised."

The expected delay. He'd been drunk-dozing with the phone in his hand, set to vibrate. I could picture him, creased, struggling up from the couch, hair aloft with static, fumbling for the Gauloise. "Harley? Are you listening? The house isn't safe. Get out and go under."

"Are you sure?"

"I'm sure. Don't waste time."

"But I mean they don't know you're *here*. They absolutely do not. I've seen the intel updates myself. For fuck's sake I *wrote* most of them. Jake?"

Impossible in the falling snow to get a lock on my footpad. If he'd seen me cross he'd have got into a doorway. There was a dark-haired artfully stubbled fashion-model type in a trench coat across the road ostensibly arrested by a text message, but if that was him then he was either an idiot or he wanted me to see him. No other obvious candidate.

"Jake?"

"Yeah. Look, don't fuck about, Harley. Is there somewhere you can go?"

I heard him exhale, saw the aging linen-suited frame sag. It was upon him, suddenly, what it would mean if his WOCOP cover was blown. Seventy's too old to start running. Over the phone's drift of not silence I could sense him visualising it, the hotel rooms, the bribes, the aliases, the death of trust. No life for an old man. "Well, I can go to Founders, I suppose, assuming no one shoots me between here and Child's Street." Founders was the Foundation, Harley's satirically exclusive club, sub-Jeeves butlers and state-of-the-art escorts, priceless antiques and cutting-edge entertainment technology, massage therapists, a resident Tarot reader and a three-Michelin-starred chef. Membership required wealth but forbade fame; celebrity drew attention, and this was a place for the rich to vice quietly. According to Harley fewer than a hundred people knew of its existence. "Why don't you let me check first?" he said. "Let me get into WOCOP and——"

"Give me your word you'll take the gun and go."

He knew I was right, just didn't want it. Not now, so unprepared. I pictured him looking around the room. All the books. So many things were ending, without warning.

"All right," he said. *"Fuck."*

"Call me when you get to the club."

It did occur to me to similarly avail myself of Flamingo, since there it was. No Hunter would risk so public a hit. From the outside the night club was an unmarked dark brick front and a metal door that might have served a bank vault. Above it one tiny pink neon flamingo none but the cognoscenti would divine. In the movie version I'd go in and sneak out of a toilet window or meet a girl and start a problematic love affair that would somehow save my life at the expense of hers. In reality I'd go in, spend four hours being watched by my assassin without figuring out who it was then find myself back on the street.

I moved away from the queue. A warm beam of consciousness followed me. One glance at the glamour boy in the trench coat revealed him pocketing his mobile and setting off in my wake, but I couldn't convince myself it was him. The ether spoke of greater refinement. I looked at my watch: 12:16. Last train from Gloucester Road wouldn't be later than 12:30. Even at this pace I should make it. If not I'd check in at the Cavendish and forgo Madeline, though, since I'd given her carte blanche with room service over at the Zetter, I'd most likely be bankrupt by morning.

These, you'll say, were not the calculations of a being worn out by history, too full of content, emptily replete. Granted. But it's one thing to know death's twenty-seven days away, quite another to know it might be making your acquaintance *any second now.* To be murdered here, in human shape, would be gross, precipitate and—despite there being no such thing as justice—unjust. Besides, the person tracking me couldn't be Grainer. As Harley said, his lordship prized the *wulf* not the *wer,* and the thought of being despatched by anyone less than the Hunt's finest was repugnant. And this was to say nothing of my one diarist's duty still undischarged: If I was snuffed out here and now who would tell the untellable tale? *The whole disease of your life written but for that last lesion of the heart, its malignancy and muse. God's gone, Meaning too, and yet aesthetic fraudulence still has the power to shame.*

All of which, my cynic said, as I stopped under a street lamp to light another Camel, was decent enough, unless it was just a fancy rationalisation for the sudden and desperate desire *not to die.*

At which point a silenced bullet hit the street lamp's concrete three inches above my head.

3

COGNITIVE PILE-UP. On the one hand I was busy cataloguing the perceptual facts—Christmas cracker snap, puff of dust, clipped ricochet—to confirm I had indeed just been shot at, on the other I was already past such redundancies and springing—yes, *springing* is the correct present participle—into the doorway of a former Bradford & Bingley for cover.

One wants clean, 007ish reactions at times like these. One *wants* all sorts of things. Backed into the urinous doorway, however, I found myself thinking (along with *oh for fuck's sake* and *Harley can publish the journals* and *what will survive of us is nothing*) of the refreshing abruptness with which financial institutions—B & B among them—had collapsed in the Crunch. Ads for banks and building societies had continued to run days, sometimes weeks after the going concerns had gone. For many it was impossible to believe, watching the green-jacketed lady in black bowler hat with her smile fusing sexual and financial know-how, that the company she represented no longer existed. I've seen this sort of thing before, obviously, the death of certainties. I was in Europe when Nietzsche and Darwin between them got rid of God, and in the United States when Wall Street reduced the American Dream to a broken suitcase and a worn-out shoe. The difference with the current crisis is that the world's downer has coincided with my own. I must repeat: I just don't want, I really can't *take* (in both senses of the verb) any more life.

A second silenced shot buried itself thud-gasp in the B & B brick. Silver ammo? I had nothing to fear if it wasn't, but no way of finding out other than taking one in the chest and seeing if I dropped dead. (This was so typically unreasonable of the universe. Apart from a few days to do what I had to do I didn't *want* any more life. What's a few days after two hundred years? But that's the universe for you, decades of even-handedness then suddenly *zero negotiation*.) I got down on my belly. The concrete's odour of stale piss was a thing of cruel joy. Low, moving in tiny increments, I stole a look round the doorway's edge.

The supermodel in the trench coat stood twenty yards away with his back to me. His left hand was in his pocket. Either he'd shot at me and was now making a suicidal target of himself for my return fire, or the shots had come from somewhere else, in which case only clinical moronism could excuse him from not having worked that out. The scene was an eighties album cover, his overcoated silhouette and the snow and the odd-angled cars. I was tempted to call out to him, though to communicate what, God only knew. Possibly words of love, since imminent death fills you with tenderness for the nearest life.

Hard to say how long he stood there like that. The big moments distend, allow intellectual expansion . . . a disused London doorway in a twinkling becomes a public toilet; the lower animal functions pounce the second the higher ones look away; civilisation remains in Manichean deadlock with the beast . . . but eventually he turned and began to walk towards me.

Flush to the wall I got back on my feet, inwardly loud with calculations. Hand-to-hand with me this marionette wouldn't last three seconds but somehow I didn't see it going that way. Between here and the junction with Collingham Road thirty yards away there was cover, four cars parked or ditched on my side of the road and a pair of old-style phone booths on the corner. Risky. But unarmed in the doorway I was a sitting duck.

Meantime my pretty young lord and his cheekbones had halved the distance between us and stopped again. For a moment he frowned slightly, as if he'd forgotten his purpose. Then, precisely as I opened my mouth to say, What the fuck do you want?, his left hand came out of its pocket, languidly, holding a silenced .44 Magnum, a tool of such prodigious bulk it was hard to imagine him having the strength to lift and aim it. He smiled at me, however—big sensuous mouth and brilliant teeth in a bony face ensouled by dark mascaraed eyes—then with a surprisingly steady arm raised the weapon slowly and pointed it at me.

The body gets on with things while consciousness prattles. Without realising it I'd bent my knees to leap (and there was the great futile ghost of wolf hindquarters, a feeling of exquisite useless memory); my hands were out, fingers spread, head full of gossip *but a shame not to see the first crocuses and if there's an afterlife but no just something like your mouth filling with soil then nothing—*

His hand—hit by a bullet—jerked and spat blood as the gun flipped away. He did a queer little simultaneous yelp and hop, staggered two steps forward clutching his wrist, then sank to his knees in the snow. His face, far from the Tragedy mask you might expect, showed something like bewildered disappointment, although as I watched, his mouth opened and stayed that way. A pendulum of spittle (a phenomenon all but exclusively appropriated by modern pornography) hung from his lower lip, stretched, broke, fell. The bullet had gone through his palm, which meant bleeding from the superficial veins only. If it had severed the median nerve there might be lasting damage, but with today's surgical top guns I doubted it. He sat back on his heels and looked about, vaguely, as if he'd lost his hat. The Magnum might have been a cigarette butt for all the attention he paid it.

The sniper's message emerged: If I can hit our friend's hand from here I could have hit *you* anytime. It was as if we'd been having a conversation and he or she just said this, quietly.

"Who are you?" I said to the young man.

He didn't answer, but very sadly got to his feet, left forearm cradled close. The pain would be transforming the limb into something big and hot and beyond placation. With careful effort he bent, retrieved the Magnum, put it back into his coat pocket. Then without a word or further look at me he turned and began trudging away.

I didn't doubt my reading, my risk assessment, my temporary safety, but those first steps out from the shelter of the doorway called for force of will. I took three and stopped. Pictured the sniper watching through the cross-hairs and, since every mutual understanding gives *some* sort of pleasure, smiling. My back livened to all the clean cold space behind me for a silver bullet to fly through. The smell of the falling snow was a mercy, though I was sure my clothes had picked up the doorway's vicious scent of old piss. I took four more steps, five, six . . . ten. Nothing happened.

The warmth of being watched never left me, but I walked to Gloucester Road without incident and boarded the last Circle Line Tube to Farringdon.

Harley had called and left a message while I was underground. He'd made it to the Foundation safely.

4

IT'S HARD NOT to think of 1965, the year I saved Harley's life, as one of rising sexual anarchy. Anti–Vietnam War demonstrations brought young men and women together and revealed the erotic potential of political activism. Mailer's taboo-breaking *An American Dream* was published. Brigitte Bardot was on all the U.S. magazine covers and in England it emerged that Myra Hindley and Ian Brady got turned on by murdering children. If not quite Anything Goes, then certainly Everything's Going On.

It's hard not to think this way, but to do so is to succumb to the compressions of popular history. The facts are true, the interpretation false. The 1965 contemporary humans imagine didn't really come about till 1975, and even by that jaded year what happened to Harley that night would still have happened. It was still happening ten years later, twenty, thirty. It's still happening now.

Wayland's Smithy is a five-thousand-year-old megalithic tomb in the Vale of Uffington, a mile east of the village of Ashbury, just southwest of White Horse Hill in the Berkshire Downs. It sits hidden by a little gathering of trees fifty yards off the Ridgeway, a chalk track following the line of the Downs *Homo sapiens* have been walking (knuckles gradually leaving the ground) for more than a quarter of a million years. Local legend is that if you leave your horse by the tomb with a coin on the lintel stone you can return to find it shod by Wayland, the smith of the old Saxon gods. During the day people stroll up from White Horse Hill, take photos, poke around, lower their voices, don't linger. The stones exude meat-freezer cold. At night the place is deserted.

They'd taken Harley there to torture him.

I shouldn't have been there. I should have been behind my own bars in the cellar of a purpose-acquired farmhouse a mile away. (Ah, the machinations of those premicrotechnology days! My cell contained a cast-iron safe with the key to the door taped inside it. The safe was welded shut, but with a hole in it just big enough to admit a human hand. A *human* hand. Once I'd Changed I had to wait until I'd Changed back. The simplest solutions are always the best.) I should, I repeat, have been under lock and key, self-gaoled and self-sedated, but at the last moment I'd weakened. I was in a phase of one kill every other full moon (less ethics than fear of the Hunt, who'd been on a recruitment drive since the postwar revelations of Nazi occultism) but abstinence was agony, even with the barbiturates, the benzodiazepines, the chloroform, the ether. That night I'd paused at the top of the cellar steps, contemplated the hours ahead. You go down, you take the drugs, you suffer near-death, you come through. You're still alive and you haven't killed anyone. Well, yes. But. The bare walls, the bars, the stone-flagged floor, the cheerful solid fatuous safe. Even underground the rising full moon like the Virgin Mary on a bed saying please, please, *please* just *fuck* me, will you?

With a physical gurn and a mental *bollocks to it*, I turned and went back upstairs . . .

The initial impulse, to *descend* like the Angel of Death on the nearest farm or village, didn't last. It was a mad little fantasy born of a month without live meat. Besides, I was an old dog by this time. I'd long since rarefied into dalliance and deferral. You let the Hunger run you for a while, give the lupine lineaments a workout. The muscles fire up, allow near-complete dissolution of consciousness into animal joy. You run and the night goes over you like cold silk. I crossed the Oxford–Didcot railway line north of Abingdon, swam the icy Thames, ran east into the Chiltern Hills almost as far as the London road. The Byrds' "Mr. Tambourine Man" had that week been displaced from number one by the Beatles' idiotic "Help!" Both songs went irritatingly round in my head like a pair of unshooable flies. The Hunger does this, seizes some arbitrary detail and makes it an incantation or totem, a maddening recurrence. Eventually I killed and ate. On the edge of the village of Checkendon an insomniac old duffer stood in his back garden smoking a roll-up, gazing blankly at his moonlit vegetable patch. He gasped, once, when I knocked the wind out of him, but that was the only sound he made. He'd survived the Somme, killed a man in a brawl in Ostend, discovered the peace of growing food in his own ground, the queer miracle of tubers torn up from the soil. Love, way back, was a scrawny Margate tea-shop girl with dark corkscrewy hair who'd sent him into a Lawrentian blood-drowse of certainty. They'd walked out together for three months and the night before he joined his regiment made long, dreamy love in a friend's purposely vacated room with the window open and the smell of the sea coming in. Then war and the odd ordinariness of horrors. Limbs lying around like big doll parts. You lose things. Overhear them saying, *He's not the same.* His libido remained a creature of frisky cunning: a stash of mouldy adult magazines behind the creosote tins in the shed, a blasphemous erection the other day with one of the grandkids on his lap, even Nell's old fat arse after all these years grist to the shameless mill. God could go to hell after what he'd seen, Jones's blown-off head rolling down the trench, Sterne with maggots living in his foot where the toes had gone—

I left his remains among the blood-drenched cabbages. Slipped from the village back into the woods. Disgust came in the hour after feeding but the years had reduced it to a heavy suave embrace. Disgust doesn't kill anyone. Loneliness, on the other hand . . .

At Wayland's Smithy an hour before dawn I stopped to observe. There wasn't, really, time to stop and observe. The farmhouse (for current purposes home) was a mile away through sparse cover. This was high ground at the mercy year-round to Valhallan winds. Trees were few. Hedgerows were thin. Darkness, or at the very least twilight, would be required to get home unseen. Nonetheless. Here were the prehistoric stones roused to sentience. Here was the air dense with human stinks, jabbering with primal energies. A Cortina was parked nearby. My flesh steamed. The last of my victim's life found settlement in me.

By the entrance to the tomb—a soft oblong of deeper darkness between upright sarsens—two men were intent on something I couldn't see. A third kept lookout where the trees opened onto the track.

"Terry, *I* should have the torch," this third one hissed. "It's fucking pitch-black over here."

The balance of power was evident. "Terry," in his thirties and older by perhaps ten years than the other two, was in charge. He was the bearer of the torch. The beam swung, picked out the sentry——a small-eyed face of boyish sweetness, fair hair, one hand raised against the glare——then returned with disturbing precision to its original object.

"Arse-bandit," Terry's nearer accomplice said, quietly. "He's probably enjoying this."

"Get him out again," Terry said. "Come on, Fido, out you come."

"Oi, bum-boy, chop-chop."

"He's . . . Gimmie a hand, Dez."

Between them Terry and Dez dragged their victim into the open. A lean young man with curled-under long hair, a high forehead, slender wrists and ankles. They'd tied his hands and gagged him. His shirt was still nominally on his back but apart from this and one dark sock he was naked. He lay on his side, not unconscious, but beaten to the point where merely drawing his knees up——the reflex to protect the soft organs——was almost beyond him.

"Come *on,*" the lookout hissed. "It's going to be fucking daylight soon."

"One minute he's moaning about pitch-black," Terry said, "the next he's on about daylight."

"Shut up, Georgie, for fuck's sake," Dez said. He took a swig from a bottle of Haig, passed it to Terry. Terry sipped, poured a libation on the victim's head, then kicked the victim in the face. As if the action had tripped a switch Dez immediately kicked the young man at least half a dozen times in the stomach and ribs. This was Dez: If Terry drank a pint Dez drank six and still didn't end up being Terry.

The man on the ground made a blurred animal sound, not plea or protest, just a foghorn note of despair. Dez spat on him. Halfheartedly stood on his face for a couple of seconds, balanced, slipped off. Terry reached into his jacket and pulled out a six-inch knife with a serrated blade. "Well," he said, in the tone of a patriarch at the end of a satisfactory Sunday lunch, "we know where he likes it, don't we?"

Call it an aesthetic judgement. One admits beauty to consummate sadism, but this confused pudding of cruelty was an offence. Dez and Georgie, at least, wobbled with sentimental notions: blue-collar fellowship; the Queen; family; Mum; graft; this sceptred isle. Match days would find these two Englishmen in full voice on the terraces, open-armed, in tears. By contrast Terry had depth but lacked the courage and vision that might have usefully plumbed past it and out into the world of others. His imagination would stick forever at himself. I had a bizarre little image of him sitting on the toilet, face slack from absorption in his own schemes—then I was moving.

Fast. Laughably too fast for them. Georgie was dead before the other two even noticed. I'd torn his throat out (redundantly since I'd already broken his neck) and still had most of its wet tubing in my left hand as I approached Terry and Dez. There was nothing to be said. For me this was just the relief of walking out of a bad play. Dez tried to run. Terry sat down somewhat in slow motion, mouth open, then made an attempt to get up on noodle legs. I took one bite out of Dez's midriff as his life slipped away, swallowed, got a flash of a cobbled street corner and a plain blond woman's moist frowning face—but stopped. I'd fed to saturation already. You ingest a life, trust me, it fills you. Terry watched everything like someone who couldn't quite assimilate the surprise party even after everyone had jumped out and shouted surprise. He did say, as I stood over him trailing the warm sausages of Dez's intestines, Please. *Please.*

Harley, their victim, had dragged himself a few feet away and stalled. I squatted next to him. He was at the pitch of fear that resembles calm. I very gently eased the gag from his mouth, pressed my finger, my awful hybrid finger—*shshsh*—against his lips. He nodded, or shuddered in revulsion, at any rate didn't make a sound. I found his trousers in the doorway of the tomb, brought them to him. His face was a mob of glistening swellings. The left eye was plum-fat and gummed shut. The right tried to watch me. Untying his hands took a wearying while, what with *my* hands. His three broken fingers made getting the trousers on a dreamy labour. I daren't risk helping him with them. He was too close to the edge of himself. I remained on my haunches a few feet away. It occurred to me that I hadn't thought past ridding him of his attackers. Had he run or walked or crawled away I suppose I would have let him, though it would have meant immediate flight for me (this night's work was bad enough now that I'd killed on my own doorstep) but he didn't. He struggled to his feet, took three or four steps, then collapsed, unconscious.

The sky said maybe half an hour till dawn. I hadn't made much of a mess, considering. Quickly I got bodies and gore into the Cortina. The sleeve of Dez's shirt made a fuse, worked into the tank with a twig. By the grace of the random universe a stainless steel Ronson was in Terry's pocket. I picked Harley up, slung him over my shoulder, lit the sleeve and ran.

And the rest, as they say, is history.

5

I phoned Harley from the Zetter's lobby.

"They're not onto me," he said. "I just got a call from Farrell. They didn't know you were here. They weren't following you, they were following the other chap. Wasn't even the London unit. It was one of the French. I could have been at home *in bed,* I hope you realise."

My young man, Paul Cloquet, had been under WOCOP's Paris surveillance for a month. "Lightweight stuff," Harley said. "He'd been clocked in the wrong place once too often. Plus he was having it off with Jacqueline Delon, apparently." Jacqueline Delon is heiress to the Delon Media fortune, also a compulsive occultist and borderline wacko. I saw her once in the flesh ten years ago leaving the Burj Al Arab hotel in Dubai. She would have been in her mid-thirties then, a lean, immaculately cosmeticised redhead in a tight-fitting green dress, big sunglasses, a thin-lipped mouth suggesting outer amusement over inner boredom. I'd imagined alluring espresso breath and slight constipation, psyche a compressed mass of Freudian maggots. Her father, who'd started in shipping, was a renowned Sadean debauchee. Allegedly she'd inherited his tastes as well as his fortune. "The French agent wasn't even supposed to be in the UK," Harley said. "He was supposed to call and let us take over from Portsmouth. But this is the French. They think we're all incompetent queers."

"You mean 'They think we're *all* incompetent queers.' "

"Hilarious. Anyway, fuck knows how but it turns out Cloquet had been watching you in Paris and followed you here. Fancied making a name for himself with a big scalp. My guess is he's a rejected WOCOP applicant with a *pomme frite* on his shoulder. The French operative followed him here and ended up, vicariously, as it were, following you."

"That's not possible," I said. "If this knob had been following me in Paris I'd have known. He's not very good."

"Really?"

"Really."

Ice cubes clinked in a glass. Harley sipped, swallowed. Around me the Zetter's lobby was warm and softly lit. The murmur and tinkle of the still-serving bar was a great reassurance. Two crisp-bloused young women were stationed at reception. When I'd walked in they'd smiled at me as if my arrival was a wholesome erotic surprise. The point of civilisation is so that one can check in to a quality hotel. "Well, he managed it some-how, Jacob, I assure you. I've just got off the phone with Farrell at HQ. The French agent identified you and—belatedly—called us. Trust me, WOCOP knows you're here, but only as of ten minutes ago."

I wasn't convinced, but Harley sounded exhausted and I couldn't bring myself to worry him further. It was true I'd been preoccupied in Paris. One of my companies was involved in a large takeover and I'd had too much contact with my human proxies for comfort. It was just possible, I told myself, that I might, with a headful of irritating practicalities, have missed a tail, even the moron with the Magnum. The bullets of which, Harley had also confirmed, were pure Mexican silver. Whoever Cloquet was, he knew the nature of his quarry.

"Obviously we oughtn't meet face-to-face for a while," Harley said.

"What while? In twenty-seven days I'll be dead."

Quiet on his end. Remorse on mine.

"Don't you trust me anymore, Jake?"

"I'm sorry. Forget it."

"I don't blame you. Sad old queen with hypertension and a sore arse. We should have found you someone young by now. We should have found you someone who—"

"Forget it, Harls, please." Again quiet. It was possible Harley was cry-ing. He's prone to emotional fracture since the prostate surgery. The truth is we *should* have found someone else, or rather no one else, since I haven't actually needed a human familiar for a century or more. The real truth is I should never have let Harley in to begin with, but I'd been in a phase of deep loneliness the night I put him in my exploitable debt. Now, hearing him sniff, once, and take a big sip, I thought: This is me. Every present anger derives from past weakness. Enough. *Let it come down.* "Ignore me," I said. "I'm just miffed about this tool following me."

Harley cleared his throat. Sometimes the sound of him doing this, or the sight of him struggling to open a pickle jar, or patting his pockets for the specs that are resting on his forehead breaks my heart. But what's heartbreak? A feeling. I've had it with feelings, even if they haven't had it with me. "Well, there's no point leaving the Zetter tonight," he said. "They already know you're there. Why don't you call me tomorrow morning when you've had some sense fucked into you?"

"Why don't I do just that?"

Another pause. There are these silences in which I can feel him restraining the word "love."

"Who is it tonight?" he asked. "Not the one with the plastic twat?"

"That's Katia," I said. "This is Madeline. No plastic. All real."

6

A VAMPIRE HAS written: "The great asymmetry between immortals and werewolves (apart from the obvious aesthetic asymmetry) is that whereas the vampire is elevated by his transformation the werewolf is diminished by his. To be a vampire is to be increased in subtlety of mind and refinement of taste; the self opens the door of its dismal bed-sit to discover the house of many mansions. Personality expands, indefinitely. The vampire gets immortality, immense physical strength, hypnotic ability, the power of flight, psychic grandeur and emotional depth. The werewolf gets dyslexia and a permanent erection. It's hardly worth making the comparison . . ." For all of which you can read: *Werewolves get to have sex and we don't.*

Though I'm not a misogynist I only have sex with women I dislike. Emotionally there's no alternative, but it's tough. Not because dislike impedes desire (on the contrary, as we modernly know, as we're modernly cool with) but because *my* dislike rarely lasts, especially with prostitutes, most of whom go out of their way to be likeable. Very many contemporary metropolitan escorts are ruinously likeable. Last year I hired a twenty-nine-year-old Argentinean girl, Victoria, whose soul spoke to mine in its own occult tongue within the first minute of our encounter. I had oral, vaginal and anal sex with her (in that order; I repeat, I'm not a misogynist) over a period of six hours (£3,600) then we went shopping at Borough Market and had breakfast overlooking the Thames. Crossing the Hungerford bridge we held hands and the wind lifted her dark hair and she turned her face up to mine for the inevitable kiss with already languorous knowledge of what was possible between us and I liked her enormously and she said, This is going to be trouble, isn't it? So I called the agency after putting her in a cab on the Embankment and told them never to send her to me again.

Why then, if they're so likeable, rely on prostitutes? Why not trawl the ranks of lady neo-Nazis or the register of paedophile mums? There's a deep reason and a shallow one. The deep reason I'll get to, by and by. The shallow one you can have now: In short, because nonprostitutes require reciprocal desire. I'm not an ugly man (or werewolf either, judging by some of the pug-faced lollopers I've seen in Harley's sneaked WOCOP files) but I'm a long way from taking any woman's attraction for granted. I can't hang around waiting for someone who fancies me. It's time-consuming. It's labour intensive. Therefore professional escorts, for whom, like therapists and mercenaries (and in happy contradiction of Lennon and McCartney), all you need is cash.

Madeline, white-skinned, green-eyed, with straightened blond hair, a short upper body and alert, pop-kittenish breasts, is self-congratulatory, vain, materialistic, brimming with tabloid axioms and fluent in cliché. She's been there done that, bought the T-shirt. She goes ballistic. She gets paralytic. She wants the organ-grinder not his monkey. She wouldn't piss on you if you were on fire. Amis's mouldering novelties are her lingua franca. Her telephone farewell is mm*baah*. This more than her spiritual deficits has kept my dislike going, but it can't last forever. A month in I can see the confused child in there, the gaping holes and wrong bulges in the long-ago fabric of love. There was a Doting and borderline Dodgy Dad, a fading and viciously Jealous Mum. This is the drag of having lived so long and seen so many: Biography shows through, all the mitigating antecedents. People teem with their own information and I start to get the headache of interest in them. Which is pointless, since when you get right down to it they're first and foremost *food*.

She was waiting for me in the Zetter's deluxe rooftop studio suite, albeit with a look of having just freshened-up from a quickie—moonlighted on my dollar since I'd booked her for the whole night. "Hiya," she said, raising her glass, muting the TV, summoning the feline glitter. *Extreme Cosmetic Surgery* was on. A woman was having fat from her abdomen removed and stuffed into her buttocks.

"Feel that," I said, extending my frozen hand. "Shall I put that on you somewhere?" Madeline's hand, French-manicured, was warm, lotioned and in even its moist fingerprints promissory of transactional sex.

"Only if you like hospital food, babes," she said. "D'you want champagne? Or something from the minibar?"

"Not yet. I'm going to wash the world off. You watch the rest of this. Order whatever you want."

Brutally thawed after three minutes in the shower I stood letting the hot jets hammer wolf dregs from my shoulders. Habit had me mentally busy with disappearance strategies and WOCOP blind spots (the Middle East, Democratic Republic of Congo, Sudan, Zimbabwe, all the fun destinations), Swiss bank account numbers, timer-equipped holding cells, fake passports, weapons caches, bent hauliers—but underneath it all was something like my own voice saying: This is what you wanted. Stop. Be at peace. *Let it come down.*

Not that I could hold either line for long. It had been ten days since I'd fucked Madeline. Ten days takes my kind to the edge. On the Curse you're desperate for sex with a She (if you're straight, that is; there are, naturally, gay werewolves—one resists "queerwolves"), while off the Curse your regular libido's amped up by the frustration of not having *had* sex with a She. It's a numbers problem. Infection rates for females have always been low, WOCOP estimates one to every thousand males. As you can imagine, we don't run into one another. I've never met one. In *Buffy* there'd be a howlers' singles bar or dating agency. Not in the real world. The Internet's no help: WOCOP's set up so many entrapment sites (infamously werewolffuckfest.com, from which they wiped out almost a hundred monsters—all male; no females, if there were even any left, responded—in one month back in the mid-nineties) that no one dares take the risk. For the longest time the romantic explanation for low rates of female infection endured: Possession of a womb, it was supposed, conferred a gentleness which simply could not bear the viciousness of a lycanthropic heart. Female werewolves, masculine idiocy maintained, must be killing themselves in crazy numbers. First full moon they'd Change, devour a loved one, be unable to live with the guilt, slip away somewhere quiet and swallow a silver earring. It's quite extraordinary, given the wealth of historical evidence to the contrary, how long this fallacy of the gentler sex lasted, but the twentieth century (years before Myra and the girls of Abu Ghraib put their two penn'orth in) pretty much did away with it. Now we know: If women don't catch the werewolf bug, it's certainly not because they're sugar and spice and all things nice. Whatever the reason, there have never been enough Shes to go round. It's one of the universe's great sexual tragedies. It's one of the universe's great sexual farces too, because none of this souped-up concupiscence serves an evolutionary purpose. Werewolves don't reproduce sexually. Howler girls are eggless, howler boys dud of spunk. If you haven't had kids by the time you're turned you're not having any, get used to it. Lycanthropic reproduction is via infection: Survive the bite and the Curse is yours.

But here's the thing, the old news, the stale headline: No one *is* surviving the bite anymore.

According to WOCOP not for at least a hundred years. Mauled victims die within twelve hours. It's a mystery. I was turned in 1842 and it's possible I was the last werewolf made. WOCOP, giddy with scientific incredulity, has captured werewolves and *given* them victims to bat around—without successful transmission. For the last century the species has been on a fast track to extinction, with or without WOCOP's exterminatory zeal. By the year of the Great Exhibition we were down to fewer than three thousand. By the time Queen Victoria died just under two and a half. And by the time of the first moon landing we were a list of 793 names. Within WOCOP the Hunt's become a joke, the guys who did their job so well they did themselves out of a job. Yearly their funding dwindles. A veil of melancholy has fallen. You'll be Grainer's swansong, Harley had said. His late masterpiece.

I turned the shower off, voluptuous from the heat and the perceptible pulse of Madeline's waiting body. One hard straight fuck, *allegro,* to kill the fizz and settle me, then the second, third and fourth movements, *adagio, ritardando, grave.* This is acute desire and acute boredom in the same glass. I do what I do with the glazed despair you see in the superobese as they chomp rhythmically through their tonnage of chocolate and fried chicken. One of the things I've been hanging on for is the death of my libido. I've lost interest in everything else, so why not? But it just keeps, as it were, coming.

A pre-coitus glance in the mirror showed the drearily familiar calm dark-eyed face (every time I see it these days I think, Oh, Jacob, do yourself a favour and *stop*) then I joined Madeline on the bed, where at my request she turned the TV off and lay on her back and opened her white-stockinged legs and placed her arms slave-girlishly above her head and for some fifteen minutes endured the increasingly painful realisation that I wasn't going to get an erection, while simultaneously doing everything in her power to give me one. Eventually, emphatically soft, I accepted defeat. "Hilarious though this sounds," I said, "we've just made history. This has never happened to me before."

Her professional self was miffed, and not very good at hiding it. After a clipped exhalation and a flick of the blond hair off her clavicle she said: "Do you want to try it another way?"

It's official.

You're the last.

I'm sorry.

It's called delayed shock for a reason. Until getting on top of her I'd been ethereal with not having taken it in, or with having doublethink-ingly taken it in and rejected it at the same time. But I'd put my hands on her waist and felt her nipples touch my chest and the softness and heat of her breath had in the way of such mysteries returned me to full and nau-seous mass. It was as if I'd been ignoring a shadow on my peripheral vision only to turn and find it was a thousand-foot tidal wave, heading my way. You're the last.

"Maybe later," I said. "It's not you, incidentally." She pulled her chin in at the absurdity of that, glanced away to the invisible documentary-maker who's always with her. Madeline's narcissism reconfigures awk-ward moments as opportunities for into-camera astonishment. Er, he*llo*?

I'd slid to rest with my head on her thigh, and now lay inhaling the smell of her warm young cunt with its wreath of Dior Addict. The last image before I'd quit flubbing her was of flak-jacketed Ellis holding up Wolfgang's giant severed lupine head while a Hunt colleague filmed the whole thing for the WOCOP annals.

"How about I give *you* a massage?" I said. If this was Hollywood I'd be dismissing her fully paid and heavily gratuitied in preparation for a night's heroic solitary brooding, a sequence of fade-shots wet-eyed Pacino would do with baleful minimalism, staring out at the city, lit ciga-rette, bottle and glass, the face tranquilly letting all the death and sadness gather with a kind of defeated wisdom. But this wasn't Hollywood. The thought of being alone all night released dizzyingly wrong adrenaline and a second phase of denial. It didn't bear thinking about. I removed Madeline's stockings.

"Is that nice?" I asked, a little while later. I'd turned the lights out but left the blinds open. It was still snowing. The yellowish grey sky and white roofscape yielded a moony light, enough for the glimmer of her earrings and the oil's sheen on her skin. I had her left foot in my hands and was working it gently.

"Nnnn," she said. "Lush."

I massaged in what would have been silence if not for her occasional groans, certain that if I stopped I'd be unable to tolerate my own hay-wire energies. I recalled how tired Harley had sounded on the phone, reread it now as the first sign of his willingness to let me go. Certainly my death would bring him up against his history, leave nothing between him and the horrors he'd helped conceal, but it would release him, too. He could retire from WOCOP. Go his ways. Chug down every day a little of what he'd become and hope to live long enough to ingest the whole ugly mass. At the very least find a place somewhere warm where he could sit straw-hatted with his bare feet in the dust and listen to what the emptiness had to say. If I needed an altruistic rationale for dying, there it was.

"Tell me some more werewolf stuff," Madeline slurred. I'd been at it for almost an hour without fear of her conscience kicking in: There's no boon or pleasure she doesn't peremptorily gobble up or absorb as part of her birthright. As far as she was concerned I could have gone on pampering her all night, all year, for the rest of her life. The truth is she's not a very good prostitute.

"I thought you were asleep."

"Tell me about the first time you killed someone."

The Werewolf Stuff. For Maddy it's another client quirk, but one she's hooked on. In the posteverything world it turns out humans can't kick the story habit. Homer gets the last laugh. "A lovely young girl lies on a bed in the dark listening to a fairy tale," I said. "But she's naked and the storyteller's hands are all over her."

She didn't speak for a moment, then said: "What?"

"Nothing. I seek objective correlatives for the times. Never mind. I killed my first victim on the fourteenth of August, 1842. I was thirty-four years old."

"1842 . . . So that's . . ."

"I'll be two hundred and one in March."

"Not in bad nick then."

"Human form sticks at the time of turning. It's the werewolf gets arthritis and cataracts."

"You should go on telly with this stuff."

Tell me about the first time you killed someone. For the monster as for the man life's one long diminishing surprise at how much of your wretched self you find room for. But there are the exceptions, the unique unpleasantnesses, the inoperable tumours . . .

"A month before taking my first victim," I said, "I was on a walking holiday with a friend—my best friend at the time, Charles Brooke—in Snowdonia. The year, as I said, was 1842. We were wealthy, educated gentlemen of neighbouring Oxfordshire estates, therefore we went about the trip as we went about everything else: with an air of good-humoured entitlement. Charles was engaged to be married in September. The summer before I'd shocked my little world by marrying a penniless thirty-year-old American woman I'd met and fallen in love with in Switzerland."

"What were you doing in Switzerland?"

"Charles and I were on a European tour. Not as in the Rolling Stones."

"What?"

"One went to Europe and saw the sights, it was the done thing. Arabella was travelling there with her aunt, a bad-tempered old turkey but her only means of support. We met at the Metropole Hotel in Lausanne. It was love at first sight." I ran my thumb very gently over the moist crinkle of Madeline's anus. A pornographer in Los Angeles said to me not long ago: The asshole's finished. Everything gets finished. You keep coming up with crazy shit you can't believe you'll find the girls for, that'll finally finish the girls. But the girls just keep turning up and finishing it. It's depressing.

"Something there you like?" Madeline asked, arching her back.

I removed my thumb and recommenced massaging. "No, it just seemed momentarily apposite. The word 'love.' "

She lowered her backside and reached down into the ice bucket, hefted the bottle of now-flat Bollinger for a swig. "Oh," she said, only very vaguely wondering what "apposite" might mean. "Be like that then."

"Charles and I made our camp in a forest clearing some few miles from the base of Snowdon. Pine and silver birch, a stream glimmering like tinsel in the moonlight. A full moon, naturally."

"That's really the thing then, is it? The full moon?"

On our wedding night Arabella and I had dragged the bedclothes to where the window's slab of moonlight lay. I want to see it on your skin.

"Yes, the full moon's really the thing," I said. "We all stupidly thought it would stop after astronauts had been up there and walked on it in '69. There was palpable species depression when it was obvious Armstrong's one small step changed nothing for werewolves, however giant a leap it was for mankind."

"Don't go off," Madeline said. "You always do that, go off on something and I get lost. It drives me mad."

"Of course it does," I said. "I'm sorry. You're a child of your time. You want the story. Only the story. Very well. To resume: Charles and I lit a fire and pitched the tent. Despite the clear skies it was warm. We ate a supper of salted beef and plum jam, bread, cheese, hot coffee, then between us drank the better part of a flask of brandy. I remember the feeling of freedom, the moon and stars above, the old spirits of wood and water, the companionship of a good friend—and like a radiation from home miles away the love and desire of a beautiful, tender, fascinating woman. I said an air of entitlement earlier, didn't I? That was true, generally, but there were moments when I was humbled by a sense of my own good fortune."

"How d'you do it, by the way?"

"Do what?"

"Talk like this, like telly?"

It had stopped snowing. The room was a nest of appalling contemporary comfort. In the new, still, science-fictionish light we could have been on another planet. The journals are in a safe-deposit box in Manhattan. All but the current one. This one. The last one. The untellable story. Harley has the code, the spare key, the authorisation. "Practice," I said. "Too much time on my hands. Shall I continue?"

"Sorry, yeah, go on. You had the brandy and you were feeling whatever. Free."

"Charles had a poor head for spirits, and he was exhausted from the miles we'd covered that day. Not long after midnight he retired to the tent, and within a matter of minutes was snoring, softly." I lifted Madeline's hair out of the way and worked her trapezoids from scapula to occipital bone. Anatomical Latin's an unjudgemental friend if you have to rip people apart and eat them. "While Charles slept I lay by the fire, thinking of Arabella. I considered myself the luckiest man alive. Neither she nor I was a virgin when we met, but the little boudoir experience I'd had was no preparation for what followed with her. She had rich, steady, amoral passion. What the world would have called perversion was between us a return to angelic innocence. Nothing of the body was shameful. Everything of the body was sacred."

"Sounds like *lust* at first sight to me," Madeline said, not without a trace of irritation. She doesn't appreciate not being the main woman in the room, even if the competition's been dead for a century and a half.

"Certainly there was lust," I said. "The holiest of lusts. But make no mistake, we were as deeply in love as it's possible to be. It's important you understand that. It's important for what comes later."

"Umm."

"You understand we were in love?"

"Got it. Oh God, yeah, do my hands. You forget about your hands."

"If this was Poe or Stevenson or Verne or Wells I'd have been drawn away from our camp by a strange sound or glimpsed figure."

"What?"

"Never mind. It's not important. I got up from the fire and walked away towards the stream. Thinking about Arabella, you see, had put me in a state of unbearable arousal. I needed to, in the vernacular, toss myself off."

Madeline said nothing but a microcurrent of professional alertness went through her skin under my palms. Oh. Right. Back on. Here we go.

"I walked perhaps twenty paces to the trees by the edge of the stream, unfastened my trousers and with my throat turned up to the moon began pleasuring myself. I knew I'd tell Arabella I'd done this when I returned home. To her it would be one more sweet sacrament . . ." I'd started the tale with mechanical wryness but had been sucked in despite myself. I felt, suddenly, not how long a time two hundred years was, but how short. There was the werewolf beginning, like a thorn that had just this second scratched me. Yet somehow between then and now near enough two thousand victims. I thought of them in a concentration camp heap. My guts are a mass grave. It could so easily not have happened. It could so easily have happened to someone else.

"Go on," Madeline prompted. The massage had paused with the narrative. Patience isn't one of her strengths.

"It was the last moment of my life as a human being," I continued, working my hands down her thighs, "and it was a good one: the scent of conifers, the rustle of the stream, the warm air and salving moonlight. I came, deliciously, with the image in my head of her looking at me over her shoulder as I fucked her from behind."

"Getting the picture, babes."

"Then the werewolf attacked."

"Oh."

"I say 'attacked' but the truth is I just happened to be in the way. He was on the run. I still had my prick in my hand when I heard a sudden commotion in the undergrowth, and in less time than it takes to tell he was on me—giant, strong-scented, frantic with fear—then gone. For one second of clarity I felt it all, the speed and bulk of him, the scourging claws, the meat stink of his breath, the ice of the bite and a single glimpse of the beautiful eyes—then he sprang away into the darkness and I lay winded, one arm in the rushing stream, my shirt gathering the weight of my own blood. Cold water, warm blood, something pleasant about the contrast. I seemed to lie there for a long time, but in reality it can only have been seconds before I saw the Hunt. They weren't called that in those days. Back then they were SOL, the Servants of Light. On the opposite bank three cloaked men on horseback, armed with pistols and silver-tipped spears, one with a longbow and quiver of glinting arrows."

"Seriously, you should write this down."

"They didn't see me, and the noise of the gallop would have drowned me out even if I'd had strength to call to them. In a moment, they too had disappeared. For a while I lay, strangely unconcerned, between consciousness and oblivion. I don't know how long a time passed. Seconds might have been days. The moonlight on me was like an angel and the constellations came down to me in tenderness: *Pegasus, Ursa Major, Cygnus, Orion, the Pleiades.*

"The wound had stopped bleeding by the time I crawled back to camp. Charles had slept through the whole thing and some quickening nausea told me not to wake him, told me, in fact, to say nothing of what had passed. What *would* I have said? That a nine-foot creature, part man, part wolf, had burst out of nowhere and bitten me, then disappeared, pursued by three hunters on horseback? There was a little brandy left in the flask so I poured it over the wound and dressed it as best I could with a couple of handkerchiefs. I built up the fire and settled down to watch through what remained of the night. We had no weapons, but I could at least raise the alarm if the creature returned." I lay alongside Madeline now, right hand doing deft shiatsu around her lumbar vertebrae. Most of her was busy absorbing the pleasure of the massage. A little of her kept the professional motor idling. Only a negligible bit of her was being irritated by whether this werewolf stuff might turn out to be some sort of mental problem.

"Naturally I fell asleep," I said. "When I woke, the wound had all but vanished, so that for the remaining four days of the excursion I lived in fear that at best I'd suffered some sort of massive phantasm, at worst that I was completely losing my mind. Every time I thought of telling someone—Charles in the first instance, Arabella when I got home—the feeling of guilty sickness rose and I kept my mouth shut." Madeline, fine-tuned for certain frequency shifts, touched my cock very lightly with her fingernails. "This, of course, keeping the secret from Arabella, was a Calvary all on its own. My wife's eyes sought mine for the old recognition, but found there a difference that would have been less nightmarish had it been less slight."

"Hey," Madeline whispered. "Look what I've found."

"I had trouble sleeping, swung between moods of euphoria and despair, two or three times ran an inexplicable fever and increasingly, as the month since the attack passed, fought against a new violent force of desire." Madeline turned, expertly insinuated with her bottom, guided what she'd found into its cleft. "By day I was plagued by fantasies, by night I was at the mercy of dreams. Arabella . . . What could she do but pour out love? Love was what she had. It beat on me like sunlight on burned skin."

From movements in Madeline's shoulders I inferred nimble searching in the handbag on the floor. A pause. The tinkle of foil. All this via the thin muscles of her hand, arm, shoulder, to me. My heart beat against her back. She was waiting for precisely the right moment. I could feel the small difficulty she still had suppressing the part of herself that didn't want to be a prostitute. My own tumescence reminded me of how the young man's hand must have throbbed.

"Arabella had never seemed so desirable to me," I said, "yet every time I went near her something stopped me. Not impotence. I could have broken stone with the erections I had. It was, rather, a compulsion to wait, to wait . . ."

Madeline opened the condom and reached back slowly for my cock. Between us we fitted the rubber with minimal ugliness. Another dip into the omniscient handbag yielded lubricant, which she applied with measured prodigality to the first and second fingers of her left hand. I got up from the bed with great care, as if anything—a twang from the mattress—could set the moment haemorrhaging. She backed towards me on all fours, stopped at the bed's edge, knees together, arse raised in elemental submission. Whatever interest she'd had in the story, her only interest in it now was professional, as aphrodisiacal instrument. This called for wisdom, she knew; it was the sort of thing that could backfire on her. She reached around a second time to work the lubricant into her anus. "What happened next?" she whispered.

Arabella forced back over the bed, naked, a version of her face I'd never seen. Myself reflected in the gilt cheval glass Charles had given us as a wedding gift, the fantastic absurd prosaic reality of my Changed shape.

I pushed my cock into Madeline's arsehole as the image shifted to one of her, Madeline, pertly shopping on the King's Road. She made a small noise in her throat, fake welcome. *What will survive of us is nothing.* "I don't tell that part of the story," I said.

This is the deep reason I only have sex with women I dislike.

7

It was a long night after Madeline fell asleep around three, leaving me alone in the inaptly named small hours, when so many big things happen in the heart. I lay for a while on the bathroom floor in the dark. I smoked. I went out onto the suite's roof terrace, where the undisturbed fall was deep (and crisp, and even) and looked across the roofs of Clerkenwell. Snow makes cities innocent again, reveals the frailty of the human gesture against the void. I thought of waking Maddy to share the scene's queer quiet beauty—and felt the impulse immediately sucked into the furnace of absurdity, where all such impulses of mine must go, accompanied by a feeling of dead hilarity. After a while the only thing you can do with loneliness is laugh at it. I drank the minibar's spirits, one by one, with reverence for their different personalities. I watched television.

I don't tell that part of the story.

Haven't told. Yet.

Gritters worked with jovial British inadequacy through the darkness, but by the time the Zetter's kitchen started up snow was falling heavily again. Londoners would wake, look out, be grateful: not business as usual. Thank God. Anything, *any*thing but business as usual. Daybreak was the slow development of a daguerreotype. Madeline woke—she does this with startling high-energy abruptness—and made it obvious by twitching her ankles that she was waiting for the sexual all-clear. "Why don't you jump in the shower," I said, "and I'll order us some breakfast." Which was what I assumed had arrived when, fifteen minutes later (the mere preamble or tune-up to Maddy's ablutions barely begun) there was a knock on the door.

"Hey," Ellis said with a smile when I opened it. "Not room service."

He knew there was only a moment before I'd slam the door or jump at him, so immediately put his hands up and said: "Unarmed. Just here to talk." Soft voice, Californian accent. Three years ago on a freezing night in the Dolomites he and Grainer had hunted and almost killed me. He looked the same: waist-length white hair centre-parted over a candlewax face with a big concave drop from cheekbones to jaw. For a second you thought albino—but the eyes stopped you: lapis lazuli, full of weird self-certainty. At an average height he would've been a grotesquely striking man. At six-four he entered the margins of science fiction. You couldn't shake the feeling he'd started life as a willowy San Franciscan hippy girl then had his genes diabolically fiddled with. He was wearing black leather trousers and a faded Levis jacket.

"May I come in?"

"No, you may not."

He rolled his eyes and began, "Oh come on, Jake, it's—" then kicked me with high-speed gymnastic accuracy between the legs.

I've been good at fighting, in the past. I've been dangerous. I know karate, kung-fu, jujitsu, how to kill someone with a Yale key. But you've got to keep your hand in, and I haven't humanly hit anyone for decades. I did what a man does, inhaled, suddenly, through the white light detonation and dropped, first to my knees, then, parts cupped, onto my side, knowing I'd never exhale again. Ellis stepped over me in a draught of damp biker boots and mushroomy foot odour and closed the door. In the power shower, Madeline sneezed. He ignored it, sat on the edge of the bed.

"Jake," he said. "We want you to know something. Do you know what I'm going to say?"

I didn't, but responding was out of the question. Everything other than staying curled up holding my balls and inhaling more and more air was out of the question.

"What I'm going to say is: You're the last. All the resources are dedicated. There's no one else left. It's all for you."

I closed my eyes. It didn't help. I opened them again. All I wanted was to breathe out but my lungs were annealed. Ellis sat knees apart, elbows on thighs. Behind him the windows were filled with pale cloud against which the snow looked like a fall of ash. History's given snow new evocation options: ticker-tape parades; Nazi crematoria; World Cup Finals; 9/11 fallout.

"Did you know?" he asked.

I very gently shook my head, no. He gave a dismissive shrug—obviously if I'd known I'd hardly admit it and prove WOCOP had a leak—then bowed his head and rolled his neck as if to ease mastoidal tension. He breathed deeply a couple of times, loosened his shoulders, then straightened, staring at me. "I'm supposed to be the leering villain," he said. "I can feel it, a sort of narrative coercion in the ether. It's here in this room, you know, that I should get up and take a piss on you or something." His fingers were long and knuckly, possessed of the ugly dexterity you see in virtuoso lead guitarists. "Don't worry," he said. "I'm not going to. I just felt I wanted to see you before we . . . you know, come to it. The last hurrah." He looked out at the snow and said, "Jesus, this *weather*." For a few moments we both watched the down-swirling flakes in silence. Then he turned back to me. "To be honest," he said, "I'm ambivalent about the whole thing. It's all ambivalence, now, right? Grey areas. Morality reduced to approximations. I know you know this, Jake, that everyone's more or less okay, all things considered. Look at this guy whatsizname, Fritzl, raping his daughter in the cellar for years. We don't mind him, really. We know there'll be psychology, we know there'll be *causes*. It's shock-fatigue. Beyond good and evil."

In the shower Madeline adjusted the jet option to "massage" and let out a gasp. It occurred to me that Ellis was on drugs. His face was damp.

"We fluked it, you know," he said. "Finding you. An agent from France came over following a suspect, turns out the suspect was following you. We thought you were still in Paris."

At the absolute top of my held breath I said very quickly: "Why didn't the agent kill me?"

"Come on, Jake. You're Strictly Grainer. You know that. All the Hunt knows it, all WOCOP. It's like one of the Five Pillars."

The pain was diversifying: stabbings in the abdomen; a dark red headache; something devious and knifey in the colon; the need to vomit. I got up on one elbow and released a burp, which felt like a little miracle.

"I won't lie to you," Ellis said. "I'll be sorry to see you go. I don't like endings, not on this scale, not *of an era*." One of Madeline's stockings lay next to his hand. He fingered it, idly, with his awful white asparagus digits, seemed for the first time to be reconstructing my night. It was irrelevant to him. I remembered Harley's description of him: magnificently abstracted, carries with him an inscrutable scheme of things next to which your own feels paltry. You have to remind yourself it's just because he's half insane. "There's a literary anticlimax available," Ellis continued, discarding the stocking. "You and Grainer come face-to-face and he realises that killing you will take away his purpose, his identity, so he lets you live. I've discussed it with him. He didn't dismiss it straight away."

I'd been exploring positional alternatives while he spoke and had ended up (again I say God being dead, irony still rollickingly alive) in exactly the attitude Madeline had adopted last night for receipt of buggery. Humour lightens. "But he did dismiss it," I helium-squeaked.

"He did dismiss it. He considered it, he weighed it, he dismissed it. Filial honour trumps all."

Filial honour. Forty years ago I killed and ate Grainer's father. Grainer was ten at the time. There's always someone's father, someone's mother, someone's wife, someone's son. This is the problem with killing and eating people. One of the problems.

"That's a shame," I wheezed. Ellis didn't laugh. (He *doesn't* laugh, Harley had told me. It's not that he doesn't get it. It's that amusement no longer makes him laugh. He's transcended too much.)

"I agree," Ellis said. "It's a goddamned *crying* shame. But unfortunately it's not my decision."

With monumental belatedness I wondered what he was doing here, manifestly not putting a silver bullet in my brain or lopping off my head. The question troubled me, my other self, the one that wasn't filling with joy at having just managed to breathe out slightly.

Someone knocked. "That'll be your breakfast," Ellis said. "I'll leave you to it." He got up and, stepping over me again, opened the door. I heard him say: "Take it in, would you?" Then he was gone.

A young hair-gelled man in Zetter livery entered with Madeline's Full English on an enormous tray.

"Cramp," I gasped. "I'm fine. Just put it on the bed."

8

HARLEY'S PHONE WAS off when I called him, which meant he was either at the WOCOP offices or dead. I couldn't shuck the conviction they were onto him. An hour after Madeline's departure (I spent the bulk of breakfast nursing my keening plums on the bed while she ate—with meticulous greed, since she allows herself only one fry-up a month) I'd arrived at the conclusion that Ellis's visit was simply to reinforce the story of how they'd found me. The man's mental style—oblique, tangential, possibly stoned—made him hard to read but there was surely something hokey about the way he'd volunteered that *We fluked it, you know, finding you.* The only motive that made sense was WOCOP's desire to preserve the illusion that Harley's cover was intact. Which meant it wasn't.

I passed the afternoon supine with a cold flannel pressed to my forehead, tracking my gonads' slow return to quiescence, CNN on the plasma screen for the lulling white noise of the news. I'm immune to news, *the* news, breaking news, rolling news, news flashes. Live long enough and nothing *is* news. "The News" is "the new things." That's fine, until a hundred years go by and you realise there *are* no new things, only deep structures and cycles that repeat themselves through different period details. I'm with Yeats and his gyres. Even The News knows there's no real news, and goes to ever greater lengths to impart urgent novelty to its content. *Have Your Say,* that's the latest inanity, newscasters reading out viewer emails: "And Steve in Birkenhead writes: 'Our immigration laws are the laughing stock of the world. This is the Feed the World mentality gone mad . . .' " I can think back to a time when something like this would have annoyed or at least amused me, that the democracy Westerners truly got excited about was the one that made every blogging berk a critic and every frothing fascist a political pundit. But now I feel nothing, just quiet separation. In fact the news already feels postapocalyptically redundant to me, as if (silent dunes outside, insects the size of cars) I'm sitting in one of the billions of empty homes watching video footage of all the stuff that used to matter, wondering how anyone ever thought it did.

"I had a visitor," I told Harley from the Zetter's bar, when, after eight in the evening, I got through to him at last. "Ellis was here this morning."

"I heard," he said. "I'm not surprised. Hunt consensus is you need your nose rubbed in it."

"That's not what worries me. It played as an effort to deliver the official 'how we found you' story. Which means that's not how they found me."

"Jake, no. You're being paranoid. I spoke to the French chap myself."

"What?"

"The twit with the Magnum. Cloquet. They brought him in for questioning. I was there during the interrogation. He *was* following you. Had *been* following you for a week in Paris."

I sipped my Scotch. The bar was low-lit, dark tones and soft furnishings, a carefully designed atmosphere of deserved indulgence. The long white calves of a moody brunette sitting with one leg crossed over the other on a high stool opposite me offered a momentary distraction. She was doodling in her cocktail with a straw. In the film version I'd go over and open with a gambit of jaded brilliance. Only in films is a woman alone at a bar actually a woman alone at a bar. The thought added itself to the mental racket I was sick of. Every Hollywood movie now is part of the index of Western exhaustion. I had a vision of my death like a lone menhir in an empty landscape. You just walked towards it. Simple as that. The peace of wrapping your arms around cold stone. Peace at last.

"What for?" I asked.

I heard the *shick* of Harley's malachite Zippo and his first intemperate drag. "That's what we're not clear on," he said. "He claims he's a free agent with a grudge against werewolves, but he's been fornicating with Jacqueline Delon for the last year so it can't be that simple. Trouble is he's somewhat gaga. High as a kite when we picked him up. Farrell told me he'd enough coke on him to get a horse airborne. My guess is even cleaned up he's borderline psychotic. In any case Madame Delon's the last person to be ordering a hit on a werewolf. She loves you lot." He caught himself. "Sorry, sorry, sorry. Bad choice of words."

"Forget it," I said. I sniffed my Scotch. It was supposed to be Oban but it didn't taste right. "What about the WOCOP agent tracking him? Did you talk to him?"

"Broussard," Harley said. "He's back in France. I didn't speak to him, but Farrell did. Story confirmed: He was keeping an eye on Cloquet, went out of his jurisdiction, realised Cloquet was tailing *you,* and rather sheepishly called us in. Jake, seriously, stop worrying. I'm fine. We're fine. No one knows."

I'd left my room to call Harley in case Ellis had planted a bug I'd been unable to find, though I'd spent two hours looking. Perhaps I *was* being paranoid. Either way I felt tired, suddenly, weighed down again by the saddlebags of *if*s and *then*s, the swag of dead currency. There's an inner stink comes up at times of all the meat and blood that's passed down my gullet, the offal I've buried my snout in, the guts I've rummaged and gorged on. Harley's crispness reminded me we weren't seeing this the same way.

"Okay, listen," he said, as if with clairvoyance. "We've got to get you sorted. It's going to take me a week, maybe ten days to get a solid out in place. That's lousy, I know, but in this climate everything's got to be quadruple-checked. I'm thinking—"

"Harley, stop."

"Jake, I'm not going to keep having this argument."

"Funny, isn't it, how now that it's come to this we both always knew it would come to this?"

"Please don't."

One develops an instinct for letting silence do the heavy lifting. In the three, four, five seconds that passed without either of us speaking, the many ways the conversation could go came and went like time-lapse film of flowers blooming and dying. When it was over all the relevant information was in. Paradoxically, it renewed our licence to pretend.

"Fuck you, Jake," Harley said. "This is how it's going to work. I'm getting you an out anyway. If you're still bent on this absurd suicidal melodrama when the time comes then you needn't avail yourself of it. But it'll be there. It'll *be* there."

Pity and irritation curdled, gave me an inkling of the energy I'd need to fight him. Well, let be. He needed this for himself. I was secondary.

This is what I've reduced him to: a human whose raison d'être is keeping a werewolf alive.

"Okay," I said.

"I should bloody well think so."

"*Okay* I said."

"Well, for God's sake. Why do you keep sniffing, by the way?"

"I ordered Oban. I think they've given me Laphroaig."

"The crosses you bear, Jake. You ought to get an award."

We discussed immediate logistics. Naturally the Zetter was being watched. WOCOP had tried to get an agent in but an international pharmaceutical sales conference had started today and the hotel was full, would be for the next forty-eight hours. The manager knew me and could be trusted to run light interference but staff would be susceptible to bribes. We had to assume my movements were marked.

"Which suits us," Harley said.

"Because?"

"Because you're getting out of the city tomorrow and surveillance is going with you. I can't set up an out with the whole organisation watching London. I'm good, but I'm not *God*. I need their attention elsewhere."

This is how it is: You come alert, wait, feel a piece fall into place, know the joy of aesthetic inevitability. I said: "Fine."

"What, no tantrum?"

"There's something I need to do. I'll want peace and quiet. Do you care where I go?"

"What do you need to do?"

I don't tell that part of the story. She'd looked into my eyes and said, It's you. It's *you.*

"Set the record straight," I said. "Does Cornwall give you enough room to manoeuvre?"

"Cornwall's what I was thinking."

"We should change phones again."

"No time. Have to trust to luck."

"I don't even know if the trains are running."

"Every hour from Paddington or Waterloo. There's a four-by-four booked for you at the Alamo office in St. Ives. Use the Tom Carlyle ID. There's something else you should know."

"What?"

"Someone hit one of Mubarak's places in Cairo three months back. Guards neutralised with rapid-acting tranx. No forced entry, an inside job."

Housani Mubarak, Eyptian dealer in stolen antiquities. At one time or another half the Middle Eastern market's passed through his hands.

"Point is," Harley continued, "they left everything in place. Took one small box of worthless crap formerly of the Iraq Museum in Baghdad. Mubarak's in a state. Can't get past the fact there was nothing valuable in the box."

"So what was in the box?"

"Quinn's book."

For a moment I didn't speak. Suffered a second dreary surge of pity and irritation. Painful to see how far Harley was willing to reach. "Harls," I said, gently. "Please don't be ludicrous."

Quinn's book, if it ever existed, was the journal of Alexander Quinn, a nineteenth-century archaeologist who had, in Mesopotamia in 1863, allegedly stumbled on the story of the authentic origin of werewolves and written it down in his diary. "Allegedly" being the key word. Neither Quinn nor his book made it out of the desert. A hundred years ago tracking this document down had been an idiotic obsession of mine. Now we might as well have been talking about Father Christmas or the Tooth Fairy.

"I'm just telling you," Harley said. "It's a possibility. You've never been the only one looking for it."

"I'm *not* looking for it. I haven't been looking for it for years. I don't *care* about any of that stuff anymore."

"Right. You don't want to know how it all started. You don't want to know what it all means."

"I already know what it all means."

"What?"

"Nothing."

Silence again. The bulging insistence of the real and Harley's palpable effort to ignore it. This was how it would be between now and the end, him covering his eyes and stopping his ears and holding in the words until it was absolutely beyond denial that we were *at* the end. And then what? What could he say to me except Good-bye? Or I to him except Sorry? Sadness went through me like a muscle relaxant. So many moments bring me to the conclusion I don't want any more moments.

"Call me when you get to Cornwall," he said, then hung up.

9

A MILE FROM the village of Zennor, south of the promontory known as Gunard's Head, the Cornish coast concertinas in a series of narrow coves and jagged inlets. The beaches—it's a stretch to *call* them beaches—are shingle and stone and even a full day of sun leaves them literally and figuratively cold. The onyxy water would be mildly amused by you drowning in it. Local teenagers stymied into near autism or restless violence come here and drink and smoke and make fires and work with numb yearning through the calculus of fornication. The rocks go up steeply on either side.

"The Pines" is a tall house overlooking one of these coves, backed by a hill of coniferous woodland that gives it its name. It sits at the seaward end of a deep valley, accessed by a dirt track (NO THROUGH ROUTE) down from the B road that links the coastal villages for ten miles in each direction. A former cattle farm, now equestrian centre, lies a mile inland, and the nearest domestic household is out of eye- and earshot on the other side of the woods where the track leaves the road.

This place ought, given what I've come here for, to have special significance, but it doesn't. I wasn't born here. I didn't become a were-wolf here. I've never killed anyone here, though a victim might scream his brains out unheard by all but spiders and mice. There have, over the years, been valuables (liquidated this last half century) but none stashed here, no Holbein in the attic, no Rodin under the stairs. I acquired the property because I had nothing in the southwest and because these devilish wriggling inlets are ideal for Harley's outs by sea. For all that, I've used it maybe three or four times in twenty years.

Yet here I am. Mailer famously labelled writing the spooky art. He was right. There's a lot of frontal lobe blather, a lot of pencil-sharpening and knuckle-cracking and drafting and *chat*, but the big decisions are made in the locked subconscious, decisions not just on the writing but on the *conditions* for writing: I resolve on the one story I've never told and lo! Here I sit, holed up in a house that means nothing to me, bone-certain no other place will do. Art, even the humble autobiographer's, invokes occult necessities. The damp rooms are high-ceilinged and largely bare. Furniture, such as it is, is miscellaneous and secondhand: a cream seventies vinyl couch; a Formica dining table; a sagging bed into the mattress of which something's burrowed with what looks like sexual fury. Everything's been gnawed, nibbled, bored, colonised, webbed. Last night three foxes came up from the cellar and sat nearby on the floor, concussed by my authority. (Dog family. Anything canine succumbs. There are beautiful women in Manhattan who would have married me on the spot for the charm I had over their mutts. Wow, he normally *hates* guys. I've never *seen* him like this. Do you live around here?) The central heating works, though after my first night I drove into Zennor and bought wood for the fires. HQ is the lounge. I'm stocked up with Camels, Scotch, mini-market basics. No TV, no Internet, no radio, no books. Nothing to aid procrastination. Procrastination, it turns out, does well enough without aid: This is the third night I've managed not to write what I've come here to write. Hours have gone fire-gazing or staring out to sea or merely lying in a whiskied doze warmed by the foxes' mute kinship.

Surveillance has followed as planned. I did some token fancy footwork en route to Paddington but made at least three WOCOP agents still with me on the Penzance train. If they didn't have cars waiting they might have lost me in St. Ives, but by midnight the dark said they'd found me again. Not a comfy gig for them. You're staking out the world's last living werewolf but most of the time you're thinking about your thermos, your chilblains, your frozen butt, the heaven of getting out of the snow and back into the van. I considered inviting them in. Rejected it: more procrastination. The dial went up a notch on Day Two; I think Ellis arrived. Grainer, my gut tells me, is keeping his distance, doesn't want the tension spoiled. We're like Connie and Mellors at the end of *Lady Chatterley's Lover*, apart, chaste, happily purifying ourselves in honour of the coming consummation.

Very well. Night has drawn in. The foxes are out hunting. There's fire in the hearth and Glenlivet in my glass.

But a cigarette, surely, to gather my thoughts.

As if they're not already gathered. As if they haven't *been* gathered, in a raw-eyed mob, for a hundred and sixty-seven years.

10

New, waxing crescent, first quarter, waxing gibbous, full, waning gibbous, second quarter, waning crescent, new. In the summer of 1842 I didn't know the names of the phases of the moon. I didn't know that a complete cycle is a *lunation*, or that the full moon is full for one night only (though it might appear so for two or three) or that the phrase "once in a blue moon" derives from the occurrence of two full moons in a single month, a phenomenon you can expect once every 2.7 years. I did know, courtesy of a wasted classical education, that to the Greeks the moon was Selene (later Artemis and Hecate), sister of Helius, who fell in love with handsome young swain Endymion, had fifty daughters by him, couldn't stand the thought of him dying so cast him instead into an eternal sleep. As an Oxfordshire gentleman my country lore came via my tenants, who assured me that if the horns of the moon pointed slightly upwards the month would be fine, and that if the outline of the moon could be seen there was rain ahead. A mopey scullery maid I had reciprocal oral sex with three or four times in my late teens believed that bowing to the new moon and turning over any coins you had in your pockets would double your money within the month. The only thing I knew about the moon that turned out useful was that its Latin name, *luna*, gives us the word *lunatic*. Useful because by the middle of August 1842 I'd become one.

"This is death," Arabella said, with what sounded like detachment. "To be with you and see you and feel you but not to be known by you. I can't bear it." We were in the study at Herne House, me in a low chair, her standing at the unlit hearth. The room's closed French windows looked onto a stone terrace and flower-bedded lawn, summer colours by turns dulling and vivifying in the day's flaring and subsiding light. "And yet here I am bearing it," she said. I was staring at the faded Bengal rug. My grandfather had made the family fortune selling Indian opium to the Chinese. "Is this what it comes to?" she asked. "Bearing what one can't bear?

The melodramatist taught a lesson, passion's rhetoric cut down to size? I suppose the word 'unbearable' is a lie by definition. Unless you kill yourself immediately after using it."

Since my return from Snowdonia she'd gone through phases of her own. Initially, innocent concern. The doctor had been called twice for my fever and cramps but on both occasions the symptoms had subsided. There were other symptoms—headaches, visual disturbances, nightmares, moments of objectless entrancement—but I'd hidden them as best I could. Concealment left me furtive and sullen, led Arabella into her next phase of less innocent concern, a question or two about "any amusing fellow ramblers" Charles and I might have met on our trip, a new investigative determination in bed, something searching and irritated that morphed into fear when time after time I tore myself from her as if in disgust or contempt. Lastly, in the face of my erratic moods and inexplicable actions (I'd grab her, lock the door against servants, work her clothes loose, feel her opening to me in relieved collusion—then again recoil, curse, beg forgiveness, leave her, ride out or walk the grounds for hours) came the current phase: an almost complete conviction that the things about her I once loved were the things I now despised.

"Can I really have been so mistaken?" she asked. I could feel her looking at me but fixed my eyes on the rug. The throb of its gold and maroon kept time with my blood. "Can I really have imagined your soul so much larger than it is?" Other women would have blamed themselves. Not her. She remained in magnificent self-certainty. From deep in my fugue I blessed her rarity. "I don't believe I can have been so wrong," she continued. "Yet perhaps I was. I'm an American. We're a people diseased with progress. Jacob? Look at me."

Irony big enough for a festival: She thought I was suffering a moral reversion. She thought this, my behaviour since coming home, was a resurgence of propriety: a woman to bed but never to marry, according to the local consensus. In our first conversation over a shared breakfast table at the Metropole her eyes had advertised frank enlightened fallenness. *In Eve's place I'd have done the same and in Adam's so would you. God put His money on shame and lost. Now it's up to us to make the most of what we've won*—all while she buttered a slice of bread and we talked of Geneva and her aunt prattled to Charles and the white tablecloth filled with sunlight and the silver winked. I knew from the first moment. So did Arabella. The knowledge was a perpetual latent mirth between us. She was a brunette, milk-white and supple, a little heavy in the hips. Her father had fought the British in the War of Independence. She'd been an actress, an artist's model, once or twice a kept woman, through all a voracious reader. Eventually, penniless, she'd nearly died of pneumonia in Boston. Her only living relative, grandly dyspeptic Aunt Eliza, had swooped from Philadelphia and taken her on with the sole purpose of finding her a wealthy husband, preferably a European one, who would take her far away and off Eliza's conscience forever. Arabella's submission to this plan was part curiosity, part exhaustion. She'd had infatuations, never love. Fifteen years of never saying no to life had stripped her of fear—and convention. The first time we went to bed together we did with gentle greed all we could think of to do, which between us, once I got past my own astonishment, was much of what could be done. I hadn't known desire could dissolve selves into and out of each other. I hadn't known love's indifference, love's *condescension* to God. She was a year older than me, ten deeper. She loved in casual imperious exercise of a birthright. I loved in terror of losing her. The staff at Herne House couldn't have been more amazed if I'd married a Bornean orang-utan.

"What do you wish?" I'd asked her one morning in the first week of our marriage. We were in bed, her lying with her wrists crossed above her head, me up on one elbow, caressing her nakedness. (The flesh had infinity in it. I must know every inch by touch yet every inch renewed its mystery the instant my hand moved on. Delightful endless futility.)

"To be as I am at this moment," she said. Sunlight lay on her like a benign intelligence. "A happy creature. I want conversation and grass under my feet and cold water to drink and this"—she reached for my cock—"rising for me in hunger, and an occasional glimpse of my own death to keep me mindful of the beauty and preciousness of life. There. That is the complete desire of Arabella Jackson—Arabella Marlowe. *Mrs.* Arabella Marlowe, in fact. What do you think?"

The house's spirits were in appalled awe of her. "I think I'll be forever running to catch up with you," I said.

So for a year we'd taken and taken and calmly taken without surfeit from this inheritance which restored itself daily.

Then, in mid-July, I'd gone with Charles to Snowdonia.

The question is: How long does incredulity last? How long do you go on with *such things don't exist* after one such thing has risen up out of the darkness and sunk its teeth into you? The answer is: not very long. My mother had been a lip-licking consumer of Gothic novels, but more than the *Vathek*s and *Frankenstein*s and *Monk*s and *Udolpho*s the library's pull in my childhood was a fiendishly illustrated *Bestiary of Myth and Folklore*. It was in German (my father, a committed monoglot, must have acquired it for its fantastical plates), of which I couldn't read a word. I didn't need to. The images were sufficient. Home from Wales a day sooner than expected (Arabella was out walking) I'd rushed from the carriage straight to the mouldering stacks. It was a hot afternoon of shivering leaf shadows. There was dust in the tapestries undisturbed since the Glorious Revolution. Of course the book was still there. All these years of its quiet sentience. Now loud sentience. The King James Bible. Locke's *Essay*. A complete Shakespeare. Newton's *Principia Mathematica*. Turning the *Bestiary*'s pages I was aware of these tomes gone tense and tight-lipped, a respectable family who knew their shameful secret was about to be exposed. The room was warm and goldenly lit, laboriously aswirl with motes. My hands buzzed. One knows a fraction before seeing.

Werewulf

In the full-page engraving up on its hind legs, maw open, tongue martially curled.

You'd think that would've clinched it. It didn't. It inaugurated instead a short period of emphatic, of *relieved* scepticism. Ridiculous. Utterly ridiculous. I closed the book not as if it had told a shattering truth but as if it had exposed a preposterous lie.

A short period, I said.

Transformation's nothing to me now (all over in less than two minutes) but it wasn't always thus. The process has to learn you, search you out, find its optimal fit. Like murder, like sex, like everything, in fact, it gets easier the more times you do it, the more times it does you, but there's no standard, no consistency. It gets the hang of some in three moons, others are still going through hell decades after First Bite. But however long transformation takes to bed down, *debut* transformation's something no howler ever forgets.

In my dreams a small wolf slept inside me and it wasn't comfortable. It moved its heels and elbows and paws, struggled to make space between my lungs, stomach, bladder. Occasionally a scrabbling claw punctured something and I woke. What were you dreaming? Arabella wanted to know. I knew what *it* was dreaming. It was dreaming of being born. The form and scale of its occupancy shifted. Sometimes its legs were in my legs, its head in my head, its paws in my hands. Other times it was barely the size of a kitten, heartburn hot and fidgety under my sternum. I'd wake and for a moment feel my face changed, reach up to touch the muzzle that wasn't there.

Days passed and being awake guaranteed nothing. You hold a teacup or the rein of your horse and there's your hand, your arm, looking just the same as always—but the mass is wrong, the reach, the grip. On the outside it's you. On the inside . . . not. It's not *you*, Arabella kept saying. It's still me, but it's not you. I kept moving out from under her touch, her look. Falling in love makes the unknown known. Falling out of love reverses the process. I watched the mystery of myself thickening between us into a carapace. Once you've stopped loving someone breaking his or her heart's just an unpleasant chore you have to get behind you. My God, you really don't love me anymore, do you? No matter your decency the victim's incredulity's potentially hilarious. You *manage* not to laugh. But breaking the heart of someone you still love is a rare horror, not funny to anyone, except perhaps Satan, if such a being existed, and even his pleasure would be spoiled by not having had a hand in it, by the dumb, wasteful *accident* of the thing. The Devil wants meaning just like the rest of us. Once, in the small hours, when I'd thought she was asleep with her back to me, Arabella had said, Put your arms around me, and I had, cupped her breasts and buried my nose in the warm down of her nape—and felt another bit of her faith die because despite my skin against hers something kept us apart. Me. Can't you come to me? she said, holding tighter. I'm still here. I'm waiting for you.

The simplest tasks required immense concentration: descending a staircase, opening a door, pulling on a riding boot. I had memories not my own. Waist-deep mist dividing around me. Trees rushing past. Moonlight on a mountain tarn. A young girl on a forest floor with her thigh torn open, naked white doll body on a bed of dark green ferns, eyes wide, dead. Jacob, where *are* you? Arabella wanted to know. Are you seeing something? I certainly was. Harebells crushed under his wrinkled quivering heel. The three moonlit horsemen like a living Uccello. Mucus in his snout had rattled. I fell asleep in my chair with my arm hanging down and woke feeling the stream's soft cold flow and my shirt warm-heavy with blood. I had to keep getting up and leaving the room, the house, *her*.

So the two weeks since my return from Wales had passed and every day I'd suffered the torture of torturing the woman I loved, the woman who loved me. At moments of supreme self-pity I'd hated her for it. Last night, woken mouth open, tongue out, body at tearing point over the simmering shape of the wolf, I'd left her asleep and gone out onto the lawn. The moon knew. The moon knew I didn't know what. The moon was an inscrutable pregnancy, a withheld alleviation, a love more cunning than a mother's. The moon had a secret to share. But not yet. Not quite yet. I'd wandered the fields, crawled in dew-damp before dawn. For Arabella, waking to find me gone had torn off a further layer of denial.

"This will almost, but not quite, kill me," she said now, still with the ominous neutrality, as the small-faced parlour maid crossed the doorway carrying a vase of white roses. "That love's no match for the whispers of English neighbours. Marlowe's American whore. Do you remember laughing about that? Do you remember calling it *quaint?*" I did remember. I remembered how that "quaint" had liberated me into superior benevolence, how with that one word the harness constricting the world—Blake's *mind-forged manacles* (the erotic revolution had resuscitated dead pictures and poems)—had dropped away. Now she believed I wanted something else. How could she not? I did want something else. *More blue-veined, more soft, more sweetly white / Than Venus when she rose / From out her cradle shell.* Together we'd celebrated the bliss of the Fallen flesh. Now I knew there was a Fall further, into the bliss of devouring it. (And a fall further than *that*. Or so the moon told. Or so the moon withheld. Not yet. Not quite yet.)

"Where are you going?" Arabella said. I'd risen from the chair and crossed to the French windows. "Jacob? Will you not look at me? For God's sake."

My legs gave. I went down slowly onto my knees, one moist hand slipping from the door handle. She rushed to me—or the creature did; the ether tore a moment and I couldn't tell which. Then her arms and orange blossom perfume were around me, my face close to her white breasts *take her life take her life take her life please God make it stop let me die take her—* "Don't," she said, as I pushed myself upright. "Don't try to get up." But I was on my feet again as if a spirit had hoiked me by the armpits.

"I must go," I said. I knew how insane that sounded to her. "I'll go and see Charles." Her detachment, I now saw, had been an experiment, a toe dipped in the emotional waters she might have to enter. In fact she was still waiting for me to return to her. And still I hadn't. She stared at me, forced into her eyes suspicion, anger, concern, potential forgiveness; to admit outright incomprehension *would* be a death. A few drops of sweat showed above her top lip. I thought of the look she gave me when I came inside her: sly welcome that segued into infinite calm relished confirmation. For a man a woman has no greater gift to give. And here I was destroying it. "It's not you," I managed to get out. I'd opened the door. The smell and weight of the lawn was a gravity I could flow into. "It's not you. I love you."

"Then why—"

"Please, Arabella, as you love me believe me there's nothing . . . I must be . . ." I stepped out onto the terrace—and vomited suddenly in one hot gush and splatter. The sound was a gash on the still afternoon.

"Jacob, for pity's sake come in. You're *sick*." Some relief, naturally, at the recurrence of a physical symptom: Better my guts than my soul, than *me*.

"I'm all right," I said, straightening, searching for my handkerchief. "That helped. Disgusting. Forgive me. Please, just let me be awhile. Let me walk over to Charles's. I'll stay there tonight and tomorrow everything will be different, I promise. Just give me this one night to clear my head." I could hear the precise degree by which my voice didn't sound right. My body laboured under invisible soft weights. With a superhuman effort I hauled the version of myself she needed to the surface, turned to her, saw hope ignite in her eyes, took her hands in mine. "Don't think what you've been thinking," I said. "You wrong both of us in thinking it. Something is troubling me, something . . . On my life, Arabella, I can't stay here tonight. You must let me go. Tomorrow everything—I swear everything will be different. Please. Let me go."

For days I'd been unable to meet her eye. Now I did and saw she was still warm and open to me. Her look was of steady entreaty, to return to collusion, to renew the silent vows, to *recognise* her. Summer had brought out a sprinkle of freckles under her dark lower lashes. In Lausanne we'd lain stunned on the bed after first lovemaking. She'd said, Goodness me, that was nice. "Whatever it is, Jake," she said, "you know I'm equal to it. I'm not asking you this, I'm telling you something you already know."

For a moment I felt completely normal. It was her. It was me. We shared an outrageous exemption. The distance between us burned away. These last days had been an absurd inversion.

"I know," I said—but the blood rushed hardening up from the soles of my feet and I saw the girl's thigh like a disgorged treasure of rubies and felt already though it was barely three in the afternoon the moon's slow-ascending joy. I turned and walked away across the lawn.

22

THEY'VE KILLED THE foxes.

I heard something outside and went to look. The severed heads had been left on the back porch facing the door, two with eyes closed, one— the youngest, ears too big for his head, like a bat—with eyes open. A single set of footprints in the snow from the tree line twenty feet away. *We can come all the way up to the house without you hearing.* I stood in the door- way and looked out into the woods. Nothing visible, but the darkness full of consciousness. I assumed Ellis. To stave off boredom and impress the juniors. To refer to Wolfgang. To advertise the product. I'm supposed to be the leering villain, he'd said back at the Zetter. If this was his work it would've been done with affectless efficiency. The man's centre of self is remote. I imagine Grainer watching his protégé in action and conceding with a sad fracture inside that the torch has passed to a strange new bearer.

I'll bury the heads in the morning. It's too cold now, and it won't make any difference to the foxes.

•

It was six miles cross-country to Charles's, and I stopped—doubled-up, glazed, queasy, for periods bereft of any kind of will—many times en route. When I lay down on it the land was a continuation of my skin, full of frantic whispering life. The *WEREWULF* engraving shivered from the grass, from the boles of trees, from the air's buzzing atoms. In a wood on the edge of Charles's estate I got down on all fours and cooled my hot face in a shallow stream of water-polished pebbles. The wolf's shoul- ders flirted with mine, his haunches, the scroll of his tongue. For all this there were interludes of sanity. Enough religion remained so that I went into and out of the belief that this was a punishment, superficially for carnal excess but really for living in a love that rendered God negligible, optional, obsolete. Thou shalt have no other gods before me. Yahweh's First Commandment and one he wasn't shy of fleshing out—Thou shalt not bow down thyself to them, nor serve them: For I the LORD thy God am a jealous God . . . He had every right to be jealous of Arabella. It wasn't the fucking, the licking, the sucking, but that with her these acts livened the soul instead of deadening it, elevated being instead of degrading it. Lest ye become as gods yourselves. The serpent's reading of the Edenic proscription was correct. We were our own divine images, not graven but flesh and blood, and God shrank in the light of our divinity. Christ was born of a virgin and died one himself. What did *he* know? The truths of the body were ours, not his. Human love didn't eradicate God, but it put Him into His proper distant second place.

And for this, for thy wretched arrogance, I have turned thee into a monster. At times I half-convinced myself I could hear—in the trees' susurrations, in the chuckle of water, in the soft clamour of thin air—the Almighty's condemnation. But the feeling was always displaced by a worse feeling: that where should have been God's booming petulance was in fact a slab of silence the size of the universe. This intimation, of the night sky like an abandoned warehouse of stars, of the earth heaving up flora and fauna in epic meaninglessness, was a horror so unexpectedly huge I turned back to the conviction of God's wrath with a kind of relief. *Did He who made the lamb make thee?*

It was dark when I reached Archer Grange, the two-hundred-year-old pile Charles shared with his mother, older sister, deaf uncle, three bull mastiffs and a staff of twenty-four. Mother and sister were summering in Bath. (A mercy: Lady Brooke disapproved of my mercantile origins and Miss Brooke disapproved of my wife.) I had a struggle with Charles. My story was that Arabella and I had had our first fight, that I'd said absurd hot things and stormed out, that what I needed was a bottle from the Brooke cellar and a bed for the night, that the walk over here had given me time enough to realise I'd been a fool, that tomorrow would see me return in conciliatory penitence. All well and good, but my friend wasn't blind. I was wet with sweat and shaking. For God's sake, I looked as if I'd been brawling with a bear. We must have Dr. Giles. A servant would be despatched . . . I argued him out of it, but the effort nearly killed me. Only the artfully sheepish admission that I'd slipped and fallen in the stream and bruised my knee and the concession that I'd take warm brandy and one of the housekeeper's legendary herbal compresses to an early bed kept the doctor out of it. Even then Charles insisted on ministering to me himself. Soon to be married, he wanted details of the fictional domestic spat, and while he bound on Mrs. Collingwood's malodorous poultice I in disbelief bordering hilarity concocted nonsense about my wife's madcap tastes in interior décor and my irrational reluctance to alter any of Herne House's furnishings. It was quite a performance. I was in the largest guest bedroom, overlooking the Grange's ornate front gardens and fountained lawn. The moon would come up over the line of poplars at its edge. Less than an hour. Twice the urge to rip Charles's face off with my hands nearly got the better of me. Only the brandy—of which I'd drunk half a bottle by the time he left me to my rest—saved him.

It seemed a long time I lay there waiting for the thing I didn't believe would happen and believed would happen and knew couldn't happen and knew must happen. The scent of honeysuckle trellised just below the open window mingled with the room's odours of old wood and lavendered linen. For some reason I decided to fight the impulse to get up and pace around. The poultice felt like an enormous tick. I ripped it off and threw it in the chamber pot. I grabbed the bedside candlestick to see if the wax would melt in my hand. It didn't. I dropped it on the floor. I left my body for a few moments, long enough to look down at it shivering on the bed. Pale, sweating, knees pulled up. Charles had lent me a nightshirt. Pulling it off seared and abraded me. Crazed American ideas of style, I'd said. It made me laugh out loud. She wouldn't have cared if we'd lived in a shed. Her dark eyes were flecked with reddish gold. When I fall asleep with you, she said, it's like I'm sleeping *in* you. I drifted back down into my body. He wasn't a man and he wasn't a wolf. Harebells crushed under an appendage neither foot nor paw, a leathery hybrid. One jewel eye a steady gleam of the lives he'd taken. His eye said, The deepest nourishment, something like love. Something like love. You'll see. You'll see.

The moon rose.

Blood dragged itself upwards, the whole bodysworth packed tight under the top of my skull, an impossible accommodation, a gathering breath before brutal redistribution. I saw my mouth open and my fingers working during those moments of tantalising semifreedom from my carcase. I tore out, strained, was yanked back in. This was a new frank dark sacrament, something no-nonsense, sure of itself. There were flecks of resistance—I imagined dashing my head on the stone mullion—but the other thing swept them aside. The other thing. Indeed. A brother, a tall twin from before birth with an agenda of brisk recalibration. He arrived with nonnegotiable needs—or needs negotiable only in their potential expansion: Enough now was no guarantee of enough later. My shoulders shifted, not without difficulty learned the strange game of osteomorphosis, bore the hurried tectonics, the sensation of turning to ice and the shocking thaw that left a new grammar of movement. Shoulders, wrists, ankles—first to Change, last to Change back. I rolled onto my side. Fairytaleishly too big for the bed, since everything was growing. The not toenails nor quite claws had scarred the inlaid rosewood. I dropped onto the floor dizzied by the inrushing night's symphony of smells, from the garden's shut roses to the fields' wealth of dung. An acre of wheat in the south crackled and splashed. Invisible giant hands gripped my neck and twisted in opposite directions, the schoolyard bully's Chinese burn writ large, a necessity it turned out for the head's jerky magic into its more blatantly predatory lineaments. My lupine twin was impatient. A being was no good without a body. The slow hindquarters tested his tolerance of delay and mine of pain. My new skull shuddered and my bowels disencumbered themselves of a piping hot turd. It was still him and me but we eyed each other knowing everything depended on bridging the gap. Cooperation would come, the two strands would plait so that *we* would become *I*, but it was his birthright to take the inaugural moment by force. *Do as I say. You will do as I*—many of his early utterances were cut off by the inarticulate urgency of animal need. It came down like a guillotine. I knew what the need was. There was no not knowing. There was nowhere to hide the thought that I wouldn't . . . that I would *never*—

Many of my utterances were cut off, too.

For a moment I squatted on new long hairy haunches in the open window. Matter, raped and rearranged, murmured its trauma in the quivering cells. Consciousness, it transpired, was tender, could be hurt by something rough shoving itself in next to it. *He forced himself inside me.* I thought of history's violated maids—and got his sharp correction like a slap: No anachronisms, idiot. The old world's dead.

A pause, as if a muted bell had clanged. The night's soft tumult stopped. Complete silence and stillness. This was sufferance on his part, a moment allowed to mark the passing of the life I'd known. (For him *this* was the heartbreak chore to be got out of the way quickly.) I looked out at the moonlit topiary, the pale flowers, the lawn holding its breath. I waited. Nothing. Here again was the colossal silence where God's, someone's, anyone's voice should have been. Learn this lesson now, my brother said, I shan't teach it twice. There is nothing. It *means* nothing. Then the night exhaled and flowed again. I knew with clairvoyant weariness I'd go back countless times to the question of why, how, but knew too I carried the answer inside. It had gone in like an inhaled spec of toxic dust. Life is nothing but a statement of what happens to be. *That* is all ye know on earth and all ye need to know. A few seconds wasn't much to swallow a universe of pointlessness, but it was all the time I had.

A breeze stirred the honeysuckle, the hairs on my ears and delirious wet snout. My scrotum twitched and my breath passed hot over my tongue. My anus was tenderly alert. I pictured my human self jumping the twenty feet, felt the shock of smashed ankles and slivered shins—then the new power like an inkling of depravity. I leaped from the window and bounded into the moonlight.

12

FIELDS ROLLED UNDER me. Summer dry grass and the fruit-sour of cowshit. Daisies and buttercups frail lights in the land's umber. Cattle and sheep fled, shrank, huddled at the hedgerows. *Not these.* All right, but the air was plump and beating with bodywarm life and its stink of fear and the moon was a woman whose smile and wide-openness seared with generous demand. My long jaws and hybrid hands ached with what they could do. Orion swung up over the woods and the question how far back do we . . . ? Greeks? Egyptians? The myth of Lycaon. And hadn't I read somewhere that the American tribes—but the trees closed over me and soon too soon the pork-sweet and ironish odour of human flesh and blood stunned me into a swooning halt.

My brother was a capricious gravity. At moments his pull had been light. Now I fell to him as if a trapdoor had opened under my feet.

Bragg was Charles's gamekeeper.

This was his cottage.

Bragg was out hunting poachers.

This was Bragg's wife.

This was no. This was yes. This was him. This was me.

Nature doesn't judge. An earthworm curled and uncurled under my foot. The air gave its odours—sage, sawdust, wet wood, compost, lavender, charcoal—as I crept towards her. Fifteen paces. Ten. Five. Close enough to see through the window. She was standing in profile at a tin sink scouring a skillet with soot. The scrubbed table showed the remnants of supper: a torn white loaf, steamed onions, a muslined cheese, yellow butter, a pewter tankard flecked with suds. A bright fire burned in the limewashed hearth, livened the room's half dozen bits of copper and brass. A dark-haired child of two or three years sat on the floor playing with a box of empty cotton reels.

The woman was barely out of girlhood, pallid, mouse-faced, with greasy hair pinned up under a mobcap. Thin hands raw from too much cold water. I wanted her name. Sally? Sara? I'd spoken to her once, when——

It was as if he'd been holding in check the force of what we were to maximise its impact when he let it go. Not that he fully let it go. Instead he kept just enough back so I could feel my own helplessness in the torrent of our will. *Do you see?* Yes, I did. A rush of appetite skewered my salivary glands and like a single stroke of expert lewdness raised my lupine cock into hitherto unknown hardness—but within seconds I was soft again. No, not that. Only if she were to become. You think—but it's not. It doesn't——

I could feel my brother's irritation, as if I fit him like a too-tight collar. My ignorance was a maddening labour to be got through with gritted teeth. *If you tried that it wouldn't work—This is not what we——*

My cock stiffened again as she blew her fringe off her moist face—but a second time softened. A moment of complete inner silence, then sudden loud Hunger, the other Hunger, booming like a kettledrum. Understanding went in: Lust was a mistaken reflex, an adjustment phase, soon burned through. The new desire made the old seem a whim. Only if she were to become. Only if she. To fuck to kill to eat. Fuck kill eat. There *was* a Trinity mystery, but only if . . . but only if——

He upped the drum's rhythm. Thinking slid and fell like snow thawing from a roof. Her thin arms were bare from the elbows down. Collar open. Neck tendons rose when she scrubbed. White negligible girlish legs floating either side of rutting Bragg like the antennae of a confused insect. Forlorn pale toes. A shallow whorl of a navel. A quiet girl. Humans wear their histories like microclimates. She'd never shone among her eight siblings, had been vaguely loved only when noticed, had remained unformed until Bragg then seen her chance for a single leap into identity. And still her centre didn't hold. Even giving birth hadn't established her; it had gone through her like a fire through a field, a random agony that had left her hurt and curled around herself. She spent hours unanchored, drifted through by what felt like other people's daydreams, though she washed and cleaned and looked after the child and opened her legs for the man.

You don't just get the body. You get the life. *Take a life.* Into yourself. The deepest nourishment. Something like love. You'll see. The space between you swells with untenable potential. Her little breasts the size of apples and her thin-skinned throat with its pounding jugular were already in my hands, between my teeth, taut and turgid, ripe for rupture. I stood outside. I saw how it would be. Nothing but my brother's grip on the rein kept me back.

Not her.

He let the thought stand alone, unembellished.

Not her.

23

HE RAN. I ran. We ran. All persons, the plural and two singulars justified. They grappled, sheared off, bled into each other, enjoyed moments of unity. Out of the woods moonlight painted me nose to rump, a palpable lick of infinitely permissive love that asked of me only that I *be completely myself.* What more generous request can a lover make? It's what I'd asked of Arabella. It's what she'd asked of me. Until now.

He ran. I ran. We ran. At moments the triumvirate dissolved and was neither him nor I nor us but an unthinking aspect of the night, inseparable from the wind in the grass or the odours in the air, a state—like getting lost in music—recognisable only by coming out of it.

Herne House.

Home.

A hundred yards away I smelled the stabled horses sweating, heard them shifting their feet in the stalls, a lovely sound, the *clop-rasp* of iron on stone. I leaped the gravelled drive and walked up the rollered front lawn. From butler to tea boy the house held seventeen human hearts. Moonlight silvered the casements. The master bedroom was on the second floor. These warm nights we slept with the window open. And there it was, open. The eighteenth heart.

There's a view that the only thing to do with atrocity is chronicle it. Facts, not feelings. Give us the dates and numbers but stay out of Hitler's head. That's all well and good when the chronicler is outside the atrocity. It won't wash when the chronicler *is* the atrocity.

She was asleep, lying on her front, face turned towards me, one bare arm and shoulder in moonlight so bright I couldn't believe it hadn't woken her. The scene's painterly sumptuousness registered, peripherally: her long dark curls against the ivory pillow, the shut lilac buds of her eyes, that white Aphrodite arm on the damask counterpane. Peripherally, because what I could see mattered so much less than what I could smell:

her vinous breath and orange blossom perfume, a fraught day's sweet-salt sweat (she'd bathed cursorily) and barely touched food (poached salmon; a summer fruit compote; coffee), her fearless female blood, a thrilling whiff of shit and the sleepwarm tang of her clever silken cunt. And what I could smell mattered so much less than what I knew: that for a moment I'd be closer to her than ever before, that every secret would be revealed, every treasure yielded, every shame exposed, every shred of self surrendered. I knew—it was passed from him to me, the old dull divine truth—that no ecstatic union compares with killing the thing you love.

My wife didn't wake until I was fully inside the room. I was both raw with awareness and buried in the Hunger like a lone seed deep in the ground. You're the thing you don't want to be and it's a joy. She ought to have screamed. According to fiction she ought to have screamed. But people never do what fiction says they do. Instead of a scream she opened her mouth and made a small noise of giant shock and revulsion, almost a hiccup. As if she had all the time in the world she lifted herself on one elbow. Her face had always had this distended version of itself—terror—but I was only seeing it now. I put a claw in the bedclothes and dragged them off. My cock rose again at the sight of her naked. My own drool fell on it. The spectacle forced a weird hiatus. Then she turned to fling herself off the bed and I grabbed her ankle and pulled her towards me. At the touch of her my member shrank. Fuck kill eat. Fuck kill eat. Fuckkilleat. But not with—

She lashed out with her free foot, missed, because I had so much time to move. I was so fast it was like having the gift of foresight. Then she did open her mouth to scream—and recognised me. It was what I'd been waiting for. You don't know what you've been waiting for until it arrives. We froze. She looked into my eyes. She said, "It's you."

Then, because I knew she knew me, and because I could kill everything in her before killing her, and because that was the trick that led to the peace that passeth understanding, and because the only way was to begin with the worst thing, I let it come down.

The flesh of her thigh opened with a spray of warm blood. She looked sprinkled with garnets. She repeated, "It's *you*," and I grabbed her by the neck and drew her to me. The Hunger fits like a womb. You deliver yourself from it. You must be born. Savour this, he warned. Savour it because too soon you won't taste the details. I wished I could speak to her. Wished with all my heart I could say, "Yes, it's me." That I couldn't left the tiniest fraction missing from her horror, and though it was tiny we felt it, my brother and I, like a splinter. I cut off the air in her throat and looked into her eyes. Goodness me, that was nice. *Savour this*—but I didn't have his restraint. The smell of blood was a finality. My knees loosened. When I couldn't stand it anymore I pushed her down onto the bed and sank my teeth—*that first, fine, careless rapture*—into her throat.

There *is* the frenzy (our unatrocious chronicler would list the postmortem facts: severed trachea, carotid and femoral arteries; massive tissue loss from the torso, thighs, buttocks; bowels ruptured; kidneys, liver and heart gone; lacerations of the breasts, vagina and perineum) but the frenzy holds a centre like the eye of a storm, and here something else is happening, an entranced consumption. Here you're taking a life. You can't swallow it whole. You get strands, bites, glugs, chunks. The life of Arabella Marlowe, née Jackson. She was at approximate peace with herself. Delivered into it through the troubled labour of shedding constraints. Still the odd flash of self-loathing—*slut, whore*—like distant lightning, but powerless, really, against her bigger, her wiser, her more wholly human self. Memories: her mother's smell of flour and lavender. A red ploughed field under a blue sky. A painted carnival horse. A dead possum in the yard. Her limbs lengthened. The arrival of her breasts filled her with maidenly pride. The shocking little pearl of pleasure down there. *Dost thou love me? I know, thou wilt say—Ay; And I will take thy word.* Her father had a complete Shakespeare. She learned lines and entered characters. There was some incompletely hammered-out contract between art and God. Male attention went to her. Once or twice something shy and fierce in a man that hinted at what love would be, an index of the body's maddening insufficiencies. She took her clothes off for painters, sculptors, lovers, learned poker, the rough friendship of rye whisky. Knowing the dangers she pushed forward into experience, suffered, caught on fire, rolled in the dirt to put herself out. She pushed harder and got sick. Pneumonia. Aunt Eliza she hadn't seen for fifteen years. She emerged from the interrogation by death knowing she'd never be quite as awake as she'd once dreamed. Then Europe, Switzerland, white mountains, me. Love at first sight.

I swallowed it, stole it, the wealth you never count till it's taken. It went into me, an obscene enrichment, a feast of filthy profit. She fought me, such as she could. She wanted life. Unequivocally she wanted life. She couldn't scream. I'd gone through her vocal cords in the first bite. Five seconds. Ten. Twenty. Instinct tells you when they're going. (As a kindred instinct tells you when they're coming.) I looked at her, gave her my werewolf face dark with her blood, my fangs dressed in her shredded treasures. She was past pain now. Her eyes said she'd gone on from it, was standing at the rail looking back at the dock. Embarkation. I could never have not loved her without becoming someone else. But I had become someone else. She blinked, once, languidly. Her lips moved. One wet gobbet of her own raw meat winked red on her cheek. Dark brown eyes flecked with gold. These eyes said: I'm going. She was past the old language: murder, morality, justice, guilt, punishment, revenge, the words were valueless currency on her voyage. Her eyes said: So, this is it. In the moment before they closed she made the last shift: At the true end of life one doesn't care how one's come to death. I wasn't Jacob, or her husband, or her killer, or a monster; I was just the thing that had unlocked the door. Now she saw through me and the matter of this world into final solving darkness or annihilating light. I was no longer important. Her eyes widened once, then closed.

At some point our struggle must have clipped the bedside table because the lamp had fallen, smashed, spilled, spread a little pool of flame. One bed drape had caught. The fire moved in leisurely consummation up it, across to its neighbour. I only noticed the heat because hers had gone. Once the body's light's out the Hunger admits a strand of disgust, a post-coital realism before the act is complete. You eat fast, in a worsening temper, with contempt for God's creative vulgarity in yoking consciousness to meat. You eat fast because revulsion's chasing you. When it catches you—seeks you out like the long arm of the law—you'll have to stop, you won't be able to go on.

The fire bloomed. In one gesture of flame the whole rug was ablaze. I caught sight of myself for the first time in the cheval glass, hunched over the gored body. It was a hideous composition, a pornographic companion piece to Fuseli's *The Nightmare*—or a satire on its excesses. Her left arm hung white, slender, supple, miraculously untouched, the hand half open, fingers arrested as if in mid-evocation of something delicate and elusive. Goodness me, that was nice.

Satiety ambushed me. Too much too soon. A delayed expansion to accommodate the haul. Fed on her flesh my own silted. The stolen life went over my consciousness like hurrying cloud shadows. I found I'd lifted one leg off the floor for balance. It took effort to put it back down. Imbibed blood goes molasses-thick. You lug it for a while, awkwardly. Get out, now, before the fire stops you. Heat beat on my back. Already one curtain was aflame.

I let what remained of her fall from my arms back onto the now burning bed. Let it go. Let it all go. At the window I paused just long enough to feel my right side singed and my left salved in the moonlight, then jumped down, fell, got up and ran.

14

THE FIRE CLAIMED half the house and killed nine of the seventeen staff. Also, as subliminally intended, overwrote the true story of how Arabella died.

Poor Charles suffered, not just the loss of my wife (whom he was at least inordinately fond of and at most guiltily in love with) but of my friendship. In the days immediately following the blaze I was as he saw it understandably remote. But remoteness became estrangement, then absence. I put my estate manager in charge of reconstruction and left for Scotland within a fortnight. I had no plan, merely a reflex to get as far away from people as possible.

I took with me a single souvenir.

The little ground-floor room overlooking the western end of the garden had been Arabella's study. There wasn't much in it: a bookcase; a walnut bureau; one of the tattiest of the Indian carpets and an enormous armchair in which my late wife was wont to curl up with her journal and scribble away for entire afternoons. The journal was kept in the bureau in a queer little iron lockbox with a handful of talismanic trinkets from her risky life, and though the desk had gone in the conflagration the casket—and diary—had survived. It's in the safe-deposit box in Manhattan now, along with my own chronicles, but in the weeks and months that followed the fire I came to know much of it by heart. Only a few lines are necessary here.

His behaviour grows daily more disturbed. Others would condemn me for keeping my secret, but he is so erratic I fear the effect of a mistimed disclosure. So many moments this last week I've been on the verge of telling him. The words are gold under my heart, honey under my tongue: Jacob, I'm carrying your child.

i5

LAST NIGHT, NOT long after I'd laid down my pen (*quad scripsi, scripsi*) it started raining. It rained all night and it's still raining now, late in the afternoon. The very last of the daylight shows a low sky of soft dark cloud passed under occasionally by lighter white shreds ("pannus" to meteorologists, "messengers" to fishermen; two hundred years, idle moments, books). The sea looks like marbled meat. Against it the gulls' white has detergent ad purity. The rain's destroying the snow, obviously. There's still plenty out here in the valley, in the woods, but in Zennor pavements are reemerging. By the time I get back to London tomorrow the magic will be almost gone. The city will be brisk and miserable, derisory of its lapse, its little dream of things being different.

"Have you done what you needed to do?" Harley asked on the phone an hour ago.

"There was a gap in the record," I said. "I filled it. Shall I send it to the PO box or the club?"

He understood: This journal would be the last. No more record because no more me. A bad way to start the conversation. I pictured him closing his eyes and jamming his jaws together before letting himself start again.

"Everything's set up," he said. "But I can't get you out of the country till the seventeenth. Cutting it close, I know, but there's no choice. You've got three car-changes between the city and Heathrow. You're booked on the afternoon Virgin flight to New York with the Tom Carlyle ID. That's the interference. You'll actually be flying private charter to Exeter as Matt Arnold. These are brand-new ID packages. Passports, driving licences, NI numbers, the whole fucking caboodle. From Exeter—"

"I'm going to Wales, Harley."

"What?"

"You heard. Snowdonia."

"Don't be absurd."

"Go out where I came in. Full circle."

He paused again. Laboriously lit a cigarette. "From *Exeter*," he went on, quietly, "you've got options. You can fly to Palma and on to Barcelona or Madrid, or, if you're not absolutely convinced you've shaken them, I've set up another two car changes between there and Plymouth. Reggie'll wait for you until midnight of the seventeenth. He'll get you over the Channel, then you're on your own."

"You've done the work, Harls," I said. "You're a rock star."

"Yeah, well, don't give me this Wales bollocks then."

I let it go. He knew. I knew he knew. He knew I knew he knew. Standing at the Pines lounge bay window looking down through the rain to the cove I felt the familiar fondness for him being gnawed at by impatience. The longer I hung on the worse it would get. You can't live solely for someone else without sooner or later hating them. I started to ask about a drop for the new fake IDs, but he stopped me.

"I'll give you the documents myself," he said. "I don't want any fuck-ups."

"That's a stupid risk for you."

"I won't rest until I've put them into your hands personally. Do this my way, Marlowe, please."

Which was his concession. If you're going to die then I want to see you one more time. One last handshake before the end.

"Anything more on Cloquet?" I asked him. It was the first time I'd thought of the young man with the Magnum since leaving London, but now that I had I felt uneasy again.

"We let him go," Harley said. "He's got nothing. We bugged and watched him for a day or two after his release. He bowled around a bit, nursing his hand, which by the way we treated for him, then eventually he made a penitent call to Jacqueline Delon herself. She was furious with him for going after you. He was told to stay put in his hotel until one of her lot came and escorted him back to Paris. Twenty-four hours later two guys—Delon's—showed up and did just that. Case closed."

"You know why they invented the phrase 'case closed'?"

"What?"

"So that the audience would know it wasn't."

"Have it your way, Jacob. You're chasing shadows. You should be worrying about Ellis."

"Not Grainer?"

"Grainer's patient. He'll wait for the full moon. But Ellis down there watching you with fuck-all else to do . . . There are a couple of trigger-happy juveniles with him, too."

"They beheaded my foxes."

"What?"

"Never mind."

"Just be careful, that's all I'm saying."

The cloak-and-dagger arrangements, superfluous though we both know they are, are in place. Graham Greene had a semiparodic relationship with the genres his novels exploited, a wry tolerance of their exigencies and tropes. Unavoidably I have the same relationship to my life. False IDs, code words, assignations, surveillance, night flights. Espionage flimflam. And that's before we even *begin* on the Horror Story trappings. If it were a novel I'd reject it along with all other genre output that by definition short-changes reality. Unfortunately for me it *is* reality.

There is the elephant in the room: I killed and ate my wife and unborn child. I killed and ate *love*. Which left two alternatives: expand or die. Kill yourself or live with it. Give it up or suck it up, in the modern idiom. Well, here I am.

It was a mistake. I don't mean morally, I mean strategically. I should have turned her. That was my chance. *That* was my chance. She would have made a better werewolf than I. She was bigger, braver, more blasphemous. Her potential would have been released. *She* would have led *me*. My brother in his haste missed the cure for loneliness. It was in his arms and he couldn't see it. *I've been happily married to my wife for eleven years. We have two lovely children. I have a good job and a beautiful home. She's my soul mate in every respect—except one. In bed, I like to . . .* Cathedral-sized marriages crumble because she won't pee on him or he won't tie her up. Nothing holds love together like shared vice or collusive perversion. In the years since I murdered and devoured her I've had plenty of time to think of what might have been with Arabella, under, as it were, the moon of love. I picture her in pale stockings in a sunlit Edwardian window seat, a cigarette in a long holder, reading aloud: " ' . . . The history of human civilisation shows beyond any doubt that there is an intimate connection between cruelty and the sexual instinct . . .' Hang on, that's not the bit— ah, here it is: 'According to some authorities this aggressive element of the sexual instinct is in reality a relic of cannibalistic desires—that is, it is a contribution derived from the apparatus for obtaining mastery, which is concerned with the satisfaction of the other and, ontogenetically, the older of the great instinctual needs . . .' There, you see? I *told* you. What time are we supposed to be at this shindig anyway?"

We would have killed together and we would have *shone*.

All appearances to the contrary, I haven't left good and evil entirely behind. Absurdly or otherwise I still subscribe to atonement. I killed love. Some short while after ripping Arabella and our little foetal secret to pieces my psyche passed sentence on my heart: Henceforth you will endure, without love. You will kill, without love. You will live, without love. You will die, without love. Doesn't sound like much of a proscription, does it? Try it for a couple of centuries.

As I say, there has been and still is vestigial ethical craziness. Over the years I've sought out and helped the human oppressed, from fugitive Jews in the forests of Poland to terrorised peons in the hills of El Salvador. I funded labour movements in Chile and ran guns for the anti-Fascists in Spain. Big deal, I know. Even the SS didn't use *silver* bullets. You'd think the occult nuts among the *Reichsführer*'s people would've insisted, but no. Still, I saved a lot of lives, and, when I got my alignments just right, killed a lot of scumbags. My fortune (reduced by 31 percent in this latest meltdown) has dished out kidney machines and scanners, put food into the bellies of the starving and inoculants into the blood of the at-risks. The philanthropy's self-sustaining now, the foundations, the trusts. All built (God being dead, irony still etc.) on the Indian poppy. My father, a London director of the East India Company until just before the first Opium War, had followed my grandfather's lead in the trade and left me a formidably wealthy young man on his death in 1831. There was land, there was property, there were shares in John Company itself. Opium became cotton became coal became steel became . . . it's a long story. I diversified. The 1930s hit me hard, but I recovered. Renounce love and you can achieve demonic focus. Once I'd made the decision to stay alive other decisions made themselves. I'd need mobility, anonymity, security. Or in other words sustained wealth. But earlier journals cover this. The point is I make no apology and ask no forgiveness. I'm a man. I'm a monster. A cocktail of contraries. I didn't ask to become a werewolf but once it had happened I got used to it pretty quickly. You surprise yourself. You surprise yourself, then realise even the surprise was a bit of a sham.

For a hundred and sixty-seven years I've put off writing of Arabella and the death of love. Now that I've done it, what? Do I feel unburdened? Purged? Ashamed? Absolved?

Something's happening to this business of talking about feelings. It's becoming moribund. The analysand on the Manhattan couch opens his mouth to begin "I feel . . ." and knows that if he had any decency he'd close it again straight away. Humans are moving into a new phase, one based on the knowledge that talking about their feelings has never got them anywhere. The Demonstrative Age . . . I shan't be around to see it. *That,* since I asked the question myself, is how I feel, surer than ever that my clock's been right all along, that I've had enough, that it's time to go, that I really can't stand it anymore, the living and the killing and the wandering the world without love.

16

I'm journeyman scribbler enough to know a natural stopping point when I see one, so I doubt I'd have written any more yesterday, even if the vampire hadn't turned up.

In my lupine form his stink would have been blatant. As it was I didn't catch it until, alerted by an anomalous creak from the upper floor, I was halfway up the stairs.

The faintest draft of snow-flavoured air said he'd got in through one of the bedroom windows. I backtracked on cartoonish tiptoe, mentally racing through the house's furnishings for anything that might do service as a wooden stake. (It's really the wooden stake thing then, is it? Madeline would doubtless ask. Yes, it's really the wooden stake thing. Or sunlight, or beheading. By all means arm yourself with crucifixes and holy water and garlic and Latin—then prepare for fatal disappointment.) My ghost *wulf* hackles rose. In fact let me deal with this as straightforwardly as possible: Werewolves and vampires don't get on. Mutual repulsion is visceral and without exception—and that's before we get into the bloodsuckers' survival strategy, their realpolitik, which, in the spirit of disinterested analysis, I'm forced to admire: Almost three hundred years ago the fifty most powerful vampire families formed an alliance and made a deal with the Catholic Church. (WOCOP—or SOL as it was then— was originally an ecclesiastical offshoot, though by the mid-nineteenth century it had become a secular corporation with a private army.) As well as paying a percentage of all vampire profits to God's representatives on earth (nocturnals are peerless businessmen) they agreed to keep their world population under five thousand, give or take. Which means, since there are always a few rebels and rule-breakers who can't resist creating brand-new vampiros, annually doing away with a number of their kin. Picture adult seals clubbing their own pups. In return, the Hunt allows the Fifty Families to operate uninterfered with. There have been flare-ups, of course, there have been spats (and naturally some cheating on the numbers) but by and large the deal's held. The vamp Dons retain control of their households and the WOCOP cash registers sing. Half the "reconstruction" contracts for postwar Iraq went on no-bids to vampire-owned companies (whose funding favours, dear President Obama, the Republicans will be calling in about now). One of them, Netzer-Böll, has a weapons manufacturing subsidiary that specialises off the record in SDS—Silver Delivery Systems. A handful of particularly cynical boochies actually *work* for WOCOP. The Hunt uses them as trackers. Of werewolves. Grainer, Old School, will have none of it.

So what the fuck was this one doing here?

You speed-whittle a log—no, a chair leg—no, a broom handle—no, a pencil—no a—God *dammit* . . . In the kitchen I turned the solitary wooden stool on its side, braced it with one foot and stomped on it with the other. Nothing. I stomped a second time. A faint sound of stress from the joint. I picked the bastard thing up and dashed it against the chimney breast. (Oh for that saloon-brawl furniture of cowboy movies!) Nil effect except a terrible rubbery shock to my wrists. I put it back on the floor and prepared for a third stomp—by which time it was too late.

He stood in the kitchen doorway, a lean pug-faced young vampire in combat trousers and leather bike jacket with eyebrow piercings and bleached white hair cropped close to his skull, holding a bulky rifle. I say "young," but for all I know he could have been alive since the days of Gilgamesh. He raised the weapon and pointed it at me.

"Wait," I said.

"Can't," he said, and smiled. Before what happened next happened I had just time to think: No, he's a young one. The eyes haven't gone dead. Time hasn't done its thing. An elder wouldn't even have paused to say "Can't." Then what happened next happened.

From outside came a feminine shriek, cut short with a shocking abruptness.

A silence of uncomfortable richness for two seconds. Then a severed female head smashed through the kitchen window and bounced uglily across the tiles, before coming to rest at the foot of the oven. The long dark hair fell back to reveal green eyes, semi—rolled back, mouth horribly slack. Spittled fangs. Her skin was already beginning to blacken.

"Laura?" the vampire said, quietly. Then a wooden spike tore his chest open from the inside with a wet crunch. He frowned. Dropped his weapon with a clatter and sank to his knees, the capillary webbing of hands and throat and face darkening. Ellis, in winter combat fatigues and holding a top-of-the-line Hunt Staker, stood behind him. The long blond hair had been pulled back and bound into an extraordinary solid bun.

"Hi, Jake," he said. "You all right?"

I exhaled, slowly, set down the wooden stool. "Come on in," I said. "Join the party."

"Well, now that you mention it," he said, "I could murder a drink."

"What the fuck is going on here?"

"I really don't know."

He stepped around the crisping corpse of the vampire and called out of the window: "Russell?"

"Yo!"

"We good?"

"We're good."

"Okay. You've broken Mr. Marlowe's window, however."

"Apologies, boss. Exuberance."

Ellis didn't answer. Instead picked up the severed head and tossed it back out. Sounds of amusement from the juniors. The skin on the darkening corpse crackled softly. "Let me get rid of this for you," Ellis said. He grabbed the cadaver by its bike jacket collar and dragged it out the back door. Vampire decomposition isn't the screen-friendly instantaneous transformation to ash heap Hollywood peddles, but it is quirkily rapid. In an hour or two there'd be nothing but bloodstains to show the boochies had been here. I went into the living room, tossed a fresh log on the fire, lit up a Camel and poured a couple of straight Glenlivets.

"No hard feelings?" Ellis said, when he came back in and I handed him his glass.

"Let's not get carried away."

"Understood. L'chaim, anyway."

"Chin-chin."

He sat down on the arm of the couch and propped the vampire's rifle alongside him. I, cold and queasy from truck with the undead, remained standing by the fire. Surrounded by surveillance, the house had retained its feel of fragile sanctuary. Now, with icy air coming through the broken kitchen window and Ellis actually *in* here, the magic was gone. Just as well I was leaving tomorrow.

"So?" he said. "What's your theory?"

"I was hoping you might have one."

"Nope. Presumably you've got enemies in vamp-camp?"

"I wouldn't have thought so. I don't have anything to do with them."

"But you used to, right? My understanding is that for a while in the fifties you were something of a thorn in their side."

True. See under *Werewolf Philanthropy*. Vampire-run businesses had paid the Nazis a fortune for ill-gotten genetics data during the war (their search for a solution to the problem of nocturnality goes on) and the Allies a fortune for what remained up for grabs after it. They'd *made* a fortune fencing treasures appropriated by the Reich, augmented by a highly profitable sideline smuggling war criminals out of Europe. (Decades later, naturally, there was additional money to be made selling the whereabouts of these ancient Nazis to interested Jews, but by then I'd given up interfering.) Back in the early postwar years I was the money behind and frequently leader of a disparate dozen groups convinced that direct action against certain organisations served their disparate causes. Communists, anarchists, animal rights supporters, vigilantes, conspiracy theorists—for a decade or so anti-vamp activism was rationalised by me into *protecting the human,* to make up for the losses I was inflicting on the poor old human myself. Crazy, I know, but true.

"I threw a few stones," I said. "Petulance, really. Anyway, it's ancient history."

Ellis took a sip, looked around the room, unblinking. Nothing, apparently, disturbed the man's air of having his mind on something more important than you. You wanted to slap him. "Yeah, but these guys are the grudge club," he said. "Fifty years? What's that to them? It's yesterday. It's five minutes ago."

"Well, maybe you should have a word with them. Tell them there's a queue."

"They weren't trying to kill you."

"What?"

He set the glass down on the couch and picked up the rifle. Or rather what I'd thought was a rifle. The creepily nimble long fingers went to work, popped the chamber and took out the ammunition. Held it up for me to see. A dart.

"Tranquilizer," I said.

"Tranquilizer. If it wasn't for us you'd be fast asleep and on your way."

"On my way where?"

"Pennsylvania."

"*What?*"

Ellis smiled—alarmingly, since it brought a sudden nude babylike quality to his face. "My sister teaches second grade. One kid's telling his buddy about Count Dracula. Says he lives in a big spooky castle in Pennsylvania. You know, instead of Transylv—"

"Got it. Hilarious. Did you know these two?"

He stowed the dart in one of his jacket's innumerable pockets. Retrieved the Scotch. Now that the smile was gone it was as if it had never been. "The girl," he said. "She's maybe Mangiardi. The guy I've never seen."

Mangiardi's one of the Italian houses, one of the Fifty Families. I might have bombed a couple of their labs back in the day, but couldn't believe this was a belated revenge attack. Vampires don't go in for that sort of thing. Not on any kind of principle but because nine out of ten times they just can't be bothered. All motivation derives from the primary fact of mortality. Take mortality away and motivation loses its . . . motivation. Thus vampires spend a lot of time lounging around and staring out of the window and finding they can't be arsed.

"Well, it means nothing to me," I said. "But I suppose I ought to say thank you. Whatever they want me for I don't imagine it's pleasant."

"All part of the service, Jake. But listen, if you're really grateful, there's something we should discuss."

"What?"

"Mutual benefit. We've got som—" His headset clicked: a squad communiqué. The white waxy face and lazuli eyes very still while he listened, processed, concluded. "Roger," he said. Then to me, covering the mic: "Christ, they can't be left alone for five minutes." He swallowed the last of his drink and stood up. "This'll have to wait. But look, we'll find a time, seriously, okay?" His tone would have been just right if we'd been minor studio executives.

"I didn't appreciate the gesture with the foxes, by the way," I said.

"I know. I can only apologise for that. These rookies. I'm sorry, Jake, really."

"And now you've broken my window."

"We'll fix it up first thing tomorrow. And again, seriously, I'm sorry about the foxes. Critters can be such a comfort. I'd love a dog, but with my life? It's not fair on the animal. We'll talk again."

The temptation, immediately Ellis had left, was to call Harley. I resisted: Again, the Hunter could have planted a bug. I'd been sloppy to leave him unsupervised even for a moment, but the vamps had thrown me. Besides, a report would go to WOCOP this evening; Harley would get the story without my help. Which wouldn't do me any favours, now that I thought it through, since he was already in anxiety overdrive. This latest—vampires are after Jake—would only give him something else to waste time and energy fretting about. I sent him a text: "Audio compromised. SMS only until further notice. Small incident here. You'll get it from Ellis. DON'T WORRY. I'M FINE."

Vampires are after Jake. It's ridiculous. I haven't *seen* a vampire in more than twenty years. A mistake? Or some new Hunt twist? But there, beyond argument, was the tranquilizer dart. If it wasn't for us you'd be fast asleep and on your way.

On my way where? And for what?

Here it is again, the wearisome thing, life's compulsion to woo, the suitor who won't take no for an answer. Vampires, Jake. What's *that* about? Stick around. Find out what happens.

Yes, well, I know what happens. *More* happens. Variations on the same half dozen themes. There are only six plots, Hollywood says, or twelve, or nine . . . whatever the number it's finite, it's small. If this is life trying to narratively intrigue me back in, it won't work. I'm not coming in, I'm going out.

I went around the house closing all the curtains. The darkness outside was loud, now that I listened, with the sound of Life's indefatigable random plotting, the gossipy simmer of a new assault on my resolve. It gave me a peculiar tender sad thrill of emptiness, as when you catch your wife in bed with another man and realise you don't care, haven't for years, feel a little pity for them, wish them both a little luck.

Back on the couch with a fresh Camel and a topped-up Glenlivet I kicked my shoes off, stretched my legs towards the fire and yawned. It was only six in the evening but the booze and hullabaloo had made me sleepy. In a concession to Life I thought back over my years of antivamp activism, sifted memories for high-ranking bloodsuckers I might particularly have ticked off. I couldn't come up with anything compelling. Certainly Casa Mangiardi didn't ring any bells, and I'd never seen the lately beheaded Laura or her young companion before, I was positive.

I swallowed the last of my Scotch, put my feet up, rested my eyes. Fuck them, anyway, whatever they wanted. Under Grainer's orders (God being dead, irony etc.) the Hunt would watch my back. I had a suicidal date with WOCOP's werewolf-killing maestro just over a week from now, and boochies or no boochies I intended to keep it.

EVEN BY MY own efforts I make a pretty convincing woman, but for the rendezvous with Harley back in London I had professional help.

"Are you sure this is necessary?" I asked. "I mean, why can't I wear trousers? Women do wear trousers, after all."

"In trousers you'll move like a man. The body language will give it away." This was Todd Curtis, a friend of Harley's, and he was waxing my legs from the knee down. I'd been instructed to shave them before leaving the Zetter. The waxing was an extra—and in my view—unnecessary precaution.

"Look, if they get that close I don't think it's the legs that'll—Ow! Jesus *Christ*."

"Three more and you're good to go."

Todd, good-looking, understatedly muscular with dark curly hair cropped very close and a thin face of calm Mafioso cruelty, was the sort of gay man very few heterosexuals would be able to tell was a gay man— though on discovering his profession they'd start to wonder. He and his team specialise in elite transvestism. For film, stage and television, yes, but also for private clients and drag competitions. Turnover last year, he told me, was just under a million euros.

"The weather's on our side," he said, selecting a three-quarter-length fake chinchilla from the rack his assistant had wheeled in. "The coat will do a lot of the work. How are the shoes?" We were in a massage cubicle at a health and beauty spa in Knightsbridge. Conditions were cramped and the air-con was set for nudity. The wig didn't itch (my wigs don't itch, Todd had said, calm as God) but the makeup caused mild claustrophobia. I'd been tailed from the Zetter but had given the two agents the slip in Covent Garden. WOCOP's hooked into a lot of the city's CCTV but Harley knows the blind spots. These, plus four cab changes, made it virtually certain I'd reached Halcyon Days unmarked. Virtual certainty notwithstanding, Harley's life was at stake. Hence Todd, hence the new me.

"Wow," I said, looking in the full-length mirror. "Maybe I'll just take myself back to my hotel."

"Yeah, you're hot," Todd said, without apparent emotion. He'd worked the transformation with a sort of impersonal concentration, and now it was done I very much had the impression he had other places to be, other men to turn into women. "Go up and down in here a few times to get used to the heels."

The disguise followed my natural dark colouring. I looked like a plain big-boned woman who'd availed herself of maximum cosmetic assistance but about whom there remained something eerily unfuckable. No denying slight titillation. The tights in particular delivered secret arousing snugness. An erection halfheartedly threatened. You'll be delighted to hear, dear Harley, that—

Todd's assistant put her head round the door. "Car's here," she said.

The vampire attack in Cornwall had put WOCOP in a stir, though Harley's snooping had thus far turned up nothing. Calls had gone back and forth between the London HQ and most of the Fifty Houses, but the head families, Casa Mangiardi included, were feigning ignorance, or *were* ignorant. Laura Mangiardi, allegedly, had forfeited familial rights by running around with pariahs, illegally made vamps who'd eluded the annual cull. The Dons' line was they were just as irked as WOCOP. Efforts would be redoubled, controls tightened. A regrettable glitch, no harm done, long tradition of mutual respect blah blah blah. Harley, of course, remained sceptical. It doesn't matter, I'd told him. None of it matters. In seven days—

Shut the fuck up, will you? he'd said.

The male receptionist at the Leyland made two assumptions. First, since I went straight to the lifts with barely a glance at him, that I was a prostitute. Second, since I wasn't attractive, that I was a prostitute of dizzying kinkiness or filth.

"Your concierge thinks I'm a hooker," I said to Harley by way of hello. He was standing, leaning heavily on the bone-handled stick. "A coprophilia specialist. And these fucking shoes, I don't mind telling you, are killing me."

Harley smiled, but we both knew my tone wasn't up to the task. I'd been in the room five seconds and already the atmosphere was frail. (Don't come onto the platform with me, we say, knowing how it'll be: the

forced levity, the nonconversation, the minutes that can't be left empty.)
The suite was large, dully corporate, decorated with too much navy blue:
drapes, bedspread, corduroy couches. The window looked over puddled
roofs, air vents, skylights, the rear yard of a pub with its umbrellas closed
and plastic furniture wet. A few dirty scabs of snow remained, irritating
now that the big white dream was over.

All the ID documents were crisp, to my eye flawless, but once Harley
had tossed them to me where I sat on the bed we didn't mention them.
They'd been his last hope, talismans to bring the dead magic back to life.
He'd done everything he could—and proved that nothing he could do
was enough. For what felt like minutes we remained in silence, me on the
edge of the bed with nyloned legs crossed, him in profile by the window,
all but silhouetted by London's milky grey afternoon light.

"What will you do?" he said.

"Go to Wales. Snowdonia. I never have been back, you know."

He opened his mouth to say something—an objection reflex—then
closed it again. Both of us had imagined there would be things to say, that
we'd *find* things to say, but Harley stared out over the shivering roof-
lakes and I knew he was getting the first true flavour of his life without me
in it, an effect like the rubbery antiseptic taste of a dentist's surgery. *All
those people Marlowe killed.*

"The vision I have of you," I said, "is in South America. White cotton
pyjamas. Mango trees. A dusty courtyard. Hot blue sky and half a dozen
static pure white clouds. You go where there's beauty. You think God will
never forgive you, but the only God is beauty and beauty always forgives.
It forgives with its infinite indifference." I lit a Camel, watched myself
in the mirror, a noirish unattractive woman, sitting on a bed, smoking.
Somewhere in the back of our minds had been the belief that my being in
drag would leaven the horror. *And if I laugh at any mortal thing / "'Tis that
I may not weep.* It had failed in the way that comic music at a funeral can
fail. He sat down on one of the blue corduroy couches and set the walking stick between his knees and abstractedly lit a Gauloise and slowly
scratched the big dome of his forehead.

"I can't believe this," he said.

"Harls, come on."

"A parent doesn't expect to bury his child." Cigarette smoke swirled as if struggling to form a representation of something. The room's memories were of masturbating sales reps and adulterous couples.

"I'm sorry," I said. Saying it gave me my first inkling of *how* sorry, of how exhausting this leave-taking had the capacity to become. It was as if the decision to die had taken the energy required to get me to death.

"I'm leaving too," Harley said, then with satirical brightness: "A month's holiday. Don't want to be here when they cut your head off, do I?"

"Where are you going?"

"Caribbean. Barbuda. A Ballardian enclave. The bored wives of neurosurgeons. Retired astronauts. Pharmaceuticals executives. The brochure looks like a virtual world. White concrete and ultramarine sky. A pristine end point of modernity. I imagine silence that's really the low hum of air-conditioning and humidors."

"Well, you've got the wardrobe for it. I still think you should go to Brazil. For the boys if nothing else. You're not dead, Harls, so live."

"Yes, well, physician heal thy fucking self."

A silence began to solidify between us. Unaffordable. I stood up, with a wobble on the high heels, saw him immediately thinking not yet, not so soon, not like this, wait.

"Nothing's going to be the right thing to say," I said. He stared at the carpet. Cigarette ash fell on his trousers. "We're hanging around waiting for this not to seem so painful when the fact is it's only going to get more painful the longer we hang around."

He didn't move. His eyes were filling. He took an aggressive drag on the Gauloise, exhaled through his nose. A tear fell, with an audible *putt* onto his lapel. The moment demanded action and all we had was paralysis. *The heart of standing is you cannot fly.*

"I'll just ask you this once," he said. "So I know I did ask."

I waited. Someone pushed a cleaning cart past the door. Outside, London was set in frowning concentration, dourly focused on getting through the economic migraine. Heavy on me was the weight of the world's ability to keep going, producing day after unique day, heaving up wars and conversations, bloodily popping out babies and silently swallowing the dead. The collective human unconscious can't stand it, the thought of *stuff* going on forever, so has decided (collectively, unconsciously) to bring the planet to an end. Eco-apocalypse isn't accident, it's deep species strategy.

"Don't do this," Harley said. "Don't leave me to myself. I haven't got what it takes for suicide. You know that. What's another decade to you? I'll be dead by then. Just stay."

"I can't."

"You're a selfish cunt, do you know that?"

"Yes."

Again he opened his mouth, saw the futility, let it go. He pulled out a wrinkled white hanky and dried his eyes. Very slowly put the glass down and stubbed out the cigarette. When he looked at me I saw his fear of everything beyond this moment. The future held a horror—himself—and he wouldn't look until he had to, until he had no choice, until I was gone. His face shivered like the water on the flat roofs.

"So what?" he said. "We just say good-bye?"

"We just say good-bye."

"You've got another week. You'll change your mind."

"Come here."

He felt like an old man in my arms, skin and bones in a baggy suit, thinned hair and the smell of scalp. Something medicinal too, tiger balm or Vicks. Out of habit I searched my feelings, turned up sadness, regret, something like loss but also undeniably boredom and a kind of impotence of the heart. My inner voice repeated, *enough, enough, enough.*

At the door I turned and looked at him. He had nothing to say, or too much. He just stared, wet-eyed, hands heavy, filling as I watched with the sand of his future. Every act of leaving feels like a victory. The thrill of this one was tiny, faint, dud, almost nothing.

Harley remained still, unblinking. Leaving him alone with his conscience was like leaving a child alone with a paedophile.

"You've been a good friend to me," I said. He didn't respond. I turned, opened the door, stepped out into the hall and closed it behind me.

18

I HAD IMAGINED, crossing the border into Clwyd under a low sky of dark cloud, that finding the exact spot I was attacked a hundred and sixty-seven years ago wouldn't be easy. I'd pictured hours poring over Ordnance Survey maps and picking local octogenarian brains, flailing in bogs, getting lost in the woods. But this is the twenty-first century. I simply hired a car and drove north from London, then west through Snowdonia National Park to Beddgelert (the *dd* pronounced as a voiced *th* in Welsh), a village some five miles south of Snowdon and a comfortable three-mile walk from Beddgelert Forest, where after only a single afternoon exploring I found the clearing in which Charles and I had made our camp all those years ago. From there the twenty paces to the stream, the site of the attack, the line the Hunt or Servants of Light had ridden. I sat on a rock by the bank and smoked a cigarette. That's all there was to it.

Beddgelert hasn't much to offer so I booked myself into the Castle Hotel in Caernarfon, a half hour's drive northwest of the forest, overlooking the unsavoury waters of the Menai Strait.

Five days to kill before dying.

All the practical work was done long ago. The companies pass under the control of their boards. A percentage of profits stream to the charities. Real estate sale proceeds likewise. Personal wealth (I've off-loaded the art, the trinkets, the antiquities over the last fifty years) will be divided among certain individuals known to me (though I'm not known to them) by virtue of some outstanding quality: compassion, talent, kindness, humour, conscience. Some of it will go to ordinary folks I just happen to have met and liked. None of it will go to the families of people I've killed and eaten for the simple reason that finding out where the money came from (a possibility, no matter how many precautions) would drive them insane, since they wouldn't want to part with it but would have to and would end up hating the dead person.

There are probably a dozen things you could think of to do if you only had five days left to live. I doubt they'd include visiting the Inigo Jones Tudor Slateworks, or the Caernarfon Air Museum, or Foel Animal Park, or the Sea Zoo. Nonetheless, partly in an act of self-ridicule, partly out of unexpected vacuity, I spent a day taking them in. I ate an ice cream in the drizzle. Fed coins into a delirious fruit machine. Drank a cup of tea in a café full of damp pensioners. I brought this journal up to date. All feeble distraction from the quickening Curse, which, indifferent to the winsome farewell drama, foreplayed my blood in obedience to the swelling moon. And on the subject of swelling and blood, my libido was going nuts. I had thought, given the near failure of my last date with Madeline and the days of sexual quiescence in Cornwall (nothing, not even a hand job), that desire was finally done with me. Thanatos advances, Eros retreats. Not so. By the end of my second day I was walking around in a more or less permanent gurn. To join a queue was to risk arrest.

Pocket Internet consultation revealed Caernarfon served by not one but four escort agencies, with which I made do until, around midnight of Day Three, incredulously taxied two hundred miles at my expense and toting a Louis Vuitton overnight bag, Madeline arrived. I'd promised her triple time and a generous sayonara bonus. Yes, I was Going Away.

"You are *so* one can short of a six-pack, babes," she said, when I opened the door. "What are you *do*ing here?"

"Dying. Here's some champagne. Drink it and get into bed."

"Crikey. Can I take my coat off first?"

"If you think it's necessary, but please hurry."

Maddy wasn't the only thing up from London. I'd practically advertised my departure from the capital, so naturally WOCOP surveillance had followed. I'd clocked agents everywhere, though Grainer and Ellis declined to show themselves. I wondered what they thought I was doing, this swanning, this insouciance. To them it must look like prep for the biggest fugitive sleight of hand in history. Visibility this brazen could only be the dummy to an extraordinary escape. God alone knew what machinations they imagined I had planned.

"Ow," Madeline said, having rolled over on something not soft in the bed. "It's your bloody phone." It was late afternoon on Day Four and we'd just woken up. The curtains were closed and what was left of the light was going. The night had been taxing, for Madeline because I'd fucked her six times with preposterous staying power, and for me because no amount of fucking her could suppress the psychic quartet of fear and boredom and sadness and hunger that took turns being me and sometimes didn't take turns but nauseously swelled together like a mesmerising special effect. I had a champagne head and cocaine guts, but more pressingly the first blood-shudders and muscle-hiccups of wolf, of the coming transformation. The Last Curse.

"You've got voicemail, by the way," Madeline said. "Here. I've got to pee. God, I feel like death."

The phone, of course, was *the* phone, the Harley phone. Battery almost dead. Message icon flashing. The clipped nonperson female voice (a slightly retarded descendant of the Speaking Clock) said: *Mess*age. Rec*ei*ved. *Yes*terday. At. *Se*ven. *Four*teen. a.m.

It was Harley.

"Jesus Christ, Jake, listen. There's—"

That was all.

I played it again, pointlessly since I'd heard it perfectly the first time. The cutoff was absolute, technological. I dialled the number. Voicemail. I dialled again. Voicemail.

A little more of the light seemed to go. The room smelled of hotel carpet, flat champagne and sex. Adrenaline shimmied and bucked in my shoulders and wrists, went through my scalp, balls, knees. I stood there staring at nothing, trying to see through walls, miles, hours, other people.

I dialled again.

Voicemail.

Maddy emerged from the en suite. She'd washed her face and brushed her teeth and pinned her hair up with clips. In ten minutes she'd look as good as a new car. Her recovery time's astonishing. "Look at *that*, thank you very much," she said, turning her cheek and showing me a tiny lovebite on her pliable young neck. "That's a *mark*, isn't it?"

"Get dressed," I said. "I'll give you an extra thousand but only if you get dressed and go down to the restaurant right now. I just need a few minutes."

"I can't go down looking like this."

I found last night's dress and tossed it to her. "A grand on top of the rest. Go on. I'll be down in a bit."

Alone in the room when she'd gone, I stood (dressed, brutally awake) with all the lights on and the mobile in my hand trying not to panic.

Jesus Christ, Jake, listen. There's—

There's what?

It was a risk, but I called the Earl's Court house. You've reached Elite Antiquarian. Please leave your name, number and a brief message, and we'll return your call as soon as possible. Thank you. "Yes, hello. This is Mr. Carlyle. I'm told you've recently acquired a sixteenth-century *Malleus Maleficarum,* which I'd be very interested in taking a look at. Please do call me back on . . ." No point not leaving the hotel number. WOCOP knew I was here, and if they were monitoring Earl's Court calls then they already knew about Harley. I hung up and called the foundation. No, Mr. Harley wasn't there at the moment. Was there a message?

Jesus Christ, Jake, listen. There's—

It wasn't beyond Harley to try a ruse. Drag me back to London for another assault on my resolve. He was desperate. Desperate enough to leave *that* message? Possibly. You're a selfish cunt, do you know that? Said in the way we said such things, implying affection. But underneath he'd meant it. Why not? It was true.

I lit a Camel. Parted the curtains and peered out. Dusk. Rain. Car headlamps. Pedestrians under umbrellas. Every now and then you look out at the world and know its gods have gone utterly elsewhere. Its personality shows, the kid abandoned horribly early who's survived at too great a price.

There was a knock at the door.

"Who is it?"

"It's me," Madeline said. "Let me in a sec."

"For fuck's sake."

I opened the door. Had a split second to register Ellis holding a fire extinguisher and Grainer holding Maddy—then the fire extinguisher hit me in the face.

19

I WASN'T KNOCKED out but I was knocked over, and in the aftermath of the blow's red detonation sufficiently dazed for Ellis to get my hands cuffed behind my back. Grainer steered Madeline at silenced gunpoint over to the couch, sat her down, then stood behind her with the weapon resting against the back of her skull. The room's furnishings achieved sudden taut sentience. To her credit, Maddy was keeping her mouth shut. I had the impression it wasn't the first time she'd been around men with guns, which made me feel tender towards her, sorry I hadn't kissed her more.

Grainer had lost weight since I'd last seen him and looked handsomer for it. Oily thick dark hair flecked with grey, a broad face, small hard brown eyes, pockmarked skin. Native American blood in there somewhere giving the good cheekbones, the inscrutable distance. In the Dolomites he'd been in lightweight Hunt fatigues and night-vision goggles. Now here he was like a spruce gangster in dark casuals and a quality black overcoat.

I spat out a bloody front tooth. My nose was broken. "Don't worry, Madeline," I said through my mashed mouth. "It's me they want."

Ellis found the dimmer and turned the lighting down slightly, for no reason, it appeared, beyond his own aesthetic sensibilities. He took the desk chair, placed it opposite me and sat down. In a film he'd start cleaning his nails or peeling an apple. In reality he just sat, elbows on knees, in a state of relaxed readiness. The long white hair was ponytailed today.

"So here's the thing," Grainer said. "We know about Harley."

Instant structural shift. As if a wall or door had gone for good and now cold air came in.

"Is he dead?"

"Don't try'n drive this, Jake. You're the passenger."

You think horror enters spectacularly. It doesn't. It just prosaically turns up. Even in the first seconds you know you'll find it a room. I thought (how not?) of Harley's face at our farewell, of how delicate he'd felt in my arms. Weariness tingled through me, as if the heart had released a stimulant that wasn't working. Simultaneously there was a dreary bodily certainty that something would be demanded of me, that I'd have to *do* something.

"We're aware of your intention for tomorrow night, Jake," Grainer said. "To take it lying down. We don't like it."

"No challenge for you."

"Exactly. Do you know I've been *dreaming* about it? In this dream, you're sitting—fully transformed in broad daylight—all alone at one of those picnic tables in a forest. When I come out of the trees you're pleased to see me. You *wave* at me, for Christ's sake. I mean I do it, I cut off your head, but you're just sitting there, smiling, nodding. It's depressing as hell. I don't want that."

"How long have you known about Harley?"

"Years. You two were pretty slack. That wasn't much of a challenge, either."

"Surveillance?"

"Everything. The phones, the mobiles, the Earl's Court place, Harley's club. Jesus, Jake, we've had *you* bugged a dozen times."

Some relief, naturally. You can't live in dread of something for long without beginning to crave it.

"So the French story, this idiot Cloquet, that's bullshit?" Questions stacked up. Only one mattered: What had they done with Harley? Jesus Christ, Jake, listen. There's—

Grainer shook his head. "That guy, God what a loon. No, the story you got from Harley was true, as far as it went. Cloquet was tailing you in Paris, and the WOCOP agent was tailing him. The only thing Harley didn't know was that we knew all about it. We've known your whereabouts more or less continuously since 2003. Harley's *been* your surveillance, albeit unwittingly. Anyway, when it became apparent Cloquet was planning to take you out himself he was stopped. By me, as a matter of fact. As you know, I consider you my responsibility. Exclusively."

"And Cloquet is?"

"Jacqui Delon's boyfriend, or one of them. Cokehead wastrel. That's all we know. She seemed pretty pissed when she found out he'd pulled a gun on you."

"Are you a spy?" Madeline asked me, quietly.

"No," I said.

"He's a werewolf, honey," Grainer said. "Surely you've told her, Jake?"

"As a matter of fact I have." I felt tired again. Maddy's look of fraught computation. I sincerely hoped they wouldn't kill her. Surviving this experience might be just the epiphany to get her out of prostitution.

"It's no way to end a war, Jake," Grainer said. "Sit there and just . . ."

"Let it come down?"

"Let it come down. Doesn't ring the right bell in the universe."

"This is the way the world ends," I said.

"Not your world. You're the last of a great species. You owe the narrative something better."

"There is no narrative. You know that."

"There's the one we make. It's our responsibility."

Ellis nodded. "Just because life's meaningless doesn't mean we can't experience it meaningfully," he said.

"Wow," I said. "You should patent that. I've got one too: You don't have to be mad to work here, but it helps." Anger, after all, was rising through the blood vessels. Not at Ellis's banality (nor Grainer's arrogance) but at being forced into something when all I wanted was nothing.

"So," Grainer said, "Madeline's going to come downstairs with us for a moment. You'll stay here. We'll send her back with the key for the cuffs, and the information you'll need."

"Information?"

"About Harley. Madeline, do that and you're absolutely free to go. Fuck it up or try anything and you're dead. Understood?" Maddy nodded, swallowed. Her little nostrils flared. Under the gun's gentle direction she got to her stilettoed feet. The faintest tremor in her knees. Ellis stood, replaced the chair. "Sit tight, Jake," Grainer said. "She'll be back soon."

I waited. The room waited. Tomorrow night's full moon tugged and tweaked and smacked. There are these pretransformation shenanigans, ghost spasms, the muscles and bones getting ahead of themselves. The monster knows the length of its wait as a dog knows the length of its leash, but like the dog it pulls and chokes. My front tooth was already starting its grow-back with a fibrous tickle. Information about Harley. They had him somewhere, presumably. This is the deal: He stays alive as long as you do. Give up and he gets it. Ellis's idea, I was sure. A scheme of simple symmetry handed down from his remote height. I'd imagined . . . What *had* I imagined? Kneeling like Anne Boleyn while Grainer's blade caught the moonlight? Sitting full-lotus smiling down the muzzle of a silver-loaded gun? At any rate I'd imagined *yielding*. Stillness, stars, reverence for the last benignly indifferent details. A happy death.

The door opened and Madeline entered, unaccompanied, carrying a small leather holdall. Also the handcuffs' key. She closed the door behind her and put the bag on the floor. Then she helped me to my feet and unlocked the restraints. All done I could tell in accordance with specific instructions. She radiated moist heat. In the cleavage of the black halterneck her breasts were wet. One of the clipped-up strands of hair was down. Poignant to see her this way, stripped of her professional self, a human, afraid. Dangerous, too: Artless humanity made her wrongly appetising. Now that she'd been forced into depth I'd want to kill and eat her. One way or another my time with her was over.

"I have to say something," she said. "What they told me. They said to say to you: 'Think of it as an incentive.' Now you're supposed to open the bag."

She hadn't opened the bag. Had been told not to. She would have carried it up in the lift denying it was there, denying her own hand holding it, her arm, her shoulder, that whole side of her body. Because of course the lower animal in her knew. The lower animal knew and the higher animal threw up the ice wall of denial. She said nothing now as I knelt and opened the zip, only leaned back against the door, bare shoulders held a fraction higher than usual. Instinct warned her this was a big moment. She might not be able to carry on being herself after it. The possibility gave her an aliveness she'd never known, as if she'd suddenly been lifted a thousand feet in the air. In spite of everything a part of me wondered what she might become. This is the slow, grinding compulsion I'm sick of, this inevitably getting interested in people. You love life because life's all there is, Harley had insisted. There's no God and that's His only Commandment.

Inside the holdall was a second bag made of tough transparent plastic, tightly sealed with tape. Inside that was Harley's head.

20

THERE WAS A note stuck over his mouth with a message written on it in black marker: IT WASN'T PAINLESS. IT WASN'T QUICK.

"Oh my God," Madeline said. She stood with her bare white shoulders slightly hunched and her hands pressed against her midriff. "Jesus fucking Christ."

The face had been beaten. At leisure, I imagined. Creases in the plastic held bubbles of blood, as with vacuum-sealed beef in the supermarket. They'd made sure his eyes were open.

Just stay, he'd said.

It would be heartening to say I broke down in tears. I didn't. The moment merely updated the inventory of all the things I should feel but didn't. I very carefully opened the seal, reached in and peeled the note from his mouth. Like it or not the image of myself sticking it across Grainer's lips after I tracked him down and killed him came to me, which of course was the idea. Grainer's idea after all. Ellis would have kept Harley alive. Ellis's money was on guilt, conscience, responsibility—mine. Grainer's was on eye-for-an-eye vengeance—mine. New and Old Testaments respectively.

"Jake?" Madeline said. "Is that real? That's not real, is it?"

I closed Harley's eyes. You have to. Open, the eyes of the dead are a travesty, a parody, make a fool of the deceased. Open, the eyes of the dead perform that most indecent subtraction, show the person without his life. I knew now all the times I'd pictured Harley's recuperative solitude after my death I'd never really believed in it. The worst horrors confirm a suspicion you've hidden even from yourself.

IT WASN'T PAINLESS. IT WASN'T QUICK.

I'm used to the body as a thing separable violently into its constituent parts. To me a torn-off arm's no more searingly forlorn than a chicken drumstick is to you. Still, it was Harley, what was left of him, a blunt testament to the defilements he'd suffered. A farcical testament, if you let yourself see it that way. Naturally torturers giggle while they work: The body's dumb obedience to physics (pull hard enough and this comes off, squeeze tight enough and that pops out) against which the nuances of the victim's personality count for nothing has in it one of the roots of comedy—the spirit's subservience to the flesh. You can cut a head off and shove it in a bag, stick it on a pole, play volleyball or footie with it. Hilarious, among other things. This too is what I'm tired of, the friability of boundaries, the nearness of opposite extremes, the depressing bleed-ability of grief into laughter, good into evil, tragedy into farce.

Meanwhile Madeline was filling with unruly energies. I knew if she stayed shock would wear off and the demand for coherence take its place. With careful handling I put the head back in the holdall, zipped up gently, found myself out of deep inane habit hoping the darkness would come as a relief to him.

"You should go," I said to Madeline.

"Who is that?"

"Never mind."

"We have to call the police."

"It's best if you just go. The police aren't part of this."

"But—"

"No one will harm you, I promise. Just go and let me deal." My window was that her system had temporarily crashed. I grabbed everything of hers I could find and stuffed it willy-nilly into the Louis Vuitton. She remained stalled by the door.

"That guy said you were a—"

"It's a code word. It's a word agents use."

He's a werewolf, honey. Naturally that had gone in. Naturally she'd made the connection.

"But *you*'ve said . . . All that stuff. It's not true. There's no such things." This last utterance without much conviction, almost a question.

"Of course there are no such things," I said. "That's just a routine of mine, a gimmick. It's nothing. Come on. Here, take the cash." Six thousand. She took it, but numbly. Her face was clammy, her white hands lovely with veins. I had to keep pushing her forward against her need to stop, rewind, go over, make sense. In the end I half-propelled her through the door. I knew there was every chance she'd go straight to the police.

From which followed my own hasty pack-up and check-out. I put the holdall with my bag in the boot of the Vectra and drove. South. No specifics, just the sudden claustrophobic need to get out of the town's clutter to the clean spaces of the coast.

It was dark, raining. I kept imagining discussing all this with Harley—then realising Harley was dead. It was a mental loop, augmented by the windscreen wipers' two-syllable mantra, *wichok, wichok, wichok.* I must have been feeling something like grief (or self-pity) because I took the car's responsive steering and smell of new vinyl as anthropomorphic sympathy. I didn't cry. Real things don't make me cry. Only false or sentimental things can do that. In this respect I'm like most civilised humans. Instead I drove, fluently, with reverence for the small actions, still going through the same loop of imagining talking events over with Harley then realising he was dead. When the loop faltered a giant contained emptiness took its place.

The road ran down the coast. To the west, Caernarfon Bay and the Irish Sea, occasional boat lights, a tanker or two. East and south the land rose into another stack of vowel-starved hills: Bwlch Mawr; Gyrn Ddu; Yr Eifl. Of course I was being followed, had been since leaving the hotel. A black transit van, which was unusual for the Hunt, who normally use something quicker.

You were pleased to see me. It was depressing as hell. I don't want that. Of course he didn't. Forty years he'd been building up to avenging his father's death. Not much of an avenging if the murderer was going to be grateful to him for it. Therefore provoke the murderer into something other than gratitude.

The question was: Had it worked? Was Harley's death (or as I must infer, torture and death) incentive enough to bring the wolf out fighting?

Human standards would convict me of obscene weakness if the answer was no. Harley, a man who'd devoted his life to my protection, who'd loved me, whose love I'd exploited when it suited and stonewalled when it didn't, had been mutilated and killed for my sake. I knew his killer or killers, I had the resources and experience to avenge the crime, and if I didn't do it no one else would.

But my standards aren't human. How could they be? The thought of resisting Grainer tomorrow night weakened my hands on the Vectra's wheel. Revenge entails a belief in justice, which I don't have. (You can't count my monster philanthropy, my werewolf good deeds. That's vestige, habit, a moribund personal accounting system. It doesn't derive from a principle, it just provides the moral equivalent of hand relief.) I knew what I *ought* to feel. I knew Grainer (and Ellis, since he would have joined in) ought to be made to pay. But *ought* and I parted company when I murdered my with-child wife and ate her and carried on living.

I turned off the main road at Trefor and the WOCOP vehicle followed, stopped a token fifty feet behind me when I pulled over at the seaward edge of the village. I was sweating. The Curse played preview blasts of free jazz in my blood, my goosefleshed skin. The hand I lifted to wipe my face was the impatient ghost of the other hand, the hybrid thing, heavy, elegant, claw-tipped. Transformation was less than twenty-four hours away. My body heat filled the car. I got out.

Better. Cold wind and rain. Hands, throat, face, scalp, all cooled. The beach was near. A pale footpath led down to it. I took it, overcoat flapping. A WOCOP van door opened, closed. *This* would very soon become intolerable, this low-tech, this *panto* surveillance, ordered surely by Grainer, an extra satirical irritant, but I couldn't think about it now. There was only the one thing to think about, the one thing to decide.

It wasn't painless. It wasn't quick.

Knolly turf gave way to shallow sand dunes. A sudden rough fresh odour of the sea. The old Somme survivor stirred: Margate's salt air had come in through the open window and mingled with the lovely between-the-legs taste of his girl. (Their memories clog me like arterial fur. I'm *full*, I said to Harley. I have achieved fucking *plenum*.)

A marker buoy clanged, muted by wind and rain. The lights of a tanker twinkled, conjured a vision of a snug galley, cable-knit sweaters, tin mugs, roll-up-fag smoke. I could hear a helicopter somewhere inland, a sound like an endlessly discharging machine gun.

What's my moti*vation?* lousy actors want to know. Grainer had given me a legitimate one. *I killed your friend, now you want to kill me.*

It almost worked. The fuse leading to the appropriate emotional bomb lit, crackled, glowed, dazzled for a few heartbeats, then faltered, sputtered, died. I couldn't make it mean enough. I couldn't make it mean anything. Vengeance for the murdered supposed the dead enjoyed sufficient afterlife to appreciate your efforts. The dead enjoyed nothing of the kind. The dead didn't go anywhere, except, if you were the monster who'd taken their lives and devoured them, into you. That's the gift I should have given Harley, or rather made him give me. At least that way we would have been together at the end.

I turned inland, light of heart and heavy as the Dead Sea, thinking, So thank you, dear Grainer, but no—when two things happened.

The first was that I put my hands in my coat pockets and felt in one of them the woollen hat Harley had insisted I take that night in the snow. Your fucking *head* will freeze, moron, he'd said. Because he'd loved me and I hadn't loved him we'd cast the relationship as irascible doting father and moody son. It had begun self-consciously, facetiously, but like so much that begins that way acquired some of the emotional substance it lampooned. And this memory, in the perverse way of these things, did pierce me, set an ache in the empty place where the energy to go after Grainer should be.

The second was that the agent, who'd followed me and was now down on one knee not twenty feet away, fired his weapon directly at me.

I felt a single icy stab in my thigh, an eternal three seconds of something like mild outrage—then all the lights went out.

21

WHATEVER THEY USED they didn't get the dosage right the first time. I floated up to consciousness just long enough to deduce—from the tremor, the noise, the shape of the ceiling—that I was in the helicopter. Restraints pinned my arms, legs, chest, head. A man's voice (definitely *not* a vampire's) said in French, Fuck me, he's awake—then I felt the scratch of a needle, and darkness closed over me again.

•

Transformation woke me to the smell of rust and fuel and seaweed. I was lying on my spasming back on a metal table and the restraints were gone. So were my clothes. Shoulders, shins, head, hands and haunches shunted blood and hurried bone to meet the Curse's metamorphic demand. My circus of consumed lives stirred. The world felt strangely undulant. I thought, Well, I hope you're ready for this, kidnapping fuckers, whoever you are. Then, throbbing with Hunger for living meat, I howled and rolled over onto my side.

Bright halogen lighting showed I was in a cage.

In what looked like the hold of a ship.

Being filmed.

Beyond the bars three men and a woman stood between a pair of tripod-mounted motion-sensitive cameras. One of the men was the agent who'd tranquilized me, early thirties, with a sullen, guinea-piggish face, wearing a nose stud and a black woollen cap. The other two were large skinheads in unmatching fatigues and Timberlands. One, arms covered in golden fuzz, was worryingly glazed. The other was baby-faced, with surprised eyes and a dimpled chin. Both were equipped with automatic rifles and side arms.

The woman, in tight white trousers and a clinging bloodred top, was Jacqueline Delon.

She hadn't changed much in ten years. Slender, petite-breasted with a tiny abdomen and a lean face. Short red hair in the boyish style only French women seem able to carry off. The last time I'd seen her, outside the Burj Al Arab in Dubai, big sunglasses had hidden her eyes, and my inference—of constipation and usefully disturbed sexuality—had been drawn (wishfully, lazily) from the thin-lipped mouth and the patent narcissism of her deportment. Here, however, *were* the eyes, narrow and dirty green, full of insomniac intelligence, a bright front of compulsive playfulness over God only knew what, fear of death, self-avoidance, money-guilt, loneliness, hunger for love—possibly just immense boredom.

"Can he talk?" the baby-faced skinhead asked, *en français*.

"No," Jacqueline said. "But he understands. So don't say anything you might regret."

Without the faintest twitch of warning I flung myself snarling at the bars.

To her credit, Jacqueline barely flinched. The men—to a man—leaped backwards, the two meat-goons with guns raised, the Tranquilizer with a priceless falsetto shriek.

Immediately, I subsided, stood down, shook my head *dear-oh-dear* fashion, a portion of dignity regained. The table I'd woken up on was, I now saw, a huge metal crate. I sauntered back to it and lay down, hands folded on my belly, ankles crossed. Jacqueline laughed, with charming subdued musicality.

"Fuck *me*," the baby-faced skinhead said.

"He's playing with you," Jacqueline said. Then to the Tranquilizer: "For God's sake, don't be such a baby. Turn off the cameras."

Apparent nonchalance notwithstanding, I was booming with Hunger. And in a cage. Mentally I flashed forward a few hours to the cold turkey scene from every heroin-addict movie. Please, man, just some*thin*, you gotta give me *some*thin. I'm not gonna *make* it. Oh God, it hurts . . .

Jacqueline stepped forward and wrapped her red-nailed fingers (blouse-matching) around the bars of the cage. "Jacob," she said, in English, "I'm so sorry for all this. It's not what it appears, I promise. I know you can't answer me, so just let me talk for a moment. My name is Jacqueline Delon. I've wanted to speak with you for some time. I have a proposition for you. But that can wait. You must be wondering where you are."

I didn't move. The cage was bolted to the floor. Other than a few wooden crates, some heaps of rope, rolls of tarp and half a dozen oil drums the hold was empty.

"You're on board the freight ship *Hecate* and we're en route to Biarritz where I have a comfortable place and where I hope we can have a mutually rewarding conversation. Aside from this current indignity, for which I apologise again, I intend you absolutely no harm or discomfort, and as soon as you're no longer a risk to myself or my crew, which should be"—she looked at her watch—"in approximately eight hours, your liberty will be restored to you, and I will personally do everything in my power to compensate you for this inconvenience. In the meantime, as a peace offering, please accept my gift to you. You'll find it in the container you're lying on."

She stepped away from the cage and said quietly, "Let's go."

"You sure?"

"I'm sure."

"The cameras?"

"Leave them off. I've got what I wanted."

The men went ahead of her. At the hold door she turned and looked back at me. "I'm so excited to meet you at last," she said. "You're everything I hoped you would be. I know this can be the start of something exceptional."

After she'd gone I forced myself to lie still, listening to the Hunger turning the volume up in my blood, heartbeat the buzz-thud of a car with the stereo's bass set to max.

Lie still.

An idiotic injunction.

Lie still.

Because you and I know.

Lie still.

What's underneath us in the box.

22

IT'S NO ACCIDENT that the great moral philosophers invariably wrote on aesthetics, too. Figuring out what made something Right (or Wrong) was akin to figuring out what made something Beautiful (or Ugly). These days scientists are in on the act: At the unprovable cosmological fringes beauty swings it. Now mathematical models are like supermodels: They have grace, symmetry, elegance. It's hardly surprising. Modernity having done away with Absolute Moral Values and Objective Reality, there's only beauty *left*. What theory won't we espouse if it's beautiful? What atrocity won't we excuse?

Or what instinct (to stick, as Madeline would have it, to the story) won't we overcome?

For a while, standing with my warm lethal hairy hands wrapped around the cold bars of my cage, I resisted opening the container. Truth was I felt slightly seasick. The tip of my snout was dry. Beyond my confines the full moon made its inexhaustible suggestion, sent down its unbankruptable love, weirdly mingled just then with the memory of Jacqueline Delon's thin face and tightly red-wrapped breasts. *In the meantime, as a peace offering, please accept my gift to you.* Clearly she'd moved beyond customary limits. Courtesy of wealth. *You're everything I hoped you would be.* The remark was an affront, subject and object in each other's seats. *I* live up to *her* expectations? Who the fuck did she think she was?

This, of course, was the embarrassing heart of the matter. I was an animal who'd been caught, caged and observed on camera. My scrotum shrank from the shame of having been seen changing—worse, of having been *filmed* changing. And now left to perform, to do what it was in my nature to do. I was *l'objet d'une voyeuse.* Even the lion knows his debasement, mounting his mate while the bored zoo crowd looks on. To kill and eat here, now, in captivity and on show (I suspected the cameras despite

Madame's instruction; I suspected *other* cameras, CCTV, spyholes) would be a rich and vulgar degradation, an aesthetic (dear Maddy) offence.

Thus the Hunger got its first inkling that resistance was on the table. You're kidding, right? the Hunger said. Then a little more sternly, You are kidding, *right?*

I moved quickly to the container and threw open the lid.

Inside was a naked, white, epicene young man of perhaps twenty, gagged, bound, and judging by his pupils heavily drugged. Dirty blond greasy hair and tiny nipples. Junkie arms and a long thin penis. Whatever the drugs they weren't proof against the vision *I* must have presented. His sore-looking eyes first focused then bugged. He roared behind his gag. An odour of fear on his nostril breath like bitters.

Oh, the Hunger said. Oh you sweet, *sweet* thing.

In their cellular prison my devoured dead roused. (A consequence of eating people: The ingested crave company. Every new victim adds a voice to the monthly chorus.) Ganymede's ankles and wrists were blood-bruised where he'd fought his restraints. Blue circulatory webbing showed through the white skin of his belly. Terror's mouth-watering secretions crept from his pores. My salivary glands duly discharged. In the face of such . . . such *meat* the thought of eight hours ahead without feeding made my teeth and nails hurt. My *hair* ached. Mentally, weakness worked its angle: Resistance would be futile. I'd crack, I'd kill him and devour him and Jacqueline Delon would watch while getting head or smoking a cigarette or eating a crème brûlée or filing her nails.

And yet.

There remained the profound aesthetic repugnance. Or less loftily, self-disgust. At getting so feebly captured. At finding myself the Entertainment. At the decades spent sick of Being a Werewolf. At carrying on regardless. At costing Harley his life. (His poor head must still be in the Vectra's boot. The locals would notice a smell. It would make the news, pass to the world via the anchorman's autocued disbelief: "In the Welsh village of Trefor today police discovered the *severed head* of . . ." Christ, the exhausting predictability of it all.)

My young man thrashed, screaming behind his gag. The ship did something, offered some large tilted response to the sea, and I genuinely thought (God being dead etc.) I might vomit over the wretched creature. I let the lid fall shut. Then worried lest he suffocate. Jacqueline opening the case to find him not mauled but asphyxiated was hardly the denouement I was after. A quick check revealed air holes in the steel flank. Very well. But the Hunger had twigged I was serious. No barbs, no bennys, no chloroform, no laughing gas. No chains, no time locks. No teasing or dallying. Just Jake Marlowe, cold turkey, saying *No.*

There was an inner silence while the Hunger took this in.

I went back to the bars (thinking of Tantalus, of Christ in Gethsemane, unjustifiably of Samson at the Philistine Pillars), wrapped my monster fingers around the steel, closed my eyes and waited for the agony to begin.

Second Moon

)

Fuckkilleat

23

READER, I ATE HIM.

About three hours after resolving I wouldn't.

Throughout the dull solo feast the refrain from Tennyson's "Mariana" repeated in the hot spaces of my gorging head:

She only said My life is dreary, He cometh not, she said.
She said, I am aweary, aweary, I would that I were dead.

I would that I were—Yet here was the flesh that took my teeth in helpless succulence and the warm sour fountain of blood, the puncture moment that never gets old but stops being enough. And afterwards the swollen headache of my unsurprised self, the old exhausted cognisance of all the times I've vowed it was the last time and all the times it wasn't.

Don't misunderstand me: There was no guilt. Only the cavity where guilt used to be. This and the weight of my own still-hereness slumped on me like a corpse. For a long while I lay in the recovery position, eyes closed. Total self-disgust is a kind of peace.

At dawn Jacqueline returned, accompanied by the baby-faced skinhead. Both wore rubber boots over surgical scrubs. From the doorway they unrolled a length of plastic to form a walkway up to the cage. A hosepipe was unwound from a corner of the hold. I understood: a murder scene in the age of CSI. Leftovers were in the crate. The kid's half-eaten carcase in a gelid blood soup. Wolf remnants wriggled under my human skin like rats in a sack. My fingernails, as always after the withdrawal of their wolf counterparts, hurt like hell.

"It's warm water," Jacqueline said. "Do you mind? I'll help as best I can, with your permission."

I sat (naked, obviously) in profile to my captors at the side of the cage with my back to the bars, knees drawn up, face smeared and sated.

I was full-bellied, heavy in the human-again limbs. The wolf's ghost dimensions played with me when I moved, the snout's weight and the long hybrid feet, the haunches still struggling to unload their late mass. The goon had his gun levelled at my belly, but at his mistress's gesture lowered it.

"Here," Jacqueline said, handing me a squeezy bottle. "It's just a sterilising detergent. Would you prefer it if he holds the hose?"

"Decorum and I don't keep company," I said, my throat howl-sore. "Besides, the role of prison guard suits you. Go ahead."

"I'm so sorry," she said. "Really I am. I promise this is the very last discomfort you'll suffer as my guest. Please forgive me."

To repeat: Total self-disgust is a kind of peace—because further ignominy can add nothing to it. Standing there washing myself in front of her I made an intellectual concession to the debasement, but it was only moments before I was enjoying the soft soap and perfectly adjusted heat of the water. Put the right music behind this, I thought, and I could be advertising shower gel.

I dried off with a white towel that might have been manufactured in heaven. The flesh can't help it. The flesh merely reports. When I'd finished I was tired and roseate and curiously pleased with the ongoing failure of myself.

"The ammunition is pure silver," Jacqueline said. "I tell you this not as a threat but only so that you know you'll die if you decide to attack me the minute I open the door. I wouldn't blame you. You must be furious with me. But there's a helicopter waiting which will have us at my home in thirty minutes. Once there, I promise you nothing but luxury, rest and conversation. If you prefer, I can make arrangements for you to be taken to any destination you choose, and I'll never bother you again. But I so much hope you'll agree to hear what I have to say. Is it safe for me to open the door?"

The heroic thing would have been to refuse. Take her at her word and get the chopper to drop me at the nearest airport. *Fuck* conversation. But I was exhausted. The appeal of putting myself in someone else's hands bordered the sensuous.

"I assume you keep a full bar at home?"

"Three full bars."

"Then it's safe to open the door."

When we stood facing each other on the plastic she offered me her hand. I was tempted to take it and bite off a finger (leftover wolf aplenty for that) but settled for a gentle squeeze. "Now we can be relaxed," she said. "I'm so pleased to meet you."

I followed her to the doorway. The gargoyle with the gun stayed put. In the short corridor facing us was a little fold-out table, on it, my clothes (including the woollen hat Harley had given me) washed, dried, pressed. She opened a door on her left, which revealed a small locker. I saw a shower unit, a plastic chair, a dress the colour of wheat on a hanger. "I just need to get out of these," she said, indicating the scrubs. I was checking the overcoat's inside pocket for the journal. It was there, along with passports and wallet. I didn't waste time wondering if she'd read it. "And?" I asked.

"Fascinating," she said. "But let's discuss it over a drink."

24

JACQUELINE DELON'S VILLA sits a few miles south of Biarritz on a wooded hill a little west of the tiny town of Arbonne. Modern, white, glass, oak and steel, surrounded by eight private acres. The trappings you'd expect: helipad, infinity pool, tennis court, gym, CCTV, a combo-staff of domestics and security personnel. The rooms are big, full of light, ornamented with artefacts reflecting her obsession with the occult. From the upper floors (there are three, plus roof terrace) you can look down over the tops of the evergreens to the pale beach, the surf line, the ocean. In the basement there's a library to rival Harley's. All the tech hardware is up to the minute. There are indeed three bars—lounge, pool, master bedroom suite—and it was to the first of these Mme Delon and I retired alone on our arrival.

I lit the first deeply needed cigarette since transformation (a softpack of Camels on the counter; she'd done her homework) while my hostess fixed drinks. Tanqueray and tonic for me (too much sunlight in the room for whisky), a Tom Collins for herself. Nicotine and alcohol embraced in my system like long-parted siblings, grateful to me for reuniting them.

"It's ages since I've made drinks," she said. "There's always someone else. But I thought it best for it to be just the two of us." She'd taken a seat—the bar had six high swivel chairs of white leather—next to mine, and was poking at her cocktail's ice cubes with her index fingernail. The wall to my left was glass, and looked out onto a patio of terra-cotta tiles and a cactus garden. Soil red as chilli powder. It was only mid-March but the sky was clear and the air still. You could feel the blinding brilliance summers would have here. Small birds whirred to and from a feeder bracketed to one white wall.

"So," she said, "I must explain myself. What it comes to, Jacob, is . . ." She looked down, smiled, had a brief inner dialogue with herself, let her shoulders sag, then slid from her stool and stood in front of me. "Come with me," she said, offering me her hand. She might have been a nine-year-old with a tree house to show off. "Come."

I took her hand (retained the Camel, the G&T), got to my feet and followed her.

Through two large rooms (one with a central circular designer fire pit and a large standing stone but little else) down a corridor to a steel door with keypad entry. Beyond, varnished oak stairs led down to the formidable library. Air-con and the feel of soundproof walls. Other heavy doors, also keypadded, led off. Jacqueline paused at one of them, looked me in the eye for a moment, then punched the access code and opened the door.

The room it revealed was small and windowless. A filing cabinet, a desk, a computer—and the wall above it covered in press clippings. All of them related one way or another to me. BODY OF MISSING GIRL FOUND. CORAL INDUSTRIES ESTABLISHES SUB-SAHARAN AIDS CHARITY. VECTOR IN AGGRESSIVE BUY-OUT. MUTILATED BODY DISCOVERED. FAMILY MASSACRED IN MANSON-STYLE ATTACK. MYSTERY DONOR FUNDS PIONEERING CANCER RESEARCH. WHO RUNS LAERSTERNER INTERNATIONAL? "WEREWOLF" EYE-WITNESS IS CLASS-A DRUG-USER. UNNAMED DONOR INJECTS NEW LIFE INTO VACCINE DISTRIBUTION. "SILVER BULLETS" FOUND AFTER NIGHT OF MYS-TERY GUNSHOTS. VECTOR NOW TO TRADE AS HERNE. FULL-MOON MURDERS ARE COINCIDENCE, POLICE MAINTAIN.

"Press Enter," Jacqueline said.

The animal remnants don't like small spaces. I forced myself past it and sat down at the desk. Hit the key as instructed. Instantly footage began to run. Me coming out of International Arrivals in Tokyo. Caption: JM Tokyo, 07/02/06. Me leaving the Algonquin. Me on the beach at Galveston. Me going into Harley's Earl's Court house. Me strolling down the Rue de Rivoli. Me in a Cairo café. All shot in the last three years. The last sequence: me dressed as a woman, getting out of a taxi and entering the Leyland Hotel.

"I take it I'm supposed to be surprised?" I said.

"Not at all," she said. "Just convinced of my dedication."

There was nothing to put my cigarette out in, so I downed the Tan-queray and dropped the butt in the glass. "Well, you've got the transformation footage now. Essential for a name-and-shame operation. The kill too, no doubt. Congratulations. Prepare yourself for the weight of public indifference."

"Please don't insult me. You know that's not what this is."

"Then what is this?"

"A chance for sanctuary."

"What?"

"I want you to stay alive. I'm offering you protection, indefinitely. *Serious* protection," she added, seeing the dismissal forming in my face. "Not that—not what you're used to. I don't think you have any understanding of what a subtraction from the world your death would represent. You're something magnificent, Jake. There's such little magnificence left."

"Thank you very much. I think I'll be going now."

"Listen to me, please."

"There's nothing to discuss."

"You must give me a chance to—"

"Don't be fucking absurd."

She fell silent. Little-girlishly dropped her head, picked at a hangnail. A performance of compressed sullenness. I remembered the small turgid breasts and inviting abdomen. Blood in my cock twitched. Of course it did. The post-Curse horn. Again: The flesh can't help it. Laughter, desire, boredom and exhaustion did what they do as a team, cornered me into a unique paralysis. My hands in my lap like two dead crabs. *Just stay*, Harley had said.

Whatever else was wrong with Jacqueline Delon her sexual instincts were fine. She took the two steps necessary to bring herself within my reach. For such moments to work, knowing when not to speak is crucial. In silence she very carefully placed her legs either side of my knee but remained standing. Thus just above my left dead crab hand was the hot skirt-space. Into which the now livening hand slowly ascended (will always ascend, must ascend, though the gods have gone and the planet's dying and the human race has ironied itself into terminal indifference and it wasn't painless and it wasn't quick) through the zones of deepening heat to the lace-enflowered tender sly swelling of her cunt.

25

SHE HAD THE complete repertoire, the full gallery of sexual personæ, and though boosted by cocaine we flirted with several of them, it was only when I lay on top of her and she stared dead-eyed at me while I went into her that we managed something like alignment. Tender and Curse-hungover I remained in danger of segueing into hysterical laughter or a crying jag. Even when I came (she gave me the raised eyebrows and half smile of sinisterly maternal triumph) it was with sad fracture, a frail sense of the poor old world's injuries and might-have-beens and my own wretched list of losses. Closely followed by a feeling of deep fraud: Beyond the mawkish moment I remained as sick of the stinking planet as I was of my threadbare little self.

Old habits of decency dying hard, however, I got her off, orally, without the remotest illusion she cared very much, though she held my head and bruised my lips with her pubis and made a masculine noise of apparent satisfaction when she came.

"I'm going to have some food sent up," she said. "You don't want anything, I know." We were in the master bedroom suite on the villa's sunlit top floor, a large rectangular deep-carpeted Chanel-scented space, again with one wall entirely glass. Décor was ivory, with here and there a big statement: a cowhide chaise longue; a chandelier of red glass; an original Miro. It was still only early afternoon, though already the *Hecate* seemed weeks ago. Less than forty-eight hours had passed since I'd held Harley's severed head in my hands. My whole life's been like this, too much experience crammed into too little time. Two hundred? You feel two thousand.

"You know?" I said.

"You're still full. It'll take a week at least before you're hungry. It's why you smoke and drink so much. The boredom of the mouth. I was watching, by the way. It seems dishonourable not to tell you now."

Watching my feast in the hold, she meant. Dishonourable now that we were going to be friends.

"We're not going to be friends," I said.

"Aren't we? I assume you'd like another drink, at least?"

She rang for service. Pâté de foie gras, fresh fruit, yogurt, a selection of cured meats and cheeses, brought by a dark-skinned gold-earringed boy of perhaps thirteen dressed in crisp white pyjamas. In smiling silence he set the platter down on a low Japanese inlaid table along the wall of glass. In smiling silence he exited. Jacqueline, in a pearl-coloured silk robe (cover up; give the gentleman's postcoital imagination fresh incentive), fixed drinks at the minimalist wet-bar. I lit a Camel.

"Tell me something," she said. "Why did you give up the search for Quinn's journal?"

Oh God.

"What?"

"You heard me. Quinn's journal. Why did you give up?"

My palms needled. Forty years wasted. When I started searching for the wretched book Victoria was on the British throne and Tchaikovsky was debuting his 1812 Overture in Moscow. When I stopped George V reigned and *The Waste Land* was Europe's massive tumour of enlightenment.

"Who wouldn't have given up?" I said. "One gets tired of not finding what one's looking for."

"But you believed. Otherwise why bother?"

"I don't know what I believed. I wanted answers. I wanted the story. Who doesn't want the story? If someone had told me there was a blind and deaf one-legged washerwoman in Siberia who knew the origin of werewolves I'd have hired myself a yak and set off. There's a period of being bothered with big questions. It doesn't last forever."

"I'm still bothered," she said.

"You're French. If you lot stopped bothering the coffee and tobacco industries would collapse."

She chuckled. Brought me my drink, administered a light fingernails caress to my thigh, then paced silkily away to the Japanese table. She knelt and began undaintily helping herself. Veins showed in her white hands and ankles; my cock stirred in dumb irritable reflex. She wasn't falling-in-love material but the thought of eating her was already, as from a great distance, starting to appeal.

"Werewolves are not a subject for *academe*," she said, "but you know what the professors would be saying if they were. 'Monsters die out when the collective imagination no longer needs them. Species death like this is nothing more than a shift in the aggregate psychic agenda. In ages past the beast in man was hidden in the dark, disavowed. The transparency of modern history makes that impossible: We've seen ourselves in the concentration camps, the gulags, the jungles, the killing fields, we've read ourselves in the annals of True Crime. Technology turned up the lights and now there's no getting away from the fact: The beast is redundant. It's been us all along.' "

"Yes," I said. "I keep telling myself I'm just an outmoded idea. But you know, you find yourself ripping a child open and swallowing its heart, it's tough not to be overwhelmed by . . . the concrete reality of yourself."

Another smile. She was enjoying this. Worse, I was slightly enjoying it myself. Still, the mention of Quinn's journal and reminder of my hot years when Meaning meant something had disturbed long-settled dust.

"And in any case," she said, "there remain vampires. If the human psyche's so at ease with itself why are *they* doing so well?"

"I don't concern myself with vampires," I said.

"They regard you as primitives," she said. Then, looking away: "It's the absence of language, naturally."

The second drink had gone down with shameful ease. Your fucking *head* will freeze, moron, Harley had said. Poor Harls. Once, heartbroken by a brilliant and toxic young Bosey he'd drunk himself into a semicoma that lasted two days. When he came round and realised *I*'d been there the whole time, looking after him, he'd said, confusedly: My goodness, aren't you kind? Then he'd fallen asleep again.

"Sorry," I said, having lost Jacqueline's thread. "Say again?"

"Werewolves can't talk. *Les vampyres* think this is hilarious."

"Yes," I said. "Of course they do." One of the great subcurses of the

Curse, this loss of speech. It's a failure to achieve full monstrosity. Certainly it's deeply pleasurable to open your victim's belly with an index claw, but not as pleasurable as it would be to be able to talk to him while you did it. It's you, Arabella had said—and animal dumbness had denied me the apotheosis of saying, Yes, it is. Purest cruelty requires that the victim knows she suffers by your free choice. It's you. Yes, my darling, it's me. Now, observe.

"They're inclined to snobbery to start with," Jacqueline said. "This business of werewolf inarticulacy is the great justification. They do have such a large body of literature."

This has been one of the great vampiric contentions, that they constitute a civilisation: They have art, culture, division of labour, political and legal systems. There's no lycanthropic parallel. The yeehaw explanation is we're too busy chasing meat'n'pussy, but the truth is the language of the *wer* is anathema to the *wulf*. After a few transformations your human self starts to lose interest in books. *Reading* begins to give you a blood-brown headache. People describe you as laconic. Getting the sentences out feels like a giant impure labour. I've heard tell of howlers going decades barely uttering a word.

"Yeah," I said to Jacqueline, as I lit another Camel, "we're not great ones for belles-lettres."

"Yourself excepted."

Well, yes. Obviously *I*, anomalously, still can't fucking shut up. I blew a smoke ring. "Since you've read the journal there's no point my denying it," I said.

"How do you explain it?"

"I must like a whore unpack my heart with words."

"Of course, but why?"

"Congenital logorrhoea."

"Jake, *please*. It's so obvious."

"And yet I don't see it."

She shook her head, smiling. Popped a strawberry into her mouth, chewed, swallowed. Wiped her hands on a fat napkin. "Yes, you do. You're just embarrassed by it. You've held on to language because without language there's no morality."

"Ah, yes, I spend a lot of time considering morality, when I'm not slaughtering people and gobbling them all up."

"I'm talking about testimony. I'm talking about *bearing witness to yourself.* What is this—what are the journals—if not the compulsion to tell the truth of what you are? And what is the compulsion to tell the truth if not a moral compulsion? It's perfectly Kantian."

She presented a peculiarly annoying attractive figure sitting there in her ivory silk robe with her legs tucked under her. "What was your phrase? 'God's gone, meaning too, yet aesthetic fraudulence still has the power to shame . . .' *Aesthetic* fraudulence, notice. Telling the truth is a beautiful act even if the truth itself is ugly—and my dear man, you can't stop caring about beauty. *That* is your real predicament, your real curse."

"Fascinating the way other people see things," I said. "But I really must be going." I swung *my* legs over the edge of the bed and reached for my trousers.

"I have Quinn's book," she said.

There's a distinctive aural quality to lies. This didn't have it. It cost me some effort to hold—after the briefest hesitation—to my purpose with the trousers. I stood and pulled them on. You pull your trousers on and everything seems fractionally less desperate. Nonetheless I felt sick. You get used to no one having anything (except their flesh and blood, except their *life*) you could possibly want. You take your sufficiency for granted. You forget it's contingent. You forget it's a luxury.

"Good," she said, observing. "I see you know I'm telling the truth. That saves us some time."

"How did you get it?" I asked, though I was pretty sure I knew. The memory of Harley—*someone hit one of Mubarak's places three months ago*—like the punch line that draws a groan.

"Oh, that's too long a story for now. Stay for dinner and I'll tell you. Right now I absolutely must take a shower." She got to her feet.

"This is the technique then, is it? Keep me dangling?"

"Well, if you're not going to see reason."

"What makes you think I give a fuck these days? I don't give a fuck, actually, now that I think of it."

"Then feel free to leave. If you genuinely have no interest then walk out the way we came in. You'll find my driver at the gate. He's instructed to take you wherever you care to go."

"What *do* you want from me?" I asked her.

She turned, one hand in the pocket of her robe, and looked out through the wall of glass. "I told you," she said. "I want you to live."

26

I FINISHED DRESSING. Sunlight filled the perfumed room. I went to the huge window and, as she had, looked out. Dark conifers swept down to the pale line of the beach and the sea's glitter. Blue cloudless sky, London's recent snow a world away and a century ago, though this was still Europe, still early March. The sex had carried us into late afternoon. My shoulders ached. The junkie's gobbled life was finding room, incredibly, the last seat in a packed arena, that solid deafening crowd of living dead. Somewhere among them an unripe foetus the size of a plum, my daughter, my son.

There were two explanations for what I was doing here. One was that Jacqueline Delon was sufficiently bored and unhinged for the keeping of a werewolf as an erotic pet to seem a rejuvenating novelty. The other was that she had a motive as yet unknown which required, in addition to the palaver of kidnapping me and accessorising herself to murder, temporary dissemblance. A woman of intriguingly acute ambiguity even without the bait of Quinn's book.

Oh Jesus, Quinn's book.

Thirty-seven-year-old Alexander Quinn went out to Mesopotamia for the third and final time in the spring of 1863. A double first in classics and ancient history from Oxford ought to have bricked him into academia for life, but by the time he left Kings in 1848 he was ravenous for the world beyond college walls. Brief failed stints in the British Museum, the Foreign Office (Burma) and the East India Company (Bombay) finagled by his Old Etonian dad confirmed the futility of sticking him behind a desk, and by 1854 he was on his first archaeological expedition to the Middle East under the Bacchic eye of Lord William Greaves, a known occultist roué, whom Quinn (no sluggard with the ladies himself) had met and befriended as a fellow whorer at Kate Hamilton's. Greaves, a collector of religious antiquities and student of the Black Arts, had been thrilled to read of Botta's discoveries at Nineveh and Khorsabad and was convinced ancient objects of talismanic power were there for the taking if one merely had the money, leisure and inclination to go and dig them up. Quinn, desperate to get his hands dusty and put his colloquial Arabic to use, pretended an interest in diabolism and offered his services as an interpreter-cum-right-hand-man. Which, over the next nine years, is exactly what he became. Along with site management and the cataloguing of finds Quinn greased the requisite bureaucrats, landowners, tribal elders and customs officers and still found time to score opium and girls for his lordship.

How do I know all this?

Because I spent time finding it out.

Why did I spend time finding it out?

Because before his death in 1863 Quinn claimed to have discovered the origin of werewolves.

It's a ridiculous story, of course, but history's full of ridiculous stories. *You can't make this shit up,* one finds oneself saying, whenever the seemingly prosaic old world lifts the veil on its synchronicities. Meanwhile the seemingly prosaic old world shrugs: Hey, don't ask me. I just work here.

As so often with Great Finds, the man looking was looking for something else. Quinn had travelled to the town of Al Qusayr, whence rumour had reached the archaeologists of an underground temple fifteen miles away, literally fallen into by a retarded goatherd. Greaves, sceptical (the natives had learned quickly there was money to be made selling "information" to eccentric Europeans), had given Quinn the site as a pet project, and the protégé had set off from the camp in Al Qusayr with camels, a guide and two servants, one of whom was to be despatched with the guide back to his lordship to summon hands and equipment should the rumours turn out to be fact.

Which, to everyone's surprise, they did. The subsequent excavations at Gharab revealed not just a temple but an entire sunken village dating from the third millennium B.C. Lord Greaves cleaned up his act and led the dig, partly because the wealth of artefacts shocked him into a renaissance of genuine interest and partly out of respect for the good man he'd lost.

For Alexander Quinn never made it back to camp. He and his little scouting party were ambushed by bandits on their return journey. Quinn, the guide and one of the servants were killed. The other servant, John Fletcher, though left for dead, survived a knife wound to the shoulder, wandered delirious for a day in the desert, then was picked up by a merchant caravan. On the strength of the only word they understood, "Qusayr," the merchants returned him to Greaves there two days later, where, having made it through fever and miraculously dodged infection, he told his lordship the whole story.

The night before the attack, Fletcher reported, the party, camped by the temple site, had been startled by the arrival of an astonishingly old man in rags, who'd come crawling on hands and knees out of the darkness. Skeletal and half blind, he spoke a dialect even the guide only partly understood, but they didn't need the translator to see the old fellow was close to death. When Quinn made to send for help the old man stopped him. No point. Time to die. But listen. Keep story. No children so tell you. You write down. Keep story. He'd laughed when he said this, at himself it seemed. Fletcher had supposed him mad. Quinn, unwilling to simply let the man die, sent the servants back to the village for help, but by the time they returned the old man had expired. In those two hours he had told, Quinn claimed, an extraordinary story, a story which, if its provenance was genuine, had been passed down from the days before Etana and which would provide the oldest account of the origin of a near worldwide myth—of humans who became wolves.

Quinn, via the guide's translation, had written the whole thing down in his journal.

That wasn't all. But for the rags on his back the old man's only possession, wrapped in the remains of a gunnysack, was a piece of stone, some ten inches by eight, clearly a fragment of a larger tablet, bearing hieroglyphs Quinn couldn't decipher, but which, according to the old man, was proof of the truth of his tale.

Which isn't much, is it? Hardly sufficient, you'd think, to form the basis of a neurotic obsession for the better part of forty years. Because *for* forty years the thought of Quinn's lost journal—and the story of the Men Who Became Wolves—never ceased being a drain on my energies.

There's a limit to what one can do. I interviewed John Fletcher, Lord Greaves, all the surviving members of the 1863 expedition. I travelled with an interpreter to Al Qusayr and on to the excavated temple at Gharab. I sought out bandit chiefs and offered rewards for information. I retained half a dozen dealers in antiquities and rare books to keep an eye on the market, despite the laughably overwhelming likelihood that Quinn's diary had simply been deemed worthless and chucked away to be long since swallowed by the desert sand. It all took time, money, mental illness. I knew it was a ludicrous fixation. (One knows one's madnesses, by and large. By and large the knowledge is vacuous. The notion of naming the beast to conquer it is the idiot optimism of psychotherapy.) When the *Times* reported the story in May of 1863 I'd been a werewolf for twenty-one years. The big questions didn't, it turned out, go away. Once a month I transformed into a monster, part man, part wolf. Fair enough. I killed and devoured humans, starting with my wife. Very well. But where did it all *fit in*? Was my species God's handiwork or the Devil's? Darwin's *Origin*, published four years earlier, had said, effectively, neither, but old habits died hard. What would happen to me when *I* died? Had I still a soul? Where and when did werewolves begin?

Of course I'd *read*. Folk tales, compendia of myth and superstition, academic studies. Lycanthropy, even a cursory investigation will reveal, has a place in many cultures. I'd travelled to North America and learned what I could of *Wendigo* and the skinwalkers, to Germany, where rustics still kept silver handy and cherished wolfsbane (which, by the way, though toxic to humans and pretty much every other animal, has absolutely no effect on us), to Serbia to hear of the *vulkodlaks* and to Haiti to learn what I could of the *je-rouges*. None of it conclusively convinced. I was a werewolf but the werewolf stories still sounded like fairy tales to me. I began to wonder if my scepticism was congenital, if the howler was naturally equipped with a nose for his own true provenance, or at least his own false biographers. The stories left me with the same depressing doubt the growing youngster begins to feel about Santa Claus and the Stork, those uniquely deflating intimations of the world's somehow *just not being like that*. (These were still the days before I'd actually met any other werewolves, by the way. Not that the half dozen I've met since have been any use. One was four hundred and three years old and refused to speak at all. One was the founder of a [failed, naturally] werewolf society in Norway, a sect based around the worship of Fenrir, the illegitimate wolf offspring of Loki and Angrboda, which ruled him out of serious conversation. To the other four—one in Istanbul, one in Los Angeles, one in the Pyrenees and one, incredibly, on a Nile cruise in 1909—each monomaniacally desperate for a She, I was simply unwanted sexual competition and lucky to escape with my life.) Whereas, against all likelihood, John Fletcher's story of Quinn's encounter rang . . . if not true then at least not wholly false. Its very inaptness—werewolves in Mesopotamia?—lent it a whiff of mad authenticity.

One meeting with Fletcher was enough to convince me *his* story was true (what he was telling us was what Quinn had told him) for the simple reason that the man was incapable of making something like that up. So, granted the veracity of Fletcher's testimony, what did Quinn write in his journal? What was the five-thousand-year-old story of the Men Who Became Wolves?

What I expected, what I realised I'd *been* expecting ever since the words "I have Quinn's book" left my hostess's mouth, was a deep, a bodily certainty that I no longer cared. What makes you think I give a fuck these days? I don't give a fuck, actually, now that I think of it. Brave words. In fact I felt sick. Sick*ened,* by the combination of knowing it was all too late and knowing that even now it wasn't too late. "Quinn's book" was simultaneously an outgrown childhood fetish and a miraculously resurrected dead love. I knew what a liberation it would be to get up and walk away, with a sad smile, as of a final renunciation that brings peace.

The beauty of chronic ambivalence is that even tiny shifts of detail have the power to tip the scales. Jacqueline turned the shower off and exhaled, heavily, and the sound rushed me up out of my stupor. Suddenly the uncertainty of my status here—was I a prisoner or not?—was intolerable. *I have Quinn's book.* She wasn't lying (and even now the thought of it within reach after all these years was like a violent drop in blood pressure) but I couldn't stand the thought of simply *waiting to see how things played out*. With the abrupt cessation of the water's flow and that one female sigh the weeks of passivity caught up with me and yanked me to my feet (without intending to, I'd gone back to the bed and sat down) in a contained paroxysm of self-disgust. I crossed the soft carpet, picked up my overcoat from where I'd dropped it by the door, then quietly let myself out of the room.

27

JUST WALK OUT OF HERE was all I had. Not much, but enough. Take her at her word and see how far I got before someone stopped me. Before someone *tried* stopping me. That was what I wanted, something concrete to launch myself at, physically, partly for the relief of not having to think, partly to get out from under the weight of shame that had accumulated. She makes a fool of you and you lick her hand. Holds up the baby toy of Quinn's book and you dribble and coo. Meanwhile it wasn't painless and it wasn't quick.

The house was solid silence. If there were staff they were hidden, though there was no mistaking the weird protoconsciousness of CCTV following me from room to empty room. Behind the butch front I was still talking myself out of looking for Quinn's journal. It wouldn't be visible, and if it was it wouldn't be accessible. And in any case what was the point? Suppose I found it and it said werewolves came on a silver ship out of the sky five thousand years ago, or were magicked up out of a burning hole in the ground by a Sumerian wizard, or were bred by impregnating women with lupine seed—so what? Whatever the origin of my species it would no more make cosmic sense than the origin of any other. The days of making sense, cosmic or otherwise, are long over. For the monster as for the earthworm as for the man the world hath really neither joy, nor love, nor light, nor certitude, nor peace, nor help for pain, and we are here as on a darkling plain . . . I found the lounge, opened one of the glass doors and stepped outside.

The house was built, I now saw, on the flat summit of a series of landscaped terraces. At the front a little red-earthed cactus garden led via white stone steps (one flight on the eastern side, one on the western) down to a tier of olive and cypress interspersed with lavender and thyme, with more steps down to a paved mezzanine over the garages, beyond which the white gravel driveway through the dark evergreens began.

I stood at the top of the first flight and scanned the grounds. No one visible. The indoor silence continued out here, gravid, surveillance rich. I pictured goons manning a closed-circuit console. He's just exited the lounge, Madame. Do we intercept? Not yet. Is everyone in position? Good. Wait for my command.

In less than half a minute, unmolested, I stood on the driveway. The sun had dropped below the top floor of the house and the little sweat of self-contempt I'd worked up was cooling on my skin. Ahead the conifers made a dark green resinous tunnel, an odour like a nightmarish overdose of Christmas. I began walking.

Off the drive a floor of dead needles and the firs embracing like mourners overhead. A memory of being in my mother's wardrobe as a child, the thrill of secret enclosure. Presumably a Freudian enactment of a return to the womb. The realisation that I hadn't thought of my mother for years. In a universe sans afterlife the dead soon become negligible. Unless they're the dead you've killed and eaten. Then you *are* the afterlife, the overcrowded spirit prison, the packed ghost hotel.

I walked slowly with my full-of-thinking head down—yet when the attack came I was prepared for it. In spite of myself recent events had rebooted the defence systems, dusted down the schema of combat. Jake in reverie at a stately pace, yes, but with aura madly vigilant, trip-switched, motion-sensored, hair-triggered, so that when the figure launched itself from the trees' murk I was ludicrously ready.

It happened very fast, the reversal. One moment he was barely arm's length from me, silver-tipped javelin on a collision course with my chest, the next (the silver forced a rush of sickness, as if I'd looked down to see my feet an inch from the cliff edge) he was on his belly groaning into the gravel. There had been a vertiginous second when I grabbed the weapon but I burned through it, snatched the thing from him, spun it Little John–style and struck low to take his shins out from under him. Since he'd flipped facedown with his legs invitingly parted I kicked him hard in the balls—terrible squish of testes on bone—then with some irritation at how inadequate a release this had been put my foot on the back of his neck and jabbed the point an inch or so into his left buttock. He wriggled, soundlessly, since he couldn't breathe. I removed the spear and gave him a second jab next to the first. More silent contortion. I removed it a second time, got my foot under his hip, hoofed him over onto his back. Recognised the big-lipped young man formerly armed with a Magnum, Paul Cloquet. Wearing the same trench coat, the same ridiculous mascara. His right hand was now grubbily bandaged.

"Oh, for God's sake," I said. "You?"

Speaking was temporarily beyond him, what with the testicular trauma and ass-stabbing. He brought his knees up and rolled over onto his side, facing the tips of my shoes. I checked him for further weaponry, found none. Instead a gold cocaine tin and spoon, a crumpled pack of Marlboro reds, a copper Zippo, loose matches, an iPhone, a pair of binoculars, a hip flask, a credit card–filled wallet and five hundred euros in cash. Also, touchingly, a pack of cashew nuts. Since he was going nowhere I took a minute to establish there weren't accomplices lurking. The forest's lush consciousness said no, just this nut job. We were in quiet partnership against the purely human, me and the forest. Nature livens to the latent animal, concedes you contain a divine fragment of the pantheistic whole, that you are, at least in part, part of it. A mere domestic dog lolloping through the woods knows this, feels it, is happy.

"Well?" I said, returning. "Let's hear it."

He closed his kohled eyes, spent what seemed to me an inordinately long time parting and bringing together the Jaggerish lips over the excellent large teeth. Shook his head, slowly: Can't talk yet. The balls. Must wait for the balls. I got down on my haunches and began slowly rubbing his back. It was what I'd wished someone could've done for me when Ellis mashed my nuts that morning at the Zetter. As is the way of it once two men have shared the intimacy of violence, Cloquet took the gesture as if it were the most natural thing in the world. His eyes opened.

"Why are you trying to kill me?" I asked him, in French. "And why are you so superhumanly shit at it?"

Still no dice. He just kept swallowing. His breath was bad. Aware of our conspicuousness I half-carried, half-dragged him off the drive and in among the trees. I'd left my smokes in Jacqueline's boudoir so filched one of his Marlboros and lit it. Incredibly, he with trembling hands found his coke accoutrements and took a couple of hefty toots. It first dazed then steadied him.

"Better?" I said.

He nodded. "Don't kill me," he said, in English. Then added, with something like tenderness: "You fucking cunt."

I hadn't heard anything to make me laugh for a while. This did. Plus there was the standard French insult of ignoring your French and answering in English. "Hot tip," I said. "If you're trying to get someone to not kill you, avoid calling him a fucking cunt."

He smiled, reached for the coke again. I snatched it from him and put it in my pocket. "Enough of that," I said. "Quid pro quo, understand? You don't get this back until you tell me what I want to know."

Something ended in him, visibly. Though still lying more or less on his side, now semipropped against the flared bole of a tree, he sagged. The bright cosmeticised eyes said no sleep for a long time. "Quid pro quo, Clarice," he said, in a Hopkins-Lecter impersonation of surprising accuracy.

"You've got it. Now. Why do you want me dead?"

"Because she wants you alive."

"Jacqueline?"

"Did you fuck her yet?"

God only knows why, but I lied. "No," I said.

"Her cunt's got a mind. It knows you. Everything about you. Like Lucifer. God is omniscient but he can't separate out the useful knowledge. You know? He can't *distinguish*. For that you need the Devil or her cunt."

"Why does she want me alive?"

"For the vampires."

"*What?*"

"You don't know anything. I can't believe you've lived this long. I'm not talking to you. You're beneath me."

I got up off my knees and crept back out to the drive where I'd left the javelin. "I can use this in a number of ways," I said when I returned. "They won't kill you, these ways, but they will hurt. You're fond, I imagine, of your right eye? I mean, you've gone to the trouble of putting makeup on it." I lined the tip up with the object in question.

Tears, to my surprise, welled and hurried down his cheeks. Ignoring the silver point of the weapon (it was as if he genuinely didn't recognise it was there) he reached up and tenderly covered his eyes. "Oh God," he said, quietly. "You don't know what it's *like* with her."

"For the love of Mary," I said. "I get it, she's got a nifty twat. Tell me what I need to know and you can go up there and try'n get back into it. What is this about vampires?"

He dropped his hands, snuffled up his tears, laughed as if at an irony visible only to him. With the now-smudged mascara he looked like Alice Cooper. "I thought I was large," he said. "Until I met her. Little sins you're so proud of. Nothing. Crumbs on her table. Now there's no going back."

"I can't believe you're going to make me do real damage to you," I said, raising the javelin. "But if that's the only—"

"Helios Project," he said. "You know about the Helios Project?"

"Well, I know what it *is*," I said. Hardly a secret: The Helios Project is the ongoing attempt by vampires to get themselves immune to the destructive power of daylight. One way or another they've been working on it since the Ten Commandments.

"Well, I know what it *is*," he parroted, in satirical falsetto. "Do you know, *loup-garou*, that they now have three recorded cases of sunlight tolerance?"

"No."

"No. Of course you don't. So far it hasn't lasted more than seventy-two hours, but you can imagine their excitement. Know what all three cases have in common?"

"What?"

"Werewolf attacks. The vampires who showed massively increased resistance to daylight had all been bitten by werewolves."

I sighed. I probably hadn't sighed in thirty years, but right then it was just the thing. See, Jake? Life said. See how things just start *taking shape* if you stick around long enough? Dots were becoming visible; I knew with weary certainty the next few moments would join them into *some* sort of bastard picture. Still, one goes through the motions.

"Doesn't make sense," I said. "There have been plenty of bites down the years. We're like cats and dogs."

"Yes, Clouseau, but what happened a couple of hundred years ago?

Werewolves stopped multiplying. Victims stopped surviving the bite. A virus, WOCOP says. Who knows? But whatever it is when it's passed to a vampire it confers, to however small a degree, resistance to sunlight." He reached for the Marlboro. I let him light one up. In the time since leaving the house late afternoon had become dusk. The forest around us was suddenly wealthy with darkness. The white gravel of the winding drive would be the last light to go. "The vampires are kicking themselves because it took them so long to spot it," Cloquet continued. "Now that they have spotted it"—the big lips widened to free the equine grin—"*O Fortuna!*—there's only one werewolf left." He laughed, huskily, softly blasted me with the louche breath, forgot not to put weight on his bottom, yelped, curled back onto his side. I rather wished I'd stabbed him somewhere less awkward.

"Look," I said, "I don't dig vampires but they're not stupid. It can't possibly have taken them this long to work this out."

He was searching his pockets—for the hip flask it turned out. I helped him unscrew the top. After a glug and a wince he said: "But of course it can. For one thing the cases are so far apart. One in 1786, one in 1860, one in 1952. In the 1952 incident the vampire never told anyone he'd been bitten. He was embarrassed. A minion found it in his journal last year and reported it. Plus you're overstating the case for werewolf-vampire contact. The reality is that when you meet each other you just turn and go in opposite directions, no? Actual conflict rarely occurs." He shook his head. "It's too funny. They're *livid*."

I sat back on my heels. *Jesus Christ, Jake, listen. There's—presumably—a vampire plot to get you. Werewolf failure to infect is the result of a virus which when passed via a bite to a vampire confers on him a resistance to sunlight.* The impulse to laugh started then immediately died. I closed my eyes. The little combat flurry had left me with a postadrenaline heaviness, worsened now by the predictability of the picture revealed by joining the dots. "Aging Jacqueline's selling me to the boochies," I said. "For immortality."

"The immortal cunt. *Le con immortel.*"

"So you kill me and there's nothing for her to sell. Dear God help us. Then what? You send her flowers and a vat of Botox and she takes you back?"

He wrinkled his nose, as if conceding a minor snag. Then smiled. He had a sort of likeable stubborn idiocy.

"Quinn's book," I said. "Does she have it?"

"Ah, the Men Who Became Wolves. The place where it all began! Not a very wholesome story from what I hear. Wild dogs and dead bodies. Fucking disgusting."

My scalp went hot. I pressed the javelin's tip against the tender meat of his throat.

"Okay, okay, fuck. Ow—"

"Does she have the book or not?"

"She has it. The stone too."

"The stone? The original stone?"

"You can't get to it. It's in a vault underground. You have no clue. It's like Fort Knox under there."

"How did she get it?"

"How does she get anything? You know what you're dealing with. She has the uncanniness. You know Crowley? Do what thou wilt? She has the . . . Things *align* for her. She bought a lot of the looted shit that came out of Iraq in the war. She's got contacts in the military, Blackwater, the CIA, the U.S. State Department. I told you: Her cunt is a giant intelligence. What are you going to do now?"

I stubbed out the Marlboro. Just on the edge of audibility the sound of an approaching car. "Well," I said, "at the moment walking out of here still seems a luminously good idea." *Except you don't get the book, the stone, the beginning.* Nausea redux, the earlier untenable simultaneity of knowing it was too late and knowing it wasn't too late. A five-thousand-year-old story. A story. A fucking *story.* Wild dogs and dead bodies. I told myself I was imagining it, the bone-deep, the *cellular* recognition, the old blood taste of shame. Not, Jake, mythic resonance or species memory or ringing a bell or striking a chord. Just, dear Jake, the desperate desire not to die a mystery to yourself. Wild dogs and dead bodies. A disgusting story's better than no story at all.

"How did you get in here?"

"I shot the two guards on the south gate."

"With what, for God's sake?"

"My gun. It's probably over there. I dropped it." He indicated the spot of his failed ambush. A quick search turned the weapon up, a silenced CZ 75 B cal. 9mm Luger, serial number erased. I checked the ammo: silver bullets.

"Why didn't you use this? I'd be dead by now."

"I know. But I had the javelin custom-made. You see this running down the shaft? That's my name and hers in Angelic script."

The car was nearer. The car—there was no denying it—was Coming Here. "That's them," Cloquet said, trying to get to his feet, managing only to struggle onto all fours, with a look of being about to vomit. I pocketed the handgun and dragged us farther in under the trees. The vehicle—a black people-carrier with mirrored windows—went past slowly over the pale gravel, around which the darkness was now complete. "Why didn't they pick me up from the ship?" I said. "I was already in a cage."

Cloquet shook his head. "I don't know. I thought that was the plan. Keep you on board until sunset. She must have worried the Coast Guard bribe wouldn't hold. Maybe WOCOP had a vessel close. I don't know. Maybe she just wanted to fuck you. You fall in love with her because she shows you straight away she'll never feel anything for you."

We had to work our way around through the woods to get a downwind view, a struggle for Cloquet, who hobbled, one hand covering his stabbed backside, the other his discordantly singing balls. When we stopped under tree cover not far from the front of the house he dropped to his knees and threw up, quietly. Quietly repeated *merde, merde, merde* until I hissed at him to shut up.

Five vampires got out of the car. Three males, two females. Beyond that it was too dark for details. Jacqueline Delon, flanked by two armed goons (ammo'd with what? wooden bullets?), appeared at the top of the steps in a pale dress to meet them.

"What happened?" one of the vampires said. The characteristic boredom (a version of seen-it-all teen tedium, forgivable, since so many of them have seen it all) was missing from his voice.

"Come up," Jacqueline said. "Just come up. We'll talk."

Four of them went up the stairs. The fifth, one of the females, stopped halfway and turned. Looked directly at us. I felt Cloquet holding his breath.

Realised I was holding mine. Since I couldn't feel her she shouldn't, by rights, be able to feel me. I'd left enough distance between us. Even down-wind her scent was very slight; mine would be imperceptible. But there she stood, alert. The odour of Cloquet's vomit, perhaps?

Oh, for fuck's sake: the blood from his wound.

It's the obvious things you don't think of.

She hesitated, lifted her head, took her hands out of her pockets, took a step forward and leaned into the darkness.

"Mia, get up here."

For a moment her extended sense groped at the edge of our aura. Then it passed, missed us, shrank back to its centre. She turned and went quickly up the steps.

28

"Now what?" Cloquet said.

Good question. What I really wanted was to lie down there on the soft dead needles under the pines and let myself drift into a deep sleep, come what may. There was profound comfort in it, that phrase, *come what may.* "I'll tell you something," I said. "You'll find this hard to believe, but all I'm trying to do is stay alive until the next full moon so that a man whose father I killed and ate forty years ago can cut my werewolf head off or put a silver bullet in my werewolf heart."

Cloquet was on his knees and elbows next to me, apparently a position that maximally relieved his butt, nuts and guts. "I don't feel well," he said. "I've lost a lot of blood."

"Hardly any. Don't be a baby. Here, have a toot." I handed him his coke tin. A pause. Two snorts. A businesslike groan of pleasure.

"*C'est bon. Aie. C'est beau.* Will they kill her?"

"Who knows? They probably won't be able to summon the requisite vim."

"Vim?"

"Energy."

"But what are we going to do?"

"Nothing. Watch and wait. And who the fuck are 'we'? Starsky and Hutch?"

He chuckled, wheezily. The cocaine had cheered him. "In a way," he said, "I wish you had fucked her. Then you'd know. Then you'd know the sublime . . . Her asshole, for example. It's like a stern coquettish spoiled secretary working for Himmler—"

"Shut up, will you? I need to think. Give me a cigarette."

The sensible thing would have been to break Cloquet's neck and slip away. Vampires wanted me alive—so what? It added to the vocabulary of my predicament but the grammar remained unchanged.

Except for Quinn's book. The disgusting story. Wild dogs and dead bodies and the iron taste of ancient memory. Proximal enlightenment was a throbbing headache that wouldn't subside.

I cupped the Zippo, lit up, took a ferocious drag. The facts remained, no matter how long I stood there shuffling them: Either the story's true or it's false. Either Jacqueline has the book or she doesn't. If she has it, either I get it or I walk away. If I get it, either it will make a difference to me or it won't.

Simultaneously (in the inner voice of a female American cultural studies professor): Only meaning can make a difference and we all know there's no meaning. All stories express a desire for meaning, not meaning itself. Therefore any difference knowing the story makes is a delusion.

Cloquet was now lying on his side with his knees pulled up. In the darkness I could just discern the large wet black blinking eyes and the glimmer of the hip flask. "I'm starving," he said. "I don't suppose you've got anything to eat, have you?"

I remembered the binoculars and began going through his pockets for them.

"There's a little place in Le Marais," he said, not seeming to mind the manhandling, "that makes the best *choux* pastry in the world. I could kill for one of their vanilla éclairs right now. This is the beauty of not modelling anymore. I can eat whatever I want."

"You really were a model? That's hilarious. Here, have these."

"My cashews. Thank God. But what I really want is something sweet. When she comes, you know, she looks at you with such pure and remote clear hatred. The contempt . . . It's the con*tempt*. I spent so many years looking for a woman who truly despised me."

The binoculars didn't help much. Mme Delon had science-fiction technology in her windows, which were now, without the aid of curtains or shutters or blinds, completely opaque. Three of her security men in puffer jackets and combat trousers were visible: two on the ground, one on the roof. They paced, chewed gum, smoked, exchanged occasional quiet words. The firs were a dark fraternal presence around us. Cloquet munched his cashews, breathing through his nose. It got uncomfortably cold. An hour passed.

"She'll negotiate," Cloquet said, availing himself of another two hits of coke. "You don't know how she operates. Do you know about the African kids? Angola, Nigeria, Congo. Kids accused of witchcraft. She takes them off their parents' hands, pays handsomely too. Then what? What do you think she does with—"

"Quiet! Fuck, I nearly missed them." I'd been watching the front of the house but the vampires must have come from an unseen exit on the garage level below. Only the sound of the people-carrier door opening alerted me. I put the silencer to the back of Cloquet's head. "One squeak and you're dead."

The ridiculous, of course, waits only for the moment of intense seriousness. In a tiny whisper Cloquet said: "I have to sneeze." Hardly surprising after the barrel of coke he'd inhaled. I dropped the gun and the binoculars and grabbed him, one hand pinching his nostrils shut, the other clamped over his mouth. One of the vehicle's side doors slid closed with a rasp and a thud. The female vampire, Mia, lingered, again with her nose lifted in our direction. In the light from the van's interior I saw a young high-cheekboned face and shoulder-length yellow-blond hair.

Cloquet's moment was near. I tightened my grip—too much. He wriggled, desperately. I rolled on top of him as if for buggery and held on. Mia got into the front passenger seat. Legs and high heels that would have been at home in an ad for luxury stockings lifted in gracefully. She reached for the door handle.

Chssʒn! With an almighty effort Cloquet wrested enough of his nose free to release his bizarre sneeze—by the mercy of the gods precisely synchronised with the clunk shut of the passenger door. I nearly broke his neck there and then. But the engine started and the people-carrier, carrying its immortal people, swung round and pulled away.

A gobbet of Cloquet snot clung to the back of my hand. "Thanks for that," I said, wiping it on his lapel. "Now. On your feet, soldier."

"What?"

"Get up. Back against here, please."

Improvisation. His belt secured his hands around the tree trunk behind him. He didn't protest much. Evidently he had a penchant for surrender. A little moment formed between us when I'd fastened him. He looked at me.

"What?" I said.

"You lied. I smelled her cunt on your fingers."

"Oh. Yes. Sorry about that."

"You're going back for more. Everyone goes back for more."

"I'm going back for the book."

"You think you're safe. You're wrong. She already knows what you're thinking."

"I'll take my chances. I'll also take your Luger and our friend the custom-made javelin here." I balled up his five hundred euros, shoved them in his mouth and appropriated half the wrist bandage for a gag. God only knows why I didn't kill him. He was too absurd to murder. The cashews and the mascara and the abandoned modelling career. That sneeze.

"I may be gone some time," I said.

29

WHEN YOU NEED a plan and don't have one a retarded giddy indifferent faith takes over. Improv comics know this, criminals, soldiers too. Self dissolves into the flow and will reassemble on the other side of the job— or not. Either way you're doing it. Either way you're *in*.

Moving low, I worked my way silently through the trees, back past where Cloquet and I had first left the drive and on to the very edge of the conifers. From here twenty feet of open ground separated me from the garages. Darkness ample to foil the naked eye but if one of the guards should chance to raise a pair of night-vision binoculars . . . I went across in an absurd tiptoeing sprint, got my back to the wall below the mezzanine's overhang, caught my breath. An accommodating deus ex machina would have been to find one of the garage doors open, and inside the garage a second door to the villa's basement. I did check. All three were locked. I wondered what Jacqueline drove, got a mental snapshot of her in a '65 ivory Mercedes convertible, red leather interior matching her lipstick and nails.

A pleasing image, but not helpful. I hunted for something to throw. You throw something and according to screen fictions the noise takes at least one guard out of position to investigate. There was nothing to throw. What had I expected? Loose plant pots? Rocks? Empties? *Some* goddamned thing. Welcome to the downside of dissolving into the flow.

In the end I threw Cloquet's binoculars. Up across the mezzanine onto the steps on the eastern side of the terrace, where they landed with a (surely?) intriguing clatter. A guard or better still guards would come to check it out, leaving the stairs on the western side free for my stealthy ascent.

"Hear that?"

"Heard it. Call it in."

I was already on my speedy-tiptoe way (something like the goosestep touchdown celebrations of American footballers) to the western stairs.

Clear. I passed the mezzanine and since there was no reason not to hurried on up the next flight to the level of olive and thyme just below the cactus garden and the villa itself. There, hunkered in a well of shadow between balustrade and trees, I halted to take stock. One guard had indeed descended to the mezzanine, automatic rifle readied, and was cautiously poking about. The roof guard was scanning with (night-vision!) binoculars, but looking in entirely the wrong direction. The second ground-floor guard was less than ten feet away, just above me.

"It's a pair of fucking binoculars," the investigating guard said. "Did you call it in?"

"Yes, I called it in."

"I think someone's in the woods," the roof guard called down. "Definite movement in the woods. Nine o'clock."

Movement in the woods? Was it possible Cloquet had got free?

"Who's with the boss?"

"Marcel."

"What can you see?"

"Movement."

"What kind of fucking movement?"

The guard nearest me was a coward, God bless him. He should have done an immediate sweep of the western side. Instead he went to the top of the eastern stairs and called down to his mate. "Get back up here."

"Movement in more than one place."

"What *is* it?"

This was my chance. Not one of them was looking my way. I crawled out from my hiding place and leaped swiftly—balletically in fact, albeit with neck-tendons straining—up the last set of stone stairs.

At precisely the moment I reached the top a door in the wall of glass opened and the guinea pig–faced goon from the ship—Marcel, evidently—stepped out directly opposite me.

30

NATURALLY WE LOOKED at each other. Naturally the single second that passed was more than enough time to enjoy a purified intimacy, to note each other's details and feel the exact weight of each other's history. Naturally our essences, peremptorily denuded, exchanged a stunned glance.

Then I shot him in the face.

It was a near thing. A near thing that he didn't shoot me first, I mean. His weapon's muzzle was on its way up, certainly. I was aware of this empathically, as if it were my own arm raising it. In fact my own arm, as if it were the weight on the end of a piece of gym equipment worked by someone else, came up in a perfect 45-degree arc to level the Luger at his head, whereupon my hand—another part of a precision mechanism in someone else's control—pulled the trigger.

The silenced bullet went into his forehead (a large messily applied *bindi*) and he collapsed with barely a sound. Jacqueline Delon, in a silk dress the colour of buttermilk, stood in the room a few feet behind him. She was wincing and her shoulders were hunched, as if she'd just heard someone drop a priceless piece of glassware. A quick check to my right revealed the two ground-floor guards now both with night-vision goggles trained on the trees. They hadn't heard.

Nil time to think. I sprang across the patio, pulled Marcel's body in from the doorway and closed the plate glass behind me. This was the lounge we'd had our first drink in that morning, and aside from Jacqueline, myself and the late Marcel it was empty. Mme Delon's shoulders came down slightly. A gesture with the Luger made her position plain: If she made a sound, I'd shoot her. I did shoot people. Witness Marcel here. Her eyes said she understood. Her shoulders came all the way down. She relaxed. "My goodness," she said. "I thought I'd lost you forever."

"No horseshit, please. I know about the vampire deal. I'm here for

Quinn's book and the stone. Vault in the basement. No time to lose. Chop-chop. Yes?"

She raised her eyebrows. There was music playing softly. Dusty Springfield's "No Easy Way Down." Also an unusually strong scent of patchouli. It hadn't smelled like that this morning.

"It's not quite so straightforward," she said. She was making what looked like an effort not to really look at me, or indeed at anything in particular. Outside one of the guards said: "No, Marcel's with her. We need two more up here right now for a full perimeter sweep. Copy?" I went to her and grabbed her by her hair and put the gun under her chin, a move which required dropping the javelin at my feet. "Don't fuck about. *Please.* Let's go. Right now."

"You misunderstand me," she said. "I don't have the book. Or the stone."

"Since this morning. I think not."

"It's true. They're in someone else's possession."

"Just for a laugh," I said, "whose?"

Certain tensions rustle up clairvoyance. I knew she was going to look up, over my left shoulder, behind me. She looked up, over my left shoulder, behind me. "His," she said.

I took a moment to concede there was no point saying, You don't seriously expect me to fall for that, do you? Then I turned around.

He'd been there the whole time, "he" being a vampire and "there" being thirty feet up with his back against the room's ceiling directly above the door. A senior, I inferred, gravity defiance being an elite sport that takes, allegedly, centuries to master. As I watched he descended, slowly, a neat slender man in what ought to be his early fifties (though he'd probably rubbed shoulders with Rameses) with artfully cropped greying hair and an elegant calm little face. Grey-green eyes and a thin mouth. The hint of a cleft in his delicate chin. Black close-fitting trousers and black rollneck sweater. I remembered the days when seeing someone move through the air like that would have been a thrilling shock, the days before we'd all seen it countless times in the movies. Modernity's mimetic inversion: You see the real and are struck by how much it looks like a tediously seamless special effect.

"Since you know about the vampire deal," the vampire said, when his feet touched the polished oak floor, "let's not waste time. Donate your services voluntarily in exchange for access to Quinn's book and the friendship of the Fifty Houses for the rest of your life."

No point saying: Or what? Now that I could see the vampire I could smell him, too, suggestible schmuck that hybrid perception is. Stubborn pockets of wolf shivered and heaved. Here was the all-but-overwhelming limbic imperative to rip his boochie head off. Here, too, packed tight in the phantom animal haunches, was coiled flight. A migrainy ambivalence: Get him. Run. Get him. Run. There was a burst of automatic weapons fire outside, from the roof guard, I guessed.

"What's going on out there?" Jacqueline said. I still held her by her hair. Hot scalp and the odour of shampoo. The room's overdose of patchouli had been to mask *parfum de vamp*. He stood perfectly still, feet together, hands by his sides, no smile, just the trademark physical economy and the intolerable self-possession of a mime artist or juggler. He'd spoken English with an Italian accent. Casa Mangiardi? It didn't matter. What mattered was that I hadn't counted heads getting into the people-carrier. Four departed, one stayed behind. In a moment he'd make his move, a move so fast I'd be living in its upshot (doped, gagged, bagged and cuffed) without realising it had happened. In wolf mode I would have been a match. Human, I might as well be a blow-up doll.

"Jacob, please," Jacqueline said. "That's really hurting."

Surrender made itself sensuously available, a lover who'd stolen up behind me and put her arms around me and pulled me close and was breathing on my ear. Here, if I wanted it, was the peace of dissolving into the bigger will. Cloquet's peace with Mme Delon, no doubt.

"Jacob, please," Jacqueline repeated. "Please." I relaxed my grip on her hair. Let her go. She moved away. A small woman with an elfin head and a body just beginning to lose the fight. I thought of Cloquet's enthusiasm for her anus, and smiled.

"Very good," the vampire said. "Shall we?"

No illusions. I was going willingly or I was going after a touchingly brief struggle, but I was going. A mad cinematic montage burgeoned, of myself assimilated into vamp-camp, prisoner, yes, but civilly treated, swapping monster yarns by the evening fire, gradually rewiring revulsion, finding the common ground, investing in Helios for the sheer science, against all odds—against *nature* starting a verboten interspecies affair, the glacial Mia and her lovely legs—jump cut to a shot of myself in lupine form spread-eagled on a brushed-steel slab, limbs shackled and head clamped, screaming, attended by white-coated boochies and state-of-the-art invasive gizmology, blood running from my ears, nose, rectum . . .

More gunfire from without. Shouts. A helicopter. I wondered where poor Cloquet was in all of it, whatever it was. Wondered too, since for a few moments now the javelin had been a modest little sentience next to my foot, whether I could get down to it and hurl it before the vampire did to me whatever he was going to do. Of no more practical use (obviously, since it was metal, not wood) than giving him the finger, but in my fey state the punk pointlessness of the gesture appealed.

"Take me with you," Jacqueline said to him. "I know it didn't go precisely to plan, but after all you're getting what you wanted. I swear you won't regret it."

"Don't speak," the vampire said, not looking at her. Then several things happened very fast.

An explosion shattered the wall of glass and a bolus of smoke and flame *woofed* into the room and almost immediately retreated again. The force of the blast blew all three of us off our feet. I smashed into the stools by the bar and felt a rib crack. The javelin went too, missed my head by six inches, buried itself in the bar's mosaic flank behind me. The vampire, closest to the detonation, sailed spectacularly *over* the bar, and went into the mirror-backed brilliant bottles with a flailing crash.

Jacqueline Delon was on her hands and knees two stools down from me. A large shard of glass protruded bloodily from her outer thigh. Another from her shin. Another from the side of her head. She reached up and gently plucked this one out and looked at it. It occurred to me I might be similarly inconvenienced. Sure enough, dreamy investigation discovered a large scalene fragment sticking out of my left shoulder. I followed Jacqueline's example and tenderly extracted it. Blood welled and hurried out. With a sort of abstracted apathy I took hold of the javelin. The out-of-sight helicopter was a deafening evocation of *Apocalypse Now*. The explosion had filled the room with heat, briefly; now cool air rushed in like an angel. The javelin wasn't budging. I struggled to my feet. Jacqueline, in the silence of freakish stoicism or deep shock, hauled herself via one of the stools onto hers. One stiletto had absconded. Even in her state the imbalance was intolerable. She reached down and removed the remaining shoe. We looked at each other as if we'd both just been born.

The vampire appeared behind her. He wasn't there, then he was. This is the way of it. Fast. Too fast. His natty little face was glass-flecked, glass-studded, beaded with blood. He wiped it, *swiped* it, actually, as if it were covered in maddening flies, though his expression of compact enlightenment remained intact. "Shall we go?" he said.

Then the helicopter appeared. Descended in profile like Miss Muffet's spider. Thudding chop and the room's lethal wreckage crazily aswirl. A WOCOP Bluebottle, lightweight, fast, handleable. The bulbous smoked-glass head dipped, once, as if in decorous greeting—Ellis beamed out at me from the pilot's seat—then turned through 45 degrees to face us with its brutal lights.

I knew what it was packing. So did the vampire. So, most likely, did Jacqueline. They call the ammunition "hail": eight-inch hickory darts discharged at the rate of thirty per second. They call the gun, naturally enough, "Mary."

He didn't get away clean. At least a dozen shots hit him—I saw one go straight through his throat, another struck just below his eye—but he was fast enough, *just* fast enough, to cover his vulnerable heart.

With the nearest shield to hand.

Two seconds, no more. I got one glimpse of Jacqueline's floodlit body magically covered in quills before the vampire launched himself—and her—backwards, shot over the bar's shattered remains and smashed through the window on the other side of the room, out into the night.

I wasn't surprised, when Ellis killed the floods, to see a stubbled Grainer in full combat gear sitting with grand masculine casualness half out of the passenger seat, a Hunt Staker resting across his knees, a cigarette slotted semisatirically into the corner of his mouth. It wasn't painless. It wasn't quick. He gave me a salute, index finger to forehead, smiled, then turned and nodded to Ellis, who pulled the chopper back, swung it slowly around, lifted it up and away above the trees.

It started raining.

I DIDN'T HAVE much fun getting myself out of the villa. There was the removal of two more bits of glass for a start, one in my left calf, one—excruciating when I took my first steps—in my right knee. For a few minutes I just lay on one of the elephantine couches bleeding and feeling sorry for myself. It was pleasant, curled up with manageable pain, listening to the rain fall. These are the first minutes of peace, I thought, with a miffed snuffle, I've had in bloody ages.

But that, obviously, wouldn't do. I hobbled to what was left of the bar, took a fortifying swig of Kauffman's, retrieved the Luger from the debris and gingerly crunched my way out onto the terrace.

Except for the rain—thanks to which a lovely fresh odour of wet earth cut through the smoke—the Delon estate was silent. The two ground-floor guards lay sprawled nearby, bloodied, dead, one of them still clutching Cloquet's binoculars. No sound from the roof. Grainer would have shot the lookout up there through the cross-hairs from fifty yards away. The called-for reinforcements weren't visible, had looked at each other, I felt sure, and with earnest cowardice wordlessly agreed: Fuck reinforcement.

Which meant avoiding them if they were now, tightly wound with safeties off, poking around.

Transportation was the pressing issue. I certainly wasn't walking, not with my bleeding bits and stove-in rib. (Ribs, plural, I now thought; too much pain for just one.) It was possible Cloquet had driven here, but no less likely he'd arrived by parachute or camel or space-hopper. In any case, who knew how far it was to "the south gate"? No. I needed motorised transport, which, since one of the many things I haven't got around to in my two hundred years is learning how to fly a helicopter (Jacqueline's ship-to-shore sat ready on its asphalt pad), meant finding my way to the garages and hot-wiring whatever was in there.

It took me a wearying and peculiarly indeterminate time to locate them, limping and creeping and swearing through my teeth and going around, I now suspect, in circles. I think I might have sat down and passed out for a few minutes in one of the corridors. Elsewhere I vomited dismally against a wall, presided over by a vast sub-Bosch painting of a Black Mass. The rain came down harder, as if to evoke with its hiss time boiling away to nothing. I passed a large dark room where a wall-mounted flat-screen with sound muted showed an overweight rapper performing rap hand gestures, which are supposed to project masculine cool but in fact look like a pointlessly violent version of deaf sign language. The baby-faced skinhead from the *Hecate* lay on the floor in a pool of blood, untidily dead, with eyes open and one leg bent under him. I went down more stairs than there ought to have been.

Eventually, wounds hot, scalp whispering, ribs vociferously against all this *moving around* nonsense, I found the utility room and a moment's comfort in the benign smell of clean laundry. A door from there led to a curved corridor, off which (I was under the mezzanine) were three more doors to the garages.

Goldilocks and the Three Cars. Ferrari 458 Italia in red. No keys. 1956 Jaguar XK140 in white. No keys. 1976 Volkswagen Super Beetle in metallic lilac. Keys. See, Jake? Life said. It's a comedy. Lighten up. I got in and started the engine.

WOCOP forces (if indeed there'd been anyone besides Grainer and Ellis) had withdrawn. When I stopped on the drive and rolled down the VW's window I got the forest's massy green consciousness absorbing the rain in the dark, the land's deep thirst. Nothing else.

"Cloquet?" I called. "You there?"

Nothing. God only knows why I bothered. One has these occult compulsions. He reminded me of Gollum. He'd take it hard to hear his precious was dead. Or undead, depending on vamp whim. I called again. No reply. So be it. I hit the gas.

32

THE SENSIBLE THING would have been to switch to a less conspicuous car and get to an airport. I couldn't face it. I was exhausted. My wounds had stopped bleeding by the time I drove out of Jacqueline's south gate (in human form as in lupine I heal with obscene rapidity) and by tomorrow morning would be gone. The ribs, even with my cellular speed-knitting, would take a day longer. Physically this was nothing, a scrape. Yet all of me that was not flesh cried out for repose. The vampire had left me, as I must have him, with a feeling of cloying contamination. I wanted a bath, a quiet room, a cool bed.

All of which, I record with humble gratitude, I found. An hour later, having cleaned myself up as best I could in Arbonne's public loo, I checked into the Hotel Eugenie just east of the village, where for two hundred and eighty euros I was furnished for the night with a large en suite room done in rustic chic: heated oak floor, Basque rugs, bespoke iron four-poster, wireless Internet and—God bless Monsieur and Madame Duval—an enormous free-standing bathtub. There I took meditative refuge with an iced flannel over my eyes and a bottle of 1996 Château Léoville Barton (Saint-Julien) for company. I dimmed the lights and lay back in the soft water's warmth and for a short while at least was pleasantly revisited by that sedative phrase, *Come what may . . . Come what may . . . Come . . . what . . .*

One wants not to think. One *wants,* I repeat, all sorts of things. Presently the bottle was empty and *come what may* had yielded to *what the fuck are you going to do?* Indeed. Practicalities like a little slag heap. The vampires would know where I was but wouldn't try again tonight. Too risky with me back under Hunt surveillance. Jacqueline's job had been to get me off WOCOP's radar long enough for a snatch. She'd failed. The *Hecate* must have drawn heat, as Cloquet said, hence the hasty ship-jump to the villa Delon. My cock rose through the bath foam in salute to the memory of the morning's sex—then just as smoothly sank back when I thought of Quinn's book.

Taken by the boochies in the hope that my need to acquire it would keep me alive.

Another sigh. This is what happens, I told myself. Life, like the boring drunk at the office party, keeps seeking you out, leaning on you, killing you with pointless yarns and laughing bad-breathed in your face at its own unfunny jokes.

I got out of the bath, dried myself with irritated meticulousness, donned one of the Eugenie's white towelling robes and in an act of forced jolly recklessness ordered up another bottle. Vampires? Hunters? Let the fuckers come! And while we're at it, fuck Quinn's book. If getting to it (to the *truth*, my inner romantic protested, the *truth*, Jacob, after all these years . . .) if getting to it meant submitting to the no-nonsense pricks and pokes of vampire science then the book might as well not exist. Of course I could always try force. One werewolf against the Fifty Houses of the undead . . .

Glass One of Bottle Two went down in a couple of analeptic swigs. I flicked on the TV. A French home-makeover show. A couple weeping uglily at the miracle of their cheaply redecorated kitchen. I changed channels. *American Idol*. Transformation again, this time from Nobody into Superstar. Perhaps Jacqueline was right: Humanity's getting its metamorphic kicks elsewhere these days. When you can watch the alchemy that turns morons into millionaires and gimps into global icons, where's the thrill in men who turn into wolves?

I turned the TV off. Sat on the edge of the bed. Felt the gathered tension go, accompanied, incredibly, by the third sigh of the day. (Like bloody buses or bloody Copean men, these sighs: none for ages then three at once.) Nothing, I averred, breathing with quivering drunk dignity through my nostrils, had changed. Be Quinn's book true or be it false its existence wasn't going to alter my course. If you can live two hundred years without the solution to the riddle of your nature you can die without it too. Humans go to their graves with none of the big questions answered. Why should werewolves fare better?

A fresh pack of Camels had arrived as ordered with the wine. I lit one up. The greatest gift of lycanthropy is knowing smoking won't kill you. I poured the last glass of the night. Peace returned, somewhat. Nothing, I repeated, had changed. I would sit out the twenty-nine days to the next full moon, whereupon Grainer—

Ah, yes. With cruel belatedness the image of Harley's murderer bloomed. Naturally his appearance on the chopper was a calculated provocation, the ease of body, the joyless Navajo smile, the mock salute. It wasn't painless. It wasn't quick. Come off it, Jake, I could hear him saying. You telling me you're really going to let me get away with that? It wasn't painless. It wasn't quick.

Enough. I finished the cigarette. Turned out the light. Lay down on the bed. How long since I'd slept? Forty-eight hours? Seventy-two?

Wolf-silt churned in my shoulders. When I'd ripped through the junkie's throat his body had jerked as if in violent ejaculation. Now his spirit shuffled through the packed underworld of my bloodstream, friendless in the murmuring crowd. It's official. You're the last. I'm sorry. I closed my eyes.

33

THREE WEEKS HAVE PASSED.
Everything's changed.
Jesus fucking Christ.

34

THE MORNING FOLLOWING my night at the Hotel Eugenie I took a train to Paris and spent the journey bringing these pages up to date. I clocked two WOCOP agents after transferring at Bordeaux, replaced by two more in the capital. A matter of indifference to me—or perhaps not quite indifference, since their presence was keeping the undead in check. Naturally the boochies were watching me, via human familiars during the day, in person(s) by night. Ordering a Long Island Iced Tea in a Montmartre night club at three in the morning a wave of vamp-nausea hit me hard enough to make me reel. I turned. Blond blue-eyed Mia at the opposite end of the neon-lined bar raised her glass (a prop, obviously) with a smile. Calm intelligent white hands and oxblood lipstick. A strikingly beautiful woman who smelled like a vat of pigshit and rotten meat. You appreciate the cognitive dissonance. Anyway, she made no move. I stayed in Paris a couple of days, too dull-hearted even to take a farewell turn around the Louvre. I hired a red-haired, big-breasted athletic escort and surprised myself with the vehemence of my climax. Postcoitally I tried, from a supposed correspondence between volcanic ejaculation and the capacity to affirm life, to work up a bit of feeling for still being here. Failed. Libido, I was forced to conclude, was a lone warrior flinging itself around the battlefield everyone else had deserted.

At last, five days since waking in the *Hecate*'s hold, I took a British Airways evening flight from Charles de Gaulle to London Heathrow.

•

Which is where everything—*everything*—changed.

•

Jesus Christ, Jake, listen. There's—

I know what he was going to say now.

("And you don't believe in fate?" she said to me.)

("I'll believe in anything you tell me," I said.)

Big coup for the *if* and *then* department. If I hadn't decided to take the Heathrow Express instead of a cab . . . If I hadn't stopped to buy smokes in Arrivals . . . If I hadn't taken the train to Paris . . . If I hadn't spent the night in Arbonne . . . If, if, if. Embrace determinism and you're chained all the way back to the beginning. Of the universe. Of everything.

("Not according to Stephen Hawking," she said. "I watched this programme on PBS. He sees space-time as a four-dimensional, closed manifold, like the surface of a sphere, with no beginning and no end. It's a nifty idea, but I still can't stop seeing it the old-fashioned way, as if space-time's a blob floating around in, you know, some other space, with some other time going on.")

("Come here," I said. "Come *here*.")

She was getting off the train, I was waiting to get on. Three carriage doors up from me she stepped high-heeled down onto the platform and in a moment found herself being helped up from the floor by the large-limbed Nordic couple in front of whom she'd inexplicably crashed to her knees.

Inexplicable to her. Not to me. I lip-read her going through the motions—Oh, my gosh . . . Oh . . . Thank you, thanks, yes I'm fine, I don't know what happened, I'm such a moron, thank you so much—as the enormous Swedes or Norwegians or Finns covered in blond fuzz with gigantic sunburned gentleness helped her to her feet and handed her her wheelie case and purse—she went through these motions, yes, but she was looking elsewhere, everywhere, with a contained wildness bordering panic for the source of the power that had momentarily upended reality like that.

Me, in other words.

Jesus Christ, Jake, listen. There's a female.

Werewolf.

No preparation. No warning. Just the whole slab of myself fallen flat before her and all my eaten dead shocked into stillness. They'd thought the end of things—release, final dissolution, peace—was near. Instead this betrayal, Marlowe wrenched awake in a world blasted into renewal . . .

Meanwhile, back on her feet and free of helping hands she stood trembling, gripping her purse, face moist, body discernibly awry. She had the look of a foreign correspondent caught off-guard mid-report by an explosion. Early thirties, eyes the colour of plain chocolate and similarly dark hair in two soft shoulder-length waves. A single mole or beauty spot at the corner of her mouth. White-skinned but with a warmth and suppleness that betrayed—surely?—Levantine or Mediterranean blood. Certainly not "beautiful" or "pretty" but Saloméishly appealing, visibly smudged with the permissive modern wisdoms. This was a girl who'd been loved by her parents and grown vastly beyond them. She thought of them now, with a little searing pain of celebration, as children or simpletons. I had an image of generic homesick immigrants in the U.S. standing in a tenement doorway, waving her off, full of heartbroken pride. She wore a beige mackintosh over a white blouse and brown pinstripe skirt but with no effort at all (since there was no stopping me) I could see her dancing naked but for a veil and a navel ruby. Lip-reading her with the helpful Nords I'd made her American, and something about her relationship with the luggage and the raincoat and the purse reinforced this, the casual entitlement to useful things. While I was soaking all this up her consciousness was hurrying around the tunnel hastily manhandling the dispersing crowd, knowing that somewhere . . . somewhere very close . . .

I backed into one of the platform's exits, managed—just—not to bound up and lay hands on her. *Her!* The pronoun had rocketed to primacy. Here was recognition as if from the hermaphroditic time before birth's division. First sight of Arabella in the Metropole's lobby had been a quickening of hope and fear: hope the recognition was mutual, fear it wasn't. Here, now, was neither hope nor fear, just nonnegotiable gravity, a fall to the pure animal bitch like the guillotine's blade to its block.

Jesus Christ, Jake, listen. There's a female.

She swallowed, plucked her blouse away from herself. Her scent was a hot perversion, a dirty cocktail of perfumed *femme* and the lewd stink of wolf. Fresh, of course, from transformation only four nights ago. She'd fed, too. Oh, yes. The ghost of her gorging was there in her eyes, though she retained something of the recent college grad ingénue making her way in the shocking world of work, determined to keep going, to assimilate the degradations, to master the atrocities.

A shaven-headed WOCOP agent lurked at the end of the platform. In the absence of vamp odour I had to assume a human familiar somewhere on the scene, though I hadn't ID'd him yet. Could either Hunt or Undead know about her? *Her!* Hadn't *I* known, somewhere at the back of the drift of days? Hadn't I asked countless times: What are you waiting for, Jacob?

Her nostrils flared. Becoming a werewolf had nearly destroyed her, but hadn't. Thus she'd discovered the Conradian truth: The first horror is there's horror. The second is you accommodate it. And there in the espresso-dark eyes *was* the accommodation, the submission to experience she'd made in the silence of her heart, astonished at herself, once she'd decided to accept what she was, once she'd decided to kill others instead of herself. She suffered fiery Hunger and did vile deeds now, had begun teaching herself enlarging self-forgiveness. You do what you do because it's that or death. She'd had a girlhood of secrets and now here was the Big Secret to justify them. She was—

Steady, Marlowe. For God's sake, think! Practicalities. Could they know about her? How could they *not* know about her? Harley had known, I felt certain of it, and if Harley then why not the rest of the organisation?

No way of telling. Therefore assume they don't. And from this moment do everything you can to make sure they never, ever find out.

Something else was going on. (Whatever is happening, as the late Susan Sontag noted, something else is always going on. It's literature's job to honour it. No wonder no one reads.) The something else going on here was my detached admission that the scales had tipped back—*crashed* back, with laughable immediacy—in favour of life. Detached admission—or deflated? Resignation to death at least simplified the living you had left. Now what? Complexity? Rigmarole? *Bothering* again? And something *else* was going on. (The number of these something elses is infinite, the hell literature faces every day. It's a wonder anyone writes.) Underneath the first admission was a sullen second: One whiff of her had done what Harley's torture and death could not. That was my measure, a giant standing stone of disappointment if I wanted to look at it. But there came again the sensational stink of her—dear *God*—and a new yokel leap of dick-blood. Let the factions of conscience quibble: I had work to do.

And the life without love?

My dead like a trade union in a silent phalanx with Arabella, shop steward, at their head.

The Heathrow Express pulled away. All but a handful of disembarked passengers had gone through the exits and were hurrying to the escalators. A sly peep showed me she was still there, apparently brushing at a speck of smut on her skirt, in fact with ravished consciousness still searching for the source of the scent that had felled her. My scent. Me. She had recovered herself, though her face still wore its sheen of sweat. She'd been blind-sided, yes, but now curiosity was at work, smart female lights in the liquid dark eyes. She reached up and with her little finger raked back a strand of hair that had stuck to her damp forehead. Very slightly raised her chin. She was breathing heavily, a lovely insinuation of her breasts against the blouse. *I know you're here, somewhere.*

I waited until she moved through her nearest exit, left as much of a delay as I dared, then followed her.

35

THE CHALLENGE, TRAILING her down the aerated tunnels and moving walkways into the bright lights and echoing announcements of departures, was to keep my distance. Just once I got too near and she stopped, turned and took a few steps in my direction. I had to duck into a doorway to break the connection—and do it with sufficient casualness to keep the WOCOP tail in the dark.

There *was* a vampire, it turned out, a tall black male with greying hair and a gold hoop earring looking down from the check-in hall's balcony. A further headache: I must keep close enough to my girl to blanket her scent without turning her head or treading on her heels. She'd taken off the fawn raincoat and slung it over her arm, revealing a trim figure and deportment projective of not natural but acquired confidence. I could *not* shuck the idea of her as the good daughter of immigrant U.S. parents, mindful of the toil and suffering borne to make her what she was, their bona fide American Girl, fluent in brand names and armed with education, health insurance, political opinions, orthodontic work, earning power— though this and all other inaugural projections were polluted by the vampire's presence like hands pressing down on my skull from above.

She stopped under one of the information screens. I stopped, ostensibly to make a call on my mobile. Logistical problems were stacking up: In a moment she'd find her check-in desk, get her boarding pass and go through security into the sprawling purgatory of the departures lounge. How would I follow her? Obviously, I'd buy a ticket to wherever she was going. But unless her desk handled one flight only, how would I know where she was going? I hadn't been close enough to read the label on her case. And what if she used *self* check-in?

Nothing else for it: I had to approach her now.

As soon as I moved towards her she moved away—but only as far as the queue for the Travelex window. She was fourth in line.

"Don't turn around," I said, quietly. I still had the mobile to my ear. In the twenty paces it had taken me to reach her I'd sensed her sensing my approach, forcing herself to stay calm, willing herself *not* to turn around. Heat enveloped her in a rippling aura. Her scent was a ring through my bull's nose. She was trembling. You had to be close to see it, in the high heels, in the wrists, in the hair. At the very last I pulled back from grabbing her hips and pressing my groin to her ass and filling my hands with her breasts and burying my nose in her nape.

"I know what you are and you know what I am. Do you have a cell phone?"

"Yes."

"Give me the number."

American, the accent confirmed as she recited it without hesitation. I keyed in the number but didn't store or dial. "I'm being watched," I said. "And for all I know you are too, so change some currency here then go to the Starbucks directly opposite and wait for me to call. Understood?"

"Yes."

"Don't be afraid."

"I'm not."

"You're feeling this, right?"

"Yes."

A great darkness of relief went through me. I nearly fainted. She moved to the exchange counter and opened her purse.

36

GOD ONLY KNEW if the mobile was safe. Other than to replay Harley's cut-off message I hadn't used it, but since it had passed through the hands of Jacqueline Delon I had to assume it was compromised. I copied the number onto the back of my hand and deleted it from the Nokia's screen. Travelex furnished me with ten one-pound coins and I stepped across to a pay phone.

She said: "Hello?"

"I can see you. Are you within earshot of those two guys with the back-packs?"

"No."

"Okay, good. But don't look too obviously in this direction."

"You were on the platform."

"Yes, sorry about that."

"I felt it. This is . . . Who's watching you?"

"Long story. Not here. Where are you flying?"

"New York."

"That's home?"

"Yes."

"What time's your flight?"

"Eleven-thirty." She risked a direct look. Our first transparent exchange. It silenced us for a moment, since it confirmed we'd entered the realm of inevitability. "I can miss it," she said.

You're feeling this, right? Yes. Not just the foregone sexual conclusion but the transfiguration of the mundane: luggage carts; information screens; airline logos; ugly families. Every humble atom glorified. *I can miss it.* Mutual certainty trims speech and here was our speech, trimmed. She would simply not get on the plane. All that was selfish and weak in me lay heavily upon the very little that wasn't. She'd get a room at an airport hotel. I'd lose the vamp and the copper. I'd go to the room. She'd be sitting on the edge of the bed when I entered. She'd look up.

"It's not safe," I said. "We have to know if they're onto you."

"That black guy upstairs," she said. "There's something—"

"He's a vampire."

Another first, her face and silence said. But also, after a slight delay: Why not? In fact, of course, of *course* vampires. She'd learned: The world pulled these sudden convulsive moves to reveal more and more of its outlandish self to a random cursed elite. Meanwhile Bloomingdale's and *Desperate Housewives* and Christmas and the government carried on. She was carrying on herself, in extraordinary fusion. I could see it in her tense shoulders and flushed face and the care with which she'd applied her makeup. It hurt my heart, the unrewarded courage of it, the particular degree of her determination not to fold in spite of everything. In spite of becoming a monster. It hurt my heart (oh, the heart was awake now, the heart was *bolt upright*) that she'd had to be brave all alone.

"Did you feel sick?" I asked.

"I still do, a little."

"When did it start?"

"Just now when I came into check-ins."

"But nothing before that?"

"Nothing."

"Nothing *ever*?"

"Not like this, no."

Good. If she'd never encountered a vampire before then chances were the boochie upstairs was for Jacob Marlowe only. Her scent would be churning his guts but without knowing there was another howler in the house he'd put that down to me.

"Don't look until I tell you," I said, "but there's a Bruce Willis type in a brown leather jacket and a white T-shirt standing under the information screens to your left. I need to know if you've ever seen him before. Okay, look now."

"I don't recognise him," she said. "Who is he?"

"You don't know about WOCOP, right?"

"What?"

"It's an organisation that—Shit, there's too much to explain like this. All you need to know for now is they're no friends of ours. Neither are vampires. We've got to be careful."

A pause. Then she said: "I'm not getting on the plane."

Which forced me to risk a look of my own. She was staring at me with wide-awake consciousness. Whatever else was true it was true this was a relief to her, a vindication of all the hours and days of fierce holding on: You're *not* alone. The ease with which I could hang up the phone and walk over to her and take her in my arms was a satanically reasonable temptation. I could see myself doing it, feel the lithe yielding fit of her against me. I know what you are and you know what I am.

"I don't *want* you to get on the plane," I said. "But we have to be sure they don't know about you." We were "we," already. Of course we were.

"Was it you in the desert?" she asked.

"What?"

"California. Nine months ago. When I was attacked. Was it you?"

I'd seen the file. In late June 2008 the Hunt had killed werewolf Alfonse Mackar in the Mojave Desert. Which had left just Wolfgang and me on the books. Or so WOCOP had thought.

"No, it wasn't me."

She bit the inside of her lip for a moment. "No, it wasn't you. I can . . . feel it." A mix: pleasure, embarrassment, relief. Suddenly, with the two of us in the same room, even a room as expansively joyless as check-ins, she could feel all sorts of things. So could I. The intimacy was, literally, laughable. Laughter was laughably available.

"How many are there—of us?" A struggle for her to choose which question first, suddenly faced with the possibility of answers.

"I was supposed to be the last," I said. "But now there's you. I don't know how. I don't know what it means." We kept looking away from each other, then back, away, back. It was hypnotic. For her as for me there was a vague awareness of all the things we didn't, in our perfect certainty, need to say, as if pages of TV movie script—*I can't believe this is happening . . . I knew from the first moment I saw you*—were scrolling on an autocue both of us were ignoring.

"I can't go now," she said. "You can't ask me to do that. It's ridiculous."

Imagine if a hundred and sixty-seven years ago I'd run into another of my kind at a railway station. Someone who'd lowered his copy of the *Times,* looked over his spectacles and said, Yes, I know all about it, but you'll have to wait.

"I know this is hard for you," I said. "It is for me too—" Our eyes met again and there it still was, hilarious mutual transparency, raging collusion. "But there's no other way to be sure. Please trust me. I just want to know you're safe."

"What do they want you for? Us for."

I told her what I knew, skipping all but the consequential chunks. Helios, the vamps, the virus. She listened with a slight frown, one arm wrapped around herself. She might have been a young mother hearing a report of her child's out-of-character misbehaviour at school. The dark hair framed her face in two soft crescents. A vaguely 1970s sub–*Charlie's Angels* look. I was thinking, with a mix of bitterness and joy: All these years. All these *years*.

"I'll leave the airport," I told her. "You stay. If they don't know about you they'll follow me. You take your flight to New York. I'll join you when I've ditched them. Shouldn't take me more than a day or two."

"Wait. This is crazy. What if they don't follow you?"

"They will. If they don't, I'll come back and we'll rethink."

"What if there are other vampires?"

"I'll call you in thirty minutes. If there are others here you'll still feel sick, and if one of them gets on the plane with you you'll feel *really* sick. But that's not likely. If they put anyone on the flight with you it'll be a familiar, a human. They won't do anything as long as you stay in public places, but keep your eyes open."

"What about these WOCOP guys?" she said. "How will I know if they're following me?" The charming frown of concentration remained. She looked now like a secretary taking in an astonishing amount of new instruction, forcing herself to stay calm, forcing herself to be up to the inhuman demand.

"You won't. But there's nothing we can do about that just now. In any case they won't make a move yet. They're trophy hunters. They'll wait for the next full moon." The words "full moon" made us look at each other again. All the big things we'd said nothing about. I was down to my last pound coin. I memorised her New York address.

"I can't just *go*," she said. "I need answers."

"You'll get them, just not like this. I have to know you're safe."

A piercing sweet catch in my chest when I said that, for the simple reason that it was true. Suddenly something mattered. In films someone finds a spaceship that's been buried for thousands of years and switches the power on—and the whole system flutters magically back into life, lights, gauges, indicators, drives. The lovely thrilling thought that this capacity's been there the whole time, waiting.

"Tell me one thing," she said. "Is there a cure?"

"No."

She closed her eyes. Swallowed. Absorbed. She'd grown a new glamorously deformed personality to accommodate werewolfhood but there in the closing of the eyes and the swallow was an indication of how much of the old personality remained, allowed to stay on condition she could pretend it wasn't really there. Even this pronouncement—No, there's no cure—didn't quite kill it. It would probably live for decades, holding hope in its hand like a hot coal.

"Don't be alone after sunset and don't sleep at night," I said. "You'll have to go to a club or a bar or whatever. Sleep during the day. With someone, if that's an option, but only someone you know well." Now, imprudently, we were staring at each other. The *wulf* certainty between us was as ugly and exciting as a massive haemorrhage on a white tiled floor. But there was the other certainty too, human, a shock to us both. Anachronistic in this day and age, almost embarrassing. I had an image of Ellis and Grainer and a crew of tooled-up Hunters surrounding us, laughing their heads off.

"You better fucking come after me," she said, quietly. The composure wasn't absolute. Desperation was right there, waited only her nod. The dark eyelashes and that beauty spot were her face's erotic accents.

"I will."

"Promise me."

"I promise."

"This is insane. There's so much . . . I don't know *any*thing."

"You will. Everything I know, which isn't much."

"You'll phone me in half an hour?"

"Trust me."

A pause. Eyes meet again.

"You know I do."

Moments like tiny gearings; an oiled click and the tectonics giantly shift and suddenly you're saying, Trust me, and she's saying, You know I do. Behind the immediacies—the *if*s and *then*s still swarming us—was the carnal eventuality, or rather *two* carnal eventualities: the coming together in human flesh, and . . .

I knew it would remain unspeakable, the other consummation, deliciously held in the mouth, in the heart. It had sent an intimation of itself back to us from the future that put a seal on our lips. *They'll wait for the next full moon*, I'd said, and as through the wink of a Third Eye we'd seen that nothing, *nothing* would compare to—

Then it was gone.

"I really don't want you to go," she said.

"I really don't want to go."

37

BUT GO I DID. I selected a cowboy cab from Heathrow, tipped the driver (a dreadlocked Rastafarian in a leather hat the size of a post box) fifty pounds in advance for the use of his mobile. The car, an unloved Mondeo, stank of ganja and Chinese food. She answered after a single ring.

"How are you feeling?"

"No sickness. They both followed you out."

"Perfect."

"You can't talk freely, can you?"

"No."

"I can't stand this. It's three thousand miles."

"I'll be there before you know it."

"Are we really the only ones?" she said.

"I thought *I* was the only one, but now there's you I can't be sure of anything." Except that now for the first time in half a century I'm—

"This is like waking up. I've been . . ." She sighed. I pictured her clamping her jaws together, closing her eyes, controlling herself. "Do you know what it *is*?" she said, eventually. "Does it fit into anything?" "It" being the Curse. "It" being Being a Werewolf. Did it fit into anything? Anything like God or the Devil or UFOs or voodoo or clairvoyance or life after death? There was no disguising her fear that it did, her hope that it did, her deep suspicion that it didn't.

"No more than anything else," I said. "We're here, we do what we do, that's it. You've read the fairy stories, obviously." Quinn's journal, I decided, could wait. There was enough for her to take in already without adding the ancient desert, mad dogs and dead bodies. Besides, the driver was listening. Not a vamp lackey, nor WOCOP unless their agents had got a lot better at blending in, but I didn't want him to have anything useful to say when questioned. As it was I was going to have to give him a crazy price for the mobile, or trash it and risk a scene. Few things more wearying than a stoned cabbie with martial arts delusions. "I wish there was a big secret I could let you in on," I told her, "but there isn't."

"I had a feeling you were going to say that," she said. She'd absorbed the first shock wave: me, the encounter, the confirmation of the world she'd fallen into nine months ago, the brutal attraction, the violent pitch into a new theatre. She assimilated fast, Manhattan-speed. Here already in the "I had a feeling you were going to say that" was her bigger, calmer, more sophisticated self that was always waiting after whatever temporary naïve furore had died down. Here already was the acknowledgement that whatever else this was it was the beginning of a liaison of fabulous proportions. Here already was the wry aspect, the curious, the playful. Here was the intelligence committed to life, whatever the cost. *I* was the one still inwardly flapping, grinning, hopping about with excitement. The impulse to thank God, it turned out, was still there. Something in me looked . . . upwards, humbled.

"Does anyone know about you?" she asked. "I mean apart from the vampires and the agents?"

"Not anymore. You?"

"No. There's my dad, but it would kill him. I can't."

"I understand. Don't worry. I'll help you."

"You are going to follow me, aren't you?"

"Do you really have to ask?"

"Tell me my address again."

"Not advisable. Please believe me, I have it."

The cab slowed for the Chiswick roundabout, got a green light, whipped through. It started raining. If the boochie was a flier he'd be cold and wet up there.

"I still don't see why I have to take the flight," she said. "Why can't I just check into a hotel here?"

"This country's too small. You have to trust me. I've been doing this a long time."

"How long?"

"Again, inadvisable."

"You're old, aren't you?"

"Yes."

A pause. She was realising what getting the answers would mean. Without them carrying on could be mere blind reflex. With them it was an informed decision. A werewolf by choice, as it were.

"How long will I live?"

"A long time."

"A hundred years?"

"Try four."

Silence. I could feel her effort at immense logical extension from the present (via science fiction, Microsoft, the space program) into the future. Impossible: One knows logical extension won't cover it. One knows the far future will involve unimaginable, perhaps comedic leaps.

"But you'll look the same," I said. "Does that help?"

She didn't answer. Suddenly the full weight of her aloneness—*her* aloneness, not mine—hit me. *There's my dad, but it would kill him.* Nine months she'd been living through this. They found three- and four-year-old kids who'd survived alone in their homes for days, eating sugar, ketchup, butter. You didn't want to think about what that had been like for them. They were objectionable, somehow. Unless of course you'd been through it yourself. Unless of course you were one of them.

"Shit," she said. "I need to check in. If I'm really going."

"You're really going. Remember: public places at night, okay?"

"And call up an ex to sleep with during the day."

"I'm serious."

"Okay, but the longer it takes you to get there the longer I'm going to have to put out for someone else."

"I've changed my mind," I said. "Sleep in the public library. Drink coffee. Take uppers."

"I don't even know your name."

Aliases like a whirlwind of dead leaves. Me in the middle, myself.

"It's Jake," I said.

"You're lucky. Jake's a good name."

"Whereas?"

A pause. Then, "Might as well get this over with, I suppose. My name's Talulla."

•

You mustn't fall in love with a woman because you'll end up killing her.

Not if she's a werewolf.

I didn't invent the necessities. But I am bound by them.

•

There was no appeal in taking the vampire on. Not with my new investment in not dying. Simpler to wait for sunrise and the shift change with his human proxy. Therefore I got the cabbie to drop me at Caliban's, a night club (one of my subsidiaries' subsidiaries' subsidiaries owns it, as it happens) on New Oxford Street, where I stayed, buoyed by hastily scored amphetamines, until five a.m. Breakfast of eggs Benedict (the first human food since my depressing banquet-for-one in the *Hecate*'s hold) at Mikhail's in Holborn took me through to six, whereupon a mirror-windowed Audi rolled up for the vamp and relieved him with a pair of familiars. The WOCOP tail had been replaced, too. *Three* agents, as far as I could tell. This was getting ridiculous. I left the café, bought a fresh pack of Camels at a newsstand and wandered down to Trafalgar Square. London was up and running. The rain had stopped and the sky was absurdly pretty, a single layer of floury cloudlets pinked and peached by the rising sun. Only the juvenile, the mad and the newly in love noticed. The rest of the city got its head down and ploughed tearily into another day of neurosis.

I bought a new mobile and called Christian at the Zetter. I wanted a haircut, a massage, a hot shower and a little time and space to gather myself for the laborious business of escapology.

38

TALULLA, LIGHT OF my life, fire of my loins . . . Ta-loo-la: the tip of the tongue taking a trip of three steps down the palate . . . Ta. Lu. La.

"Talulla's bad enough," she said. "Put it with 'Demetriou' and you're in the realm of the ridiculous."

It was afternoon and we were lying in bed in the Edwardian Park Suite at the New York Plaza, having just had sex for the fifth time in approximately six hours. I never had a sister but I imagine if I had fucking her would have felt something like fucking Talulla, sometime in our very early twenties, coming to it with relished capitulation after years of dirty adolescent telepathy.

"Talulla Mary Apollonia Demetriou," she said. "Even in New York you rattle that off and they think you're speaking Vulcan or something."

It had taken less than twenty-four hours to ditch the tails, albeit after a wearing epic of old-fashioned cat-and-mouse. With Christian's help I got out of the Zetter under a pile of soiled sheets in a laundry hamper, and away in the back of the cleaning company van. That did for the vamp flunkies. Not so the agent, whom I clocked still with me barely five minutes after leaving the depot. I wasn't much surprised. Christian is solid, but there can no longer be any doubt the Zetter's WOCOP moled. Three hours of Underground-and-black-cab switches (and four agents) later, I was back at Heathrow, if not certain of having slipped them then driven past caring by the force of the need to see her again. Flying business as Bill Morris (an airport-bought first class ticket would've waved a flag to anyone watching) I'd had the width of the Atlantic to coddle and thrum my lust. By the time she arrived in the hotel lobby in sunglasses and a pale pink cashmere dress I'd reached maximum agitation. Given which you'd expect a debut fuck of eye-popping gymnastics. In fact it was a thing of slow, hyperconscious deliberateness. You'd similarly expect a dive straight into werewolf biography, an immediate compulsion to compare howler notes. Not so. The deep reflex was postponement. To speak of what we were would be in the long run (but not long enough) to speak of death. We had this one opportunity to come together as if the rest of the world didn't exist. Thereafter the rose would be sick.

Wulf was with us. *Wulf* knew what was going on. *Wulf* wanted in, materially. *Wulf* prowled the blood, rushed up repeatedly only to effervesce into nothing at the surface of the skin. *Wulf* swung and tossed its head and let loll its degenerate tongue and wreathed us in its feral funk, an odour as dense as the stink of a crammed zoo. If it was getting nothing else out of us it was getting the primary admission, that we knew what we were, that we had both felt the peace that passeth understanding, that this, now, sex in human form, was the imperfect forerunner, the babbling prophet, mere Baptist to the coming Christ. *Wulf* knew how good it was going to be and would not, even in abeyance, suffer us not sharing in the knowledge. Therefore we knew. Had known from first glance at the airport. Had always known.

Six human victims, I counted. Few enough for each to be still a raw perfume, ghost-traces in the involved and generous scent of her cunt, on the hot flower of her breath. She'd tell me in her own time, we both knew. For now it was the draped obscenity. My own wailing dead in disbelief at the broken agreement had been churned back into the hurrying blood. Only the spirit of Arabella remained still, fixed me with—

Like this?

Yes, just like that. Don't stop. Don't stop.

We found ways. This is the story, the human story, the werewolf story, the *life* story: One finds ways. Kissing, slowly, was one. Though dark-haired and dark-eyed she was fair-skinned, a sensuous contrast that required continual reapprehension. *All* of her required this (or rather all of my desire did), repeatedness, over again–ness. The beauty spot by her lip was one of a dozen or so scattered over her body. My new constellations. There was no performance, no pornography, just complete conversion to the religion of each other, that erotic equalisation that mocks distinction between the sacred and the profane, that at a stroke anarchises the body's moral world. All her parents' love and spoiling were there in her parted thighs' sly confidence. She knew the measure of her riches.

The wolf had first raped then made her larger, forced on her in addition to the human gifts nauseous exemption from the moral city's ordinances and limits. You accepted the wolf and grew, or you rejected it and died. She'd had the soft toys and pink bedroom as a little girl, the ballet aspirations, the pony fixations. These had flared and mutated, books, a smart mouth, finding the balance between sophistication and sluttiness, a little material greed, the headache of being sufficiently pretty so that politicisation was a sulkily performed chore, then work, business and the daily shifting survival strategies that made the freshman small-hours ethical arguments quaint. All this was still there, dwarfed under the dark arch of the monster. The challenge was to find the devious bloody-mindedness to keep both, who she used to be and what she was now.

Fucking (the word "lovemaking" offered itself, with some legitimacy) let clairvoyance thrash about a bit between us: Here I was looking out from behind her eyes when she was eight, sitting on a back stoop twittered over by leaf shadows and stinging from some giant injustice. There she was behind mine in the sunlit library—*WEREWULF*—at Herne House. Here was a glowering sky over a dark field with a solitary Dutch barn. Here a car showroom, light bouncing off too much glass. Here Harley lighting the evening fire and saying, Well that's just fucking *non-sense*. Here her feet poking out of glittering bath foam, toenails like a little family of rubies. We lived a handful of each other's moments, or imagined we did. Coming, I gripped the soft warm hair above her nape and stared at her. She stared back. Her eyes had the cold omniscience, her cunt the hot. Her open mouth moved very slightly, a barely perceptible shape of affirmation. This and the beauty spot did for whatever Tantric resolve I was holding on to. A first climax of total dissolution, as into God or void—then the return, the humble reassertion of fingerprints, scalp, knees, tongue, heart, brain. You forgot sex could do this, cast the divine fragment back into the divine whole for a moment, then reel it out again, razed, beatified.

So the six carnal hours had passed.

But passed they had. Now we lay on the bed like starfish. It's one of the Platonic forms, lying with someone on a hotel bed after transcendent sex. Outside, Manhattan was chillily sunlit under a blue March sky.

Somewhere back down the hours it had rained. We'd been aware of it, as one harmless animal going about its business might be aware of another harmless animal doing the same. Now the air had a rinsed optimism. To be resisted, my realist warned, because already the future was groping, like a temporarily blinded giant, towards us.

"It's the Irish Talulla," she said. "Not the Chocktaw one. My mom's family came over in the 1880s. Not that it makes a difference. It's still a god-awful mouthful."

"Demetriou" from her Greek father, Nikolai, who'd come to the U.S. as a physics postgrad in '67, got sidetracked by the counterculture, barely scraped his MSc at Columbia and nearly died of a mysterious stomach infection on a trip to Mexico in 1973. He'd survived, however, and emerged traumatised, presumably into readiness for love, since less than six months out of hospital he met, fell for and married Colleen Gilaley, heiress to the not inconsiderable pile represented by *her* father's four delis and three diners spread over Manhattan and Brooklyn, a familial empire into which Nikolai was grudgingly (and unproductively) absorbed. In 1975 (Ford in the White House, *Jaws* in movie theatres, Saigon fallen, the Khmer Rouge overrunning Cambodia, *Humboldt's Gift* on the highbrow shelves, *Shogun* on the low) Colleen gave birth to what would be the Demetrious' only child, a girl, Talulla Mary Apollonia, now thirty-four, divorcée, werewolf.

"It happened to me in California," she said, speaking out of the qualitatively different silence that had formed after the nomenclatural explanation. (It happened to me in California. We were talking about "it," now. This was how it would be, I realised, these early hours would display gentle schizophrenia, the multiple realities of what there was to talk about, of what we *were*.) "Last summer. My decree absolute had come through and I'd taken a trip out there to visit a couple of old UCLA friends in Palm Springs. Allegedly to celebrate my new singledom. In fact I felt like shit. Sad and washed-up and ugly and sexually dead." The divorce had been precipitated by the discovery that her ex, Richard, a high-school teacher and aspirant novelist, had been having an affair with the deputy head's secretary. You know, Talulla had said, if it had been some nineteen-year-old twinkie with pneumatic tits I could have come out of it with a bit of dignity. I pity you, Richard, I really do. But this woman was *forty-seven*. You can imagine what a boost *that* gave me.

"Anyway," she continued, "I got sick of things in Palm Springs and took a rental car out to Joshua Tree to lick my wounds. I stayed in a little cabana motel out on Route 62, hiked in the park during the day, drank tequila with the kids running the motel in the evening. It was a comfort, the desert. I think, by the way, we should order up some Cuervo, don't you? I'm getting the feeling this is the calm before the storm, though *what* storm I don't know."

Lycanthropy had done things for her, licensed tangentiality, sanctioned intuition, loosened and altogether sexed-up the intelligence. She'd graduated with a degree in English and what turned out to be an insufficient interest in journalism. She started the career, but without much conviction, and after a couple of years drifted into helping run the Gilaley business. The education remained, humoured as a hopeless putz by the smut and savvy of her American trade self. I rang down for the Cuervo, half a dozen fresh limes, worried for the thousandth time Harley's IDs were rotten, that my flight out of Heathrow had tripped a switch, that Grainer and Ellis were already hip to "Bill Morris" over at the Plaza, bunked up in luxury with his new howler squeeze.

"Then, one night," she went on, "I wandered into the horror movie. I think it might have been the dumbest sequence of actions I've ever performed. For a start, I was driving alone at night in the desert. Off the main road too. I'd been out to Lake Havasu for the day and was determined to get back to my motel without the tedium of 62 West. It wasn't late. Naturally the moon was up. Naturally the car broke down."

The Cuervo and limes arrived. I found shot glasses in the suite's bar and set us up. These, I knew, were the high-octane minutes, days, weeks, when anything she does can pluck the phallic string. Watching her toss back the shot. The pale female throat and her soft hair fallen back to reveal the flushed ears with their pearl studs. And this is nothing, *wulf* said. You wait. You just fucking *wait*.

"The horror movie's always there," she continued. "Just needs certain conditions to firm up. Mainly human stupidity. You're driving around thinking the big thing is your poor broken heart and then suddenly the car dies and everything around you says, er, no, honey, the big thing is you're all alone out here and your phone's not getting a signal and you haven't seen another car in over an hour and in any case this is America so the last thing you should be hoping for is another car to come along. Hit me again."

I poured two more shots. Again the toss back, the taut throat, the breasts' uplift, the pearls.

"You could have been dumb and ugly," I said, as she wiped her mouth with her hand.

"So could you."

"If we both were that would've been okay. It's inequity causes the trouble."

"What if I'd been smart and ugly?"

"Initially excruciating but better in the long run. Dumb and pretty I'd have ended up killing you. Or more likely you me. Anyway go on. You'd broken down in the middle of nowhere."

She put the glass on the bedside table and lay on her side, propped on one elbow, facing me. We were over the first miraculous wave, her eyes conceded. Now a soberer relief, and the first shadows of realism. "I'd passed a one-horse town two or three miles down the road," she said. "A diner, a store, a handful of houses. I was pretty sure I'd seen a garage, too. At the very least there'd be a phone. I'd call Triple A and that would be that. So I walked. I must have gone about half a mile when the helicopter appeared."

I was studying her hand, enjoying the thought of its history, relishing in the inane way one must in these beginnings the bare fact that it was hers. Full-fleshed with long unpainted nails. She wore a big opal ring on her middle finger. When she'd touched her clit, with healthy deft modern American entitlement, the sight of this ringed finger slipping with cunning purpose through the soft dark hair of her mons had almost finished me.

"It came up about fifty yards away, I guess out of a ravine. I thought it must be the police because of the searchlight. Obviously these were your WOCOP guys."

"The Hunt."

"Right. Well, anyway, it happened incredibly fast. I could tell they were chasing someone, something, but I couldn't see what. It was bizarre standing there with suddenly no category to put the experience in. That's *why* I just stood there, like an idiot. Then the searchlight swung and blinded me and suddenly—out of nowhere—the werewolf hit me."

I thought back to the file I'd seen. Had the report mentioned a witness? It had not. Thank God.

"You'd hardly call it being bitten. More a scrape of the teeth. He really just ran me over. The claws did the real damage. I remember thinking, even in the split-second it took: Jesus, werewolves exist. You'd think you'd be stunned, wouldn't you? But I wasn't. I guess, you know, you see something enough times in the movies . . . I got one big gash on my chest and one on my cheek. It was so sudden, like a huge firework went off in my face. Then he was gone. I've never seen anything move that fast. *Had* never seen, I mean. These days I'm pretty quick myself."

I almost said: We'll see how fast soon enough, but didn't. It would have left us both uneasy.

"Then it was over," she continued. "The chopper was gone and there I was all alone in total silence again. I walked about twenty paces, in shock I suppose. Then I found the dart."

"What dart?"

"For the werewolf, but they'd hit me. In the calf. A tranquilizer, presumably, since a moment later I was out like a light."

"Did you keep it?"

"That would've been the smart thing, wouldn't it? But you find something sticking in you like that you pluck it out and toss it. Or you do if you're stupid. If you're me."

Darting? This is the Hunt. They don't dart, they kill. They *behead*. Alfonse Mackar was one of Ellis's. Grainer had been in Canada looking for Wolfgang. Was there anything in the file about darting for capture? If there was I didn't remember it.

"I don't know how long I was out," she said. "When I woke up it was still dark but the moon was higher. I wasn't quite where I remembered lying down, either. Must have crawled, I guess. I went back to the road and walked the two miles to Arlette. I seriously thought I'd died and this was the afterlife. By the time I got to the town the wounds had already started to heal. By the next morning there was nothing, no sign of any injury at all. But you know how all that works. Actually I do still get a slight pain in my chest sometimes. As if there's a splinter in there. God, that tequila's gone to the tips of my toes."

A moment in which Manhattan quietened and turned its glittering consciousness on us. I felt the dimensions of the hotel room, the streets outside and the frayed edges of the metropolis unravelling into freeways and the newly hopeful country's vast distances. And here we were on the bed together, warm as a pot of sunlit honey. With a very slight effort I could have settled wholly into peace. But now we'd gone through the first layer of sex all the wretched questions throbbed.

"The infection," she said, with mild telepathy. "Why me, now, after you're saying, what, a hundred and fifty years?"

Build a fortress. Guards. An army of dogs. Victims brought in, paid, tricked. We'd never have to leave. I sketched this and other fantasies, felt the tingle of futility, heard the world's forces like a billion-piece orchestra tuning up. Why in God's name were they darting Alfonse Mackar?

"I don't know," I answered. "My information's WOCOP information. They're the authority, or were. Transmission's supposed to have been stopped by a virus, which means either the bug's died or you're immune. Anything special I should know about you medically?"

"Nothing. I get hay fever and I'm allergic to almonds. Otherwise, nada."

"There's got to be something. Anyway it's not the priority. The priority is . . . Well, there are several."

"Not yet, please. Hit me again."

I had the long-overdue confrontation with myself in the bathroom while she made phone calls. (Three years ago her mother had died of bowel cancer and Talulla had taken on running the business ostensibly with—latterly instead of—her father. Until "it" happened. Two months after Turning she'd hired a general manager, Ambidextrous Alison, to cut herself loose.) "Honey, just ig*nore* him," I could hear her saying, presumably of meddlesome Nikolai. "I've told him he's out of it. He does it because he knows it pisses you off." I lay naked on the bathroom floor. Cold marble and the starry light of inset halogens. Things had caught up with me. Chiefly the completeness of my reversal. The universe, I said, demands some sort of deal, so you make one. In my case to live without love. With*out* love. A hundred and sixty-seven years. Was it ridiculous to speak of love now? No, it wasn't. Or only in that it's always ridiculous— on Wittgensteinian grounds—to speak of love. Everything was the same and everything had changed. Outside the city and the voluble traffic and the millions of human eyes and talking mouths and crafty habituated hands testified: The accidental epic of ordinariness goes on. A godless universe of flailing contingency—now with the hilarious difference of not being in it alone. (Suddenly I missed Harley, guiltily.) Courtesy of shared specieshood—indeed sole species representation—we'd skipped the phase of incredulous delight and gone straight to entrenched addiction. It wasn't a choice. I was for her, she for me. *Wulf* married us, blessed us, wrapped his arms around us like a stinking whisky-priest. What did I write of Arabella? "We would have killed together and we would have *shone*." Yes, and the warmth of that shining lay upon me now like an afterglow. *Fore*glow rather, since it came back through time from a future rich with murder. Talulla had looked at me when I pushed my cock into her cunt, had looked at me, I say, and sensed something of Arabella, whose spirit lived in me, whose ghost looked out through my eyes, had detected this presence and understood as she lifted her pale hips in slow and complete and victorious compliance that the betrayal whether I liked it or not of course deepened my pleasure, sold me wholly into the new female ownership, pissed on the altar, shat on the grave, dug up and defiled the beloved body in exquisite fully conscious sacrilege under the laws of Eros.

We both knew this was a juvenile phase that would pass, or, if it became a monolithic perversion, cause trouble, choke the sexual stream, breed pestilence. For now, however, she'd looked at me in rousing collusion, yes, I *know*. How not? How should she, six victims deep, not know the joy of the fall beneath the Fall?

The floor's chill had become unpleasant. I got up and took a hot shower. I wanted to go back to her clean and put my nose in her cunt, my tongue in her sweet young asshole, the cunning animal scent down there that answered the years of asking. *And the eyes of them both were opened, and they knew that they were naked; and they loved it.* But all the while and all the while and all the while the world. We couldn't stay here. That business with the dart didn't make sense. Grainer's days of live specimen capture were long over. Although of course it had been Ellis, not Grainer, after Alfonse in the desert. In any case we'd have to move. Dumb to have come to Manhattan in the first place, where among the multitudes surveillance was harder to spot.

I brushed my teeth and went back into the bedroom just as she was wrapping up her call. She looked at me. We didn't laugh, but if it was a movie that's what the script would have settled for as a way of showing it was the kind of thing where seeing each other again after ten minutes in separate rooms was a return to the only reality that mattered.

"You're all scrubbed," she said.

"Maximal contrast. I want your dirt."

"Yikes. Okay."

I went to the bed and lay down next to her. "Tonight we can luxuriate," I said. "Tomorrow we have things to do."

39

PARANOIA MADE THE decisions over the next few days. We met only four times, never in the same place. She had to prep Nikolai for her absence (he was prone to quarrelling with Ambidextrous Alison, prone to *interfering*) and I had logistical matters to attend to. California number plates, an array of wigs, spectacles, false moustaches, centrally the procurement of a fake driving licence for and the transfer of assets worth approximately twenty million dollars *to* Talulla Mary Apollonia Demetriou. The po-faced spirit of political correctness put its head around the door but my girl dismissed it. Obviously I should feel whored-out or patronised, she said. Well, I don't. I barely heard her. Even with the recent global mugging twenty million's a minor prang in my ride. It's walking-around money, I told her. I need more time to sort you out properly. Offshore. Swiss. This is just in case of . . . Yes. Well. The bad smell around the transfer of lucre was that it smacked of providing for her *after my death*. Neither of us could quite keep that out. Therefore we gave it its moment in the spotlight. I plan on staying alive, I said. But in case I don't you'll have what you need. Just promise me you'll always buy beautiful underwear. You drive a hard bargain, she said, but okay.

However, the paranoia. I had business lawyers in Manhattan (four of my companies have their head offices here) but insisted on meeting for instruction and signatures out of town. (Such meetings are a palaver. My face is rubber masked—I've been Richard Nixon; Marilyn; the Wolf-man—and I affect one of a dozen accents. The relevant identity's established first by code numbers and secondly via fingerprint-recognition technology in a portable gizmo. All tiresome, and used only when there's no alternative.) I hired a car from JFK and drove to Philadelphia. An opportunity, I deemed, to check for surveillance or pursuit. The results were uncertain. No sign of the undead, but I thought I made a couple of WOCOP agents in Philly. I left the car at the airport and took a flight to Boston, dodged around the city for twenty-four hours, then plane-hopped for three days getting increasingly dehydrated: Detroit; Indianapolis; D.C.; Philadelphia. I picked up the car, drove back to JFK and took a cab into the city.

Where I all but bumped into a vampire.

I was getting out of the cab on Fifth Avenue and he was exiting a deli, tearing the cellophane off a pack of American Spirits. The reek hit me when I was halfway out of the car. I went down on one knee on the sidewalk, an impromptu genuflection. Looked up to see him stopped in his tracks with an expression of outraged revulsion. I didn't recognise him. Tall, long-faced, with short thick hair dyed deep purple. Skinny jeans, leather three-quarter-length coat, orange Converse boots. Humanly you'd say mid-twenties cyberpunk. I got up off my knee. For a few moments we just stood and stared at each other, gorges rising. He looked as if this was new to him, this business of how Jesus Christingly awful running into a werewolf made you feel. Manhattan, needless to say, flowed around us, honked, glimmered, flashed, steamed, whistled, whooped and subterraneanly shuddered. Eventually, shaking his head, he backed, turned, and stumbled away downtown.

"An accident, right?" Talulla said. "I mean he wasn't following you?" We'd moved to the Waldorf Astoria, a suite overlooking Park Avenue. I was Matt Arnold again. Couldn't rest easy in any of the aliases.

"I don't believe he was," I said. "I'm getting it. I've assumed *all* the vampires know about the virus. They don't. This is one lot looking for leverage. Why am I so slow?"

Talulla sat in one of the room's red rococo armchairs with her feet up on a footstool. We were playing this, our condition, what we *were*, with bright circumspection. The hideous central fact informed everything we did but only took full unironic ownership of us when we fucked. In the sack *wulf* was stinkily eloquent, the odorous truth around which everything else fainted away. Out of the sack we conceded it like a childless couple who'd agreed to invent a fictional son, the premise, now that I thought of it (God *still* being dead, etc.), of Albee's *Who's Afraid of Virginia Woolf?* It was as if each of us was daring the other to admit it wasn't true. Actually it was her daring me. Or asking me. It reminded me how new she was to the Curse that she had such willingness to believe the whole thing—changing into a monster once a month and killing and eating people—might yet turn out to be a horrible dream. We'd avoided the question of what she'd gone to England for, though I knew: Five victims, however widely she'd spread them across the U.S., had started to feel too close. You go to another country—get in, do it, get out—the police are looking for a native, you're long gone. England because they spoke English. You want maximum fluency. She knew I'd worked this out. It introduced me to the guilty version of her face, the look an anchorwoman would have on air when someone in her earpiece says he knows all about the abortions or kinky photos, a slight swelling of the cheeks and the mouth momentarily without its guiding will. Sexually becoming, of course, the ghost of Eve's look, lips still wet with the juice of forbidden fruit.

Thus the obscenity remained draped. For now.

"That's good then," she said. "It means we don't have the entire species to worry about." She was wearing a grey woollen sweater dress, black nylons and knee-length black leather boots. So you got the soft of the dress and the hard of the boots. Like the soft of the thigh and the hard of the hip. Not sartorial archness, just a sound instinct for sexual accents. We were more than halfway through the lunation and her scent was yielding darker notes. Under the bittersweet glamour of Chanel No. 19 her quickening She exuded a high, tight-packed smell of predatory knowledge. Heat throbbed around her. The Hunger was a second heartbeat still a long way beneath her own. The next dozen days and nights would be the story of its rising. In both of us. Synchronised.

"Yes," I said. "But the danger is this twerp blabs. He looked as if I was his first lycanthropic run-in. An experience to discuss with his peers. If other vampires who *are* in the know are here in the city there's no reason they wouldn't hook up. He tells his after-dinner werewolf cherry story and they're onto us. No. We should go."

"Now? Tonight?"

"Can you stand it?"

She got up out of the chair, crossed to where I stood by the escritoire, slipped her arms around me, kissed me.

"We shouldn't travel together," I said, without much conviction.

"Don't be insane."

"They don't have you yet. If they get to you through—"

"Those days are over. It's you and me, now. That's all."

However ridiculous this sounds I already know there will never be a time when putting my hands on her won't palliate the certainty of death. The feel of her waist between my palms is of the deep geometry that takes you back or forward past the incarnate incidentals to the elemental realm, the realm of soul, one wants to say, knowing one's going soft in the head. Holding her is a Keatsian beauty-truth. I don't know what to do with it. I know there's nothing *to* do with it. Just live in it and let it bring what it brings.

"We could wait half an hour," I said, moving my hands to the firm flare of her bum.

"Is it always going to be this bad?"

"I don't know."

"Hurry up," she said. "Hard and fast. Please."

We quit New York that night (cab to Penn Station, Amtrak sleeper to Chicago) with very little discussion. She knew I'd put arrangements in place, but to talk them through would have been, according to the intuited werewolf proprieties, vulgar. Instead we moved around it, our giant ugliness, our unforgivable end point, dirtily enriched, like molested children, by knowing all and saying nothing. I saw in her abstracted moments that she remained disgusted in spite of the months of violent self-baptism. She'd hardened herself in blood but not all the tender remnants were dead. She was a monster, yes, but all she'd lost could still ambush her, turn her gaze back to her childhood and force her to look. You Can't Go Home Again. (*Thomas* Wolfe, Jesus how much more?) This hurt, very much. She'd been darling to so many, little black-eyed Lula with the high forehead and the beauty spot. Becoming a werewolf ought to have cut her off from all that but it hadn't. Continuity of identity persisted. It was like being tortured by an innocent child.

"How do you get around the fact that you should have died several times already?" she asked. To any but new lovers the Amtrak sleeper's three and a half foot bed width would have been a trial. The little window's curtains were open, revealing a rolling night sky of curdy backlit grey and gun-blue cloud just beginning, in patches, to break. The train smelled of filter coffee and air-con. "You were born in 1808—which is not a sentence I ever imagined saying—and here we are two hundred years later. There must have been questions to answer."

We could discuss these past practicalities. *Past* practicalities.

"It got easier," I said. "It's easier than ever now, if you've got money. It's always money. The principle doesn't change: You're paying specialists in the manipulation of identity technology. Used to be old guys in basements with loupes and inks and plates and presses, now it's young guys in lofts with computers. This is the primary level, the simple business of purchasing a fake birth certificate, passport, driving licence, social security number. You'll be surprised how far you can go with just those: bank accounts, credit cards, mortgages, loans, investment portfolios. Over a regular lifespan it's more than enough. Several lifetimes, it gets trickier. I can't believe what I did the first time. I can't believe I thought I'd be able to *go on* doing it."

"What did you do?"

"I became my own son."

"Holy moley."

"Jacob Marlowe 'Senior,' as it were, became a recluse at forty-two, in the year 1850. I couldn't put it off any longer: people were starting to notice I didn't seem to be aging *at all*."

She shivered next to me.

"What?"

"You. 1850. I think I'm used to it and then it gets me again."

"To tell you the truth I can't remember much about 1850. Dickens published *David Copperfield*. Wordsworth died. I'll have to think."

"It's not the big events, it's the ordinary stuff. A butler warming his hands. Those big damp houses. A bonnet on a chair." She was trying to picture the time when the present would be as distant to her as 1850 is to me. She was feeling the backdraft or slipstream of the far future: a cold flow. She shuddered, turned towards me, slid her right leg over my hip. "Anyway, go on. Jacob Marlowe Senior."

"Jacob Marlowe Senior went into reclusion—is there such a word? You think I'd know by now."

"No one cares, honey. Go on."

"Marlowe Senior went into reclusion if there was such a word in 1850. Not in England, but at a secret location known only to my lawyers. In fact I was rarely there. Couldn't afford to be." *Because as you know we can't let the victims pile up in one place.* She felt us duck to avoid this *present* practicality, a motion like a kite dipping in the wind. "All his business decisions were enacted through authorised proxies and lawyers, who received their instructions from him—I had codes, passwords, ciphers, the whole fucking caboodle—in writing. A rickety arrangement. Near misses of catastrophic losses when messages didn't travel fast enough. Telegraphy was a great relief when it came in. The telephone—well, you can imagine. Not long after leaving England I was 'married' and less than a year after that I had 'a son,' Jacob Junior. All fictional. A new will was drawn up—Jacob Junior would inherit everything—and that was that. All I had to do then was stay away from anyone who knew me."

"Are you serious?"

"Of course. You've got to remember it was a lot easier not to be seen in those days: Photography was in its infancy. No television, no CCTV. Half a dozen false names kept me going through Europe—and eventually here—for thirty-five years. Again, I had money. Money and mobility, that's how it's done."

"Thanks again for the twenty million, by the way. Another sentence I never imagined I'd have use for."

"You're welcome."

"And the fictional wife?"

Another kite dip. The fictional wife evoked the real one. The aphrodisiacal kick Arabella's ghost being forced to watch had given us, the promise of dark enlightenment. All apparent evil promises the same. It's a lie. There's no dark enlightenment because there's no evil. Whatever it is you're doing—raping a child, gassing a million—it's just another thing you can do. The universe doesn't care. Certainly doesn't give you divine knowledge in return. All the knowledge and all the divinity is already there in you doing whatever it is you're doing. Who knows this better than monsters?

Nonetheless my cock thickened next to the moist heat of her hand, and she took it and held it, and that was all the acknowledgement the moment required.

"Enteric fever," I said. "Poor Emily. She was only twenty-two. And Jacob Junior barely a year old."

"Birth and death certificates forged."

"Exactly. I followed them into the grave myself courtesy of heart failure in 1885. I grew an impressive moustache for my return as Jacob Junior, donned a pair of specs, got a new hairdo. My accent had changed, naturally. People see what they're told to see, by and large."

"And real kids? You must have them scattered all over the world by now."

Oh.

As soon as the words were out she wanted them back. These were the last seconds before something was gone forever. Very briefly I considered lying.

"We can't have children," I said.

I felt it go into her, find the place already there for it. Of course she'd known, and denied, and still known.

"My periods stopped."

"I'm sorry, Lu."

"Richard and I were supposed to start trying. Then I found out about the affair."

For a few moments we lay without speaking. Cradle comfort of the train's rocking. It would be peaceful segueing into death like this, I thought, the deepening lull, a tunnel that gets darker and darker until eventually you're gone out into darkness yourself. Gone out, quite gone out. I held her, but not as if my holding her could make any difference. (The fierce male embrace is invariably patronising to the female embracee.) She still had my cock in her hand. I felt grief and anger and futility going through her and her keeping very still. It was as if she were being burned and had to bear it without flinching or making a sound.

"I knew," she said. "Carried on taking the Pill in denial. I suppose the thing to say would be 'Well, it's for the best.' "

There were bigger patches of open night sky now. Stars.

Then suddenly the moon.

"And just to rub it *in* . . ." she said, feeling the unignorable insinuation of ownership where its light licked our skin. Then when I didn't speak: "At least I've got a guy who knows when to keep his mouth shut. I guess that's what two hundred years does for you."

I too had thoughts of burning, quietly and without pain as she rolled me over onto my back and climbed by degrees on top of me. Burning— or accelerated decay, like time-lapse film of decomposition, my headless trio of foxes going from plump corpses to dust via maggot orgy in grainy fast footage. It looped while we fucked (while *she* fucked *me*), interrupted when she leaned back and the moonlight ran lewd riot over her belly and breasts. Finished when I finished. A cine reel with the end of its film strip still whipping round.

She fell asleep immediately afterwards, half draped over me. Her weight had in it the finality of the new fact, a brutal peace now the thing had been faced and taken in. *We can't have children.* Somewhere in the sex she'd hated me for it, of course, and known that I'd known and made room in myself for her hatred. Somewhere in the sex was the understanding that love was among other things making room for the beloved's irrational vengeances.

40

WE ONE-WAY HIRED a Toyota in Chicago. Stayed off the freeways. My thinking was the emptier the space the easier we'd spot a vamp or WOCOP tail. Iowa. Nebraska. Wyoming. Utah. Those unritzy states of seared openness, giant arenas for the colossal geometry of light and weather. Here the main performance is still planetary, a lumbering introspective working-out of masses and pressures yielding huge accidents of beauty: thunderheads like floating anvils; a sudden blizzard. Geological time, it dawns on you, is still going on.

"But you're saying there are WOCOP exorcists," she said. "What are they exorcising?"

One returns to metaphysics, but with diminishing urgency. The assumption is that new phenomena must fill in the picture. But if the picture's infinite, what difference can half a dozen new species make? She was seeing this already. She sat with a strange neatness in the passenger seat alongside me, knees together, hands in her jacket pockets. She'd pinned her hair up and her slender bare neck gave her a look of appalling vulnerability.

"Demons," I said. "As far as I know, demons. That's the idiom. That's the terminology."

"Which means heaven and hell, right? Demons and angels. God and the Devil."

"You'd think I'd know one way or the other by now, wouldn't you?" I was struck by how long it had been since I'd considered such things, how these questions had subsided. I had only a generic memory of small-hours conversations with Harley, though I knew his view well enough, that there was a transcendent realm but that it spoke in many languages. In one of its languages Isis was a word. In another Gabriel. In another Aphrodite. All we ever got was the language. We were a language ourselves. The thing *behind* the word remained unknown. Naturally: The Word was with God. What use would that be to her?

"But you've seen this stuff?" she said. "You've seen demons?"

"I've seen someone with something inside them that wasn't them, that was definitely a separate entity. I've seen it—*felt* it, rather—go out of them."

"And it was evil?"

This, of course, is the crux. It doesn't really matter what the language is, only whether there's a transcendent moral grammar underpinning it. No one really cares what hell's called or who runs it. They just don't want to *go* there.

"It felt like it intended harm to humans," I said. "But not as if it had much choice about it. Evil has to be chosen."

She kept her hands in her pockets. Stared at the road ahead. This was the problem with talking. Sooner or later it led here. Sooner or later everything led here.

Evening on our fifth day from New York we stopped in the middle of nowhere for me to pee. Sunset was a gap between land and cloud like a narrow eye or broken yolk of light, rose gold, mauve, dusk. On either side flat prairie to the horizon, an effect that remade the earth as a disk of pale grass. Ahead the road ran straight to vanishing point; turn 180 degrees and look back, same thing. Talulla got out, stretched, leaned against the Toyota's bonnet, lit one of my cigarettes. (I'd told her smoking wouldn't harm her and she'd said okay what the hell, it's something to do.) We yet hadn't said anything about where we were going or what we were going to do when we got there, and the not saying anything was for her like flies gathering on her skin, more every hour, every day. These last two nights the Hunger had kept us awake in shivering TV light, drinking bourbon, screwing till we were sore, unable to find comfort lying still. Full moon was eight days away.

"When I was driving in the desert," she said, staring at the horizon, "I'd go a hundred miles and see nothing, just empty landscape." She was wearing a black leather jacket, blue jeans, a cream rollneck sweater. I was thinking of lines from a Thom Gunn poem: *They lean against the cooling car, backs pressed / Upon the dusts of a brown continent, / And watch the sun, now Westward of their West . . .*

"Then suddenly," Talulla went on, "in the middle of all this emptiness, like a joke, I'd see a solitary trailer. A washing line, a pickup, a dog. Someone living there all alone. I toyed with doing that, in the beginning, just get as far away from people as possible. Alaska, maybe. The Arctic." A breeze simmered in the roadside grasses. She took a last drag, dropped the butt and ground it out with the toe of her boot. "But I'm not built for it," she said. "Loneliness."

I put my arms around her and kissed her, felt the compact warmth of her under the leather jacket. Her hair smelled of cigarette smoke and fresh air. I was very aware of the precise dimensions we occupied just then, two bodies, all the miles around us. "You know what you look like?" I said. "You look like one of those actresses in an episode of a seventies cop show. *Cannon* or *McCloud* or *Petrocelli.*"

"I don't want to alarm you, but I've never heard of any of those."

" 'Guest starring Talulla Demetriou as Nadine. A Quinn Martin production.' They were so beautiful, those girls, they hurt men's hearts. It's your beauty spot and your high forehead and your centre-parting."

"That doesn't sound very attractive," she said. "And you can call it a mole, you know, since that's what it is."

I held her slightly away from me and looked at her. The Hunger had thinned the skin of her orbits but her face still had its centres of wealth, the long lashes and dark eyes, the mouth the colour of raw meat. A look of fragile control over demonic energies. It had been so much just the two of us that there had hardly been need to address each other by name, but earlier that day in a convenience store she'd said something and I hadn't heard and she'd said, Jake, and I'd loved her, a sudden access of ridiculous piercing love just because there it was in her voice saying my name, the new deep thrilling familiarity.

Later, driving again in the dark, she said, "I toyed with the other thing too, in the beginning. The radical solution."

Suicide.

"But?"

She didn't reply immediately. Cats' eyes ticked by. The Hunger's night shift was limbering up. Lust was available to me, moved as with aching muscles towards her hands on the Toyota's wheel, the small taut weights of her breasts, her knees, the beauty spot by her lip. She kept her eyes on the road. "Turns out I'm not built for that either," she said. "I didn't want to die. I put on a show of wanting to die for a while, that's all. I couldn't believe I was going to carry on, but there I was, carrying on. No point saying pigs can't fly when they're up there catching pigeons."

The universe demands some sort of deal, so you make one. Yes.

"The truth is I was a monster long before any of this. I got my mother's narcissism and my dad's immigrant overcompensation. If it's me or the world, the world's had it. Of course that's disgusting. And liberating. That's the problem with disgust. You get through it. You feel bigger and emptier."

Which observation broke some barrier in her, some last resistance to dealing in bald specifics. I felt it—we both did—as surely as we would have felt a tyre blowing out. She understood the genre constraints, the decencies we were supposed to be observing. The morally cosy vision allows the embrace of monstrosity only as a reaction to suffering or as an act of rage against the Almighty. Vampire interviewee Louis is in despair at his brother's death when he accepts Lestat's offer. Frankenstein's creature is driven to violence by the violence done to him. Even Lucifer's rebellion emerges from the agony of injured pride. The message is clear: By all means become an abomination—but only while unhinged by grief or wrath. By rights, Talulla knew, she should have been orphaned or raped or paedophilically abused or terminally ill or suicidally depressed or furious at God for her mother's death or at any rate in *some* way deranged if she was to be excused for not having killed herself, once it became apparent that she'd have to murder and devour people in order to stay alive. The mere desire to *stay* alive, in whatever form you're lumbered with—werewolf, vampire, Father of Lies—really couldn't be considered a morally sufficient rationale. And yet here she was, staying alive. You love life because life's all there is. That, ladies and gentlemen of the jury, was the top and tail of the case against her.

That night, lying on our backs side by side in a Motel 6 bed, I knew what was coming.

"I killed animals," she said, quietly.

Nine moons, six human victims. Simple arithmetic.

"Yes."

"Did you try that?"

"Yes."

It was raining. The motel was almost empty. The room smelled of damp plaster and furniture polish. A truck honked on the wet highway half a mile away. She was thinking about her parents. Her mother dead and her father living alone in the big maple-shadowed Gilaley house in Park Slope. A lot of her strength had gone into not letting the Curse rob her of the warmth between her and Nikolai, who would without thinking run his hand softly over her cheek as if she were still a little girl.

"Of course it was no good," she said. "I knew even when I was doing it it wouldn't work. You can tell."

You can indeed. Have no illusions, the Curse specifies: *human* flesh and blood. This isn't a nicety. An animal won't "do," at a pinch. Refuse the Hunger what it demands and see what happens. The Hunger isn't at all pleased. The Hunger feels it incumbent on itself to teach you a lesson. One you won't forget.

"I thought I was going to die," she continued. "Throwing up afterwards it felt like I was trying to turn myself inside out. I was relieved. I thought I'd solved the problem, poisoned myself, accidental suicide. But of course it passed."

My hand rested just above her mons. The question was whether to use what was coming next erotically. I could feel she was aware of the option. She was undecided. Mentally, too much was mingling: her mother's death, her father's loneliness, *we can't have children*, innocent victims, the prospect of a four-hundred-year lifespan.

"It got worse," she said. "The next time. After the third month I knew I wouldn't make it through another Change without feeding properly." It cost her something to get that "feeding" out. Her voice hardened for the word. It occurred to me that this was probably the first time she'd had to put it *into* words. Kurtz's unspeakable rites. "I was crazy," she said. "Two hours before moonrise just driving around aimlessly in Vermont. I don't know what I was thinking. Maybe get myself killed. Walk into a hotel and just go through the whole transformation routine in the lobby." She paused. Closed her eyes for a few moments. Opened them. "Well, of course *not* aimlessly. You know what you're doing but you pretend you don't. There was this place I knew from a vacation years back. A big woods between two little towns. Houses far apart. I picked one at random. I wasn't careful, just went straight in. The doors weren't even locked. It was a nineteen-year-old boy. His name was Ray Hauser. It was the last week of his summer vacation. His parents were in town watching a local theatre production of *Titus Andronicus*. I read about it afterwards in the papers."

I didn't say anything. Therapists and priests and interviewers know all about not saying anything. When you die and go for judgement God will sit there and infinitely not say anything and you'll do all the damning work yourself.

"Feel," she said, opening her legs slightly.

Her cunt was wet. There was the killing. There was the eating. And there was this. The central monstrosity. The way it made you feel. What it did for you. You couldn't live with it without living with this.

I kept my hand there. Stroked her. This central monstrosity had nearly made her kill herself. But she hadn't. And once you don't kill yourself it's all over.

"I'm smarter when I Change," she said. "In all the worst ways. In all the ways that matter."

"I know, Lu."

"You think some sort of red cloud would come down, some sort of animal blackness to blot everything out and leave just the dumb instinct, but it doesn't."

"No."

"I know what I'm doing. And I don't just like it—I don't just *like* it . . ."

"I know."

"I *love* it."

We left a respectful silence. Her hair was a dark soft corona around her head on the pillow. Evil has to be chosen.

"I tasted it," she continued calmly. "All of it. His youth and his shock and his desperation and his horror. And from the first taste I knew I wasn't going to stop until I had it all. The whole person, the whole fucking feast."

She moved her hips very gently in response to my stroking. The argument with herself about what she was, what she was willing to be, was effectively over. Her bigger self had gone on ahead and accepted it. These were residual emotional obligations.

"Then afterwards," she said, lifting slightly as my finger slipped into her anus. "The big talk, the promises to myself I wasn't ever going to do it again."

It'll get easier, I could have told her. It's the story, the human story, the werewolf story, that the hard things get easier. Carry on and in a year or two you'll be taking victims as you might grapes from a bunch.

"It's the worst thing," she said, turning towards me, forcing herself against my hand. "It's the worst thing."

We're the worst thing, she meant. We're the worst thing because for us the worst thing is the best thing. And it's only the best thing for us if it's the worst thing for someone else.

There are times when saying "I love you" is blasphemy worthy of the Devil.

"I love you," I said.

Much later, after we'd lain for a long time listening to the rain in the dark, I felt the last barrier between us dissolve. It was as if the night's tensile apparatus suddenly fell apart. She said: "You killed your wife, didn't you?"

She already knew the answer. Had fucked me knowing. Was lying here with me knowing. Accommodating this, even more than accommodating her own slaughters, was the proof of having entered a new world.

"Yes," I said.

Silence. But of cogitation, not shock. I could feel her trying to find a justifying angle—*because sooner or later you'd have had to, the alternative would have been turning her, which would have felt as bad as killing her, with four hundred years for her to spend never forgiving you*—then finding the unjustifiable truth: because nothing compares to killing the thing you love.

"It was good," she said. Conclusion, not question. The insight that withers the old flower and lets the new one bloom.

"Yes."

"Because you loved her."

"Yes."

And here we were at the delicate logic. I was thinking: She'll be a much better werewolf than me. (And with *this* thought came the first true realisation that she was less than a fifth my age, that half her life would be lived after my death in a world beyond my imagining.) Already she had an understanding it had taken me decades to arrive at. Very soon, a year, two, I'd be struggling to keep up with her.

"Maybe you'll kill *me*," she said, pressing her hand flat against my chest. "Maybe that's what I was hoping for."

It had occurred to me she might want this, an exit strategy. But there was that past tense: Maybe that's what I *was* hoping for. If she had wanted it she didn't now. Or at least not cleanly.

"There's something better than killing the one you love," I said. I extricated myself from her embrace, gently forced her onto her back, held her wrists above her head, got on top of her, felt her bedwarm thighs softly opening. Her eyes and earrings and lips and teeth glimmered in the dark.

"Something better?"

I eased into her as she lifted her hips.

"Killing *with* the one you love," I said.

It was only afterwards, when she slept (wondering what knowing the worst would feel like had been one of the things keeping her awake; now, having let it in and found room for it she surrendered to exhaustion, a blissful rapid unspooling into sleep) that I knew there would be no purpose served, indeed none, by telling her Arabella had been pregnant, and that in murdering and devouring my wife I'd also murdered and devoured the only child I'd ever have.

42

THE BIG OPEN spaces thin the American gods: Elvis, John Wayne, Marilyn, Charles Manson, JFK. Out there they're like frail clouds tearing, nothing behind them but blue emptiness. It sends some people mad. Americans know this and gather by collective intuition on the coasts.

Life reduced to the dimensions of a car. Lack of sleep and the deepening drift of miles blurred all our categories, yielded absurd conversational segues, from Tom Cruise's career to WOCOP genetics to Obama to the fragmentation of feminism to the history of the Hunt to the film adaptation of *The Lord of the Rings*. Meanwhile Texaco, gospel, storm clouds, scarecrows, Jack Daniels, Camel Filters (the *brand* divinities prove surprisingly resilient), fucking, stars, vending machines and the constantly tightening torque of the Hunger. She wanted to know everything, Harley, Jacqueline Delon, Cloquet, Ellis, Grainer, the Fifty Houses. And that was just the contemporary matter. I had two hundred years' worth of places I'd been, people I'd met, things I'd seen. No matter how much I told her there was always more. But she wanted to talk, too. The Curse had left her memories intact but not her sense of entitlement to them. *They* had become unspeakable. Now here I was, apparently having the cake of my past and eating it. Her unsalved grief was for the lost familial warmth. Her mother's clan had been large, featured Irish characters, clichéd Irish in some cases, colossi of drinking and sentimentality and with the great bloodstained tapestry of Roman Catholicism to wrap everything in. The Uncles. When she was a child these men picked her up in massive sausagey hands and sat her on their shoulders amid whisky vapours and wild hair and talked fabulous nonsense. The women initiated her in gossip and the arts of masculine deflation. This had been her template for happiness. This and the deep cahoots with her long-suffering father, whose little sprite she was and who indulged her, recklessly, and who had not just heroes and gods to entertain her but black holes and comets and the precise weight of the sun. Among the Gilaley tribe Nikolai's already negligible Greek Orthodoxy had disappeared.

"He started with capitulation," Talulla said. "Went through the farce of converting to marry my mother. It made him smaller in her eyes, of course, though she'd never have married him without it. She held all the paradoxes, casually. Not that I can talk, the rubbish I'm still carrying around."

"So you do believe in God?"

We were in Nebraska, south of the Middle Loup River, east of the Sand Hills. It was evening, cold, sleeting since we'd stopped for gas an hour ago. I'd seen the acned cashier give us a sidelong look. This was new. In human form I never failed to pass as simply human. Were we, together, palpably more Other?

"It's not belief," she said. "It's just what you're stuck with, the lousy furniture you can't change. The educated me knows hell's nothing, a fiction I happened to inherit. The other me knows I'm going there. There must be a dozen *me*s these days, taking turns looking the other way."

"It's the postmodern solution," I said. "Controlled multiple personality disorder. Pick a fiction and allocate it an aspect of yourself."

"But you don't think the story in Quinn's book's a fiction, do you?" I'd told her what I knew, how close I'd been at Jacqueline Delon's, the Men Who Became Wolves.

"Ridiculous, isn't it?" I said. "Let everything else have its place in purposeless evolution but let *my* lot be exempt. It's just a hangover from—" I was going to say "the days of being human," but felt how it would bring the fact of infertility close again. "It's just the same old shit," I amended. "The desire to know whence we came in the hope it'll shed light on why we're here and where we're going. The desire for life to mean something more than random subatomic babble."

"And now the vampires have it," she said. "Assuming you really think they do?"

"I really think they do."

"I know this is crazy, but I can't quite get over the whole vampire thing. That they really exist."

"It's the lameness of their having to sleep during the day. That and the not having sex."

"They don't?"

"They don't. The desire goes. I mean, they'll tell you screwing's nothing to draining a victim but that's always sounded desperate to me. It's one of the reasons they hate us."

Us. I felt the word evoke for her a tribe, a family, a *kind*—then the effect dissolved. A whole species gone to silvered dust.

"How do we really know there aren't any others?" she said, off the back of this image, rolling her head a little to ease the neck's knots of gathering wolf. "Alfonse Mackar turned me—okay. You say there must be some anomaly in me that made infection possible. But what if it was an anomaly in him? If the thing interfering with infection really is a virus maybe *he* was immune to it. In which case who's to say he hasn't turned others? There could be dozens, or hundreds—"

"Not hundreds. WOCOP would know. Harley would've known."

"A few then. It's possible, isn't it?"

This had occurred to me. But for no reason I can dignify with anything higher than the authority of a two-hundred-year-old gut I didn't buy it. "It's possible," I said. "Of course it's possible."

"But you don't think so"

"No. I'm not sure why."

Another silence, her intelligence working. Then a very slight smile. "It's because it would be less romantic," she said.

We drove long into the nights, since it gave at least the one behind the wheel some distraction from the Hunger. Our scents made a dirty brew in the car, went into us, absolutely refused to let desire sleep. Sex muffled the drum-thud for an hour or two. Then the beat struck up again—worse. Diminishing returns. I could feel her sometimes looking back to her werewolf life before we'd met and feeling a kind of retroactive vertigo or nausea that she'd survived it alone so long. It was as if the sun had come up and shown her for the first time how close to the edge of a thousand-foot drop she'd been walking in the dark. Despite which reflections (I could also feel) she was daily making the aesthetic or dispositional shift:

As long as you're still considering suicide the Curse can play as tragedy. Once you're resolved on living only comedy will do.

Unless you fall in love, Jacob.

(Harley's ghost? Arabella's? Whoever, I ignored it.)

I bought things we'd need. A lightweight rucksack. Binoculars. Clip ropes. Talulla didn't ask. Not, any longer, out of avoidance, but because for the first time in nine months she was enjoying being entirely in someone else's hands.

The early hours of our eighth day from New York found us in a Super 8 motel in Wyoming.

"The more I think about it," she said, "the more it doesn't seem possible they don't know about me. WOCOP, I mean." It was just before dawn. My head rested on her thigh. The room's one thin-curtained window was a lozenge of smoke-blue light. We were dry-eyed, wakeful. The Hunger had forced us off regular food. This, as Jacqueline Delon would no doubt have known, is the way of it: Human appetite occupies roughly the middle fourteen days of the cycle. The rest of the time you're winding down from the kill, or winding up to it. Now, four days from the full moon (waxing gibbous), we were reduced to water, black coffee, liquor, cigarettes. Even chewing a stick of gum felt categorically wrong.

"It's bothering me too," I said. "I feel sure Harley knew, and if he did there's no reason the rest of the organisation wouldn't. But you've never felt yourself being followed or watched?"

"*Would* I feel it? Surely not if they're any good."

Quite. My own sense for surveillance had had a long time to develop. She was an infant. A conviction seized me suddenly that the motel was surrounded, that any second the door would be booted in. I leaped up from the bed, unlocked, looked out. Nothing. The parking lot's winking mica. The road. The mountains, white on the heights. Clean cold air and the predawn feeling of the earth's innocence. I went back inside.

"Maybe I'm wrong about Harls," I said, as she lit us a Camel each. "It's just that when I saw you at Heathrow, the instant I saw you it seemed to complete his cut-off message. It was a tonal thing, you had to know his voice. But maybe that wasn't what he was telling me. It could just as easily have been that he'd found out the vampires were after me for the virus. Or it could have been that he knew his cover was blown, that his own people were onto him. Christ, it could have been any number of things."

"I've wondered if they even saw me that night in the desert," she said. "I mean it was a matter of a couple of seconds. The chopper was having trouble keeping the light on him. They could have missed me. I mean they *could* have. Otherwise wouldn't they have come back for me?"

"There was no mention of you in the report I saw," I said. "And in any case they'd assume you'd be dead in twelve hours. There was no reason to come back. As far as they were concerned the only thing you were going to turn into was a corpse."

She considered this for a few moments, staring at the ceiling. The effects of *we can't have children* were still going on. She was wondering where the grief might go, what shape it might take. Anger—or rather focused malice—was a possibility. I could feel her considering it, the complete devotion of herself to only a handful of her aspects: intelligence, cruelty, destruction. She could become Kali. "Well," she said, "that'll teach them to be complacent, won't it?"

Fear of pursuit grew in inverse proportion to evidence of pursuit. The back of my head and neck developed a blind hypersensitivity. I got eye ache from repeatedly checking the rearview. Abnormal scrutiny of every desk clerk and chambermaid and store manager and waitress. The world was vampire or WOCOP until proven innocent.

But the miles passed with no sign we were being followed or watched.

We drove west through the Rockies. A bad idea, *wulf* so close. The latent creature yearned and strained for the sheer spaces. Flaring mountain flanks gashed with snow. Big stone knees bent up out of pools of forest. When we stopped and got out the air was thin and mineral. Talulla suffered spells of fever, in the worst of them sweated and shivered, wrapped in a blanket, but passed from these fugues into picked-clean awareness, like a child after its evening bath. We needed less and less to speak. The dusk sky with the first sprinkle of stars became our element. Mile after winding mile of rich silence in the car. I watched her when she drove, her dark eyes' incremental submission to what was coming, what she was. It was the look of a little girl who's assimilated a secret she knows can bring the grown-up world crashing down.

Sex stopped. Without verbal agreement we found ourselves numbed, a pitch of desire so extreme, perhaps, that it nudged or bled into its opposite, as all extremes must. I could barely touch her, she me. Neither of us was surprised. *Wulf* had its occult necessities, demanded now that the great consummation was close a small fee of purity, a little swept-clean antechamber before the hall of majestic filth.

In the early hours of our tenth day from New York, road-burned and red-eyed, with the Hunger forcing lupine life through human exhaustion, we left Nevada's share of the mountains and crossed, just south of keen-aired Lake Tahoe, into California.

Transformation was two nights away.

42

MY LAST KILL in the Golden State was thirty-two years ago, in the summer of 1977. Led Zeppelin had played the Oakland Coliseum and a vanload of fans had driven up to Muir Woods after the show to drop acid and screw. I'd planned to go farther north into the Napa Valley (the woods here a tad too close to the city and occasionally ranger-patrolled) but when a young hallucinating gentleman, gamine, with pre-Raphaelite blond curls that would have given Robert Plant's a run for their money, injudiciously wandered away from his hallucinating friends and all but fell into my lap . . . Well. No pain felt he. I am quite sure he felt no pain. Had I not been long past the days of self-comfort I would have comforted myself with the thought that to him I'd been nothing more than an alarming—and final—hallucination. Altogether a lazy kill. I barely took pains to bury what was left of him. Of course the remains were found, three days later, but by then I was in Moscow.

Talulla was sick. We checked into a motel on foggy 68 just east of Carmel and I left her soaking in a hot bath. A risk, but unavoidable: Moonrise tomorrow would present its necessities. There was reconnaissance to be done. Besides, I'd seen absolutely no sign of pursuit since we left New York. We had new phones; check-in would be every hour. If she saw or felt anything—*anything*—suspicious she was to get among the public and call me. "Is it this bad every month?" I asked her. She was pale in the tub, dead-eyed, shivering. Her little breasts were goosefleshed despite the water's warmth, nipples prettily puckered.

"At least."

"Jesus, how've you managed?"

She just looked at me, jaws clamped, on behalf of womankind. My own pre-Curse blood-bubble and bone-burp routine was under way. The premature hybrid hands and feet were ghost-fucking with me (extra care behind the wheel, Marlowe), lupine previews flashing in my human shoulders and hips. I deal by keeping on the move. Sitting still makes things worse. Not so for Lula. She looked like she never wanted to move again. Her makeup was smudged. She'd started taking it off then given up. She stared at me with the baleful resignation of a seventeen-year-old suffering the sort of hangover she'll come out of with a feeling of humble spiritual enlargement—if she comes out of it at all.

"I'll wait awhile," I said. "We've got time."

She shook her head. "Don't bother. This is just what happens to me. It'll last till this evening then I'll be full of beans. Come this evening you'll wish I was like this again."

It still wasn't easy leaving her. Several false departures. "If for any reason something happens to me," I said, turning back for the fourth time at the door—then realised I didn't have anything useful to offer.

"Just go," she said. "I'll be fine."

I left her a bottle of Jack Daniel's, three packs of Camels, a dozen Advil and a pot of lousy motel coffee. Also Cloquet's Luger, which I'd hung on to, though I'd replaced the silver ammo with regular rounds. Useless against boochies (should I not be back before sundown) but fine for familiars and agents. "Anyone comes through that door who isn't me," I said, "shoot them."

She nodded, teeth chattering, then closed her eyes and waved me away. I locked the door behind me. It was just after noon.

Novelists, notoriously, are always working, eyes and ears open for anything they might be able to use. Ditto werewolves. Not for quirky characters or snippets of dialogue but for murder locations, places that lend themselves to the secret kill. I'd had this stretch of coast—the hundred miles between Monterey and Morro Bay—in the file for years. Along with the requisite geography and the ghosts of Steinbeck, Miller and Kerouac, Big Sur's got isolated houses and a glut of whacked-out residents with more money than sense. In the late sixties I'd rented a place here for a few weeks (flew to Alaska for the kill) and been struck by the potential richness of its pickings. Odd I'd left it this long, really. *You were saving it for her,* my romantic insisted—and in my new generous idiocy I didn't wholly dismiss the idea.

It's a strange craft or art, finding the where and the when and the who of the kill. Naturally one develops a nose for it over time, a sensitivity to variables. In the early years I used to spend weeks as it were casing the joint. Now you can drop me anywhere there's human habitation and in less than twenty-four hours I'll give you the optimal target.

Of course there are soft options. The Western world's so mad these days you can put an ad in the paper and some desperate self-harmer will answer it. *Wanted: Victim for werewolf. Must be plump and juicy. Non-smoker with GSOH preferred. No time-wasters.* I've had my share of drug addicts and alkies, the blind, the deaf, the crippled, the infirm, the mentally ill. I've hired escorts (male and female), doped them, driven them out to the countryside, let them wake up and make me a chase of it. All of which will *do* (the Curse being unencumbered by aesthetics or fair play) but there's a peculiar profound satisfaction in the straight—one wants to say traditional or clean-lined—mode of predation: You stalk a perfectly healthy human being, confront them, give them plenty of time to really *take it in*, then do what you do.

I spent the day driving and hiking, equipped with knapsack, bush hat, state-of-the-art Van Gorkom walking boots, binoculars and a paperback copy of *Birds of the Western United States,* officer. Tourist season was a month away and the trails were quiet. I had the place to myself. The odour of redwoods and damp earth made my eyeteeth and fingernails throb.

By three in the afternoon the fog had lifted and the sun had come out. I worked with free-form fluidity, and with an hour still to go before sundown I'd lined up a hit and two backups. It would mean a sixteen-mile on-foot round-trip and smart timing but we could do the whole thing without breaking cover once—and it doesn't get better than that.

Talulla phoned as I was climbing back into the Toyota.

"You'll be sad to hear," she said, "I've entered the full-of-beans phase."

"Good."

"Don't get excited. It's basically ADD, with fever and hallucinations."

This is another purpose of civilisation, so that we can exchange love-packed banalities over the phone.

"Everything's set," I told her. "I'll be home in an hour."

The sun was setting over the Pacific and the mountains were lit pink and gold. The car was warm with evening light and spoke in its fuel and vinyl odours of America. I drove carefully, holding focus. *Wulf* heckled, spooked my hands and face with claw and muzzle. My scalp loosened and shrank, hot and cold by turns. Close, now, brother, very close. But I drove to my beloved, carefully.

43

THE FOLLOWING EVENING we parked the Toyota, now with its California plates, in a twenty-four-hour gas station and diner just off Route 1 about a mile north of the Andrew Molera State Park. Talulla wore a blond wig while I sported a false moustache and a Yankees baseball cap. Sunglasses for both of us. The disguises felt excessive but the gas station had CCTV. It was cool and damp. Moonrise was three hours away. Lu's mode had changed again. Last night's fidgets had subsided. Now she was quiet, clear-eyed. This was her penultimate pretransformation stage. The final stage would come ten minutes before Turning. Not pretty, was how she'd described it.

It was an hour's trek to the change site I'd selected. Redwoods mixed with coastal oaks at least a half mile from the nearest trail. From there a seven-mile romp to the target. Kill. Seven miles back. Two miles to the car. Timing was the issue. Timing's *always* the issue. Moonrise was 8:06, moonset tomorrow morning at 7:14. Eleven hours and forty-six minutes on the Curse. Hunting alone I'd hold off till 4:00 a.m. Two hours for killing and feeding and an hour-fourteen to get back to base camp. Once you can manage the Hunger, whet and dandle and tease, you want the shortest possible time between werewolf crime and human flight—for the simple reason that if the remains are discovered and the alarm raised you don't want to be nine feet tall covered in hair sporting a gory muzzle and bloody claws when the sirens start to wail. But I wasn't hunting alone.

"It's coming," Talulla said.

"In here. Quick."

I lifted a branch and she ducked under. Her face was strained and sweaty. "Get undressed," I said. "Can you manage?"

No one near, according to my nose, and in any case we weren't visible. Twilight on the roads and trails was coagulate darkness under the trees.

"Oh," Talulla said, down to her underwear, holding her belly. She swallowed, repeatedly. Dry heaved, once. I got her out of the bra and panties and stuffed them with the rest of our clothes into the rucksack. Kit-checked: wet wipes, water spray, liquid soap, bin liners. I climbed fifteen or twenty feet into the oak (as rehearsed yesterday) and secured the pack with the clip cables. Back on the ground I found Lula on her knees, doubled up, arms wrapped around herself.

"Don't touch me," she said.

"Okay."

"Very close."

"I know. Me too."

They were the last words we exchanged that night.

She was quick. Quicker than me. I had assumed—as a male? as an elder? (as a *moron*, Marlowe)—I'd be fully transformed and at her service while she was still in the throes. But no. Her damp face rendered an appalling small-eyed in extremis version of itself, she vomited bile, jackknifed, rolled onto her side, curled her pretty lips and went in less than twenty seconds with an extraordinary symmetrical fluidity through the Change, while I was still untidily crunching and popping out of my human lineaments. Cutting-edge CGI versus fifties stop-motion, an embarrassing discrepancy I wondered if we'd be able to laugh about later.

Not that there was much time for wondering, what with the fully released scent of a She filling my hybrid nostrils. Oh. *Oh.* The weeks of human-leaked olfactory hints were no preparation, really *no* preparation for the merciless clout of the female werewolf stink. Standing, I nearly fell. At the first inhalation my balls filled with a riot of libidinal jazz, my cock shot up like a sprung—like a booby-trapped—device. Talulla, still on all fours with her hindquarters raised, issued a low sound and slowly spread her legs for my questing snout. And there, dear reader, wet for my wet muzzle's tip was her lupine cunt, larger, slyer, darker-skinned than its human sister, murder-silked and blood-fattened, firm and soft as a ripe avocado and releasing a sweet scent just at the evil edge of rot.

Not yet.

She growled at the injunction, delivered to both of us in simultaneous telepathy, but we knew the waste it would be to come together now, with the Hunger holding our innards at knifepoint and the gift of the kill not yet unwrapped. I let the tip of my cock nuzzle her for a moment, felt the slick entrance hotter than a fevered baby's mouth, almost, *almost* failed the dalliance test at the last—but withdrew, and watched with a sort of vicious admiration as she rose to her full height, looked at me with her wiser animal eyes, grinned, and moved off ahead into the darkness. I shot one hot arrow of piss to mark the tree, then followed her.

We understood each other. Clairvoyance that in our human form was no more than the standard new lovers' allowance increased posttransformation to near-total mutual transparency. She knew, for example, where we were going, though I hadn't told her. The route I'd traced yesterday led her like an aboriginal songline; it was there in front of her as clearly as if I'd left a trail of phosphorus. Ditto, since she was at liberty to rummage any of the relevant mental files, the image of the house I'd selected, binocular-watched and eavesdropped-on long enough to establish a lone male inhabitant for whom the sub–Frank Lloyd Wright pad was a second home–cum–recording studio retreated to at times of creative crisis. "Look, if they're going to keep changing the cue-points the whole thing's a complete fucking waste of time, Jerry." Under my surveillance yesterday he'd come out on the deck with a coffee, a joint and his cell phone. "No. No, I've got all the software here. It's the same shit. The same *useless* shit if they're going to keep changing the cues. I really . . . Seriously. Tell me how someone making his third feature thinks you can score from footage that isn't the final fucking cut? I mean . . . Exactly. Seriously. Seriously. Yeah. Well. That's the fucking indie wunderkind for you . . ." He was handsome, with dark blond hair chopped to create a look of boyish self-obliviousness, a good thin mouth, a hard jaw and a long-muscled body. More than enough success with women for resolved misogyny. Or so I thought, perhaps wishfully. I'd picked a man (and a looker at that) lest a woman complicate things for Talulla, which rationale I felt her now perceiving—she turned her head back to me with a grin—and being in equal parts touched and offended by.

Moonlight blotched the forest floor, maternally soothed us when we moved though it. Lu stopped once to look up and let her werewolf face take its cold balm and I saw my lover silvered in all her sinuous beauty, the hardened breasts and fatless belly, the long deadly hands, the thin-haired muscles of thigh and calf. I shuddered at how close to giving up I'd been. Remembered Harley in the library saying, You've got a duty to live, same as the rest of us, with London's snow hurrying and the whisky's firelit gold. You love life because life's all there is. The last two weeks, the motels, the miles on the road, Manhattan, Heathrow, all had the closed encrypted quality of a dream. *This* was the waking world, lust and hunger racing to the primal feast, my dead rapture brought back to life by the simple miracle of not having to do it alone . . .

Meanwhile we'd come too far too soon. A small stream broke into a steep valley, conifer-covered on its western wall (the great fresh flank of the Pacific just beyond it), mixed forest and stony outcrops on its eastern, snaked down through by a smooth, single-lane, new-smelling tarmac road, sparsely lit. Talulla stopped, breath going up in plumes. I stood behind her, wrapped my arms around her and filled my hands with her breasts and lightly bit her shoulder. She put her head back, licked my snout. *I'm smarter when I Change,* she'd said, and I could feel it in her, the deepened cunning and whetted nous. Inside the Hunger's red din her predator was busy with angles and shadows, lines of cover, points of entry, how far a scream would carry. I'd underestimated her, in spite of myself, out of vestigial delusions of female delicacy assumed I'd have to help her through this. She knew, sensed my embarrassment. The lick was partly *It's all right, I understand. Sweet of you. But you see what you're dealing with now?*

The house (lights on, black Lexus in the drive) was built like a chic bunker into the side of the hill, two storeys, a basement, a pool, a decked balcony running all the way round the upper floor, double garage, stone gateposts, electronic gate. Even without our advantages getting in wouldn't be difficult. The downstairs doors were shut, granted, but it was too early in the maestro's evening for the hi-tech lockdown his Shield 500XS Security System allowed. In the centre of the upper floor one of a pair of sliding glass doors was open, beyond which were visible an elephantine white leather couch and a plasma-screen TV with the sound down. Our friend, barefoot in Bermudas and a baby-blue rollneck fleece, reclined on the couch with the remote in one hand and his phone in the other, channel surfing and bitching, with a monotony implying defeated acceptance of the rest of the world's unprofessionalism, about the director.

The plan said to wait several hours. The plan was dead. Hunger and desire had unceremoniously assumed control. We felt it go, both of us, with relief. *Come what may* conferred its mantric blessing as we moved silently up the eastern slope of the valley, in a single bound each across the empty road, and on, with all lupine stealth, towards the house.

I went first. One leap got me over the gates. A second from the ground to the balcony. A third from the balcony through the open door and directly onto the couch.

Hyperbole's a writing vice, but I stand by the claim that I gave Drew (Drew Hillyard, the papers have since informed us) quite literally the fright of his life. The Old World snob in me thinks he screamed—or rather went *maaah!* in falsetto—because he was Americanly conditioned to do so by lifelong overingestion of television and movies. A woman dumps you, you go to a bar and get drunk. Someone cuts you off on the freeway, you shout "Asshole!" and give him the finger. A werewolf appears, you scream like a six-year-old girl. These are the scripts. In any case he not only went *maaah!* in falsetto but flung both arms up in the region of his head. The remote flew from his hand and sailed across the room to clatter against a chair, leaving *America's Next Top Model* to keep us company for the duration. Perhaps by profound survival instinct he held on to his cell phone. I reached out, relieved him of it, and while he watched crushed it in my own ample monster mitt, which spectacle elicited from him a strange nasal moan. His face crumpled or crimped as in preparation for grown-man toddler tears, but from the distension of his mouth and his filling lungs I knew another bigger scream was coming. I thought, We can't have that.

We didn't. Talulla's dark lovely long-fingered hand came from behind and covered the bottom half of his face.

44

YOU'LL WANT ORDER, sequence, categories. I sympathise. But the trinity mystery of fuckkilleat collapses distinctions, swipes aside the apparatus separating *this* from *that* and introduces with the transcendental equivalent of a Gallic shrug *a completely new form of experience.*

There was, for example, deep turf, frost-hardened, fracturing with a soft crunch underfoot. Turf? Where? We were in his living room. We moved languidly, two creatures gone into by the drift of dark water alongside us, neither river nor sea and with no opposite shore. Stars came all the way down to the horizon, nestled in the water. Which isn't to say I don't remember Talulla's black-clawed thumb tearing his neck, a mastoid opening, a fan of blood and his sealed-up roars. The landscape was nowhere and it rolled out from the room. Bits of it fizzed or crumbled away to reveal the deity it belonged to, not God but one of his aspects, the great clean spirit of Predation, to whom *we* belonged, of which we contained a fragment or flame like a portion of pure joy.

We looked at each other and everything became still. Which isn't to say the white leather couch wasn't smeared red where his hand went hurriedly back and forth, as if waving or trying to erase something.

Between us was the shared certainty of escalation, a speeded-up version of the ticking of roller-coaster cars climbing the hill to the Big Drop. *You're feeling this, right?* Yes. Meanwhile Drew's life in vivid chunks like the "Previously, on—" opening of a soap: his mother's large blond-haired head, blue-eyeshadowed and coffee-breathed, blotting out the light over his pram and coming down to him like a benign planet. His fingers' ache stretching for the piano keys and the keys themselves clues from the time before birth. A dark-haired twelve-year-old girl biting her lip and the feeling like Christmas and birthday of his young hand creeping under the elastic of her pants her pants her actual pants, and Rheingold saying, You've got talent but no star quality, and he was right.

A million-page flick-book of TV images, cowboys lightsabres Coke car-chases *Friends* the Twin Towers. That dream he'd had of swimming to what he thought was the shore except it was the flat edge of the pre-Columbus earth and suddenly he was being sucked to where the ocean poured its wrecks and sharks over the rim into black empty space not even stars just nothing and then waking covered in sweat and the escort wasn't next to him as instructed but sitting in the window seat sending a text message on her BlackBerry and the thing with women now was purely transactional probably always had been they pretended to want sex but it was always some other fucking thing and it was amazing how you could at forty-one accept that the thing with women from now on forever was just going to be transactional he would still like to have a son and teach him music.

In spite of the moon the television's light perceptibly twitched and shivered, a blond green-eyed contestant on *America's Next Top Model* wept glitterily, half her face obscured under the screen's pancake of con-gealing blood.

Talulla turned from what she was doing and looked at me. *It's close. Can you feel it?*

Sky and water shifted or swivelled their occult constituent parts and like the solution to a visual riddle the stars yielded a new constellation describing the figure of a wolf, a diagram showing that there was no rea-son for us, only the certainty *of* us, and understanding this was like tak-ing the hand that would lead us to peace. The night in the room agreed, through the drifting water and the smell of frost.

Which isn't to say we weren't wet with blood or that Talulla didn't arch her back or that my hands didn't cup her breasts or that her legs didn't open with sly animal capitulation. I'd thought I loved her before, and so I had, the woman. But this was the monster and the monster was magnifi-cent. I got an unmanning glimpse of the depth of my capacity for worship, drew back from it as from the edge of a cold-aired chasm. She saw that, too, and sent me, *It's the same for me, don't you see?*

Her question turned out to be the tipping point. A second of absolute balance—then down from the fulcrum moment I went into her as her eyes rolled back and her tongue curled in martial or erotic triumph (detonating however absurdly Dante, *And now a she-wolf came, that in her leanness / seemed racked with every kind of greediness*)—while the sudden plunge tore us out of our bodies and for an unmeasurable moment returned us to the thing that wasn't God but the aspect of him that was ours, and in which infinitely generous archetype there was neither her nor me but only the rapture that calls you home to unity with the sweetest song and painlessly burns away the straps and buckles of the suffering self.

Bliss.

Bliss defies description, obviously, since it annihilates you, since you're not there to experience it. You get the lead-up and the comedown, never the zenith. We went to the place. We came back—spoiled, made ruined addicts at a stroke. From now on nothing less would do. I thought: Two hundred years of ignorance; now this. And only two hundred years to repeat it in.

I love you, the moment instructed us (as Drew's life, like the last lights off the black West, went), was for the human sphere. Here, humbled and filled with tenderness for the newly restored finiteness of arms and teeth and lips and bellies, we brought our noses close, lapped, nuzzled, paused, looked, saw into each other and knew for better or worse we'd been consecrated, not just our unholy marriage but our aloneness together in the world. A condition both of us calmly conceded might lead to complete mutual hatred. It was a great comfort to know this, to understand it, to allow all the possibilities. We felt like modest little gods ourselves, beating with fresh love for life and humble in the face of the possibilities. Would have laughed if we could.

Time had misbehaved, disguised hours as moments. I'd lost track. Unforgivably let myself unravel. Fuckkilleat came at the price of caution and control. *America's Next Top Model* had been replaced by the *Good Morning News*. (The standard U.S. double act of paternal toupéed golfer fluffered by twentysomething L'Oréal dummy. The wigged father fucking the waxed daughter is okay as long as both maintain calculated incredulity and restrained outrage at *what's going on out there in the world*.) Now, as if it had been caught asleep on duty, the moon woke and began sending its warning, a dragging (menstrual, for all I know) sensation in the lower body's blood. We might have been two heavy fish on a weak line being reeled in by an invalid—but a magical invalid, since the thin force was irresistible.

As one we left what remained of our victim (not much) and bounded like dog-food-ad dogs out of the open door and over the balcony's rail into the collusive forest and the vapours of the waning night. My restarted inner clock said less than sixty minutes to moonset.

45

WE RAN, PASSING his spirit back and forth like teens swapping gum. Mist clung. The woods went by in a resinous blur. Half a mile from where we'd set out I caught the scent of my own piss, cut hard left, plunged with Talulla close behind through a band of fog and came in a matter of minutes to the marked tree. I went up it in a single leap and there was the pack, clipped, dew-beaded, but with contents dry and filled with the odours of civilisation. A bit of trouble with the clip cables (there's not a product on the market built with werewolf fingers in mind) but I resisted *slashing straight through them,* and after a few moments' patient application had them unfastened and stowed. I dropped to the ground.

Our pelt back had left us twenty minutes to spare. We lay near each other but not touching, silent recipients of Pan's globally ignored dawn suite, a soft exhalation through turf and leaf, the whirr of small wings, the introspective clambering of beetles, the shiver of water. The world, Lula was thinking, is oozing, teeming, *crawling* with miracles. And we live in the opaque plastic bubble of television and booze. You should start keeping a journal, I sent her, but too late: The metamorphic current had caught her. Her animal receptors were frying. I reached for her but remembered *Don't touch me* and drew back. She crawled on all fours in a loose semicircle, collapsed, curled up in a ball. Out of sight the moon set, a tiny pain, like the tearing of the last fibre holding a comically loose tooth. Talulla, foetal, jaws clamped, convulsed rhythmically, as if keeping time with something. Mucus rattled in her snout.

Again she was ahead of me. Had the opportunity to observe—which she did, sitting and catching her breath—the body-popping extravaganza of Jake Marlowe Changing Back.

"Thanks for not laughing," I said, once I was confident language had returned.

She didn't answer, was still inwardly returning herself. Her eyes were big and bright, murder-purified. Helping her clean herself up (the products don't care, address blood and guts with the same floral cheer as they would ketchup and gravy) I felt the stunned regrouping of her human aspects, the shock and disgust that here, *again*, was the grossest defilement, beyond forgiveness, beyond any kind of washing away. Very soon followed (her eyes hardened) by the knowledge that shock and disgust had already proved themselves inadequate. Six times. Now seven. Which left the fact of herself she must find a way of getting along with, since it was either this or death. *I know what you're going through,* I wanted to say. I didn't say it. Aside from the psychic travails she was visibly Curse-hungover. I, old lag that I am, had forgotten how it used to be, aura peeled, consciousness red-raw. You don't want *talk*, for Christ's sake.

I bagged up the cleaning accoutrements and kicked earth over where she'd vomited last night. Rucksack on, final idiot-check of the site. Short of the fading odour of werewolf piss there wasn't a sign we'd been here.

An hour later, fog-damp, meat-heavy, we were back at the car. My calves ached. Talulla was shivering. The vehicle's interior was a tremendous comfort when the doors *thunk*ed shut. This is another of the purposes of civilisation, so that you can get in a car and close the door and be surrounded by technology-studded vinyl and drive away in conditioned air. I dropped the bin-liner (a DNA conundrum, should anyone ever find it) in a rest-stop Dumpster en route to San Francisco and replaced the number plates in an empty lay-by a little farther up the road. Two hours after that, having returned the Toyota in the city, we boarded an Amtrak bound for Chicago.

For a while we sat side by side in silence, Talulla in the window seat looking out. Sunlight warmed our hands and faces. Her pupils were small. She blinked slowly, as if each meeting and parting of the eyelids yielded its distinct portion of peace. Her body radiated exhaustion. The train's motion went into us like a sedative.

My eyes were closed when she spoke.

"I'm getting used to it," she said. Neutral statement. Gain and loss in mutually nullifying equilibrium. Her throat was sore. I didn't reply. She wasn't expecting me to.

After a while, she put her head on my shoulder, closed her eyes and fell asleep.

Third Moon

(

The Cruellest Month

46

Six days after murdering Drew Hillyard we arrived, surreal from too many time zones and too much weather, in Ithaca.

Not Ithaca, New York. *Itháki*, Greece.

We had stopped for a night in New York, however, against my inclination. Nikolai had been haranguing Talulla over the phone ever since we'd left and she insisted on putting in an appearance before we skedaddled again. There was peace to be made between her father and Ambidextrous Alison, who'd threatened, for the dozenth time, to quit if Nikolai didn't stop interfering. (There was no financial need for the restaurants now, of course, but aside from the problem of how to explain the sudden acquisition of twenty million dollars, Talulla knew the Gilaley business was for Nikolai a nexus for happy memories.) In any case, it gave us a night in a hotel bed after the torturous dimensions of the Amtrak sleeper. A bed we *slept* in, chastely. Sex on the Curse, it transpires, zeroes libido just in the way that *no* sex on the Curse whacks the dial up to max. When we touched it was with geriatric solicitousness. Of the many memories from those crammed weeks that one—of slipping between crisp cold hotel sheets with her after three nights on the train—is peculiarly vivid, the swan dive into sleep, like pitching voluntarily into death, the last friable bits of shared consciousness—is this peace? this is peace, isn't it, to be able to let go?—dissolving into darkness like a skyrocket's trail of sparks . . . There are great sleeps, sleeps of monumental innocence, and that was one. We woke with a feeling of having been popped brand-new out of a mould. It gave us a current of mild giddiness on which to make our second exit from New York.

American Airlines to Rome, then Air Italia to Cephalonia. From there a boat to Ithaca. A modest villa up a hundred rough steps overlooking the little harbour town of Konia, an off-season short-notice snip at twelve hundred euros a week. I'd been here thirty years ago, having killed a healthy young French contemporary-dance student holidaying across the Aegean in Ephesus. The place had been insinuating itself at some subconscious level, I believed, since I first set eyes on Talulla at Heathrow, and I'd fixed this sojourn before we left Manhattan for California three weeks ago.

"It's the domestic happy ending," she said. "Odysseus back to hearth and home and faithful wife. A kid could have worked that out. I thought you were supposed to be smart?"

Not smart. Happily stupid. Stupidly happy. The Jake Marlowe revolution was complete: Tedious self-knowledge had become blissful self-ignorance. All former certainties were up for renegotiation. The circuitry of detached self-analysis was fried. Here again was immersion in the good blind flow.

Not so simple for Lula. Her larger self might have moved ahead into acceptance but her smaller wasn't going without a fight. Nightmares woke her, drenched. Fugues took her, after a while gave her back. She didn't talk about them. Sometimes the entire weight of her self-loathing was compressed into the angle at which she held a cigarette. In the white bedroom I'd wake alone, panic, search, find her lying in the empty bathtub, or standing on the veranda staring at the sea, or curled up with her arms wrapped around herself on the kitchen's terra-cotta floor. These rites were necessary, in both senses of the word: There was no escaping them, and through them survival lay. She knew this, was sickened by the logic of her own continuance. That's the trouble with disgust, she'd said. You get through it.

One night in the small hours I found her—after a rise to near hysteria when she wasn't in the house, or on the balcony, or in the garden, or in the village—out to thigh-depth naked and alone in the sea. I stripped, waded, *shosh . . . shosh* (she glanced back, once, saw it was me), stood beside her. The beach was deserted. Cool but not cold. Moonlight (waxing crescent) lay in flakes of silver leaf on the water. I knew not to take her hand, not to touch. In this state she wanted touch like a woman in labour wants a French kiss.

"My dad used to tell me the story of Lycaon when I was small," she said. "He always made a big deal of the eight years proviso, how no one ever heard of any of the wolves changing back into men."

There are two versions of the myth. In one, Lycaon, king of Arcadia, tries to feed Zeus human remains in a pie at a banquet and is punished by being turned into a wolf. In another, he offends Zeus by sacrificing a human infant on the god's altar, after which not only the king but anyone who sacrifices there suffers lupine transformation—and can return to human shape only if he manages not to eat human flesh for eight years.

"What's the longest you've gone?" she asked.

"Four moons."

"How close would you get to eight years?"

"Eight years might as well be eight thousand. You know that. There's no going back."

A little while passed before she said, "No. I know."

I was aflutter with urgent masculinity, a scowling hyperreadiness to do violence to anyone or anything that might have the obscene inclination to harm her. It was very difficult not to keep putting my hands on her, my arms around her, my body and soul between her and all conceivable dangers. It was such sweetness, such an undeserved relief not to have to care about myself anymore. Only her. Only her.

"It's always going to be like this," she said. "On the run. Looking over your shoulder. Getting away with it. What a disgusting phrase that is, really. Getting away with it. I wasn't going to drown myself, by the way. *Can* we drown?"

"Yes. In both forms. And burn, eventually."

The sea's motion around our legs gave us the illusion of swaying.

"I looked at fabric swatches with my dad and Alison when we stopped in New York," she said. "We're redecorating the place on Twenty-eighth Street. And three days earlier I'd fucked you with my face buried in a man's ripped-open corpse."

She laughed, once—not, as many would have, histrionically—but because what she'd said was both factually correct and sounded like a line from a cult comedy horror film.

"Yes," I said. "That's right." I knew why she'd said it. Your unavowed atrocities kill you from the inside out. *What is the compulsion to tell the truth if not a moral compulsion?* Jacqueline Delon had asked. She was wrong. It's a survival necessity. You can't live if you can't accept what you are, and you can't accept what you are if you can't say what you do. The power of naming, as old as Adam.

We returned to the house, a silent walk through the silent village under the constellations. For the first time since the kill I felt lust flickering again between us—then realised: She'd felt it before me, knew the next phase of the cycle had begun, was faced again with its inevitable end point. Hence thigh-deep alone in the wine dark sea.

The villa smelled of our freshly washed linen and the veranda's potted lemon and thyme. We undressed with a strange placid precision and slipped naked between the cool sheets.

"Don't you find it strange that I've taken your word for it about the drugs?" she said. Somewhere on the road trip we'd covered narcotic suppressants, my old days of the cage, the cast-iron safe, the key. I'd told her the truth: It's possible to get through, medicined to near death, for a couple of lunations, maybe three (doing four I'd nearly killed myself—literally, I'd torn my own flesh off; if it hadn't been for the howler's accelerated healing I'd have bled to death), but there are two reasons for not doing it. First, it's the worst suffering a werewolf can go through. Second, it's pointless, because whether it's this month or the next or the one after that, unless you commit suicide *you will certainly kill again*—and again and again and again until you die of old age or silver finds you. I'd told her all this.

"I don't find it strange," I said. "You see the logic. Morally a month's abstinence here or there's meaningless."

"That's not why I haven't tried it," she said. "I haven't tried it because I remember what those first three times were like and the thought of going through that again terrifies me. It's not seeing the logic. It's cowardice."

"I'm no different. It terrifies me, too. Plus the last time I tried it I failed."

"But you've done good in the world. You've counterbalanced."

"Money gestures. Which is nothing if you've got the stuff to burn. Besides, it doesn't work. Money's not legal tender in the moral world."

My cock had stirred next to her hand. I knew she knew. Was readying herself for the exquisite capitulation. Through sorrow and shame into warmth, and the peace of having no one but each other.

"It doesn't change," she said. "I keep thinking there's some way around it, but in the end it's still either kill yourself or get on with being what you are."

"Don't kill yourself," I said.

"Will you stay with me?"

"Yes."

Just stay.

"I might kill myself," she said. "It's hard to say."

"Will you promise not to kill yourself without telling me first?"

"Yes."

"Say it."

"I promise not to kill myself without telling you first."

That night I had a tumble of vivid dreams. I think we made love again, in the half-asleep way that comes close to magic. Then more dreams. One of being repeatedly stung in the neck by an elusive insect. I thought, I must tell Talulla about this when I wake up. I must—But the thought fell off suddenly into darkness.

And when I woke, late, the room was filled with sunlight and a sea-smelling breeze, and before I lifted my head from the pillow I could feel the emptiness in the bed where her body should have been and Ellis's voice said: "Jeez, Jake, it's about time."

47

HE WAS SITTING in the room's one rattan chair at the foot of the bed
with his back to the French windows that opened onto the veranda, hands
clasped over his belly, one leg crossed at a wide angle over the other.
Trademark black leather trousers, steel-toe-capped boots, pale denim
jacket. The waist-length white-blond hair was down today. A movement
of air brought me his marshy foot odour. A tuning-fork hum in my teeth
brought me silver rounds in the shoulder-holstered firearm. I sat up to
face him.

"We've got her," he said. "Do you want Q&A or shall I just roll it out?"

"Tell me," I said.

Ellis nodded, briefly, as if to confirm his private guess at my reaction
had been correct, then he got to his feet, made a *just a sec* gesture, went out
onto the veranda and came back a moment later with two cups of freshly
brewed coffee. He handed me one then returned to his seat.

"First, let me reassure you," he said. "Talulla's alive, well, completely
unharmed. She's far from here, in a location I can't disclose yet, but you
need have absolutely no anxieties about her comfort. This I promise you,
Jake."

I set the coffee down on the bedside table. My hands were trembling.
Walking back from the beach last night under the stars she'd taken my
hand. Neither of us had said a word but the gesture had made both of us
think, gently, of death. Now I had an image of her sitting with her knees
drawn up on a spartan bunk in a windowless cell. *Alive, well, completely
unharmed*. I had to believe him because not believing him left me nothing.

"I can't do this naked," I said.

"I understand. Go ahead."

I got to my feet, felt the perfect vacuum where any concession to or
interest in my nakedness would with anyone else have been, and dressed,
quickly, in yesterday's clothes. Then sat on the edge of the bed and lit

a Camel. My in-love self like a straitjacketed lunatic sobbed and rocked back and forth repeating *They've got her. They've got her. They've got her.* There was a sore spot on my neck I couldn't resist rubbing.

"Still stinging?" Ellis asked. "Tranquilizer dart. We've got this new guy, calls himself the Cat. Justifiably, if he got up onto your balcony without waking you. You didn't hear anything?"

A dream of being stung by an insect. My own uselessness lay on me like a passed-out drunk.

"Just give me the information," I said.

"Right. So we've got her. You can have her back and live happily ever after. All you've got to do is kill Grainer."

I looked up at him. His face was peaceful, dark blue eyes lucid. He returned my stare. "You heard me correctly," he said.

"Why Grainer?" I asked.

Ellis took a sip of his coffee, swallowed; his Adam's apple moved in his gullet like a little elbow. "Jake," he said, "it's like this. For some time now I've been involved with a movement within the organisation. This is a group of people—some from Hunt, some from Tech, some from Finance—who've read the writing on the wall. I mean it's pretty big writing on a pretty big wall: We need you. Literally, you're our reason for being. Not just you, obviously. The vamps, the demons, the reanimated, the voodoo kids, the Satanists, the djin, the poltergeists, the whole crowd. Problem is the crowd's getting a tad *small*. You see this, right?"

Post-9/11 wacko-rumour said the Bush administration had launched the attacks itself, the reward being carte blanche for oil-savvy aggression and a shot in the already steroidal arm for the military-industrial complex. No fear, no funding. Ergo al-Qaeda. Same principle here.

"The guys who did their job so well they did themselves out of a job," I said.

"Exactly. My friends and I aren't prepared to let it happen. It's okay for Grainer, he's got money and he's sick of all this shit anyway. But what's a guy like me going to do? Flip burgers?"

Not just funding, then. Identity crisis too. Ellis didn't know anything else. Porn stars talked of the industry as a loving family. The Hunt, I could well imagine, played the same role.

"FYI," Ellis continued, "there are now two WOCOPs. World Organisation for the Control of Occult Phenomena, and World Organisation for the *Creation* of Occult Phenomena. We're not out. In all likelihood we never really will be. But under our influence things are going to change. We're going to save what's in danger of being lost forever."

"By killing Grainer?"

"You have no idea, Jake, how much *clout* the guy has. It's not just him. There's a nucleus, a damned junta. They're controlling funding, recruitment, research, policy, media. Half of them are cynics robbing the organisation blind and the other half are zealots who don't realise they're cheerleading themselves into redundancy."

"I had you pegged as a zealot," I said.

Ellis shook his head with a sort of benevolent disappointment. "I'm a pragmatist, Jake. Always have been. I thought you knew that."

"And when you kill Grainer—sorry, when you get *me* to kill Grainer—what then? A coup d'état? Or are you picking the generals off one by one?"

"We don't want a bloody revolution," he said, then swallowed the last of his coffee and put the cup down on the floor. "The organisation's too unstable and our numbers too small. We're looking at three, maybe four key deaths in the U.K. cabal. A dozen in the States. We don't want to overdo it. We're looking at *quietly making our presence felt.* Gentle steering. You see how this would work? The zealots, admittedly, have got to go, and Grainer's a zealot to the core, but the cynics can be persuaded. Either to go voluntarily or to stop abusing the organisation. Not a bloody revolution, but not an entirely velvet one, either."

"Then you don't need me," I said. "Just kill Grainer yourself. In fact you have to for the threat of your group to be credible."

"I *am* going to kill him," he said. "It'll be me replacing the silver ammo with regular shit. You just provide the camouflage, Jake. It's the perfect faux cover. We have to let these guys know we did it without giving them the means to prove it. They're connected in the straight world. We could face regular *legal* prosecution if we don't get it right."

"You've left it a bit late, haven't you?" I said. "I mean, there's only me left. What difference is keeping me alive going to make?"

He looked at me, almost smiling. "Nice, Jake. But there's you *and* her. You didn't know if we knew about her. You had to find out. We do."

A slender hope, but worth a try.

"Grainer knows about her?"

"No. Just my people."

My inner strategist was working through the terror. Grainer doesn't know about her. Is that any good? Can we use that? Not sure. Give me a minute.

"Okay," I said. "So there's me and her. That's two of us. Big deal. Hardly enough for a Hunt renaissance."

For a moment Ellis didn't reply, indeed seemed to attend to some frequency only he could hear. Then returned, with a short sigh. "Jake," he said. "Oh, boy. You have no idea what's going on. I don't even know where to start."

My scalp shrank. I didn't *want* him to start. The details, in any case, wouldn't matter. All that mattered was that some giant First Principles error had produced fantastic false ramifications. Now everything you thought you knew . . . Everything you were sure was . . . Didn't you see this coming? You, the big *reader*?

"We've cracked the antivirus," Ellis said.

The temptation to say "*What?*" though I'd heard him perfectly was all but overwhelming. I resisted, just.

"Serendipitously, too," he said. "I guess it's always like that with the big discoveries, a bit of raw meat falls on the fire and *voilà!*—cooking. Anyway, we've got your girl to thank."

For the werewolf, but they'd hit me. In the calf. A tranquilizer, presumably, since a moment later I was out like a light.

No, angel. Not a tranquilizer. Jesus Christ.

"Is Alfonse Mackar dead or not?" I asked.

"He's dead," Ellis said. "He died the night he ran into Talulla in the desert, though he wasn't killed by us. Some local amateur outfit in a fucking *Jeep*. Can you believe it? We had to recruit them to shut them up. Seriously, Jake, it's a circus out there, a free-for-all. Every teenager with a smelting kit and a diploma in *Buffy*. I mean there was a time when—"

"Would you just tell me what's going on?"

He held up his hand. "You're right. I'm sorry. Let me get a refill. You want?"

I did not. While Ellis fixed himself a fresh cup I picked up the few items of Talulla's clothing that lay scattered around the room and put them out of sight. Covered the bed, too. It was horrible, him seeing the evidence of our intimacy now that it was wrecked. I couldn't stop thinking of the way she'd taken my hand last night and neither of us had been able to say anything. As if we'd shared a premonition of loss.

Ellis put his head round the French window. "You want to sit out here? It's a beautiful day."

Teeth clenched, I joined him on the veranda in dazzling light. The sun said maybe three o'clock. Below us a scatter of small white houses dotted the hill down to the village, where Konia went about its absurdly picturesque business. A brown-skinned fisherman sat on a capstan mending a net. A waiter leaned against a lamppost, smoking. Four teenagers lounged around an orange Vespa. I took the seat opposite Ellis with the light behind me. The sun's heat fit the back of my head like a hellish yarmulke.

"Okay," he said. "Research on werewolf infection stopped officially five years ago. Unofficially, our boys carried on. It was tough, with the shortage of live specimens—but we had Alfonse Mackar. Alfonse was our golden goose—until he got away. *Escaped,* for Christ's sake. Can't believe we were so slack there. Some of those young guys . . ." He looked away, shaking his head. "Anyway," he continued, "that night in the desert we were trying to recapture him. Failing that, get a shot of the latest version of the antivirus into him. What happens? The shooter hits Talulla with the dart by mistake." He leaned forward, eyebrows raised. "And who is the shooter? Me! Fucking Dead-eye Dick!" He relaxed and leaned back again, smiling. "Serendipity, Jake, every time. All along we'd been trying to treat the werewolf. Suddenly, accidentally, we treated the victim. Talulla's the first person to survive the bite—and Turn—in more than a hundred and fifty years. She survived and Turned because the meds our eggheads cooked up actually work. We still don't know if they kill the virus in an established lycanthrope, but they obviously kill it in a new one. A dose of this when you're bitten and bingo—brand-new werewolf. That's Poulsom's thinking, anyway. He's the brain. These are exciting times."

"It doesn't make sense," I said. "You killed Wolfgang. *You*. You're Grainer's surrogate son. You've killed *loads* of us."

He nodded again, lowered his head. Ridiculously, *sighed*. "You're right, Jake," he said. "It took me too long. I was under the man's spell. He's got the gift, you know, the charisma. He *has* been like a father to me. But I had to stay close to him to find out who the crucial players in the organisation are. He's got access to everyone. Even now the thought of him not being around makes me a little ill, and it's a year since I joined the renegades. There's the ghost of ambivalence like a spirit that can't cross over. It's the price of double agency."

I felt ill myself. Not least because it was clear Ellis was mad. His inner universe was impenetrable. He might be telling the truth. He might be suffering a protracted hallucination. The fundamental reference points and parameters weren't there. You had to make a decision to take him at face value. Easy enough, since the alternative was a void where another explanation should be.

"By the way," he said, "it's only fair to tell you: You've had the antivirus yourself. The new one. More than once."

"What?"

"Drinks at the Zetter. Again in Caernarfon. Poulsom's still after a version that destroys the virus in the biter. Talulla got bitten, and got the antiviral, and as a result Turned. But we still don't know if she can Turn anyone herself. Plus, having the drug that allows successful infection in the bitten victim gets us nowhere in the big picture. I mean, think about it: We'd have to *be there* every time someone got bitten to administer the drug. It's completely impracticable."

There was a memory of a Scotch at the Zetter that hadn't tasted right. I ordered an Oban, I'd said to Harley. I think they've given me Laphroaig.

Harley.

My life, I thought, is a list of people I've failed.

"Trouble is of course you haven't bitten anyone," Ellis went on. "That's another condition of the deal, obviously. You're going to have to start leaving survivors. We're thinking two living for every one dead. You guys are going to be in clover while the numbers go up again."

The light sheeting off the white veranda was irritating my eyes and the heat was an angry sentience. In spite of their irrelevance the details maggot-tickled my brain.

"Why didn't you take her?"

"Say again?"

"Talulla, in the desert. Why didn't you take her in then?"

Ellis's phone rang. He glanced at the number. Ignored it. "We would have," he said, "but another unit turned up. Regular WOCOP with one of the goddamned Directors on board. They didn't know what had gone down, obviously, no clue a civilian was involved, but they wanted us to get Alfonse's body out of there ASAP. Poulsom had gone back to surgi-tag Talulla, but beyond that there was nothing he could do on his own. The Director transferred to our chopper to fly Alfonse back to the Phoenix HQ. Poulsom had to leave her where she was and hightail it. We picked him up a mile from the highway."

"What do you mean 'surgi-tag'?"

"It's a bug," Ellis said. "A transmitter. 'Bout half the size of your pinkie nail. Surgically implanted. It's in her chest. Poulsom was curious about what effect the antivirus would have on her. I guess even then he had a hunch. The guy's uncanny with these things. Anyway, we lost her. We thought she must have died like all the others because for the longest time we got nothing. Then, two months back, *beep . . . beep . . . beep.* I wanted to bring her in right away but the vote was against me. Rumours were rife we had a mole ourselves. Climate of paranoia. One of Poulsom's guys had disappeared. The whole movement nearly collapsed. But we waited it out."

Actually I do still get a slight pain in my chest sometimes. As if there's a splinter in there. God, that tequila's gone to the tips of my toes. The thought of them knowing where we were the whole time, all the miles across the States, all my pointless caution, gave me a feeling now like sensual capitulation.

"Why didn't you tell me any of this when you came to see me at the Zetter? Or in Cornwall?"

He nodded, lips pursed and eyes lowered, as in admission of a weakness. "Fear and unpreparedness," he said. "Grainer was supposed to meet me that morning at the Zetter. We knew you'd start to wonder if Harley's cover was secure. The suits' thinking was the story of the French idiot needed reinforcing. Then at the last minute I got a call from the office say-ing Grainer was tied up with something and that I should go ahead on my own. To this day I don't know whether they were testing me. They could have bugged the room, or there was your escort, whatsername, Madeline, who for all I knew had been recruited. Anyway, I didn't like the setup and I wasn't going to put my head on the block. Too much riding on it."

"Madeline's not WOCOP, is she?" I asked, with a genuine feeling of fracture. Maddy not being what she seemed would be a uniquely dismal disappointment, the sort of thing that makes you say, Jesus, is *nothing* sacred?

"Pure civilian," Ellis said. "A nobody. Forget her."

Small mercies.

"Okay, but what about the stakeout in Cornwall?"

"That was just shit luck. I was literally just about to spill the beans to you when I got a message from the crew that two more vampires had been spotted. I had to go. FYI, we killed another three that night, but it *took* all night—and in the morning you hauled ass back to London before I had a chance to speak to you."

"You're not in charge of this, obviously," I said.

"Holy crap, no way. Wouldn't want the headache."

A transparent lie—we both knew he was on the path to remote supremacy—but I ignored it. "So who is?"

"Come on, Jake, that's classified. Why should you care?"

Madeline would have said: *Because I want the organ-grinder, not his monkey.*

"I'm not sure," I said. "Maybe it's because you seem to move back and forth between sounding deeply rational and completely insane."

He nodded. "It's a difficulty of manner," he said. "I'm oblique, they tell me. You know I'm an orphan, right?"

"No, I didn't."

"My mom left me in a Kmart in Los Angeles when I was less than a year old. I still dream of the place, a kind of blurry Christmas glitter."

His consciousness was like a lethal ocean undertow. Before you knew it you were in colder water, miles from shore. I stood up. "Enough shit," I said. "Just tell me what to do."

"Cool your heels, Jacob. Nothing, yet. Seventeen days to full moon. Grainer still wants the animal. As far as he knows you're off-radar. In a couple of weeks you'll contact him and lay it out. Revenge for Harley. You and him, winner takes all. Stick with your original site in the Welsh forest. We're set up for that. I'm leaving three guys with you in case the vamps pick up your trail, but keep your own wits about you, will you? Oh, and don't waste your money trying to buy her location off my boys. They don't know it. You're on a flight to London tonight. Here's a new phone and charger. You keep it clear 24/7. The only person ringing you on it will be me. For the time being you just go home and sit tight."

"That's it?"

"That's it. Trust me, Jake, everything's going to be fine. We're both going to come out of this winners."

His own phone rang again. This time he answered, said, "Go," then paused for a moment before holding it out to me. "Here," he said. "Talk to your lady."

48

THE SKY SUFFERED a particle surge, briefly went a deeper blue. Sweat bloomed in my palm as I took the phone.

"Lu?"

"Jake?"

"Are you all right?"

"I'm okay. Where are you?"

"You're not hurt? They haven't hurt you?"

"No, I'm not hurt."

"Don't be afraid. I'm going to get you out. Everything's going to be okay."

"Where are you?"

"I'm at the villa still. You don't know where you are?" I could sense Ellis peripherally with the face saying, Come on, Jake, don't be silly.

"I don't know. I think I was on a plane. It's like a hospital. There's a doctor here, or a least a guy dressed as a doctor."

"What have they done to you?"

"Nothing. Took a blood sample, a urine sample. Everyone's very solicitous."

"Lu, listen. They're going to keep you for seventeen days. I'll be able to talk to you on and off—" I looked at Ellis. Not very often, his face said. "But just sit tight. I'm going to get you out, okay?"

There was a pause in which I felt, like a sudden drop in temperature, how afraid she was. "Promise?" she said.

I had to swallow. And turn away from Ellis. "I promise. I'm going to get you out. Just wait for me."

"Okay, I'll try."

"They want me to—" The line went dead.

I spun on Ellis. "Jesus fucking *Christ,* get her back. Get her back *right now.*"

"Jake, Jake, calm down. Calm *down*. You know the way these things work. You've spoken to her. You've established it's your woman. You know she's okay. I promise you nothing's going to happen to her. I've seen the room she's being held in and you know what? It's *nice*. She's got a TV and a comfortable bed and her own little bathroom with a shower and everything right there. So seriously, stop fretting."

He reached out for the phone but I held on to it. Her voice had come through it, felt still there in my hand.

"Come on now, Jacob. Don't be an ass."

I gave him back the phone. "You listen to me," I said. "I'm not doing anything for you until I've seen her. Understand? With my own eyes, in the flesh. I see her *in person* or you get dick. Nonnegotiable."

Ellis got to his feet. Looked at me curiously for a moment, then turned and rested his hands on the veranda's rail, looking out over the red roofs and white boats to the shimmering blue of the Ionian. "Jake," he said. "You're in love with her, aren't you?"

I didn't answer him. My head throbbed. A smell of raw fish came up from the village. A Jet Ski thumped across the bay. I was aware of having done something stupid.

"It's okay," he said. "It's cool. I'm intrigued. I mean you've been around for two hundred years. I'm assuming the Death of the Heart at some point. The End of Love. I'm assuming decades of emotional . . . What's the French word? *Longueurs*. Look at that, I surprise myself. Decades of *longueurs*, then suddenly ζammo, this, love again."

His tone hadn't changed much, but it had changed enough. I remained silent. The sun and the heat like a million spider bites.

"Don't make me make them do anything," Ellis said, quietly. "With sulphuric acid or anything. On her leg or someplace."

"Please," I said—but he held up his hand.

"You don't have sufficient power to dictate terms, Jake," he said. "I understand the impulse, but you're not, you know, congruent with reality."

The leg or someplace. Someplace is somewhere else, her face or breasts or between her legs. Acid makes a sound like a sigh of relief or ecstasy. It would heal but it would hurt so much and they can just keep doing it and this is the possibility you sign up for with love as Arabella had signed up and said, It's you it's *you,* so of course this would be the long-winded justice but not Talulla just me not her just do whatever it is to me.

"You'll get to talk to her again," Ellis said. "And we can discuss you seeing her once—*maybe*—before you do your part. But Jake, seriously, come into line with things, you know? The tone, man. The *tone*'s all wrong."

In films a soldier looks down between his feet and sees he's millimetres from a mine. He looks farther. Mines everywhere. From now on every step is a matter of life and death.

"Okay," I said. "You're right. Emotions. I understand. But can I just make a suggestion, an observation?"

"Of course. Shoot."

"You don't need to do this. You don't need to keep her. Let me explain. In fact let me ask you a question: Why was Harley killed?"

"To get you riled up," Ellis said. "Although between you and me I thought we'd have done better to hold him, alive, until you were willing to play ball."

"Exactly. Harley was killed because you knew I needed an incentive to make a fight of it. And you were right. A month ago I'd had enough. A month ago I didn't *want* to live." He was already nodding, slowly, with a smile. "Now everything's different. Now I have her. I'll kill Grainer anyway, with satisfaction and relief, because as long as he's alive he's a threat to the woman I love."

The smile wasn't just advance comprehension. It was the recognition of a fellow strategist. "That's nice again, Jake," he said. "The logic's sound. I like it. And for what it's worth I believe you. But you know it's not going to fly. Aside from the fact that it's still just you trying to negotiate a concession we have zero reason to make, it's not even my call. As I said, I'm not running this."

Silence. Mentally the equivalent of someone trapped in a room repeatedly trying the doors he already knows are locked. Blood and urine. Why? Everyone's very solicitous. Solicitous captors worse than brutal ones in the long run. We know this. She knew it. It had been in her voice.

For what seemed a long time Ellis and I stood without speaking, him looking out into the blue-silver bay, me with my face and wrists and fingers full of useless life. He had the air of a man thinking sentimental thoughts. Engendered, perhaps, by the memory of being abandoned in a Kmart. Then he turned to me and stretched out his hand. Sunlight blazed in his white-blond hair. "So," he said. "Do we have a deal?"

49

THERE WAS NO talking him out of the three-goon bodyguard but I managed to get a break on London quarters: After a low-voiced call to whoever was running the show it was agreed I could hole up at Harley's place in Earl's Court—and thus, after passing through the first hours of pointless incredulity, I've spent thirteen of the seventeen days confined here, brought takeout food by the agents (a fourth drafted in for rooftop duty when the attic skylights were discovered), working my way through Harley's whisky, bringing this journal up to date and living for the rationed phone contact with Talulla.

"Half the problem's boredom," she said, yesterday. "You know what the other half is." Three-quarters into the lunation she, like me, had stopped eating. I'd told Ellis she'd need cigarettes, booze, water, and he'd promised me, apparently in good faith, to make sure she got them. But a higher authority had intervened. Poulsom, I inferred, the sound of whom I liked less and less. Water, yes, but no alcohol, no nicotine. Instead she was offered sleeping pills and muscle relaxants, which, after two nights on the Hunger's rack, she'd accepted. Aside from the loss of her liberty this was, according to her, the first hardship she'd suffered in their custody. (Unless one counted kidney ultrasounds, of which she'd had three. Poulsom suspected stones.) She'd had the situation explained to her (by Ellis, whom she said treated her with a sort of ludicrous medieval politesse), understood there was no (avowed) intention to harm her, and that as soon as I'd delivered on my part of the deal she'd be released. Aside from the ultimate question of whether either of us would make it through this alive was the nearer mystery of what they were going to do with her come full moon.

"Poulsom says they've got it covered," she told me. "Whatever that means." False uncertainty. We knew what it meant. Either they were going to kill her or they were going to restrain her or they were going to put her in a cage with a live victim—and most likely record the spectacle for the breakaway WOCOP archives.

"Anyway, they're taking care of me," she said. "I've got Luxury Bath and Shower Gel from Harrods and a brand-new set of enormous white towels. Also a hundred-plus TV channels. I'm now an aficionado of *East-Enders* and *Coronation Street* and—"

The line went dead. Sudden amputation lest we forget who's in charge, lest we forget by whose grace we live, lest we forget there's a job to be done.

To deal with the obvious matter first. Ellis has no intention of letting Talulla go. And if he does, Poulsom doesn't. Assuming there's a genuine agenda to kick-start a new lycanthropic generation (and this I *can* believe), the science is in its infancy. Talulla survived the bite and—courtesy of the antivirus, apparently—Turned. Very well. But the big question, by Ellis's own admission, is whether she can Turn victims of her own. And *that* question will be tackled in the laboratory. Poulsom et al. aren't going to release her into the field when they can feed her test victims in a controlled environment.

Which means—try not to laugh—Me Rescuing Her.

Which in turn means either gangbusting her out by force or smuggling her out by guile. Sliced any way, it means me finding out where the fuck they're holding her.

Enter: money. This is where money comes in. Thanks to the recent boom in military subcontractors one can, with sufficient resources, buy one's own little army. (As is now widely known, the Bush administration bought one—Blackwater—and sprinkled it just above the law all over Iraq.) My resources are sufficient—but still, *I don't know where they're holding her.*

There is one infallible way of finding out.

Meanwhile my life here is a dentist's waiting room. A rhythm soon established itself: dayshift agents handing over to night, evenings in the library, jagged bits of sleep, raw-eyed mornings, the shift change, the daylight hours of pacing or lying on the couch. Harley never had a TV, so I can't keep my love company in Soapland, but of course I'm surrounded by books. This afternoon I leafed through a 1607 Dutch-German edition of Ovid's *Metamorphoses* illustrated by Crispijn de Passe. Market value, according to a 2006 index, eight thousand pounds. I have no idea what Harley intended for the collection, whether he'd made a will, what'll happen to the place now he's gone. Not that the world has a clue he's gone. Grainer & Co. have seen to the cover-up of his murder (God only knows what became of the severed head in the Vectra's boot) though it can only be a matter of time before a utility company or Council Tax office starts chasing a payment. Harls had no living relatives. There's a solicitor in Holborn, but since I've no intention of getting involved in a homicide investigation there's little point in contacting him. Instead I wear my deceased friend's clothes and drink his supply and pass the tight-wound time with his books. Of late I've found myself leaning, at idle moments, on his bone-handled cane.

I have little truck with my minders, who've been schooled to keep shtoom, and in any case I'm not disposed to chat. A few words exchanged with the arrival of cigarettes or firewood, but otherwise I remain mute and they talk among themselves, quietly, over their headsets. There's a man stationed on every floor. The miserable roof detail rotates, since no one wants it. I've offered to take a turn myself (the Hunger with no fresh air is a soft close hell) but no dice. Sorry, chief, can't be done. This is Russell, the one responsible for lopping off Laura Mangiardi's head back in Cornwall, who has an appealing liveliness and who is by now so bored that he *would* talk to me if I didn't keep making it obvious that I wished to be left alone. Instead he smokes and does Sudoku and thinks up wretched jokes with which he torments his fellows—What do you call a small robot vampire? Nosferatu-D2—and strips and cleans and reassembles his personal arsenal two or three times a day. The team's firepower is a mix of conventional automatic hardware and antivamp kit: night-vision goggles, long- and short-range Stakers, UV sticks, a miniature version of the Hail Mary for whoever's on the roof. Russell packs a small flamethrower, too, though I recall Harley telling me most Hunters regarded even the compact versions of these units—"boochie-burners" ("BBs" for short)—as obsolete. Thanks to Sigourney Weaver's turn in *Alien* there had been a revival in the eighties, but the hard maths of weight-to-efficacy had soon reasserted itself, and now they were seen as an affectation. In any case young Russell wears one from time to time, and is wearily mocked for it by his compadres. With all this equipment dedicated to my protection I ought to feel safe. I don't.

Outside, London goes about its business like a virile degenerate old man. By the fire's light I sit in the window seat with a straight Macallan (two bottles remain from a case of twelve) and a Camel, watching the traffic—sudden halts and surges like blood through a complex valve— and the self-involved comings and goings of humans. As always most are full of energy, riddled with their own details, asimmer with schemes and regrets, fears, secrets, hungers, sins. Occasionally love. A very young dark-haired couple came out of a deli, not dreamily or holding hands or in any way obviously rapt but deep in conversation and glimmering with the shared wealth of each other. My in-love heart tautened to see it. In love. Oh, indeed I have the condition. Verily, reader, I am fully, absurdly sick. Life, grinning like a great white, is enjoying the joke: Years of incrementally getting ready for death and now all he wants is life. Come on, Jake, you've got to laugh.

I can't. Not with my in-love heart on perpetual pleading duty, inwardly audible at every gap in my self-distraction: *Please . . . Please . . . Please . . .* There are specifics—please don't let them hurt her; please let me see her again; please let me find out where they're holding her—but this pleading is an emotional whole greater than the sum of its parts, addressed to the God who isn't there, to the benignly indifferent universe, to the spirit of Story, who we know these days has a soft spot for the dark ending. *Please . . . Please . . . Please . . .*

My inner dead are asleep, sleeping very badly, dreaming of release. Love, it appears, has the power to force them under. They toss and turn. Their murmur builds, threatens a swarm into wakefulness, dies back. Love's crude spell holds them down, just. Arabella's ghost endures in seared wakefulness, knowing something's over. I keep turning away from her. I keep turning my face away. For the first time in a hundred and sixty-seven years a hundred and sixty-seven years ago doesn't seem like yesterday. For the first time in a hundred and sixty-seven years the present matters more than the past.

It's seemed, these thirteen days, that I've left real time behind, drifted into a suspension or loop where seconds bulge and minutes warp, taking their normal shape only when I hear Talulla's voice on the phone.

•

It's seemed. Until a couple of hours ago. Ellis has been.

I was pouring myself a drink when the library door opened and he entered, smelling of wet London. He had a painful-looking stye on his left eye and was wearing an excess of ChapStick. The effect was of a creepily humanised waxwork. "Wouldn't mind keeping you company with one of those, Jake," he said, before taking the armchair opposite the couch, which received him with a leather gasp. "It's miserable out there." I poured a second Scotch and handed it to him, suppressing a shudder when our fingertips met at the glass. "Jiminy," he said, after slug and lip-smack. "That's better."

The impulse to do violence to the man was powerful, reflexive and held absolutely—Talulla on her bunk, eyes wide in the TV light, trying to see through the wall, the night, the unknown miles, to me—in check. I put another log on the fire, pokered it a bit, pointlessly, then sat down on the couch, facing him. Obedience. You keep her alive with obedience.

"Okay," he said. "Operational instructions. Two days from now, on Wednesday morning at nine a.m. precisely you ring the WOCOP office in Marylebone on this—here: It's a completely clean phone with a trace blocker. Don't mix it up with the other one. Grainer will be at the office. You won't get him, obviously, you'll get the usual bullshit from whoever's on reception. You tell them to give Grainer the message to call you on the clean number in one hour, then you hang up. Grainer will call."

"How do you know?"

"Jeez, Jacob, just *listen,* will you? He'll call because you're all he fuck-ing *thinks* about. You think I'm making this up as I go along?"

"Okay, okay."

"I'm under pressure, dude."

"Okay. I'm sorry."

He closed his eyes for a moment. Held the heel of his hand against the stye. "When he calls you, you set the meet. Full moon's Friday, moonrise 18:07. This you know, obviously. Don't let him change the location. Wales. Your forest, okay? We're set up for that. You head out for the Pyrenees or someplace and we're screwed. Got it?"

"Got it. When do I see Talulla?"

No reply. The blood drained from my scalp. My knees and hands were adrenaline-rich, giddily ready to do something. There was nothing I could do. "I have to see her," I said. Then added, with no need to pretend careful desperation, "Please. For God's sake."

Ellis exhaled, heavily. The brightness, the look of heightened sensuality, was, I now saw, exhaustion. I hadn't realised he was so near the edge. "Oy, Jake," he said, shaking his head, like a benevolent rabbi I'd disappointed with my weak will. "Impatience. Seriously. I know this is hard for you . . ." He glazed over. Drifted a moment. Went through something in his impenetrable interior . . . "Actually I *do* know this is hard for you. I'm sorry. I'm not using my imagination. That was my New Year's resolution, you know. Work on standing in the other fellow's shoes. That and to read one poem every day."

The feel of the poker I'd used was still phantomly there in my hand. Perfect for splintering a human skull. I didn't move.

"Okay, listen," he said. "The hotel you stayed at in Caernarfon, the Castle Hotel. You're booked in there Thursday night. Same room. The room that overlooks the street. You get there Thursday and wait for my call. You stay in the room. You don't go anywhere or see anyone. No hookers, nothing."

Again I thought of Maddy—or Poor Maddy, as she's become in my lately sentimentalised memory, her terrible comprehension (and flawed denial) when Grainer had said, He's a werewolf, honey. On the back of which flashback something suddenly nagged—but I had no time for it.

"You'll bring her to the room?" I said.

"No, Jake, we won't bring her to the room. You just check in and wait."

"Don't fuck with me, Ellis. Seriously. I'm not—" I stopped. Ellis sat very still, the awful long-fingered white hands at rest on his knees. "Sorry," I said. "Sorry. The feelings. God dammit."

He rolled his head on his neck a couple of times, easing tension. I held my tongue between my teeth. To my good fortune Russell appeared in the doorway. Ellis looked up.

"Land Rover went past again, sir," Russell said. "You told us to let you know."

"Okay," Ellis said. "Get a trace on the plate. It's probably nothing."

"On it, boss."

"And tell Chris I'm coming out, will you?"

"Roger that."

"What Land Rover?" I asked, after Russell had gone.

"It's nothing," Ellis said. "Been seen twice. Now three times. Probably just a local resident. These guys are getting bored." He swallowed the last sip of his drink and leaned back in the chair, for a moment turned his face to the fire and watched the buckle and snap of the flames in the hearth. "We'll do a slow drive-by, Jake. You'll see her. You'll talk to her on the phone. That's it. Don't push it. This is a favour. This is goodwill. In lieu of future cooperation."

"I understand. But Ellis?"

He looked at me.

"I want to level with you about something."

The blond eyebrows raised. Eyes lapis lazuli buttons. "You do?"

"Yes. Listen, and don't flip out: I know they're not going to release Talulla. Wait——" when he opened his mouth to protest. "Wait. Hear me out. Don't say anything till I've finished. You and I both know the egg-heads want her in the lab. I'm buying that you want werewolves back, but not that people like Poulsom are going to take their chances with natural selection. I know the odds are I'll never see her again, even if I survive Grainer—unless you take me in too. Look, for all I know that's the plan anyway. I off Grainer for you and your boys are waiting with tranqs and a cage. In which case fine. In which case go ahead. If the only way I get to live out my days with Talulla is as her fellow lab rat then so be it. I'd rather share her fate than live without her. Now you can laugh if you want to."

He didn't laugh, but the eyebrows were a long time coming down. Eventually, he smiled. "I'll tell you what, Jake," he said. "I like you. I really do. You've got the clarity. So many of the fuckers I deal with are just blundering around in a *fog*." He shrugged. "Of course you're right. They want to keep her until they know transmission really works. They want to get the numbers up to fifty in captivity, then everyone gets out and the game begins again. Frankly, I don't know why they bothered trying to sell you anything else. I was against it. Won't be like that when—" He stopped himself. *Almost* blushed. *When I'm in charge,* he'd been going to say.

"And me?" I said. "What's supposed to happen?"

"They want you, too, of course, if we can get you in safely."

"Then *get* me in safely, will you?"

He stared at me with what looked like collusive delight. "That I can promise you, Jake. You have my word on it."

Operationally there wasn't much to go over. I'd given him the Beddgelert location soon after arriving here and he'd prepared an Ordnance Survey map showing a half-mile radius around the spot where, a hundred and sixty-seven years ago, my life as a werewolf began. I was to stay within it. The bodyguard wasn't going with me to Wales. Ellis thought there was a good chance Grainer would put surveillance of his own in the area once I'd made the call: A glimpse (or word) of me in the company of WOCOP personnel and he'd know something was afoot. The climate of paranoia was extreme. Therefore Thursday morning a private car would pick me up and drive me, alone, directly to Caernarfon. Yes, I'd be exposed for a few hours at the hotel, but it was unavoidable. Ellis himself would be with Grainer.

"He'll want you there?" I asked.

"He's always said I'd be with him. I think he wants a witness. You have to understand, this is his whole life. The culmination."

Mentally there was much going on. Chiefly file-rifling for who I'd need to contact and how to move the requisite fees fast, whether I'd be able to get past the phone and room taps at the Castle, but also stubborn currents of doubt that Ellis really had it in him to murder his mentor. Pointless currents of doubt. There was no other way to get to Talulla.

"Here's the Marylebone office number," Ellis said. "Wednesday, nine a.m. Okay?"

"Okay."

50

THE BLOOD ON these pages is mine.

He turned for the door.

"Ellis?"

"Yeah?"

"Is she really all right? I mean, no one's done anything to her?"

He looked at me again. For a moment all veils fell and I could see what he really thought: that I'd been weakened, that in some fundamental way I'd let him down. As of course had Grainer. As of course had his mother before that. He was, I now realised, the most singularly alone human being I'd ever encountered. In the purified moment between us I saw his future, the rise to despotism, isolation, eventual madness, most likely suicide. All without love. We both saw it. And as if the universe was invested in proving there was no end to the perverseness of the heart (even the werewolf heart), I felt a flicker of pity for him. He felt it too—and in a reflex of terror shut it out.

"She's fine, Jake," he said. "She's cool. I promise you. Stop worrying. You okay for supplies here?"

•

It's three in the morning. The night-shift boys are at the nadir of their boredom. The fire in the hearth is low, hissed into occasionally by rain coming down the chimney. For days now I've been circling my predicament—our predicament, mine and Talulla's—trying to will a better way out of it. There isn't one. It's a relief to accept it, finally. In thirty hours, with a prayer to the God who isn't there, I'll make the call to the Marylebone office.

51

THIS MIGHT BE the last I write. If it is, I hope whoever finds this journal carries out my final wish (see inside front cover) and gets it to you, angel.

On Wednesday morning I made the call. Got the call back, from Grainer himself. The trick, I'd decided, was not to oversell it.

"Jacob," he said. "I'm aghast."

"I don't want a conversation," I said. "Friday moonrise. Have you got a pen and paper? Beddgelert forest, Snowdonia. OS Grid SH578488. You get what you wanted."

"All things considered," he said, "it's really the only fitting—"

I hung up.

The day was a churning and excessively detailed nightmare. It rained, continuously, cold skirls blown and dashed by an icy wind. Brollies dislocated. Car headlamps came on. A drain in Earl's Court Road blocked and made an iridescent black lake. The Hunger was a long-nailed hand raking my insides from gullet to anus. Desire, too. Oh, yes. Plans to hatch and a lovesick heart to comfort were matters of indifference to the pre-Curse libido, which, having reached apotheosis with Talulla last full moon was making it clear it would never again settle for less. I had to watch the booze, too, though by Wednesday evening the last of Harley's Macallan was gone. Diminishing anaesthetic returns. I hadn't left these rooms for more than two weeks. Perhaps a little craziness was setting in, but I was convinced I could feel Lula reaching out telepathically. Maddeningly just on the edge of clarity. I'd asked Ellis to let her call me but he'd claimed it was out of his hands. Said he'd stuck his neck out as it was to get me the drive-by.

My own phone had been confiscated and Harley's disconnected. I had no doubt the two I now had from Ellis were bugged and alarmed, but it was a ticklish trial to resist taking the chance. Every hour was an hour I could have spent getting the mercenary ball rolling. As it was I'd have to find a way of getting a clean line out from the Castle Hotel, which would be my only chance to act unwatched. I've had moral offsetting recourse to hired guns before. I used them against the Fascists in Spain, the Nazis in occupied France, the Khmer Rouge in Cambodia, the death squads in El Salvador, most recently against government forces and Janjaweed militia in Darfur—and in every instance absolutely *nothing* moves without money. A lot, up front. I have half a dozen SCOAs (Security Codes Only Accounts) in Swiss banks but even with my access and contacts setting up an operation in less than twelve hours would be a trip to the border of insanity. But it was all I had. I'd never see Talulla again without getting into WOCOP myself, and I'd never spring us without professional help from outside.

The vampires had other ideas.

Just after midnight I heard Russell outside the library door saying: "Andy? You reading me?" Pause. "Andy, come back." Pause. Then loudly: "Andrew, put your twatting headset back on."

Nothing.

"What's going on?" I said.

Russell put his head round the door. "Sit tight in here," he said. Then into his com: "Chris, I'm not getting anything from Andy. Go up there and check, will you?"

Andy was on roof duty. Chris on the floor immediately below him. Russell was on the library level with me, and fourth man Wazz (I hadn't enquired into derivation) patrolled the ground floor. "Wazz? You copy all that? Yeah. Look lively."

I'd got up from the couch and was about to advise being given a weapon just in case, when what happened next happened.

Very fast.

A (literally) staggering stink of boochie. Clamped salivary glands and the surge of nausea. One foot came off the floor for a moment while the room tilted. I found myself back on the couch. My vision clouded. Someone upstairs screamed.

When my sight returned I saw Russell in profile through the library's open doorway. He was looking at something out of shot and his face was the face of a child in deep distress. In an admirable testament to Hunt training his hands were doing what they'd been drilled to do and searching his belt for optimal weaponry. I saw his fingers close on a UV stick and begin to draw it out—before the sound of flesh and bone rupturing followed a split-second later by a spray of blood that covered his face and chest stopped him. He groped, blinded, managed to get the UV stick out—then jerked and dropped it, undetonated, both hands ascending with a strange slow grace to his throat, where what was unmistakably one of the Hunt's own wooden stakes had buried itself.

Flung or fired by whatever was coming along the landing towards him. He went with what looked like deliberate slowness down onto his knees, eyes wide, mouth open, trying and failing to swallow, *khah . . . khah . . . khah.*

The black vampire from Heathrow appeared on the landing. Seductively calm long face suggestive of immense patience and capability. In his left hand he held a Hunt Staker, lately discharged. With his right he dragged the body of Chris, the second-floor man, by its spinal column, which had been yanked through the abdomen and ribs. In with the stench of vampire I caught a poignant whiff of shit from the gashed human bowels.

Two rapid computations. First, that only Wazz downstairs remained alive. Second, that only a dozen paces stood between me and capture.

The library had a second door connecting to a bedroom, from which another exit took you back to the landing. The question (posed in the distended dreamscape of perhaps two seconds, while the vampire dropped Chris's corpse, moseyed over to kneeling Russell and took the young man's skull gently between his hands) was which door to go for.

A person steps into the road, turns, sees a truck about to hit him, seems to freeze. The freezing is the amazingly quick brain making its honourable start on the avoidance mathematics, the geometry of *getting out of the way*. And even the amazingly quick brain is too slow. The first trajectory calculations are barely—BAM! Good night.

Ditto here. I was still in the early trigonometry when the vampire with a deft twist snapped Russell's neck, turned and launched himself at me.

One finds oneself flying through the air. That's quite something. Time stretches to accommodate peripheral details: my foully smouldering Camel abandoned in the onyx ashtray; the empty Macallan bottle on the floor; a signed first edition of *American Psycho* one of the agents had brought up from the contemporary collection downstairs; the bellows I gave Harley for Christmas twenty years ago.

Nearer details were regrettably vivid too: the vamp's dark eyes with whites tinctured brown, his bad meat odour and long calm face, the feel of his cold left hand around my throat (a nail had already drawn blood) and his cold right in a grab that pinched the flesh of my chest through my clothes. Overwhelmingly the power discrepancy. Overwhelmingly his being able, now that he had hold of me and we were flying through the air, to do pretty much whatever he wanted.

Not that revulsion wasn't mutual. His face's calm was forced. *The werewolf,* a vampire has written, *smells like the Platonic form of a filthy animal.* I wondered—as I had such liberty for wondering, while we sailed across the library—if vampires ever threw up. Throw up what, though? All they had was blood. Harley would have known. (Poor Harls. He hadn't much liked *American Psycho*. Savage satirist or twisted fuck? he'd asked me, when he'd finished it. Both, I'd said. It's a false dichotomy. The romantic days of *either/or* are over. Who'd know that if not me?)

As one we crashed into the chimney breast and fell, just to the right of the hearth. Something brittle snapped under me. *My spine,* I thought, since the vertebrae had taken the brunt of impact—but in the moment it took him to slash four fingers across my face (white heat, blood welling in my left eye as if half the world were having a red cocktail poured into it) I knew both that it wasn't a bone and that it was my only chance of escape.

We'd ended up with me propped at an angle against the wall, him sitting astride my thighs. His face had a sprinkle of dark skin-tags or moles (that in a genuine horror evocation brought Lula's fair torso with its beloved beauty-spot constellations) and a likeable outcurve from nose to top lip. Black typecasting would have him as nirvanic drug lord or philosophising janitor. He put his hand over my face and I writhed as if trying to get out from under him—in fact trying to get hold of the thing that had snapped under my back.

I wasn't, quite, quick enough. Before I could make my move—my one move, my first and last and only resort—his other hand had torn through my shirt, executed a deep screw manoeuvre into the flesh of my chest and come away with a bloody gobbet of pectoral muscle, hardly Shylock's pound but more than enough to take my scream (for a moment I thought my poor *nipple* had gone) to the comedy edge of falsetto.

It probably worked in my favour, that scream, pleasurably diverted enough of his concentration so that my wriggling under him played as just more futile struggling. I'll never know. Because having at last got proper purchase on the top half of Harley's bone-handled walking stick, which had been left propped against the wall when I'd poured the first of the day's drinks, and had snapped under me when we fell, I whipped it out from behind my back and with a blurred prayer to the God who wasn't there drove it with all my strength into the vampire's heart.

As at all such moments the prosaic din of things subsided out of respect for the magnitude of our event. Time paused and space solidified around us. For a moment we were figures in a paperweight. He managed a look of nude surprise—a sudden, a cartoon change of expression, as if he were exaggerating for the benefit of a child—when he lifted his hands to see their veins blackening as if hurriedly filling with ink. What he couldn't see was the same phenomenon at work in his neck and face, the blood vessels showing as a darkening web, the magical roadmap of his death. He stiffened, paralysed first by incredulity, second more literally by . . . well, paralysis. I jerked my hips up, swiped, knocked him off me. He went over with a lightweight or taxidermed rigidity onto his side, knees bent at ninety degrees, hands fixed as if readying an invisible basketball for a shot. His eyes closed.

I got to my feet. The face and chest wounds were burning. Obviously I'd heal, but the pain was determined to show its stuff while it could.

However. This was a chance. Russell & Co. all had mobiles. I'd just doubled the time I had to set up a rescue. (There remained the question of how, once inside the renegade WOCOP facility, I was going to let my guys know where that facility *was,* but again, since there was nothing to do but trust I'd find a way, that's what I did, wondering, with haggard realism, whether mobile phones were small enough these days that I might conceal one up my arse.) I hurried out onto the landing.

Cold air and the sound of heavy rain came down from the floor above.

The boochie must have taken out roof-man, Andy, and got in through the skylights—whereupon I remembered young red-haired Wazz, as yet unaccounted for, who'd been on watch on the ground floor. If he was alive he'd be on a hair trigger. I didn't want him shooting me by mistake. Also, depressingly, I'd have to kill him if I was going to take full advantage of the phones.

I stepped over Russell and Chris's remains and took a cautious peep over the banister. Blood crept down my face like the hot tears of childhood.

"Is this what you're looking for?" a female voice said.

I spun left. The blond vampire, Mia, stood on the landing maybe fifteen feet away. The bottom half of her face was covered in blood in just the supposedly endearing way a Kodak toddler's is covered in chocolate (or a scat star's in shit, I always think every time I see one of these revolting infants) and in her hand she held the raggedly severed head of the unfortunate Wazz. His tongue protruded lewdly from between his lips and his eyeballs had rolled back in their sockets. He looked as if he'd died just as he was about to blow a halfhearted raspberry, to express extreme tedium.

Mia, on the other hand, in black boots, black suede skirt, black nylons, black satin blouse and black leather jacket, appeared superabundantly alive, smiling through the blood mask. Her blue eyes—not the dark lapis lazuli of Ellis's but somewhere between periwinkle and turquoise—glittered with what looked like joy. A vein in her temple showed. She was white, even by vampiric standards. From her name and the company she'd been in at Jacqui Delon's I'd made her Italian, but now that I mentally replayed *Is this what you're looking for?* the accent, though elusively mixed, put her roots a long way east of Trieste. A Russian with Norse colouring—but why not? Scandinavian marauders sailed down the Volga and took charge of Novgorod more than a thousand years ago. For all I knew she'd been there when the Vikings raided Constantinople.

All of which redundant speculation laboured under the perceptual paradox of a beautiful woman exuding a smell of decomposing meat and ripest pigshit. Initially her teammate's odour—less faecal but gamier—had obscured hers. Now I got it clear and unmingled. I sank to my knees, put a hand out to stop myself from complete collapse, slipped in Russell's lake of blood and fell facedown next to his corpse.

There was very little time. No time, really. Any moment now she'd drop Wazz's head and be upon me. Any moment now it would already have happened.

Nonetheless I'd made certain calculations. (Whatever is happening, something else is going on.) Russell had ended up on his front with his right arm trapped under him. That put most of the kit—including the UV stick he still had in his hand—out of reach. The Staker's holster was empty, the Staker itself lay five feet away in the library doorway. Getting at the *stake*, still buried in his throat, would require three seconds more than the one I'd actually have from the moment I made my move. The only weapon within reach was the flamethrower, and I wasn't sure how to—

I heard the head drop and felt the air shift. She Is Coming. Hopeless hopeless hopeless but I rolled and plucked at the BBs' gun-unit holstered at Russell's thigh—not fast enough. Her boot heel gouged a divot from the side of my skull as she went past in a blur. I collapsed a second time.

Stay put.

Not only because the blow, a rude and deafening *bok,* had dazed me but because the position concealed my Braille navigation of the flamethrower. She hadn't seen that. Didn't know the weapon was there. What I needed from her now was the Bond villain's soliloquising delay. I wasn't going to get it. She was here to kidnap, not to kill.

"Uhhhr," I said, not entirely faking. The head gouge was in the transitional stage between very cold and very hot. The wound in my chest was a rose of fire. I opened my eyes to see her descending gently to the floor. Flier. Fuck. Closed them again. Forced nimbleness into my fingertips. *It's basically a glorified water pistol,* Harley had said, knowing not whereof he spoke. Two triggers, one for fuel release, one for ignition. Ergo I'd need both hands. The odds had just worsened.

"Phil?" Mia said.

Flying over me she'd passed the library doorway. Peripherally registered its lone occupant. She hadn't known.

Two-thirds out of the holster.

She stood with her feet apart and an ugly hang to her limbs, face slack, staring at the crisping corpse by the hearth. Rain was a continuous exhalation against the house.

The weapon's nozzle was caught on something, I couldn't tell what. Talulla's voice said quietly in my head: You're running out of time.

Closing my eyes would've helped my fingers but Mia turned in the doorway and looked at me. "You?" she asked. I opened my mouth to lie but she said: "Don't bother." In the brighter light of the library her face's colours vivified: red; blue; white. Very calmly she bent—one nyloned knee ticked, humanising her—and picked up the Staker that lay by her feet.

"You want me alive, don't forget," I said. She stood over me. I looked up at her. Here was the submissive's camera angle of choice for his dominatrix, the perspective all boot and thigh and hip narrowing to the remote worshipful contemptuous head like a mountaintop divinity. I took a breath for reiteration—and she shot a stake through my left leg.

Pain, yes, sheet lightning, but also a peculiarly schoolboyish sense of injustice. She'd clipped the femur but not broken it, gone instead at an angle through the quadrilateral and vastus externus. No major arteries, but the sciatic nerve violently wronged already playing the *Psycho* shower scene strings in shock, a sensation that went all the way up to my molars.

Paltry vandalism as far as her ladyship was concerned. Something to keep me busy while she, tossing the Staker downstairs and turning with an expression testifying to the effect of *my* odour on *her,* took out a mobile and dialled. "It's me," she said. "I've got him." Pause. "Phil's dead."

I wrapped my left hand around the stake, bit down on Russell's leather elbow guard, pulled. One wonders why grimacing's a reflex, since it can't possibly help. In any case a few Popeye gurns and gurgles later I got the bastard thing out. No blood-spurt but a fart or squelch from the wound. The sciatic nerve was heartbroken, unable to do anything to comfort itself except sob. I lay, groaning, now practically on top of the Hunter's body—and straight back to concealed woozy frantic work on the stuck flamethrower.

"Bring the van," Mia said. She'd taken a few paces away and was now, with her back to me, searching her skirt pocket for something.

The weapon came free of the holster.

"Nothing serious," she said into the phone. Having extracted from her pocket a white handkerchief she held it up to her nose. Her next utterance was muffled. "Four of them." Pause. "What do you think?"

The little fuel unit in its bulletproof case remained strapped to Russell's back. No time to get that off. Whatever I was going to do I'd have to do from where I was. Very well. Kneeling, I lifted the gun unit and hit both triggers.

Nothing happened. Or rather, the thing I wanted to happen—the throwing of flame—didn't. What happened was that a quantity of unignited fuel squirted out of the nozzle and spattered the back of her leather jacket. Not surprisingly, she turned to face me.

I looked down at the weapon as if it were a child of my own who'd turned me in. Then I looked at Mia. The moment I had before she came at me again was courtesy first of her surprise and second of her embarrassment: She'd got cocky, turned her back. If Don Mangiardi had seen this . . . Shame enriched her. The white skin didn't blush, but the access of professional guilt sensitised it. Her stink deepened.

Meanwhile I fumbled mentally with a handful of engineering components and a sketchy cross section: fuel hose, gas pipe, fuel-release trigger, valve plug, ignition trigger, spark plug, battery, ignition valve.

Ignition valve. Lets compressed gas into the business end of the gun where it mixes with air and fuel released through small holes in the nozzle. Unopened, there's nothing for the ignition trigger to ignite.

I opened the valve.

She was in midair when the flame-jet caught her, spectacularly, in the chest. Momentum kept her coming but I held the triggers down. She veered and crashed into the library doorway—oddly silent. Fat heat filled the landing's space. My face felt tight-skinned. I released for a second. She scrabbled and thrashed like a short-circuiting robot, threw herself backwards into the library. I hit the triggers again. Her arms flung petals of flame. She got airborne, jackknifed, dropped to the floor. A bookcase was on fire. So was the couch. I'd taken the hose to full stretch from the tanks on Russell's back but she was still, just, in range. I released and fired again, the dregs of the fuel, I could tell. The smoke alarms went off. Into perhaps the last margin of her strength, she launched herself straight at the window, crashed through it and disappeared, upwards.

Fire was thriving in the bookcase, living it up on the couch. The room was a box of priceless kindling.

Sorry, Harls.

No time for elegy, however. The couch's conflagration had spread to the rug, where my journal (this journal, dear reader, dear finder and I pray honourer of the dead) lay within a hand's span of the flames. I leaped in, snatched it, leaped out again. A quick frisk of Russell's carcase yielded his phone. Ditto headless Wazz's after I'd more or less fallen down the stairs. I grabbed an overcoat of Harley's from the hall, threw a chair through the kitchen window (the boys had kept the place locked and there was no time to hunt for keys), cut my shin on a shard getting through and, with *on top of all this* the Hunger raking my guts, made my escape through the sodden back garden.

52

AN HOUR LATER I lay on a king-sized bed in a double room at the Grafton Hotel in South Kensington. Checking in had been delicate. Harley's overcoat hid most of the bloodstains but the singed hair and four diagonal stripes across my face, though already semihealed, gave the desk clerk pause. "Don't ask," I said, snapping the Amex Platinum (Tom Carlyle) down on the counter. A tactical simultaneity: brusque tone and class plastic. It worked, just.

"What the fuck, please, is going on?" Ellis asked, very calmly, on the Ellis phone. (I now had the Ellis phone, the Grainer phone, the Russell phone and the Wazz phone. The Grafton phone—untapped!—had made the latter two redundant.) His team hadn't called in. He'd rung *their* phones, obviously. I'd deemed it prudent to answer only the one I was supposed to have. "I mean," he said, still very calmly, "what the fuck, *please*, is going on?"

I told him about the Attack of the Vampires. I did not tell him that I'd already called my contact at Aegis (the U.K.'s version of Blackwater, former SAS, MI5, army and navy) and woken the dozing funds at three of the Swiss banks.

"You're a lucky sonofabitch, Jacob," he said.

"Yes, well, I recommend you make flamethrowers compulsory kit."

"I don't mean that. I mean you're lucky we had one of our guys in the local force."

"The police?"

"Think about how this would look: four Hunters dead and Jake Marlowe miraculously at large in perfect health. It would look, would it not, as if you'd done my boys in yourself and fled."

This hadn't occurred to me. A worry: What else hadn't occurred to me? The hotel room was deep-carpeted and thick-draped. A small part of me thought how wonderful it would be to lie down to sleep here and never wake up.

"Fortunately for you," Ellis continued, "our agent verified the vamp remains, once they'd got the fire out. There's not much of Harley's library left, I'm afraid."

I opened the curtains a couple of inches and looked out. There was a break in the rain. Wet London breathed, half asleep, twitching here and there where night-drama neurons fired: a woman getting raped; a junkie expiring; someone proposing; a baby slithering out. In the daylight the city's all brash bounce, no question of not going on. Nights you feel the exhaustion, see the going on for what it is: terror of admitting the whole thing's been a mistake.

"I'm not in perfect health, as it happens," I said. "I got staked in the leg. I've got a gouged skull and a hole in my chest the size of a tennis ball." All of which were healing—the whispering knitting circle, the cellular cabal—even as I spoke.

"I should have been there," Ellis said. "I would have made a difference."

"Maybe. It happened very fast. Did you get a trace on the Land Rover?"

"What? Oh, that. No. Guess Russell flaked on it. I clean forgot myself. Anyway it was the vamps, evidently."

"Looks that way," I said, although Mia, I quite clearly recalled, had said "bring the van" not "bring the car." Competition for my attention was fierce, however, and the Land Rover question was lightweight.

"We're going to have to redirect the pickup," Ellis said. "Where are you?"

"Tell your guy ten a.m. outside the Masonic headquarters in Long Acre."

"Jake . . ."

"Listen, Ellis, I've had more than two weeks of not being able to go for a piss without someone's say-so, and then with someone else listening in while I'm having it. You can give me one night of privacy. You know I'm not going to run. You're still holding the cards. I just need to get my head together. What's your driver's name?"

Over the phone I could feel his will to autonomy. There was someone he should okay it with, someone he didn't like. Whoever this person was their days of unchallenged leadership were numbered. Ellis liked *me* more than he liked them.

"Okay," he said. "But don't dick me, Jacob. You know the cause-and-effect reality."

"Hundred percent."

"Driver's name is Llewellyn. He'll know you, but just in case, he's in a BMW four-by-four license plate Foxtrot Tango six seven two Echo Uniform Delta. Code word is *lupus*. Ten a.m. Don't let me down. Don't let your lady down. And no"—as I drew breath to ask—"you can't talk to her now. You'll see her tomorrow. Trust me, she's fine. She's comfortable."

I spent what was left of the night on the hotel phone.

53

THE DRIVER, LLEWELLYN, young, fair, leanly muscled, with the cleanliness and near-skinhead haircut of a Mormon proselytiser, was precisely on time. The code word seemed redundant but I asked for it anyway and received "lupus, sir" in reply. *Sir*. Okay. Picked for this job because he followed orders to the letter. *You will treat Mr. Marlowe courteously, but you will not engage in conversation.* Fine. I was in any case itchy with sleeplessness and inwardly ajabber with Hunger. "I'm going to have to chain-smoke, Llewellyn," I warned him. "I hope that's not going to be a problem for you?"

He opened the rear nearside door. "Not a problem, sir," he said. "We're partitioned in any case."

Indeed. Bulletproof glass, by the look of it. Ditto the windows. "Are we expecting to be shot at?" I asked him, giving it a rap.

"Fitted as standard on these, sir," he said. "Do you want the radio on or anything?"

He called in to let whoever it was (not Ellis, the ether said) know I was on board, then we were on our way. It was a pretty morning. Blue spring sky and lively sunlight and a breeze that shivered the puddles and set London's buds nodding on their stems. Not that much of it got through to me, quietly bearing up as I was with the Curse's foreplay, the phantom elongation of snout and finger, the compressed spasms, the importunate erections, the occasional prescience in toenails and eyeteeth. My teeth *chattered*, actually, as in the first phase of the flu, prompting Llewellyn to remind me I had my own heat controls in the back. Meanwhile Piccadilly, Park Lane, Marylebone, the Westway, the M40. I tried to sleep. Failed. Instead pictured the effects of the dumped money, the fertility of the down payment. Impossible to know yet how many men a breakout would need, but I'd paid Aegis for a squad of fifty up front, nonrecoverable. My guess was that wherever they had Talulla there wouldn't be a large defence. Ellis's London renegades couldn't number more than five hundred and the majority would be carrying out regular WOCOP duties as normal. Poulsom's installation would rely on concealment rather than a standing force.

Alongside these ruminations I kept up a more or less continuous self-harangue. You fucking idiot, you're going to get yourself killed. They'll torture Talulla and rape her and do experiments and mate her with animals and if you're not already dead force you to watch and this whole fantasy of rescue and survival you've cooked up is obscene and preposterous and even Charlie at Aegis had trouble not laughing at you down the phone and only didn't because he knows you've got the money and it's your fucking funeral you stupid cunt she's going to die and so are you—

The Ellis phone rang.

"Jake, you're en route I hear."

"Is she with you?"

"Not yet. *Calmez-vous.* You'll see her tonight. Now listen. To confirm: Moonrise is 18:07 tomorrow. It'll just be me and Grainer. He's already up there, so don't deviate: Stay in the hotel. Llewellyn'll pick you up at 14:30 tomorrow and drop you in Beddgelert. You're on foot from there. Obviously you know the way."

"Aren't you going to be on the drive-by tonight?"

"Can't. I'm going up to meet Grainer now. After that he'll want me with him. I do the weapons check. There's a routine, a set of rituals. Don't worry, Jake, she's in safe hands, I promise. Just stay in your hotel room until you get the call."

The rest of the journey was febrile peaks and troughs. Moments of vividness—the huge wheels of a truck very close; a crow flapping up from fresh roadkill; a green verge covered in crocuses—and long blurred stretches, pre-Curse hypersensitivity that amounted to perceptual distortion or fuzz. My face tingled, eyes itched, limbs lost their edges to the pins-and-needles ghost of the wolf. The memory of killing with Talulla was a root that clutched from balls to brain. Neither fear nor fatigue obscured it. *Wulf* went out from it, ranged to tearing point, searching. She was here, somewhere, close, somewhere . . .

Just after three o'clock, under a pied sky of cumulus and silvery blue, we arrived in Caernarfon.

54

I MANAGED AN hour of reiterative calls to Aegis before the batteries on Russell's and Wazz's mobiles died within minutes of each other, like an ancient couple who couldn't bare to be parted. Daren't risk the room phone. It's probably bugged, but there's also the possibility they'll call in on it for the drive-by with Talulla. Either way I've left it alone.

Of course *without* the calls there's nothing to do but wait. Smoke. Pace. Write. Look out. Drink. I've allowed myself one bottle of Scotch between now and tomorrow afternoon. Eighteen-year-old Talisker's the best the Castle's got. Shame not to go out on something classier, if going out's what I'm doing.

The room is as I remember it. Seems a decade ago. Poor Maddy's white shoulders hunched and her face full of immediate belief though she'd said, Is that real? That's not real, is it?

It wasn't painless. It wasn't quick.

I'm sorry, Harls, for the mess I made of your life. For *costing* you your life. Vengeance, now, late, shamefully overdue, but vengeance nonetheless. Grainer. Ellis too, eventually. I'm sorry it's taken so long. I'm sorry the bare fact of what they did to you wasn't enough. I'm sorry it took loving someone. Someone else.

•

Dark. I watched the last of the light over the Irish Sea. Now the window shows only the street. No call.

•

The whole of one's being reduces to listening for the sound of a ringing phone.

•

Something nags when I think of Madeline here. This room's hauled it to the edge of memory but can't quite heave it over the border.

•

22:50. Still no call. It's raining again. I'll have to open the window to see her clearly.

•

Thank God.

I was beginning to give up hope. Just after midnight the room phone rang. Not Ellis. An older-sounding male.

"Take the handset to the window. ETA two minutes. Now hang up."

Time, as the twee verse has it, is too slow for those who wait. I opened the sash. The two minutes swelled and warped. Car after car that wasn't them. Then a mirror-windowed people-carrier pulled up across the road. The handset rang again.

"Hello? Lu?"

"Listen carefully," the male voice said. "You get thirty seconds, precisely. Not negotiable. Go."

The vehicle's rear window went down—and there was Talulla's face, awake, expectant, full of her nimble consciousness. Not *quite* fully disguising fear, though I could see even in that first glance the work she'd put in not to let it show. She smiled at me.

"Are you okay?" I said.

"I'm fine. Are you all right?"

"I'm fine. I'm getting you out, okay?"

"Okay."

"It won't be long, I promise."

"Be careful. You have to be careful."

"I will. I'm coming for you."

"Promise you'll be careful."

"I promise."

"What happened to your face?"

"Nothing. A scrape. You look so beautiful."

"I love you."

"I love you too. You're sure they haven't hurt you?"

"They really haven't. I miss you."

"You'll be seeing me very soon."

"I could feel you close all day."

"Me too."

"I wish I could come to you right now."

"Oh, Jesus, Lu, I—" A hand wearing a black leather driving glove took the phone from her. I saw her face's effort collapse. You think: I should have spent days just holding her, kissing her, looking at her. The electric window closed. One last glimpse of her straining to see over it. The soft dark eyes.

"That's it, chief," the voice said—and hung up. Seconds later the people-carrier was gone.

55

SOMETHING'S HAPPENED TO ME. I've stopped abstracting. This is love: You stop bothering about the universal, the general, get sucked instead into the local and particular: When will I see her again? What shall we do today? Do you like these shoes? Theory and reflection are delicate old uncles bustled out of the way by the boisterous nephews action and desire. Themes evaporate, only plot remains. Madeline was right in her priorities all along.

I hadn't realised my conversion until reading back over these pages, and now, when they ought to present themselves, conclusions desert me. For a werewolf facing what might be his last few hours your narrator finds himself woefully short of summative maxims. The great mysteries endure, unsolved, unseen-into (except love, which is really not a mystery but the force that eases mysteries into the hard shoulder); I don't know where the universe came from or what happens to creatures when they die. I don't know if the whole thing's an unravelling accident or an inscrutable design. I don't know how one should live—but I know that one *should* live, if one can possibly bear it. You love life because life's all there is. And I only know that because I happen to have found—again—love. There's no justice: *that* I know. Precious little to show for two hundred and one years.

My skull aches from where the moon spent the night under its cranium, like a lozenge of slowly melting ice. In a few minutes Llewellyn will arrive to take me to Beddgelert. I haven't slept but in spite of the pre-Curse torments I've showered, shaved, trimmed my finger- and toenails. There are no clean clothes so I washed my socks and underpants in shampoo and dried them on the room's radiator. Ellis tells me there'll be fresh gear for me when the deed is done. I drank the last of the Talisker around noon. Since then coffee and Camels, the occasional glass of tap water. It's raining, halfheartedly. This seat by the window's become a dreary home.

Its view is of the town's grey edge: a road, passing cars, headscarved old ladies, dog walkers, now and then a flushed jogger. Beyond this a low grey wall, a narrow strand, the shifting colours of the Menai Strait, Anglesey.

Not for much longer.

My inner dead make their presence felt now like a silent congregation. Arabella, their priestess, has gone, so lately they're still in shock. There's a tenderness around her absence, like the soft blood-filled cavity of a pulled-out tooth. What can it mean that I killed and consumed my wife and unborn child and now have love in my life again—except that there's no justice and that one must, if one can bear it, live?

Enough. My nerves are bad. Reflection no longer becomes me, has no place alongside love.

Besides, here's Llewellyn with the car. For better or worse it's time to go.

56

No one raped me. First because they were all scared of Poulsom and I guess he'd taken anything like that off the menu. Second because raping me would have meant killing me: A woman you've raped tracking you down is one thing, a *werewolf* you've raped is another. Within hours of my first abduction I stopped worrying about it.

Then the second abduction happened.

Seeing Jake had been hard. He looked terrible. Those scratches on his face like an insult. He seemed so alone standing there in the hotel window. His shirt was wrongly buttoned, just one button out of line, the slightest effect of crookedness. The makeup on my face felt obscene. I'd wanted, among the million other things, to look pretty for him—and perversely the universe had cooperated. Earlier, back at the place they'd held me—"the white jail," as I thought of it—one of the female guards had slipped me a paper bag with cosmetics in it. Eyeliner, mascara, lip gloss, eyeshadow, blusher. "I know you're seeing your guy tonight," she said. "Don't say where you got it." She was embarrassed. What was weird was that until then she'd been utterly stony. Hardass, I'd nicknamed her. I was so stunned I didn't say a word. Afterwards, sitting on my bunk, I cried. I read somewhere that when you're a kid it's people's cruelty that makes you cry, then when you're an adult it's their kindness. I hadn't realised until that moment how completely I'd given up any entitlement to kindness. And then when I saw Jake, so visibly strung out, looking so totally alone, the makeup felt cheap on my face, a stupid *girl*'s gesture. (The girl's still in there, waist-deep in the blood and guts of the monster's victims. There might be something out there that'll kill the girl but if so I can't imagine what it could be.) *Are you okay? I'm fine. Are you all right? I'm fine.* Weeks of waiting and then when the moment comes you trade the plainest words. The nearness of him hurt, my heart, my head, my breasts, my *womb,* it felt like, started the wolf trying to tear itself free. Memory of the kill we'd shared in California opened in me like the warmth of hard liquor, starting in the chest and hurrying outwards, a secret ecstasy in my hands and teeth and scalp. Poulsom said, Careful, you'll hurt yourself. On the cuffs, he meant. I hadn't known I was straining against them.

I wish I could come to you right now.

Oh, Jesus, Lu, I—

Thirty seconds, we'd been promised. It felt like three. A glimpse. A blur. A joke at love's expense. Then the car was pulling away, my neck twisted to see out the back, Jake in the lit window getting smaller. Going. Gone. That feeling like the first day at school, a ball of emptiness in my stomach because my mother had seen me crying but still turned and walked away to the car, the silver Volvo I couldn't stand after that. You learn early the basic thing is loss. Then spend the rest of your life trying to forget it.

Jake says he stopped abstracting. Seems I've started. Writing this isn't easy. I haven't kept a journal since UCLA. Back then we all kept them, miles of young women's handwriting like barbed wire, the full-time job of self-dramatisation. *I don't care what he says now. I've been fucked over by that asshole for the LAST TIME!!!*

I supposed they were taking me from Caernarfon back to the white jail ("they" being Poulsom and two guards, Merritt and Dyson), wherever the hell the white jail was. I knew we were in Wales, but that was pretty much it. My European geography's the standard American shambles and the place-names I'd seen on the way—Llandovery, Rhayader, Dolgellau—could've been in Wonderland for all they meant to me. The headache I'd had since first being captured was knowing I had to do something and knowing there was nothing I could do. I hadn't bought the line that I'd be released once Grainer was dead any more than Jake had, but there was no choice except to play it out. The rationed phone minutes had carried Jake's message in the spaces between words: Sit tight. I'll get you out. In the good moments it was like having a powerful talisman in my pocket. In the bad it was like a voice (Aunt Sylvia's, in fact, that bitch who fell on childhood optimism like acid rain) repeating, He won't come, you stupid little girl, you're dead. And these *were* bad moments, now, after seeing him. He'd looked so tired. Those scratches and the wrongly buttoned shirt.

We'd been driving maybe twenty minutes—a narrow winding road bordered by woods on both sides—when we found the way blocked by a traffic accident. A silent ambulance with lights sadly splashing the trees, two medics tending a helmeted motorcyclist down on the ground, the bike on its side nearby.

"Er . . ." Poulsom said. He was in the back with me and Dyson. Merritt was behind the wheel.

"Inconvenient," Dyson said.

"Reverse," Poulsom said. "Immediately."

What happened happened very fast. There was the tiny precise sound of a bullet going neatly through plate glass—and almost simultaneously Merritt's head lolled on the back of his seat.

Intense dreamy fumbling followed: Poulsom wrangling his gun out of his shoulder holster, Dyson trying to clamber over both of us to the door on the opposite side from the shot, me trying—dreamily knowing it was pointless—to get out of the restraints. It would have looked like the Three Stooges if anyone had been there to see it. I took Dyson's full body-weight—one booted foot on my thigh—as he launched himself through the rear door, then he was out, stumbling for the cover of the trees.

He didn't make it. A short burst of automatic gunfire dropped him six feet away. In the silence that followed I felt Poulsom's body next to mine softening into acceptance.

"Get out, slowly, Poulsom," a man's voice said. "Hands where we can see them." I looked past Merritt's body through the windscreen. The medics and the motorcyclist were now on their feet by the open back of the ambulance, armed with rifles. It had started raining.

"Well, Talulla," Poulsom said, quietly, "this is going to be bad for me, I think." He got out. I sat very still. Not that I had much choice: In my white jail cell I'd been free to move around, but for transportation they'd put me in Guantánamo-style restraints, the I-shaped wrists-and-ankles arrangement that allows short steps only. From the ankles another set of cuffs attached me to the bolted base of the seat.

"Drop the weapon," the voice told Poulsom. "Get on the ground face-down, hands behind your back. Do it now."

Looking to my left through the open door I watched Poulsom follow the instructions. A moment after he'd assumed the position an athletic guy in full black combat fatigues melted into view from the darkness behind the trees. A WOCOP Hunter, from the gear, with a dark crew-cut and heavy-lidded eyes. He genuflected onto Poulsom's neck while he cuffed him, then helped him, gently, to his feet.

"Miss?"

I started. The motorcyclist—helmet removed to reveal a young, cheerful face with a goatee and a silver nose stud—was at the other open door on my right, holding a heavy set of wire cutters. Cold wet air touched my face and throat. I was suddenly very thirsty.

"Don't be alarmed. I'm just going to get your legs free. Excuse me." He bent, and with hardly any effort clipped through the cable that fastened my ankle restraints to the seat. "Have to leave the others on for a moment," he said. "If you'd like to take my arm, I can help you out of there. That's it."

In spite of the adrenaline rush and frantic figuring (was this Jake's doing? Was I being busted out?) it was good to stand straight after the cramped hours in the car. I lifted my face to the rain. The night air was delicious with the smell of damp woodland, streaked with the odours of wet tarmac, cordite, diesel and the seductive whiff of the motorcycle leathers. This close to transformation the Hunger goes through me in surges that take all the strength out of my legs. I swayed, almost fell. The surge subsided. We were under thick cloud but the moon knew I was there. I get it in the roof of my mouth, my teeth, the palms of my hands, my belly, my cunt. (One of the hells of jail had been the dumb persistence of sex. Jerking off under the covers or in the shower even though I was sure there were cameras, despite Poulsom's assurances otherwise. He'd said, "I know rising libido is going to be a problem for you as we enter the waxing gibbous phase." For a terrible moment I thought he was going to offer me the use of his men, or a vibrator, or, God forbid, himself, but he went on: "Please understand, Talulla, surveillance stops at the door to your room. The space you occupy beyond it is one of complete privacy, I promise you. We have absolutely no desire to make things any more difficult for you than necessity dictates." Which presented one of the other hells of jail: trying to be civil to Poulsom. Truth was I hated him on sight, and he knew it, but he also knew I wasn't going to risk pissing him off. I read an interview once, someone—an actress—complaining that Christopher Walken—or it could have been James Woods—smelled or maybe even *tasted* of formaldehyde. Either way I could believe it, and Poulsom had the same deal, the fish eyes and the waxy skin, that look of having been under fluorescents too long . . .)

The Hunter spoke into a headset: "Okay, we're good here. Come ahead." An armoured van crept from a concealed gap in the trees and pulled up behind the people-carrier. While the medics were closing the ambulance doors and setting the bike upright, Poulsom and I were escorted to the van's rear, where the motorcyclist opened the doors. The vehicle's interior was occupied by a steel cage, snugly fitted and bolted down. No sign of lock or key, only a mystifying plate of what looked like dark glass in a metal housing where the lock should be.

Not mystifying for long. The Hunter pressed his palm flat against it. With a string of blips and a gasp of what sounded like hydraulics the cage door popped open.

"Inside," the Hunter said. Poulsom clambered in, gracelessly, and in a moment had been seated on the floor and secured, cuffs to bars. The motorcyclist helped me in, fastened my wrists to the cage, then released and removed the ankle cuffs altogether. "Better for you like this," he said. "Save you getting tossed around like a lettuce."

The Hunter leaped up into the van and stood over Poulsom. Shouldered the automatic and pulled out a pistol from a side holster. Pointed it at Poulsom's head. "Phone," he said.

"What?"

"Call in. You've drawn heat. You're going round about. They wait for your update but Ellis is green for go. That's all."

"They'll know—"

"They won't know shit without any of the alert words, all of which you know *I* know. Are we clear?"

Pause.

"I'm not going to ask twice."

Poulsom opened the phone.

"I dial," the Hunter said.

Poulsom's performance was surprisingly convincing, considering he had a gun at his head, a blend of tension, weariness and irritation; he was the horrifically overworked dictator who had to suffer shit luck and universal incompetence.

"Good," the Hunter said, pocketing the phone. He gave the motorcyclist a nod, not looking at me. Palpable contempt came off him. Not for me personally but for all women. I had an image of him choking a young girl while sodomising her, his face testifying that it wasn't enough, nothing was enough. My nose has sharpened for these things. He knew I knew, which made a disgusting claustrophobic intimacy. It was then I began worrying again about getting raped. Rape was his default. To him the only obstacles were practical. But fear was a practical obstacle. He knew what I was. This, I had to hope, would keep him off. Another surge of the Hunger went through my thighbones. My face was hot. He turned and jumped down from the van.

The motorcyclist produced a small capped syringe from his pocket. "Bobo time, doc," he said. Poulsom's face quivered—fear and a look of sensuous revulsion—as the motorcyclist approached him. "Relax. It's a sedative, that's all. Hold still."

"Whatever you're doing," Poulsom began—but the motorcyclist belted him, hard, a backhander; my armpits went suddenly hot—across the face.

"Hush. And relax. There we go."

"Where are you taking us?" I said.

"Can't tell you, miss. Sorry. Not far, though. Don't worry." He saw me eyeing the syringe. "You're not having any of this." He winked, then went to join the others. Poulsom's eyes had closed.

"Let's move ourselves, gentlemen," the Hunter said. I heard the people-carrier doors slam and the ambulance start up. The whole ambush had taken no more than two or three minutes.

A slight weight shift said our driver had left the armoured van, and a moment later a man in his early forties wearing Securicor overalls appeared alongside the Hunter. "Thought you should know, sir," he said. "Looked like a tail a couple of miles back. Can't be certain. Probably paranoia."

"Vehicle?"

"Land Rover, white, Alfa Lima two five five Juliet Papa Romeo. Single male driver. Nothing, really, one mile too many, maybe."

"It's because it was white," the motorcyclist said. "You notice white more. It's the Moby Dick effect. What sort of moron tails someone in a white car?"

"The world's full of them," the Hunter said. "I'll let the boss know anyway. Let's go."

57

WE DROVE FOR what felt like fifteen or twenty minutes. There was only a small opaque glass window in the back door, and the Hunger soon had motion sickness to keep it company. I was close to throwing up (or dry heaving, since I'd eaten nothing for a week) by the time we stopped. The van's rear door opened and the Hunter palmed the cage's lock. The Securicor guy climbed in to unfasten me and put the leg cuffs back on. Over his shoulder I could see the motorcyclist dismounting. Poulsom, still out cold, was left shackled where he was.

Hard to make out detail in the dark. We were outside a small stone farmhouse with no lights showing. The land around felt empty. I had a sense of deserted fields, remnants of dry stone walls. No cattle, no sheep, nothing.

"Get her inside," the Hunter said, not looking at me.

The farmhouse was L-shaped, low-ceilinged, damp, furnished with junk-shop crap from what looked like the 1930s. A dark wood bookcase with no books. A green couch you didn't want to sit on. An armchair with stuffing coming out like ectoplasm. A faded floral carpet. All the curtains were closed. They lit a log fire in the stone hearth. My shins ached. Wolf in my finger- and toenails like the dull biting shock you get from an electric cattle fence.

"I suppose it's pointless me asking what's happening?" I said to the motorcyclist, when the Hunter was out of earshot.

"'Fraid so, miss," he said, with the diamond smile and alert friendly green eyes. His curly hair was surfer two-tone, blond and brown.

"Or how long I'm going to be held here?"

"I wish I could tell you, I really do. Try not to worry about it." He was tearing the cellophane off a pack of Marlboro. Poulsom had forbidden me cigarettes and booze, but since his reign was over . . .

"Any chance of bumming one of those?"

We lit up. "Thanks," I said. "Now all I need is a bottle of Jack Daniel's. Maybe you could have a quick rootle arou—"

"Carter," the Hunter said. The motorcyclist turned. "Outside. Check Poulsom in an hour. If he's not quiet when he wakes up, give him another shot."

When the motorcyclist—Carter, evidently—had gone, the Hunter approached me on the couch. I thought, excruciatingly, of myself jerking off in my cell. In the dark, yes, but there must have been infrared. A terrible feeling of disgust came over me. He put his hand in his pocket and pulled out a roll of duct tape. "You can agree to keep quiet—silent in fact—or I can stick this over your mouth. It's up to you. You won't be given the choice again." The space between us held information. He was up against a higher authority. He was restricted. Whatever he was capable of, he wasn't capable of it *yet*. And there was, no mistake—the curryish stink of it came off him—fear. It was causing him trouble, that he could be afraid of a woman. It didn't compute. He had to keep reminding himself this wasn't a woman, this was a *monster*.

"I'll be quiet," I said, looking straight at the fire.

It was a bad night. They rotated the watches, two men outside, one in. Obviously I couldn't sleep, with the pre-Curse fevers and the Hunger like talons trying out their grip on different bits of my insides. In the white jail Poulsom had "allowed" me muscle relaxants, which I'd taken with deep resentment. I would've taken a handful with gratitude now. I lay curled up under a blanket on the couch, shivering in spite of the log fire. And if not the shivers the sweats. Jake says shoulders and wrists feel it first but for me it's the line from the back of my skull to the end of my spine. In the deliriums (deliria? deliriæ? Jake would know) the yellow-toothed wolf from the Little Red Riding Hood book I had when I was a child comes to me—purple jacket and all—shimmering out of the wall or the fire or the carpet or just thin air, comes to me and wraps his bigger weightless body around mine and tries to get in.

The motorcyclist made cups of instant black coffee which I drank because it was better than nothing. My clothes hurt my skin. There was a pendulum wall clock in the kitchen that went *toonk . . . toonk . . . toonk* and the soft sound was almost unbearable. Jake came in and out of the fever. Sometimes *he* was the Red Riding Hood wolf, or the wolf spoke with his voice. *You'll be seeing me very soon. I could feel you close all day. Me too.* Sometimes he was just himself, invisibly next to me on the couch, the source—as in *heat source* or *light source*—of unloneliness. The way sometimes he'd put his hand in the small of my back. It was as if my consciousness was there, in my sacrum, not in my head. Or at least the bit of my consciousness that was terrified of having to go back to being alone.

Sometime in the small hours Poulsom was brought indoors so he could go to the bathroom. He was given water, then taken back to the van. He must have been freezing in there.

At dawn the Hunter and the Securicor guy came in looking raw. The motorcyclist cheerily fixed breakfast from what was in the fridge, eggs, bacon, bread, cheese, tinned fish. The smell of the fried food was nauseating. I sat in the bathroom with the extractor fan going, wafting an open bottle of bleach under my nose. There was no window to even think of climbing out of, and in any case they'd left the Guantánamo restraints on.

My escort was visibly relieved to have got through the night without incident. The Hunter opened the curtains in the lounge. A morning of low cloud and weak light. Last night's impression of the landscape had been accurate: It was empty, crossed here and there by low pale stone walls. East, the fields undulated very slightly into a distant stack of hills. West, maybe three hundred yards away, they were bordered by a forest.

I'd assumed daybreak would bring some development, but apart from the men's air of having survived the worst of an ordeal, nothing changed. I saw the Hunter standing fifty yards off talking into a cell phone. The Securicor guy took the cold breakfast leftovers to Poulsom in the van.

At four in the afternoon the motorcyclist and I smoked the last two of his Marlboros. I began to wonder whether the impossible was true, and they didn't, in fact, know that in a little over two hours I was going to turn into a monster. In which case all I had to do was request a bathroom visit as close to transformation as possible, Change—and kill them. I wondered if I was up to that. The Hunter, surely, would be armed with silver. Wouldn't he? Wouldn't they all be?

"Okay," the Hunter said, having wrapped up another fifty-yards-away cell phone call. "It's time. Get her hooked up in the van. No, wait . . ."

He walked over to me and pulled the duct tape out a second time.

58

THEY MUST HAVE given Poulsom another shot because he was unconscious when I resumed my place with him in the cage. I had to work hard not to let the tape over my mouth drive me crazy. Incredible the difference it made, being denied speech. In combination with the restraints (this time both hand- and foot-cuffs were attached to the cage) it felt like being buried alive.

The journey wasn't long but it wasn't easy. Standing was the best position, but with the short length of cable from my ankles to my wrists I could only hold on to the bars at navel height. Jolts and sudden turns flung and yanked me. Poulsom, tossed around, as the motorcyclist would have said, like a lettuce, would be covered in bruises when he woke up. If he woke up.

Five minutes before we stopped, the terrain got rougher. What had already felt like a primitive road turned into what can only have been a dirt track, full of ruts and potholes. Keeping my balance was impossible. Poulsom was the better off, loose-bodied, out of it.

We stopped. Executed a cramped three-point turn. Stopped again. The rear doors opened. The Hunter stood with his hands on his hips, looking at me. Through the bars I saw we were on a dirt road barely bigger than a bridleway that threaded between thinning trees before curving to the right about twenty feet away to run parallel with the bank of what I could hear and smell was a stream. On the opposite bank a narrow strip of grass, a few lilac bushes, then trees again. There was no sign of the motorcyclist or the Securicor guy.

"Getting hungry?" the Hunter said.

I looked past him. Concentrated on breathing through my nose. The air was loamy and damp. The cloud cover had broken and the evening star was out. My nostrils were hot and tender. Moonrise was less than two hours away. The first inkling of animal clarity was already there, a kind of vicious joy in the power that would come up through the soles of my feet into my ankles, shins, hips, elbows, shoulders. If I lived that long.

"Come on," the Hunter said. "You've got meals-on-wheels in there. Couldn't be handier."

Poulsom, he meant, obviously. *Poulsom says they've got it covered,* I'd told Jake when we'd discussed full moon, the Change, the need to feed, *whatever that means.* Whatever it had meant to Poulsom, it hadn't meant this. It cost me a lot to hold on, teeth jammed together, the tape on my mouth still imprinted with the heat and weight of the Hunter's hand.

I looked directly at him. Very slowly gave him the finger. He laughed, quietly. Then slammed the van door shut.

59

POULSOM WOKE UP, shivering, in a sweat. As far as I could tell in the little light that made it through the frosted glass his night and day in the van hadn't agreed with him. He murmured behind his strip of tape, pointlessly. Then looked at his watch.

I didn't need his reaction to what he saw to tell me how close transformation was. The last hour had taken me into the penultimate phase, the wolf looking out through human eyes with quiet blazing animal alertness. My wrists and ankles were bloody from where Hunger spasms had cut me against the cuffs, but my limbs had calmed in spite of the pain.

Had calmed. The penultimate phase was passing. Any moment the final phase—cramps, sickness, hot and cold, half an infinite minute of casually ripped-up muscles and rearranged joints—would begin. The cuffs would either burst or slice clean through me. I had an image of myself Changed but with four bleeding stumps. I knew just the sound the stumps would make, knocking against the floor and walls of the van.

I looked at Poulsom. He was shaking his head, no, no, no. Very soon, when things began visibly happening to me, he'd start thrashing and screaming into his gag and all his life would rush to the surface of his flesh and be there sweetly for the taking. It was a relief, the Hunger, its refusal to negotiate, something solid to hold on to in the uncertainty.

Suddenly I caught Jake's scent. My legs nearly buckled. I twisted myself as close to the rear door as I could get. Overrode the impulse to make as much noise as possible. *It's me! I'm in here! Jake!*

Wait. Be smart. Listen. There were voices.

"I thought you said we'd be alone," Ellis said.

"I know," a second voice said. "But something occurred to me after we last spoke."

Poulsom, presumably at the recognition of Ellis's voice, began kicking about.

"Who've you got in there?" Jake said. "What the fuck is this?"

The van's rear door opened. Standing twenty feet away were Jake, Ellis and a third man in Hunt fatigues. Mid-forties. Dark hair flecked with grey. Broad cheekbones. *He looks like a Native American,* I remembered Jake telling me—and realised I was face-to-face with Grainer.

The other Hunter, to whom Grainer, it dawned on me, was "the boss," stood close to the cage with the automatic pointed directly at me.

"Nothing silly, Jake," Grainer said—then something extraordinary happened.

Grainer took a pace backwards and another half pace to his left. He did it as if woodenly executing a formal dance step. For a second everything froze. Jake's mouth was slightly open. The shirt buttons were still wrongly done-up. Ellis seemed to very slowly reach around for the rifle that hung slightly behind him on its shoulder strap. Grainer's right hand went up and behind his head. There was a soft rasp and a flash of bright metal. Everyone observing jumped, as if we'd all been given a small electric shock at exactly the same moment: the moment the blade, a brilliant broadsword, swung—with a sound like a wet branch snapping—through Ellis's neck.

The head toppled a fraction before the legs went. The long blond hair snagged on the rifle. The corpse's collapse was curiously neat. It dropped to its knees, hesitated, then fell forward as if in a gesture of complete worship. The head, still attached by its hair to the gun, lay facedown just next to the hip, as if it didn't want to see anything anymore.

"Lu?" Jake said. "You all right?"

"I'm okay," I said.

"How did you know?" Jake asked Grainer.

"How do we ever know? We got a good gal on the inside. I've always said women make the best agents. Deceit comes naturally to them. It's hardly surprising: If you were born with a little hole half the population could stick its dick into whenever it felt like it you'd learn deceit too. Biology is destiny. You can't blame the women."

Grainer transferred the sword to his left hand and with his right took a pistol from his side holster and pointed it at Jake. I dropped to my knees and retched up bile. It was coming.

"Keep her covered, Morgan," Grainer said. The Hunter by the cage retrained his gun on me. It had drifted a little during the beheading.

"I'm sorry, angel," Jake said to me. "I was stupid."

I couldn't speak. We got a good gal on the inside. It didn't have to be Hardass. There were other women at the white jail. But the ugliness of this moment spread backwards. *I know you're seeing your guy tonight.* And me like an idiot weeping on my bunk. It didn't have to be her. But there was the cynic's version of Ockham's razor: All things being equal the shittiest explanation's the best.

"I'm so sorry," Jake said.

"It's not"—a cramp at which the reflex was to bend double, except I couldn't, with the cuffs still attached to the cage—"your fault," I managed to get out. "My fault. I'm sorry." In spite of everything, Poulsom's flesh, fear-soaked, piping hot, was a fat pulse in the confined space of the van. Morgan looked at me, smiling. "You ready to party?" he said.

Grainer looked at his watch. "Not long now, kids," he said. "By the way, before you go, Jake, congratulations. I'm sure fatherhood would've suited you."

Poulsom wriggled and roared.

"What?" Jake said—then dropped to one knee, shuddered, got down on all fours. Jammed his teeth together. His clothes started to tear at the seams. The hair was coming. Mine too.

"Yeah," Grainer continued, "apparently the big side-effect of the antiviral. Seems your old lady's nearly two months gone. Ask Poulsom. He's over the moon about it, all set to go down in history as the man who changed werewolf reproduction forever. Except of course now he's not going anywhere. Nowhere good, anyway."

Jake looked up at me. My spine shifted. The shoulders of my blouse split. Movement in the top of my skull. The waistband of my skirt went. *Seems your old lady's nearly two months gone.* It was impossible, and yet as soon as I'd heard the words it was like falling off a cliff. No smoking. No drinking. Ultrasounds. Harrods towels, television, reassurance. I thought of those Magic Eye pictures, the disturbing moment when three dimensions shiver out of two. It was impossible. But then until the antiviral so was surviving the bite.

"Talulla!" Jake called. He was more than halfway. His eyes were going. His clothes hung in shreds. Soon speech would be impossible.

Grainer, face empty of all expression, pointed the gun at Jake's head. One of my ankle cuffs broke. The other was cutting its way into the swelling flesh. Jake convulsed. Somewhere far away my clothes were disintegrating and Poulsom was screaming into the duct tape. Fear around Morgan like a swarm of flies.

"Is it better to kill her in front of you?" Grainer said. "Or you in front of her? How about an impromptu Caesarian? Morgan's pretty good with a knife."

The van was packed with the heat of my transformation. In the blur of the final spasm I'd snapped the cable free of the cage. The left handcuff was gone. The right cut my flesh with a kind of fierce boredom. In spite of which joy filled me. My mouth was hot. Jake was still in the throes. Poulsom's legs struggled to get him upright. His body heaved out its stink of fear and meat.

"Your lady's ahead of you, Marlowe," Grainer said. "She's making you look like an amateur."

Jake foetal as the details of claws and ear tips worked themselves out—then his long soft throat lifted as the last of the Changing resolved itself. He began to get to his feet.

"Good-bye, Jake," Grainer said—then two things happened simultaneously.

My second ankle cuff snapped (a surge of blood, a lovely feeling of relief) and a silver javelin, travelling at speed, struck Grainer in the chest. He staggered back a pace, dropped the pistol and fell to his knees.

Morgan spun and fired a burst wildly, hit turf and trees, involuntarily took a step backwards. I threw myself at the bars.

The step backwards had brought him—just—close enough. At full stretch I got the collar of his jacket and his nape's sweat-hot hair, yanked him, flailing, up against the cage, locked a hand around his throat, with the other ripped the automatic from his grasp, though I fumbled and it dropped to the ground. He twisted, but either by deep training or extraordinary will overrode the instinct to reach for the hand cutting off his air, instead freed a knife from a sheath in his belt and drove it into my forearm.

The pain reflex opened my hand and he tore free, went down on one knee and reached for the gun.

When Jake leaped, his trajectory made an arc that framed Grainer for me in weird vividness. He was still on his knees, propped up by the javelin, arms hanging inert, eyes half-closed, a thickened gobbet of dark blood hanging from his open mouth. The image had the remote clarity of a religious icon. Then Jake descended, fell on Morgan with a draught of the evening's moon-edged air and in a single swipe gashed him—a gesture with a sort of emphatic masculine grace—from throat to belly. The body unstrung, collapsed like a dropped puppet.

Jake wrapped his hands around the bars of the cage and braced himself to pull but I gave him through the confusion—his head was full on the upswelling joy of *pregnant can't be javelin love by love Cloquet can't be but please please let her be*—the image of Morgan's palm, felt it emerge in him amid the chaos like a developing print and felt his own giant animal delight as he went to the Hunter's corpse, ripped the arm from its socket, pressed the hand to the panel and received, like magic, the string of blips, the gasp, the open door.

We fell into an embrace. Speech had gone from both of us, but we didn't need it, not now with the wolf melding us and our bodies free and the miracle ghost-flicker (or was I imagining it?) of new life in my womb. For a moment we held each other and everything but the purest certainty of shared nature, of common blood, of *sameness* dropped away. For a moment the world was perfect.

If I hadn't closed my eyes.

Jake's written all about *if* and *then*.

As it was, eyes closed in the bliss of feeling his warm arms around me and his heart beating against mine, I saw nothing, only felt the thud-twitch of impact and heard, what seemed such a long time after, the sound of a gunshot.

60

STILL HOLDING HIM, I opened my eyes. Over his shoulder I saw Grainer, barely conscious, desperately trying to hold the pistol upright for a second shot. Slowly, I lifted Jake and turned, so that my back was to his killer. I thought: Shoot me too, then, since there's nothing left for me.

Not nothing, angel. The child.

I looked at him, felt the silver gobbling his life with nonnegotiable greed. Death taking him was like something being dragged out of me. Out of my womb. The cuff cutting into my left wrist broke at last. Blood poured over both of us.

You live, he sent me. *There's no God and that's His only commandment.*

Okay.

Promise?

I promise. Don't leave me.

His eyes closed. The seduction was heavy on him, a suave pull on his blood. His heart was going with it, I could feel, like a boat gone from its mooring. But he opened his eyes, with an immense effort of will gathered the remnants, looked at me.

This will hurt.

He held me with sudden shocking strength—then his claw went into the flesh above my breast.

In spite of everything the reflex was to pull away—the pain was small, precise, white-hot—but everything he had went into keeping me still, and in a moment it was over. A knot of blood and tissue with a tiny metal fragment protruding.

Now they can't find you.

A moment of bafflement, then I understood. In the mess of consciousness a distinct little discharge of disgust that they'd been able to do that, get inside me. Make fools of us.

Love . . .

Stay with me. Stay with me.

His eyes closed again. The tip of the full moon appeared over the dark line of the trees. The clouds had cleared. The sky was a pretty dusk blue.

No second shot came.

•

It's hard to say how long I stayed there in the middle of what had become a bloody little battlefield, with his body growing cold next to mine. Certainly the moon was clear of the trees when I got to my feet and laid him gently on the ground. In a sort of mild dream my own voice inside my head repeated without any feeling at all, He's gone, he's gone, he's gone . . . The forest was very still. Even the stream seemed to have fallen silent. The air had a pared clean quality. The armoured van, the bodies, the trees, all had a weird solid static vividness, as if they'd been carefully arranged like this to mean something.

An indeterminate surreal time passed. There were questions, but they were like vague or distant objects. What would happen to Jake when the moon set? Would his corpse stay Changed? Or revert to human form? There were three human bodies to deal with. What was to be done with them? Where was Cloquet? If I really was pregnant, what would happen if I went into labour on the Curse? What shape would the child have?

There were, yes, these questions—but overwhelmingly, as if the sound of myself was being turned up to a point I knew would cause real pain, there was the Hunger.

Sharp consciousness returned the way sharp hearing does when water you've had in your ear suddenly trickles out. A breeze stirred the young leaves. The stream breathed its odour of damp stone. My fingertips tingled. I was freshly aware of my Changed shape, the soft fit of cool air over snout and ears and throat.

I climbed into the back of the van.

Poulsom was a mess. I tore the duct tape (and, accidentally, though I wasn't particularly careful, a bit of his top lip) from his mouth. A second's delay then the pain of the ripped flesh hit him and he screamed. I put my right hand, wrist still bleeding, heavily, slowly around his throat and very gently squeezed. Just enough to silence him. I looked down and pointed to my belly.

For a moment I could tell he was trying to work out whether a lie or the truth would serve him better. It was quite something to watch the stubborn calculator still at work. Then, presumably because of vestiges of the idea that virtue will be (ultimately) rewarded, I saw him cast his lot in for better or worse with the truth. He nodded, croaked out, "Yes. Pregnant."

Not nothing, angel. The child. You live. Promise.

Well, I had promised.

61

IT WAS FULLY dark by the time I finished with Poulsom. I'd fed fast, but my appetite had had all sorts in it: grief, rage, loss, confusion. Also a kind of dumb irreverent hope. I had an image of myself holding hands with a child by the polar bear tanks in Central Park Zoo. My own earliest memory, the chance to give it to someone else.

There was nothing I could do about the bodies, even poor Jake's. If I was going to live I had to start now. I was a monster alone in the middle of Wales. Even if I got through the Curse I had neither money nor ID nor clothes nor any safe place to go. I thought of my dad and the restaurants and Ambidextrous Alison and my apartment and how sweet it would be to be back there in one piece lying on the couch with a cup of coffee and a stupid magazine. I thought how unlikely it was not only that I'd ever see it again, but that I'd make it through the next twenty-four hours alive.

But you have to. There's no God and that's his only Commandment.

So, with great difficulty (try it with werewolf hands) I set about equipping myself. Poulsom had the smallest shoe size so I took his footwear. Grainer's combat trousers and belt, Ellis's leather jacket. Between them just over a hundred and fifty pounds in cash. Jake's clothes were in shreds, but the journal, bloodstained and buckled, was there in the inside pocket of his ruined overcoat. I took it. I found a canvas bag with a handful of car essentials—jumper cables, wheel brace, jack, torch—behind the van's front seat, so I emptied it and stuffed my new wardrobe in there. I kept imagining telling Jake about all this, later, when it was all over. My wrist was already healing.

I took Grainer's pistol and three ammunition clips from his belt. Not that I had a clue how to use it. I wasn't even sure I'd identified the safety correctly. I'd found *some*thing that looked like a safety switch and moved it to the opposite setting, but there was still, I had to admit, a good chance of the damned thing going off and hitting me in the foot.

It wasn't easy to leave Jake. Twice I moved away and came back, a last look, touch, smell. Werewolves, I was discovering, can't weep. Uncried tears knotted my throat. The raw fact of my aloneness kept dissolving into the fantasy of him waking up.

Don't be sentimental. Get going. You've got work to do.

Jake's spirit, or my own fictionalised version of it. At any rate it got me to my feet and forced me, step by step, away into the trees.

I'd only gone a few paces, however, when I found Cloquet. It couldn't have been anyone else, from Jake's description, and of course there was the silver javelin, custom-made, with his and Jacqueline Delon's names entwined around it in angelic script, now buried in Grainer's chest. He didn't seem particularly surprised to find a werewolf standing over him, nor, to his credit, much afraid. He was lying propped against a beech tree with a cigarette in one hand and a half-empty bottle of vodka in the other. He'd been hit by a bullet in the left leg. The Hunter's wild burst from the automatic that had missed Jake and peppered the trees.

"*Bonsoir, mademoiselle,*" he said. Then in English. "He killed my queen. Therefore I killed him. *C'est tout.* God's in his heaven and all's right with the world. Kill me if you like, but don't make me suffer."

You saved my life, I wanted to say, but of course I couldn't. The impulse to help him was strangely acute, partly for Jake's sake, somehow, since I knew they'd shared an odd camaraderie—but what could I do?

There was the armoured van, but it held Poulsom's messy remains, and in any case I couldn't face going back there. The motorcyclist's rhetorical question came back to me: *What sort of moron tails someone in a white car?* This sort, evidently. Not quite believing what I was doing, I pointed to him then mimed holding a steering wheel. Repeated the gesture. *Where is your car?*

Not surprisingly, it took him a few moments to get his head around what he was seeing. When he did, he laughed, one half-cracked burst of hysteria that started and stopped abruptly. I felt Jake's spirit like the sun's warmth on my back.

"*Un kilometre,*" Cloquet said, pointing behind himself. I could tell his light had come back on. Until this moment he'd thought he'd reached the end of himself. Now here was life again. A werewolf offering help. I held out my hand to him. He laughed again, then became slightly teary, then took it.

•

Which really completes the job I set out to do here, to finish Jake's story. I wanted to stick strictly to the events, to leave *feelings* out of it—but I find reading back over these few pages that I haven't quite managed that. It's surprisingly hard (dear Maddy, as Jake would have said) to stick to the story. Of course there's *another* story (among other things of how to get a nine-foot werewolf into a Land Rover) but it doesn't belong here. There might be time for that later. I get the feeling I've caught the writing bug, in honour of Jake, yes, but also from psychological necessity. Talking to yourself might not cure loneliness, but it helps.

A month has passed since that night in Beddgelert forest, and though I've survived it hasn't been easy. I couldn't have done it without Cloquet's help—but again, that's a story for another time.

Tomorrow, if all goes as planned, I leave for New York.

In the meantime there's the Curse to get through. Tonight's the full moon, and the Hunger doesn't care what you've been through or what your fears are or where you'll be next week. There's a comfort in it, the purity of its demand, its imperviousness to reason or remorse. The hunger, in its vicious simplicity, teaches you how to be a werewolf.

Maybe that's the best way to end this postscript, with a statement of final acceptance. My name is Talulla Mary Apollonia Demetriou, and I am the last living werewolf on earth.

Until my baby's born. Then there'll be two of us.

ACKNOWLEDGEMENTS

A big howl of appreciation to: Jonny Geller, Jane Gelfman, Melissa Pimentel, Nick Marston, Jamie Byng, Francis Bickmore, Sonny Mehta, Marty Asher and all at Canongate and Knopf; to Stephen Coates for musical genius and free psychotherapy; and to Kim Teasdale, without whom none of it would be any fun at all.

For the sound track to *The Last Werewolf* by The Real Tuesday Weld, go to: www.tuesdayweld.com/thelastwerewolf.

A NOTE ABOUT THE AUTHOR

Glen Duncan is the author of seven previous novels. He was chosen by both *Arena* and *The Times Literary Supplement* (London) as one of Britain's best young novelists. He lives in London.

A NOTE ON THE TYPE

This book was set in Fournier, a typeface named for Pierre Simon Fournier *fils* (1712–1768), a celebrated French type designer. His types are old style in character and sharply cut.

Printed and bound by RR Donnelley, Crawfordsville, Indiana

Book design by Michael Collica